1908 – SUMMER

Eric R Davidson

Published by Edge60

Copyright (c) Eric R Davidson 2016

The right of Eric R Davidson to be identified as the author of this work has been asserted by the author in accordance with the Copyright, Designs and Patents Act 1988.

All Trademarks are acknowledged

This work is entirely fictitious, even if set in the context of actual events. All names, characters, places and incidents have been created from within the author's fertile imagination. Any resemblance to real persons, living or dead, other than public figures, is purely coincidental.

All rights reserved.

No part of this publication may be reproduced, stored in a retrieval system, or transmitted, in any form or by any means, without the prior permission in writing of the publisher, nor be otherwise circulated in any form of binding or cover other than that in which it is published and without a similar condition including this condition being imposed on the subsequent purchaser.

As with all my books I have tried my utmost to be historically accurate in the events I portray. However, remember this is still a piece of fiction and not meant to be a history lesson, so if I have made the odd mistake, please forgive me.

My thanks, again, to my wife, Heather, and son, Adam, for their patient reading of the manuscript, correction of my mistakes and suggestions for improvements, where necessary.

Eric R Davidson

Aberdeen – November 2016

About The Author

Eric R Davidson spent most of his working life in the Civil Service before having a second career with Grampian Police in Aberdeen. His role with Grampian Police came to an end in 2013, which allowed Eric to concentrate on full-time writing, something that Eric had always wanted to do.

Eric's other main passion is Crystal Palace Football Club. For forty-one years Crystal Palace have taken Eric a rollercoaster ride season after season. 2016 – 2017 has been no different.

Previously published books by Eric R Davidson

1906 – September

1906 – October

1906 – November

MILO: The Varga File

MILO: The Assassination File

Inspector Fraser's First Case (A Short Story)

ONE

Monday 01st June

It was the first day of a new month. The year was 1908.

May had been a glorious month in Aberdeen. The temperatures recorded in the Duthie Park had reached the mid-seventies on a number of occasions and many an Aberdonian had been looking forward to a memorable summer. However, the arrival of June had put an end to all that. The first day was cloudy and cool; not at all summer-like.

It meant, as Inspector Jake Fraser, of Aberdeen City Police, made his way, slowly, up Union Street that the buildings around him looked grey and mildly depressing. The people he passed had reverted to wearing expressions on their faces more suited to the dead of winter. Only the sunshine makes people look truly relaxed and happy. The street was busy, a steady mixture of horse-drawn carts, trams, bicycles and an increasing number of petrol driven machines, which some thought might become the main mode of transport someday.

Jake was deep in thought as he made his way beyond the end of Belmont Street and continued towards the newly widened Union Bridge. The work had only just been completed and the footpath opened again a few days earlier. Jake marvelled at the work that had been done and as he crossed the bridge he found himself trying to work out where they might yet put the stairway down to the railway station below. He knew that the Council and the owners of the station were to be in talks with regard to an access being created, though as Jake paused and looked around, it seemed to him that there was not an obvious place in which to put a staircase.

He carried on his way and turned right along Union Terrace. He was making his way to Rosemount. He had been informed that a body had been found in a house there and that Sergeant Mathieson was already at the scene. It being a Monday morning, Jake had decided to take his time in getting to the premises in question. He knew that he could very well be indoors for the rest of the day and was intent on enjoying some air, all be it a chill air, for as long as he could.

Jake's thoughts were not on work as he walked past the entrance to what was now his own home. He was only a couple of weeks away from his first wedding anniversary and still had no clear idea as to what he might buy Margaret to mark the occasion. He had never been happier than the time he had spent with Margaret and he did not want to waste the occasion simply buying her flowers, or some other item that would last but a few minutes. He wanted to buy her something that would last, but he also knew that Margaret would never forgive him if he spent a lot of money on her. She didn't usually feel the need for material things and certainly nothing of any great expense.

Jake had met Margaret during a murder investigation and their relationship had blossomed in to a marriage proposal, which was accepted. They had then married in June, 1907 at which point Jake moved in to Margaret's flat in Rosemount Viaduct. Jake had, at that time, been living in Esslemont Avenue, in a flat that had been purchased by an old friend and colleague of Jake's some years earlier. It had transpired, however, that the flat had been bought with illegal earnings and in the eyes of the law, there was, therefore, no legal owner. Jake had reached an agreement with the solicitors, who had responsibility for the flat, for him to live there, but everyone had seemed relieved when Jake was able to move out and the flat would then be placed on the market and attract a lawful owner.

Jake's journey took another half hour. Eventually he arrived at the row of houses on Beechgrove Terrace and stopped at the gate where the police officer was standing. The uniformed officer saluted as Jake approached him.

"Sergeant Mathieson told me to tell you that he is upstairs, sir," the constable said.

Jake thanked him and entered the house. He made his way to the top of the stairs and then paused; there were four doors to choose from as regards to where Mathieson might be.

"In here, sir," came a voice from one of the rooms with an open door. Jake took his hat off and entered the room.

Sergeant Mathieson was standing by a large and ornate desk. Although the room was quite small it had been designed to be used as a study. Jake took in the general lay-out of the room before his eyes dropped to the body of a woman lying on the floor. Kneeling beside her body was Doctor Horatio Stephen, the man who had been the City Police Surgeon for the last year. He was bent over the corpse, studying various aspects of her appearance.

"Good Morning," Jake said, looking around the room.

"Good Morning, sir," responded Mathieson.

"Good Morning, Inspector Fraser," added Doctor Stephen without looking up. The Doctor had known Jake for a year and yet showed no sign of addressing him in any other way than formally.

"What do you have for me?" Jake then said, continuing to walk slowly around the room, looking at how it had been laid out.

Mathieson took out his notebook. "The body was found at half past nine this morning by a Martha Logan who works in the office of the Grammar School. The victim is Miss Edith McIntosh, a spinster of the Parish who taught in the Lower Division at the Grammar School. She had taught at the school for some twenty years, I believe."

"What was Miss Logan doing here?" Jake then asked, though he was engrossed, by then, in looking at a particular ornament and looked, for all the world, like someone with little or no interest in what Mathieson was saying. The fact he had just asked the question confirmed that that was not the case.

"The Rector sent Miss Logan to check on Miss McIntosh when she did not turn up for work today."

Jake nodded, as if that made sense to him. "Doctor, have you anything to add for the moment?"

Doctor Stephen remained on his knees. "I'd estimate time of death as being some time on Saturday. I can confirm that the victim has been strangled."

"And possibly with one of the curtain ties from this room," Mathieson added. "One of them is certainly missing."

Jake now noticed that half a door was visible from behind a curtain that hung in the corner of the room beside the window.

"What's in there?" he enquired.

"Nothing," replied Mathieson, "though the Doctor has a theory as to what might have been there."

Jake glanced at the Doctor. He was a man in his early fifties with greying hair and greying whiskers that looked in need of a good trim. His suit was not of the finest quality and he generally gave the impression of someone who was not in the habit of spending much money on himself. He produced a pipe from his pocket and stuck it between his teeth. Jake knew that the Doctor was in the habit of sucking on a pipe rather than ever getting around to lighting it. He had always claimed it helped him think. The Doctor stood up slowly before speaking.

"The victim's father was a doctor and I knew him briefly when we both worked as volunteers at the hospital. He used to speak about a collection of miniature paintings that he had built-up over the years. Although he never actually said in as many words I always got the impression that the collection was worth a lot of money."

Jake crossed to the curtain and pulled it back. He then opened the door and looked in to what amounted to nothing more than a cupboard with many shelves built in to it. All the shelves were empty.

"And this is where he may have kept that collection?"

"It's just a suggestion," Doctor Stephen added.

"So, are we looking at a burglar who is disturbed, panics and kills Miss McIntosh?" Jake then perused.

"Miss Logan did say that the front door was unlocked when she called this morning, sir," Mathieson then said.

"Unlocked rather than forced?" Jake asked, by way of clarifying a point.

Mathieson checked his notebook. "She definitely said unlocked."

"Is Miss Logan still here?"

"Yes, sir, she's in the kitchen with one of our constables."

Jake turned back in to the room and looked down at the body of Miss McIntosh again.

"I take it she hasn't been…….?" Jake began and then seemed to find finishing the sentence very difficult.

Doctor Stephen seemed to understand the question anyway. "She hasn't been interfered with in any way."

Jake then looked across at Mathieson. "Any sign of anything else being stolen?"

"I found the victim's purse and no money appeared to have been taken from it. I've had a quick look around the house and it's full of items, some of which could well be worth some money."

"So maybe this miniature collection was all the thief was after," mused Jake. He then turned to the Doctor again. "Do you have any idea what these miniatures might have looked like?"

Doctor Stephen smiled. "How can I describe them, Inspector Fraser? They were the type of paintings that would not be viewed in female company, if you get my meaning?"

"Naked women?"

"Oh yes."

"I wonder how many others knew of the collection," Jake then said.

Although offered as a statement, Doctor Stephen took it to be a question and provided an answer anyway.

"Doctor McIntosh certainly spoke about it to me, but how many other people were taken in to his confidence we'll never know. Doctor McIntosh died four years ago from a lung disease that struck and took him very quickly. I doubt if his daughter would have been very taken with the collection so it is perfectly possible that she sold it, in which case you don't have a burglary gone wrong at all."

"Even if she had sold the collection, maybe our thief didn't know that and came looking for it anyway. Miss McIntosh comes in to the room and he grabs the nearest item and kills her with it."

"Maybe," added the Doctor, though he didn't sound totally convinced by Jake's theory.

Jake then turned to Mathieson. "Go and speak to the neighbours, maybe they saw, or heard, something. I'll go and speak with Miss Logan"

"Very good, sir," said Mathieson, who now made his way to the door.

Doctor Stephen started to fill his pipe with tobacco. "Can I arrange to have the body taken back to Lodge Walk?"

Jake moved a little closer and studied the corpse for a moment. "I'm sure we'll learn more with her in your hands than in mine, Doctor, so feel free to get on with your work."

"I'll get a report written as soon as I can," concluded the Doctor.

"Thank you," said Jake before making his way out of the room and downstairs. He found the kitchen fairly easily and entered. The Constable and a young girl were sitting at the kitchen table; nothing was being said. The Constable immediately jumped to his feet as Jake entered the room. Jake asked the Constable to wait out in the hall and then sat down beside the girl.

"Are you okay, Martha?"

The girl said nothing for a moment, but then her green eyes looked across at him. "I spoke to her when she left the school on Friday. I can't believe she's dead."

"I'm sorry you had to be the one to find her. Can you just talk me through what happened this morning?"

Martha thought for a moment. Jake studied her in the silence that hung in the room. She was a pretty girl though clearly of a nervous disposition as she had a tendency to play with a pendant that hung round her neck. She looked younger than her years and Jake had an overwhelming urge to put his arm around her shoulder and to tell her that everything would be okay. He had never had children of his own, but this girl was bringing out the paternal instincts in him.

"I was at my desk around nine this morning when Miss Findlay said that the Rector wanted someone to visit Miss McIntosh and make sure that she was all right."

"Had he reason to believe that she wasn't all right?"

"She hadn't turned up to work and that was not like Miss McIntosh, she was always at her work."

Jake nodded, as if confirming he agreed with the Rector's decision.

"And who is Miss Findlay?"

"She's the witch who runs the office at the school."

Jake held back the smile that had nearly appeared around his lips. "Go on."

"Well I put my coat on and walked round. When I got here I noticed that the curtains were still drawn and I thought that to be a bit strange, especially as it has been light for a few hours now. Anyway, I knocked on the door and waited. No one answered, which I also thought to be a bit strange. I was about to come away again when something made me try the door. To my surprise it opened."

"So the front door definitely wasn't locked?" Jake added.

"No. I called out Miss McIntosh's name and when I got no reply I began to think that she might be ill. It seemed possible that something serious had come over her, so I entered the house and started to look around. Again I called her name and after checking the rooms downstairs I decided to go upstairs. I expected to find her in her bed."

"What happened then?"

Martha thought for a moment. "I opened the first door I came to and there she was, lying on the floor."

"Did you touch anything?"

Martha's eyes widened in horror. "Absolutely not, I just ran downstairs and out in to the street."

Jake noticed the girl becoming a little more agitated so he put a comforting hand on her arm. "Don't distress yourself, simply tell me what you did next."

"I hurried down to the police station on Leadside Road and reported what I had found. The Constable who was sitting with me came from there. We came back and I assume he then arranged for you to be informed."

Jake stood up and walked to the door. He opened it and asked the Constable to come back in to the kitchen.

"Did you do anything in particular after you'd come to the house with Martha?" Jake then asked.

The young Constable looked very nervous as he started to reply. "I opened the curtains to let more light in to the room and then checked that there was no one else in the house. It was quite clear that Miss McIntosh was dead so I waited for Constable Reilly to pass on his beat and asked him to get a message to Lodge Walk."

"You didn't touch anything else, apart from opening the curtains?" Jake clarified.

"Nothing."

"Did you notice if any of the curtain ties were lying around?"

"There was nothing, sir, I'm sure of that," the constable insisted.

"Okay, Constable," Jake then said, "would you please search Miss McIntosh's bags and pockets and try to find a key that will allow you to lock the front door. Once you can make the premises secure, would you then take Miss McIntosh's personal possessions down to Lodge Walk and get them officially recorded by someone. You can write your report while you are there and leave a copy on my desk."

"I'll get on to that right away, sir."

"And we, Martha, are going to the Grammar School so that I can have a word with the Rector. Until he chooses to make public what has happened to Miss McIntosh, I must ask you to say nothing to your colleagues about what you have witnessed this morning. Is that clear?"

"Yes, sir," replied Martha, fiddling all the more with her pendant.

***

The Grammar School was only fifteen minutes away. It was located on Esslemont Avenue, close to the flat that Jake had occupied prior to his wedding. The Grammar School had quite a history. It had originally been the school that had given Schoolhill its name. It had moved to the Esslemont Avenue site in 1863 and now occupied a building that looked as grand as the education it strove to provide.

Jake entered the building and followed Martha to the office where she worked. He was greeted by a woman whom Jake presumed would be 'the witch' and after a brief discussion was told to take a seat whilst she informed the Rector of Jake's presence. Fifteen minutes later, Jake found himself being shown in to a wood-panelled office occupied by a large bookcase, positively straining with volumes dating back many years and a desk, behind which sat a very serious looking man wearing a black gown over his dark suit.

The man stood up from his desk and came round to shake Jake's hand. He introduced himself as being Morland Simpson. Simpson was in his late forties and had been Rector of the Grammar School since 1893. He was a man of similar height to Jake, though his expression remained serious at all times. Jake got the feeling that this man had not laughed in a long time. His hair was receding and he wore his spectacles perched rather dangerously on the end of his nose. He ushered Jake in to a chair and then returned to his own.

"What can I do for you, Inspector?" he then said, his expression remaining stern. Jake instantly remembered his own schooldays and how stern all his teachers appeared to be. Was it an essential part of the job to look as if humour had left your life for good. Education may be a serious business, but surely teachers could learn to lighten up at times.

"I am the bearer of some bad news, Mr Simpson. I have to tell you that the body of Edith McIntosh was discovered in her home this morning. Miss McIntosh, I regret to inform you, had been murdered. I'm afraid that Miss Martha Logan had the misfortune to find the body and she has been somewhat distressed by it all, as you might imagine."

Simpson looked suitable affected by the news. "But this is terrible. Whoever would want to kill someone like Edith?"

"That is what I am now endeavouring to find out," added Jake. "Perhaps you would be good enough as to answer some questions?"

Simpson thought for a moment. "Feel free to ask what you want, Inspector, but I regret to inform you that I have always made a point of not knowing my staff on a personal level. To that end, I know of Edith only in her working capacity as a teacher and in that she was nothing other than professional and a lovely person to know. Having never married and having no children of her own, Edith tended to treat her class as if they were her own. She was well liked by both pupils and staff alike."

"You say she never married but did Miss McIntosh have family here in Aberdeen?"

"I never heard her talk about family at all. However, it is possible that some of her colleagues might know more about her."

"Would it be possible for me to speak to some of her colleagues?"

Morland Simpson looked rather taken aback. "You mean just now?"

"This is a murder enquiry, sir, so the quicker we build a picture of the kind of person Miss McIntosh was, the better."

"But they're teaching, Inspector and I never like to interrupt my teachers when they are hard at work."

Jake took a deep breath. He could sense his temper rising and fought to keep it in check.

"I say again, sir, this is a murder enquiry and the fact it might disrupt the odd class, here or there, does not exactly bother me. Now, would you please arrange for me to speak to some of Miss McIntosh's colleagues?"

The Rector looked like the type of man who was not accustomed to anyone standing up to him. He was more accustomed to giving out instructions and having them obeyed without question. He looked greatly offended to be receiving such a stern rebuke, but did eventually agree to Jake's demand.

"I would imagine Miss Grainger would be the best person to speak to," he finally suggested. "The ladies of the Lower School rather kept themselves to themselves."

Jake made a note of the name in his notebook. "Could I have a first name for Miss Grainger?"

Simpson had to refer to a sheet of paper, which he produced from the top, right-hand drawer of his desk. Only then was he able to tell Jake that Miss Grainger's first name was Juliet. Jake added that to his notebook. Morland Simpson then continued speaking.

"Miss Grainger works where Miss McIntosh worked in our Lower School, which is in what used to be the Westfield School. I will ask Miss Findlay to show you the way."

Simpson stood up and made his way to the door. While he was away Jake looked around the room again. Everything was in its place, with not a book out of line or a speck of dust to be seen. He was lost again in his own school-time memories when Simpson came back in to the room with the same woman who had greeted Jake on his arrival.

With Miss Findlay to show the way, they walked down the main corridor and out one of the back doors. They crossed the open area and entered another, slightly smaller building that bordered Esslemont Avenue. They turned left along a rather dark and depressing corridor until they reached a door at the end. Miss Findlay asked Jake to wait. She then knocked on the door and entered. Moments later another woman came out of the class.

She looked to be in her mid-thirties and wore her hair tied in a tight bun. She was attractive, rather than pretty and wore a plain, blue dress with black shoes. She looked a little flustered at being called from her classroom.

"I believe you want to see me, Inspector?" the woman said.

"Miss Grainger?"

"Yes."

"Is there somewhere quiet where we could go to speak?"

Miss Grainger thought for a moment. "Follow me."

They walked to a classroom on the floor above. It lay empty and they were able to find a seat in the corner of the class where no one could see them. The seats were rather low so Jake allowed Miss Grainger to sit on the teacher's chair and he perched on the corner of one of the desks.

"I believe you knew Miss McIntosh quite well?" Jake began.

Miss Grainger immediately picked up on the use of the past tense. "I still do know her," she answered with a look of confusion.

Jake went on to tell Miss Grainger about what had happened to Miss McIntosh. Miss Grainger started crying immediately and Jake offered her his handkerchief, which she graciously accepted. She quickly composed herself again.

"This is terrible news, Inspector, but who would want to kill poor Edith?"

"We believe that something of value may have been stolen from her home. It is possible, therefore, that she disturbed the thief and he chose to kill her."

"But, surely, Edith had nothing worth stealing," said Miss Grainger dabbing at her eyes with the handkerchief.

"Do you know that to be a fact, Miss Grainger, or are you simply offering me an opinion?"

"Well, I suppose it's just an opinion, but I wasn't aware of Edith owning anything of any great value."

"So you knew nothing of her owning a collection of miniature paintings?" Jake added.

Miss Grainger did not even pause for thought. "No, but then, why should I?"

"Perhaps Miss McIntosh might have mentioned it in conversation?" Jake said.

"Which she didn't; at least not in my company," added Miss Grainger. "It is interesting," she then continued, "that Edith may have been burgled. I don't know if it is, in anyway, connected, but I, too, believe I had my home broken in to a week ago."

Jake looked interested. "Tell me what happened, Miss Grainger."

"A week past Saturday I was visiting some friends and when I got home I had the strangest sensation that someone had been in my house. Nothing appeared to have been stolen but I got the distinct impression that certain items had been moved."

"Did you report this to the police?"

"No, I didn't. As I said, nothing had actually been stolen, so I didn't think there was much the police would be able to do."

"Was your door forced?" Jake then asked.

"I wouldn't have thought so. I have continued to use my key, as usual, ever since that day and my door seems as secure as it ever was."

"So the thief must have had a key to your property?" Jake then added.

Miss Grainger looked slightly upset by the suggestion. "My goodness, I hadn't considered that fact. However would someone have got a key to my door?"

"A very good question," agreed Jake. "Would you be able to offer a suggestion as to how that may have happened?"

"Absolutely not," answered Miss Grainger, looking offended by the suggestion that she would be in the habit of giving anyone a key to her property.

Jake decided not to labour the question, so he changed the subject.

"And you're sure nothing was taken?"

Miss Grainger now managed a smile. "In all honesty, Inspector, I have nothing worth stealing."

"And yet someone still saw fit to break in to your home," Jake added.

"And now the same seems to have happened to poor Edith."

"Only with greater consequences," added Jake and Miss Grainger dabbed at her eyes again with the handkerchief. Jake then continued. "Perhaps you could tell me a little more about Miss McIntosh's personal life. It might help us find her killer if we understood Miss McIntosh a little better."

Miss Grainger remained silent for a little longer, taking the time to gather her thoughts before responding to the question. Eventually she looked up at Jake and began to speak.

"I wouldn't describe Edith as being a close friend. We became friends through our shared interest in music. Although there was a ten year gap between us, we found a shared interest in Gilbert and Sullivan and other forms of music. We would go to see variety and musical acts, when they came to the city."

"So Miss McIntosh was a big fan of music?" added Jake.

The question brought another smile to Miss Grainger's lips. "She liked all forms of music, but most especially Gilbert and Sullivan. She made a point of going to see any production of their musicals, whether they be professional or amateur. She often entertained us, here at the school, by playing the piano and singing a medley of songs from the various musicals."

Jake pondered on what had just been said for a few seconds and then changed the subject.

"Did Miss McIntosh have any other interests?"

"She never spoke of any."

"Did she have any other close friends that you are aware of?"

"Edith lived alone and usually preferred her own company. However, recently she had been spending time with a male friend, which was unusual for her."

"A male friend; was there a budding romance in the making?"

Miss Grainger shook her head. "No, I don't think there was ever anything romantic in mind, they were just happy to be friends."

"Do you happen to know this man's name?" Jake prompted.

"Actually, now that I think about it, you might know him as I feel sure he was a police officer. His name is Peter Ash."

The name hit Jake in the pit of the stomach like a punch. It took a few seconds for him to recover.

"Are you talking about *Superintendent* Peter Ash?"

"I never knew his rank, I just knew his name and the fact he was a police officer."

Jake wrote everything in to his notebook. "Is there anything else you can tell me about Miss McIntosh?"

"Not really. As I said, Edith pretty much kept herself to herself. She loved her work and she loved her pupils, but outside of that she didn't do an awful lot."

"The rector said that Miss McIntosh treated her pupils as if they were her own children."

Miss Grainger smiled again. "She will be sorely missed by them all because she did tend to mother her pupils rather than simply teach them."

Jake walked Miss Grainger back to her class and then continued to the main building where he let the office staff know that he was leaving. He made his way back to Lodge Walk where he intended catching up on some paperwork and hopefully having a quick word with Superintendent Ash.

***

TWO

Tuesday 02 June

The mid-morning train from Edinburgh arrived a few minutes early in to the vast unwelcoming space of the Joint Station in Aberdeen. Passengers opened doors the length of the train and stepped down on to the platform. Porters scurried, with trolleys, to help those passengers carrying a lot of luggage. In the midst of all this activity stood a woman who seemed to be finding it difficult to orientate herself to her new surroundings.

As with everything else about this woman, nothing was ever as it seemed. Her entire life had been an act, forever playing a part to suit whatever purpose was at hand. She had honed her skills over many years and now knew that she could make other people believe pretty much anything she wanted.

"May I be of assistance?" one of the porters asked her.

She took a moment to react. She was already in actress mode; playing the part of someone new to Aberdeen. If any questions were to, later, be asked of the porters they had to report that she definitely appeared to know nothing about Aberdeen. Whatever else the police might be thinking by that time, they had to be led down a certain route so as not to confirm her identity too quickly. She eventually spoke, trying to make her tone and manner of speech appear educated and well bred.

"Yes, thank you. Could you possibly suggest a good hotel here in Aberdeen?"

The porter was greatly taken by this woman. He guessed that she might be in her early forties, but she still retained a beauty that could not be ignored. Her brown hair was tied up beneath a hat of the latest fashion and she wore clothing that indicated she was a woman of means and therefore, someone who might tip handsomely.

"The choice of hotel depends on what you can afford," the porter then said by way of gauging how much money this woman *really* had.

She looked instantly offended. "I can afford the best," she snapped, but then quickly smiled, as if trying to soften her manner.

"My apologies, I did not mean to judge," the porter said quickly, desperately trying to salvage any tip that might be forthcoming. "In that case, why not try the Palace Hotel. It is up there on Union Street," he then said, flapping an arm in the general direction of where the hotel was situated.

"Will I need to organise a carriage?" the woman then asked, looking rather perplexed as she did so.

"Not at all. There is a lift; if you'd follow me," the porter then said, lifting the woman's single, large case on to his trolley and setting off along the platform. The woman fell in to step behind him and said nothing more until they were exiting the lift on the floor of the reception area of The Palace Hotel.

As soon as she was free of the lift she suddenly drew her hand to her forehead and exclaimed that she was not feeling well. Almost at the same moment she collapsed to the floor causing the porter some concern and bringing hotel staff hurrying to offer assistance.

By the time a small crowd had gathered around her, the woman had come round again. She was assisted to her feet and led to a chair by the main door. The doorman on duty at that time, Eddie Ralston, came over to assist and soon the manager of the hotel, Cecil Bainbridge had been summoned as well. By the time the woman was sitting and ready to speak the small gathering of people had already started to disperse.

"Please, give this poor woman a chance to breathe," Bainbridge announced as he ushered the few remaining people away. He like to appear in charge of everything, even though, most of the time, he did little other than get in the way. Everyone left except for Eddie and the porter, who was still ever hopeful that a tip might be heading his way at any moment. "How do you feel now, dear lady?" Bainbridge then asked, his tone softened by the fact he found this woman to be highly attractive and most probably, rich.

The woman looked up and weakly smiled. "I fear I must eat something soon or the light-headedness will surely return."

"In that case," Bainbridge added, offering his arm to allow the woman to pull herself on to her feet again," we must get you through to the dining room and find something for you to eat. We can organise your room later."

The woman managed another smile. "How kind of you, Mr........?" she then said.

"Bainbridge. Cecil Bainbridge; I am the manager of this establishment."

"Then it could not be in better hands," added the woman, as she allowed herself to be led in the direction of the dining-room.

"Here, what will I do with this?" the porter said as everyone started to walk away from him.

"Give it to me," replied Eddie. "I'll see it's looked after until we know which room to take it to."

"But what about my tip?" the porter added, rather dejectedly.

Eddie watched the woman walking away, arm in arm with the manager and then turned to face the porter.

"I'm guessing you'll get no payment from her; you'll just have to make do with that lovely smile she gave you."

"Smiles don't pay bills," grumbled the porter as he turned and made his way back towards the lift.

Through in the dining-room the woman had now been seated at one of the tables and a breakfast ordered from the kitchen. A cup of tea had already been brought through and Bainbridge had seated himself beside the woman, his hand on top of hers in a gesture of comfort.

"How are you feeling now?"

"A lot better, thank you. I had to leave Edinburgh quite early this morning and had not had time to have any breakfast. Sometimes, if I don't eat regularly, I am prone to fainting fits. It can be quite embarrassing sometimes."

"My dear lady, how terrible. May I ask how long you are intending staying in our hotel?"

"I'm not exactly sure, Mr Bainbridge," the woman then said, taking off the small hat that she had been wearing. She also undid the buttons on her jacket, unveiling a neat, white blouse beneath that went well with her black skirt. The standard of her clothing was extremely high and Bainbridge felt sure that she was a customer worth pandering to for a little while longer. "I have some business requiring my attention here in Aberdeen, so it could take a few days."

"In that case you must take time to enjoy a nice breakfast and then we can get your details and organise a room. May I at least know your name for the moment?"

"Lucy Gill," the woman replied, taking a sip of her tea and looking around the palatial surroundings of the dining-room. Apart from a couple of staff who were setting the tables for lunch there was no one in the room other than herself and Bainbridge.

"Would that be *Miss* Gill?" Bainbridge then asked, a tone of hope in his voice as if he intended asking her to marry him there and then.

"It would indeed," replied Lucy. "I have yet to meet a man who interested me enough as to want to marry him."

"They may not have interested you but I feel sure that you interested them," Bainbridge then said, apparently taking no account of how personal his comment had been. Lucy instantly feigned embarrassment, partially hiding her face behind an upraised hand.

"Why, Mr Bainbridge, whatever do you mean?" she said, all coyly.

Bainbridge realised that he may have crossed a line with this resident, but for the moment he was lost in her brown eyes and her personable manner.

"My apologies for my forthright comment, Miss Gill, I did not mean to intrude on issues personal to yourself."

Lucy could sense that this man was showing an unhealthy interest in her. He was not the type of man who would, usually, interest her in a romantic way, but he did look the type of man who might be easily persuaded to part with a reasonable amount of money. The first step towards relieving him of that money was to play along with his apparent infatuation.

"Your comments were of a very, personal nature," Lucy then said, "however, I am sure that you meant no harm by it. Marriage is not something that has interested me in my life and certainly for the moment, I am quite content living the life that I do. Should I ever require male companionship then I merely contact my brother."

Bainbridge was heartened by the fact that the only male mentioned was her brother. Perhaps the field was clear of romantic competition?

"Where does your brother live?"

"Edinburgh. I spend much of my time there, although we also have a house in Glasgow."

At that moment a young waitress arrived with a plate of food that might easily have fed two people. The plate was placed in front of Lucy and she had to remind herself that she was supposed to be a lady who had missed breakfast, not a woman who hadn't eaten properly for two days. Instead of attacking the food with relish she had to remain in character and eat through it delicately.

"I'll leave you to enjoy your breakfast, but perhaps we can talk again later?" Bainbridge then said.

"I will look forward to that, Mr Bainbridge," Lucy concluded and turned her full attention to the plate of food in front of her.

Bainbridge went through to the reception area and organised a room for Lucy Gill. He insisted on her having one of the better rooms, though he had no intention of charging her the full price for spending time at his hotel. Once he had done that he went to his office and caught up with the morning mail. However, he had much difficulty in concentrating on the contents of the various envelopes for, no matter how much he tried, he simply could not get Lucy Gill's lovely face out of his mind.

***

Jake sat at his desk, moving around sheets of paper without taking the time to actually read anything that might have been written on them. He couldn't help thinking about Superintendent Ash's connection with Edith McIntosh and was already thinking about how he might conduct an interview with his superior officer, without offending him in any way.

He had been hoping to speak to Superintendent Ash earlier, but had discovered that morning that the Superintendent was attending a meeting with other senior officers up in Elgin. It didn't happen very often but, just occasionally, meetings were organised where officers from different police forces could meet to discuss and share details of cases. These meetings were not organised with any real intent to share knowledge. It had long been acknowledged that the big forces were more likely to have more experience of major crimes and the smaller forces could learn from that knowledge, so it wasn't so much about sharing as the small fry listening to the big fish.

With Ash away, Jake had decided to spend the day trying to learn more about Edith McIntosh. It would be a little while yet before Doctor Stephen's report would be ready so Jake decided the best course of action would be to return to her house and see if anything could be found there that might yet prove useful in the investigation. He had asked Sergeant Mathieson to make himself available from lunchtime and until then he was filling in time by trying to clear the paperwork from other cases.

It was the one aspect of Jake's job that he never liked. He appreciated the need for paperwork, after all a case could never find its way through the courts without others being able to read about the investigation and learn from the answers given by the various witnesses. Paperwork was an essential part of the job, but it was time consuming and it kept officers tied to their desks when they would rather be out solving new cases.

Jake checked his watch. It was eleven o'clock; still another hour before he planned to go back to Edith McIntosh's house. He looked down at the papers strewn across his desk and the sat back. He gave himself an option. He would either spend the next hour putting his paperwork in order or he would wander on to Union Street and find a suitable location for a cup of tea and something to eat.

The cup of tea won without having to put up much of a fight.

***

Lucy Gill was sitting in her room. She had been given one of the best rooms in the hotel, overlooking Union Street. Cecil Bainbridge had insisted that she accept his offer of a better room, whilst only charging her for something a lot more basic. Her large case had been taken up to the room for her and she was thinking about opening it as she sat at the dressing table and stared at herself in the mirror.

She didn't know how much longer she could keep on doing what she did. She was forty-one years old now and as she looked at her reflection she could see the ravages of time beginning to catch up on her. She knew she had always been attractive to men and she had used that attraction, on so many occasions, to persuade those men to part with their money in return for a procession of meaningless reasons. However, it was becoming much harder to keep herself looking as attractive as she had once been. Her face was lined and her hair had started to lose much of its colour. The passage of time always seemed so much harder on women than it was on men.

Spending time in prison hadn't helped either. The aging process seemed to speed up when the body was deprived of light and fresh air. Lucy Gill, or whatever name she chose to use at any given time, had spent a lot of time in prison. Always for short periods, but they soon mounted up and she now doubted that she could put with much more time inside. The time was rapidly approaching when she would have to find another way to make money. Perhaps she might even have to make her money legally.

For the last twenty years she had either been in prison or keeping one step ahead of the police forces of Scotland. Apart from a five year spell, from 1899, when she had worked as a housemaid and nurse in Hawick and Roxburgh, Lucy Gill had kept on the move. Now she was tired. Now she needed to be able to stop running, but that was going to be a whole lot easier said than done.

Between 1888 and January 1898 she had been convicted seven times. On four occasions it had led to six months in prison and on the other three occasions it had been sixty days in prison. Confinement had never had any effect on her. The moment she had been released she had gone straight back to the only profession she knew, that of fraudster and con artiste. She knew she was good at what she did, but all good things had to come to an end sometime. Maybe one last money-making scheme and then she could retire?

Unbeknown to the management of the Palace Hotel they now had 'The Buchan Heiress' occupying one of their rooms. In fairness to Cecil Bainbridge, in particular, he had never crossed paths with 'The Buchan Heiress' before, even though she had been in Aberdeen many times. Lucy's real name was Margaret Isabella Reid. She had been born in the north-east corner of Scotland, but she had never told anyone exactly where. In fact she made a point of never telling anyone anything about herself. Her whole life had been a lie and now she had great difficulty recalling anything truthful about herself, even if she had wanted to.

Lucy stood up and crossed the room to her case. She opened it and looked down at the stones and papers that she used to create the illusion that she travelled with a lot of fine clothing. Everything about Lucy's life was an illusion, created to make others think that she was far more important than she actually was. All that was in her case, by way of real clothing, was one change of underwear and one other dress. She also had another pair of shoes, which she had taken with her when she had left a previous lodgings. She hoped the landlady hadn't missed them yet or that would be one more report lying on a police officer's desk.

The only other item of any use, in her case, was another, smaller bag, which she would use when she left. She usually travelled light, but had decided that a large case might give an even bigger impression of wealth. From the reaction of both the porter and Cecil Bainbridge, the decision appeared to have worked.

Leaving the case open, Lucy took the dress and hung it up. She then checked the contents of her carrying bag. She had a little money in her purse and a smaller bag with a little bottle of French scent and a brush in it. The scent had also been acquired from a previous lodgings. However, the bag also contained something of, potentially, far more value. She took out some sheets of paper and laid them out in front of her.

Four sheets of paper indicated ownership of shares in the Broxburn Oil Company and two other sheets of paper were telegrams, addressed to her, which commented on money due to her from lawyers in Aberdeen. Everything looked to be in order but, of course, it was all bogus. These papers were Lucy's most recent props to making money.

All she needed was for somebody, with money to spend, to pay for the right to own shares in the Broxburn Oil Company. By the time they realised their purchases were worthless she would be long gone. She never remained too long in one place. When she did, the law tended to catch up with her and when the law caught up with her she tended to lose her freedom. At forty-one years of age she no longer wanted to spend time in prison which was why these last few swindles that she had planned would have to be her last.

She had tested the water in Edinburgh. She had met a woman in the Morningside area of Edinburgh who had turned out to be the perfect victim in her share swindle.

She had spent a few weeks getting to know the woman well enough before introducing the possibility of having shares to sell. A swindle was always guaranteed success when greed came in to the equation. Human beings are blinded by greed; the chance of making an easy penny seemed to disconnect them from the real world and they suddenly failed to see what was often staring them in the face, namely that something that appears too good to be true, usually is too good to be true.

In the Edinburgh trial run, Lucy had been able to ply eighteen pounds from the woman in Morningside for the purchase of shares that never materialised. Obviously, by the time the woman realised she had been duped, Lucy was halfway to Aberdeen. She now hoped to find a few more victims in Aberdeen and maybe earn enough to return to the Borders and put her feet up for a while.

Lucy put the papers back in her bag and then decided it was time to go out. She needed one or two new items for her wardrobe, which meant having to go shopping along Union Street. Firstly, she closed the case and pushed it in to the corner of the room. She then put on her jacket and hat, picked up her room key and headed for the door.

Down in the reception area she was greeted, once more, by Cecil Bainbridge, who wanted to make sure there had been no further fainting turns. Lucy thanked him for his concern and made her way to the door, where Eddie had it open for her by the time she arrived. She stepped through the door and out on to Union Street. She paused for a moment, looking up and down the street and deciding in which direction she should go. She knew Aberdeen pretty well but, unfortunately, some of Aberdeen, in turn, also knew of her, which meant she stood a good chance of being recognised if she were not careful.

She mentally crossed off a few shops and then decided her plan of attack. Over the next hour she would acquire items of clothing, from various outlets and all with the intention of not paying for any of them. Lucy rarely paid for anything; it had started back in the days when she genuinely had no money and had become something of a habit over the years. In fact it was now at a stage where she felt a positive charge pass through her body when she went on a shopping spree. It was fun, simple as that.

Finally, having made her mind up, Lucy set off along Union Street in the direction of the Castlegate.

***

Jake met Mathieson beside the statue of William Wallace. It was half past twelve and the clouds had parted slightly to let a hint of sunshine through the grey. It made a refreshing change from the dampness of the morning. The two men walked to Edith McIntosh's house and Jake used the key to open the front door. They entered and closed the door behind them.

The house was so neat and tidy it looked as if no one had ever lived there. Jake knew that Margaret was quite house proud, but even Margaret stopped short of having a home that looked like a museum. A house always had to carry the essence of the person who lived in it or else it became nothing more than soulless bricks and mortar.

The two men immediately went upstairs and into the room where they had found Miss McIntosh's body. Mathieson went and stood by the window and Jake remained at the door, his eyes scanning the room in silence for a few moments.

"Okay," he eventually said, "let's try to recreate what happened."

He made his way over to the corner and opened the cupboard door. He surveyed the empty shelves, then turned to look at Mathieson.

"Let us imagine that the burglar was standing here, filling a bag perhaps, when he hears the door downstairs opening. Miss McIntosh has returned quicker than he had expected and he now needs to find a way of finishing what he is doing and getting out of the house. Why would there be any need to panic?"

Mathieson gave the question some thought. "He must have heard her start to come upstairs."

"And unless the door to this room was open, when it shouldn't have been, there was still no reason to panic."

"But he knew Miss McIntosh would find him," Mathieson said.

"Okay, let's now assume that she came straight to this room on entering the building. The burglar still had time to close this door and pull the curtain. All he needed to do then was hide behind the door and wait for her to come in. She wasn't a young woman and I feel sure that most men could have overpowered her. All he had to do was tie her up, finish what he was doing and then make good his escape. There was no need for him to kill her."

"Unless she saw him?" suggested Mathieson.

"Even seeing him wouldn't have given him a reason to kill her, unless she knew who he was of course."

Mathieson moved closer to Jake. "Well that must be it, sir, Miss McIntosh knew who he was, and so he had to kill her to stop her from telling anyone."

Jake looked around the room. He then moved over and stood behind the door.

"If I'm here," he said, "I could allow Miss McIntosh to enter the room and then jump at her from behind. I could totally overpower her and I doubt if she would have the opportunity to see who I was. For that matter I could have ran out the door, pulling the door shut as I went. By the time Miss McIntosh reached the landing I'd be downstairs and on my way out the front door. Again, there would be no need to kill her."

"He had to have been known to her though, sir," Mathieson added and Jake nodded his agreement.

"It's the only reason for wanting her dead," added Jake, "even though it isn't much of a reason. In Miss Grainger's case, the burglar was gone before she returned home. Was that nothing more than her good fortune or did the burglar know what her domestic routine was to be that day? Did the burglar have similar knowledge about Miss McIntosh, only she came back early for some reason? We need to know what Miss McIntosh's plans had been on Saturday. Look around for a diary or some other record that might provide us with that information. I still have to speak to a friend of

Miss McIntosh's who may yet be able to help us but, for the moment, see what you can find."

Jake did not intend telling anyone of the Superintendent's involvement in the case until he absolutely had to. Mathieson left the room and went looking for diaries. Jake moved over to the desk and sat down. He looked around the room once more and couldn't help but feeling how masculine it was. This had clearly been the domain of her father and nothing had been changed since his death. The room felt as if Miss McIntosh would have been uncomfortable to enter. For her to have been found dead there meant that she had to have had a strong reason for entering in the first place.

Jake stood up and made his way out of the room. He went through to what he assumed had been Miss McIntosh's bedroom. This room had a far more feminine feel to it and he felt as if he was intruding to be there. None the less he started to look around. Finally he arrived at the bedside cabinets. In the top drawer of one of the cabinets he found a stack of papers held together by a piece of string. He took them out and sat on the bed to study them. He undid the string and spread the papers out on the bed. There was a mix of letters and certificates, including Edith's birth certificate and her parents' wedding certificate.

Amongst the letters were three from a solicitors' firm in Aberdeen by the name of Ward, Logan and Shinnie. The letters seemed to indicate that Reginald Shinnie was the family lawyer and Jake took a note of both Shinnie's name and the address of the firm. He thought it would be worth speaking to Shinnie as he would not only know what might happen to everything now that Edith McIntosh was dead, but also have some idea as to what else would have been of value in the house. There might even be an inventory of some kind, which would make it easier to identify what might have been stolen, over and above the miniature paintings.

Jake decided that the material in front of him might prove useful so he bundled it up again and tied the string around it. He then found a bag lying on a nearby chair in which he put the papers and left the room. He went back downstairs and in to the sitting room where he found Mathieson searching the drawers of a sideboard.

"I'm not finding anything, sir," he said.

"Leave it just now, Sergeant, we'd best get back to the office."

***

It had been a successful afternoon for Lucy Gill. Through her ability to tell a good story and the fact she looked as if she had a few pounds in the bank, Lucy had been able to get a new dress and hat without having to pay a penny. She had been allowed to open an account at Sangster and Henderson after showing them the letter she had, from her solicitor's in Edinburgh, confirming a payment of £100 coming her way. Of course there was no solicitor and there was no payment, but it worked nearly every time.

Lucy got back to her room and started to prepare for dinner. She was keen to wear her new dress and to continue to exude that air of affluence that she so enjoyed.

***

Jake was leaving the office at a little after seven to make his way home to Margaret. As he came out of the front door at Lodge Walk his attention was drawn to a man leaning against the wall, across the road. He was lighting a cigarette. Jake recognised the man at once; it was Alan MacBride, one of the main journalists at the Aberdeen Daily Journal.

The two men had helped each other out over the years and their relationship had matured in to one of mutual respect. MacBride would never knowingly print anything that might harm the Aberdeen City Police and in return, Jake would always make sure that MacBride was first to get any news springing from his investigations.

Jake crossed the road. "You really shouldn't hang around street corners, Alan, you'll be getting a reputation," he quipped.

MacBride exhaled some more smoke and smiled. "I'm hoping you'll have a story for me soon, Jake."

"About what?"

"The murdered teacher."

Jake tried to look surprised. "However did you hear about that?"

"Her colleagues. People at the school are talking. They're nervous and worried. We all get that way when death visits someone close to us. That nervousness gets magnified a hundred fold when the death in question happens to be murder."

"It's very early days, Alan, I've got nothing for you at the moment."

"But you might have someday soon?" added MacBride hopefully.

"It'll be the usual arrangement, Alan; you'll be the first to hear if the investigation starts to get anywhere."

"So, no suspects?"

"No fishing, Alan."

"Sorry, Jake," MacBride added with a smile.

The two men parted company at that point. As Jake made his way to the end of Lodge Walk and turned left, he was aware of a fog developing over the city that threatened to get worse as the evening wore on. By the time he had got home and had something to eat, the view from the window of the flat had almost been completely removed by a thick blanket of fog that clung to buildings with a dampness that would have seeped in to bones were anyone to be out in it.

It was another downside of living on the coast.

***

THREE

Wednesday 03rd June

Jake was sitting at the kitchen table enjoying a cup of tea and a freshly boiled egg. Margaret was sitting across from him, passing on the egg, but enjoy the first cup of tea of the day. Jake looked across at his wife and smiled. Margaret had grown accustomed to her husband smiling at her; she knew how much he loved her and he was forever telling her how lucky he was. The truth was, she felt lucky as well. She had given up hope of ever finding a loving husband and then Jake walked in to her life with questions regarding a murder inquiry. Not the most romantic of introductions, but they had never looked back from that day.

"I'm going to have to speak to Peter Ash today," Jake had then said. Margaret had felt sure that her husband had been mulling over something as he had eaten his egg; now she knew what that 'something' had been.

"Nothing wrong, I hope?" she added.

"No, it's to do with the investigation I'm working on at the moment. Apparently Peter knew the victim."

Margaret filled her cup from the pot and offered Jake some more tea, which he declined with a look at his pocket-watch.

"That might make life a little awkward for him," commented Margaret.

Jake smiled. "And me. Anyway, I'd better go."

"Remember I have a meeting tonight," Margaret then said.

"Another meeting with your Liberal ladies?" Jake asked, standing up and moving away from the table.

"We intend meeting more regularly now."

"Are you still discussing Liberal values or have matters turned more to acquiring the vote?" Jake then asked and received a disapproving glare from Margaret.

"You agreed not to get involved in what I choose to discuss at my meetings," she said.

"I know I did," said Jake, holding up his hand by way of apology, "but if, as an outcome of these meetings, anything happens that might require a police presence, then I'd find it impossible to stay out of things then."

"Jake, we sit and talk, why ever would that lead to a police presence?"

"You nearly did last December," added Jake.

"But we didn't," insisted Margaret and her tone was enough to tell Jake to change the subject.

"Well, I'd better be going."

Jake put on his jacket, kissed Margaret and left the flat. Outside the day was the complete opposite to the damp fog of the night before. The sky was now clear and the sun's warmth was already evident in the air. Jake felt sure that they were in for a glorious day and was already wondering what temperature might be recorded for the newspapers.

Back in the flat, Margaret sat back at the table and drank some more of her tea. She never liked disagreeing with Jake on anything and they had rarely quarrelled in the time they had been married, but there was no denying that her political views might yet create a barrier between them.

Margaret had always enjoyed her own mind. Until she met Jake she had been a single, very independent woman, who had chosen, often as not, to take her own path in life without much regard for the thoughts of others. She had been a constant worry to her parents who, whilst enjoying the fact that their daughter had a mind of her own, had always sought that safe and secure path of marriage for her. For a long time in Margaret's life she had actively stood against marriage, choosing to prove to the world that a woman could make something of her life without the need for a man.

Now that she had chosen to marry, she was finding it difficult to adapt to the fact that she now had Jake to consider in any action she might choose to take. The fact that her husband was a senior police officer further complicated matters as she never wanted to do anything that might put Jake in an awkward situation with his colleagues and superiors.

Accepting all that, however, Margaret did not want to give up on her political beliefs, particularly her desire for women to get the vote. There seemed no logical reason to her why women were still being denied a say in who should govern the country now that they were in to the twentieth century. Surely there was a need for times to change?

Jake's reference to last December had concerned a meeting of the Aberdeen Women Liberals at which the Reverend Webster had been assaulted by a group of women for trying to bring a counter proposal to their meeting, which tried to stop them discussing the vote. The women's actions had been applauded, the next day at the railway station, by no less than Mrs Pankhurst herself. Margaret had been at the station that day to see Mrs Pankhurst receive flowers from Lady Ramsay and then say a few words in support of the Suffragette movement.

It had been quite an inspiring occasion.

Being a member of the Aberdeen Women Liberals, Margaret could not understand why men were happy for her to meet and talk politics with her friends, but were unhappy about those same women having a say in which party ran the government. Why should choosing an MP be a wholly male affair? Maybe in days gone by, women had either cared little for politics, or perhaps had simply been less inclined to disagree with their menfolk.

It wasn't that Margaret really wanted to disagree with Jake, but she knew what she wanted and if that went against the wishes of her husband then so be it. She hoped it would not lead to quarrels of any kind, perhaps due more to the fact that Jake was not the type of man inclined to force his opinions on anyone. Jake was not a political animal, expressing view opinions on anything even remotely connected to government.

Margaret finally drank the last of her tea and stood up from the table. Beyond any political differences that she might have had with her husband, she knew that their relationship was, essentially, sound. They had formed a bond almost from the first moment they had met and Margaret was now more than happy to be sharing her life and her property with her husband.

She made her way through to the bedroom and opened the large wardrobe that lay against one of the walls. She then stood back and surveyed the line of dresses. Which one would she wear today, that was the question?

***

It was early evening before Jake received word from Superintendent Ash that he was free to see him. For Jake, it had been a bit of a wasted day. He had no leads on Edith McIntosh, other than her possibly knowing the Superintendent and until he had spoken to his superior officer about that relationship there was little that he could do.

Jake made his way upstairs to the Superintendent's office, which was situated two doors from that of the Chief Constable. Jake knocked on the door and entered when invited to do so.

Superintendent Ash was seated at his desk. Ash was a solidly built man in his early fifties. He had a round face and what little hair he had, grew in two tufts from the side of his head, leaving a shiny, bald track down the middle. Jake noticed a tiredness in the man's eyes; it was that look that appeared in the eyes of so many colleagues who had years of experience behind them.

The life of a police officer was hard. They saw sights that others rarely saw and they spent most of their working life rubbing shoulders with the underbelly of society. There were few laughs in the working life of a police officer and as the years went by, the accumulation of what they had seen and done weighed heavily upon them. Ash looked like a man ready for retirement and yet there had been no suggestion of him doing so.

"Have a seat, Jake," Ash said. He put his pen down on the paperwork lying in front of him and sat back in his chair.

Jake sat down. He still wasn't entirely sure how he would conduct this interview. He was not in the habit of seeking information from senior officers who might be involved in a murder inquiry. He decided to begin on a more general footing.

"Have you had a chance to catch up on what we are all doing, since you're return from Elgin?"

"Not really," replied Ash, his eyes dropping to the paperwork on his desk. "This stuff seems never-ending."

"So you don't know about the murder I'm investigating?"

"No, but I'm sure you'll keep me abreast of proceedings; you always do."

"A woman was murdered on Saturday evening," Jake then said, trying to introduce the subject in as casual a manner as possible, "and I'm led to believe that you might know her, sir."

Ash's expression changed to one of concern and he sat forward in his chair. "Really? Who are we be talking about?"

Jake paused for a moment. "Miss Edith McIntosh."

The blood visibly drained from Ash's face and he slumped back in his chair as if all the air had been sucked out of him. His eyes immediately looked towards the door of his office, as if he suspected a dozen ears were currently pressed to the other side, all intent on hearing what he said next.

A silence remained between them for a few more seconds before Ash finally said:

"Come on, Jake, I'll buy you a pint."

Nothing more was said as Jake followed the Superintendent out of the building and around to the Prince of Wales bar, where Ash bought two pints of beer and then led them to a table in the corner, at the back of the bar. Those already in the bar were perfectly aware of who the new arrivals were and as such a natural gap appeared between them and the two police officers.

Ash drank some of his beer and wiped his mouth with the back of his hand. He placed his glass on the table lying between them and then spoke.

"How did she die?"

"She was strangled, sir, probably with one of her own curtain ties."

Ash looked distraught once again. "Why would anyone want to kill someone as sweet and friendly as Edith?"

"The theory at the moment, sir, is that someone broke in to her house intent on stealing a collection of miniature paintings, which her deceased father had collected. Miss McIntosh must have disturbed him and he killed her. I have to say, sir, it's not the strongest of theories, just at the moment."

Ash looked puzzled. "Why not?"

"For a start I'm not totally sure why a burglar would feel the need to kill her. There would have been other, less dramatic, options and yet he killed her."

"Obviously she must have recognised him," Ash added.

"That would certainly appear to be the case, sir, but he could still have simply overpowered her and made good his escape. Murder seemed a somewhat unnecessary line to take. Then there is the matter of the miniature paintings themselves."

"What about them?" asked Ash.

"The cupboard, in which they were kept, now appears to be empty. However, we don't know, at present, when that cupboard was emptied. It may have been a burglary, or it may have been at a time when Miss McIntosh had decided to sell them. You wouldn't happen to know anything about these miniatures, would you sir?"

"No, Jake, I'm afraid I don't."

"Did Miss McIntosh ever mention them to you?"

Ash shook his head. "There would never have been any reason for her to talk of such things with me; we met each other for purely social purposes and were too busy having fun than concern ourselves with who might have collected what."

"How long had you known her?"

Ash thought for a moment. "It must be about eighteen months now."

"How did you meet, if you don't mind me asking, sir?"

Ash smiled, as if the memory of their meeting had been a particularly happy one. "We were both invited to a Hogmanay party at the home of a mutual friend. We had spent a lot of the time talking and realised that we had much in common when it came to what entertained us. We agreed to go to the theatre together when something of interest was on."

"Did you become close friends?"

"We were good friends, but not what I would describe as close; certainly not in terms of knowing much about each other's private lives."

"So you weren't linked romantically?" Jake then asked, choosing to ignore his beer for the moment.

"Good God, no. At our age, Jake, we were happy with companionship; there was never any thought, certainly not on my part, to change the structure of our relationship. It was nice to have dinner together occasionally, or to go to the theatre and then have someone to discuss the event with. Since Mrs Ash died I've missed having someone else with whom to simply talk. Edith filled that gap."

"What kind of woman was she?"

Ash smiled again as he recalled the memory of Edith McIntosh. "She was funny. She had a wonderful sense of humour and she loved her work. She talked a lot about her boys as if they were her own."

"Yes, her colleagues said the same thing," added Jake. "Did you ever meet any of Miss McIntosh's friends or acquaintances?"

"When we were together we tended to be in our own little world, Jake. I never saw her talking to anyone else, whilst she was in my company and she certainly never introduced anyone else to me. It was almost as if our time together became our little secret."

"Miss McIntosh didn't think of it as a secret, sir," Jake then said. "She spoke to her colleagues about you."

"Did she really?" Ash then added with another smile.

"Were you ever at Miss McIntosh's home?" Jake then enquired.

"Just the once. I went to collect her one night before going to the theatre and she invited me in for a few moments whilst she had finished getting ready."

"So you'll know that Miss McIntosh had a lot of items on show in her home, many of which are probably quite valuable?"

"I don't know about value, but yes, I did know she had surrounded herself with ornaments and other items, which she'd obviously liked."

"As far as I can see, nothing else appears to have been stolen. However, it would be helpful to have an inventory of some kind of the items that were in her house."

Ash thought for a moment. "I should imagine there would be a list somewhere, perhaps with a solicitor."

Jake nodded. "I'll be going to see Miss McIntosh's solicitor, a Mr Shinnie, sometime within the next couple of days."

Both men now drank some of their beer. Ash was staring at the table top, apparently deep in thought. Jake got the impression that the Superintendent was mulling something over in his mind.

"Is there anything else that you can tell me, sir?" he then asked.

Ash had that look of someone who was desperate to say something, but unsure as to how much he should actually say. He drank some more beer and then played with the glass as his mind appeared to be running through a variety of scenarios. He then looked around the bar, taking in the growing number of faces standing at, or around, the counter area. Many men chose to have a pint or two before going home and the bar was starting to get quite busy.

Ash eventually looked back at Jake. "You might want to have a word with Arthur Fleming."

Jake shrugged. "That name means nothing to me, sir."

"He is the brother of Tom Fleming who was hanged, around ten years ago, for the murder of Jean Maxwell."

"And you think he might be connected to Miss McIntosh's death?" Jake asked, not seeing any link himself.

Ash nodded. "About three weeks ago, Edith and I were coming out of His Majesty's Theatre when I bumped in to a man coming along the pavement. I recognised him immediately as being Arthur Fleming. I was quite surprised to see him as the last I heard he was in prison for half killing a man in a pub argument."

"I don't really remember the Jean Maxwell murder," Jake added.

"I was the main investigating officer. Much of the evidence gathered against Tom Fleming was circumstantial, but we felt there was enough to get him to court and the jury did the rest."

"Anyway, what happened when you bumped in to Arthur?" prompted Jake.

"It transpired that Arthur had only been back in Aberdeen a matter of days, after being released from prison and it was pure coincidence that we should both be outside the theatre at the same time. Having said that, he was quick to begin throwing insults at me for he had recognised me almost as quickly as I had him. Poor Edith had not known what to do. I tried to take Edith away from Fleming, but he came after us and continued to accuse me of falsifying evidence against his brother. Arthur Fleming seriously believed that it was my evidence alone that led to his brother's conviction and ultimate hanging. His last words to me were that he would find a way of making me suffer, just as he had and as he said those words, I swear to God he was looking directly at Edith."

"So you think Fleming might have killed Miss McIntosh to get back at you in some way?" Jake asked, by way of clarification.

Ash had a look of horror on his face. "I hope to God I'm wrong. I could never live with myself if it became known that Edith had been murdered because of something I had done."

"Is this Arthur Fleming a burglar?"

"He's been arrested for a variety of misdemeanours over the years. I'm sure that burglary will be in there somewhere."

"And we know he has a temper," Jake added, referring to the reason for his most recent imprisonment.

"It would certainly provide you with another motive," suggested Ash.

"Do you believe that Arthur Fleming would be capable of murdering someone just to get back at you?"

"Had he not been dragged off that man in the pub, there is every likelihood that he would have killed him. It appears that Arthur Fleming has a fiery temper when aroused."

"Does Arthur Fleming have good reason to be annoyed with you, sir?"

Ash looked as if he was about to take Jake to task over asking such a question, but then he seemed to soften and actually consider the question more seriously.

"The case against Tom Fleming had never been that strong, I admit, but nothing was falsified, I can assure you of that."

"Who worked the case with you, sir?"

"Sergeant Gauld. I'm afraid he's dead now so I'm the only target left for Fleming to vent his fury at."

Jake took out his notebook and wrote down much of what had just been said. Ash finished his beer and offered to buy another for Jake, who refused. Anymore alcohol, in a stomach devoid of food and Jake would be heading home in an obvious state of inebriation. He knew that Margaret would be less than pleased, were he to arrive home in that condition, so it made sense to head for home as soon as possible. Ash decided he'd not have another drink either, so once Jake was finished writing, the two men stood up and made their way out on to the street.

"Come and see me anytime about this," Ash then said, before he turned and walked away, towards Correction Wynd. Jake chose to briefly go back to the office. He needed to gather some information for the following day. He needed to know all that he could about Tom Fleming and his brother, Arthur.

***

FOUR

Wednesday 03rd June – Evening

Jake had still not arrived home as Margaret left the flat. It was not uncommon for them not to see each other until bedtime and sometimes even not then, if Margaret had fallen asleep before Jake climbed in beside her. The physical side of their relationship was still a bit hit and miss, with Margaret still adapting to the fact that there was a man looking at her when she took her clothes off at night. It hadn't helped that she had been nearly forty-one before she had lost her virginity. There had been many a day when she had imagined she'd have been a virgin all her life and then, suddenly, there was Jake in her life and ultimately, her bed as well.

Jake had always been so tender in his motions towards her. He had understood her reluctance to throw herself in to those more intimate moments they would share together, even though Margaret was the type of woman who threw herself in to most things. She had worried about the possible pain of love-making and she had fretted over whether, or not, she would actually be any good at it. After all, from a woman's perspective, what constituted being good at the sexual act? It had always been suggested to her that sex was an act aimed at bringing pleasure only to the male.

Prior to meeting Margaret, Jake had been having an occasional sexual relationship with a young prostitute by the name of Alice. Jake had helped Alice, in so many ways, over a period of time and the girl had felt that the only way she could pay Jake back for his kindness was to offer him her body. Over time, Jake had helped Alice to leave the life of a prostitute and she was now happily married to man called Johnnie Gordon and hopefully living happily ever after.

Margaret had no thoughts for sex as she left the building that night. Outside it was still quite light and the air was cool, though not cold. Margaret wore a coat over her maroon dress and she carried an umbrella, just in case the rain returned. Most people, living in the north-east of Scotland, permanently carried an umbrella for they felt sure that rain was never very far away.

Margaret made her way through North Silver Street and across Golden Square. She was heading for the Music Hall as the meeting of the Aberdeen Woman Liberal Association was taking place in the Round Room that night. Margaret had become involved with the Association early in 1907, after meeting a woman from London by the name of Sadie Ashton.

Sadie was a strong-willed woman in her mid-thirties. She had moved to Aberdeen five years earlier, with her husband. However, he had been killed, just before Christmas 1906, when he had been hit, whilst crossing Holburn Street, by a tram. The driver had tried to attract the man's attention, but had failed. Sadie Ashton had then considered returning to London, but had eventually decided to remain in the Granite City and play her part in helping to bring the vote to all women. The first step had been to join the Aberdeen Women Liberal Association and then to set about increasing membership numbers.

She had met Margaret at a committee meeting for one of the charities that Margaret now represented. Margaret had worked at the Sailor's Institute, on Mearns Street, but had stopped after her marriage to Jake. She had chosen to replace her employment with a series of committee meetings, at which she helped organise the running of other charitable outlets. It was Margaret's way of putting something back in to the community. She had always felt she had lived a privileged life in comparison to many others and now wanted to repay society in some way.

Sadie Ashton had felt much the same. Her husband had left her financially comfortable and now she had the time and the inclination to work tirelessly for the benefit of others. She had found, in Margaret, a kindred spirit and both women now appeared on many committees together.

Margaret arrived at the Music Hall at a little after half past seven in the evening. There were a few women already going in and the usual small gathering of men who regularly stood outside any building, in which the women held their meetings, purely so they could pass unkind comments to those attending.

"You should be ashamed of yourselves," one of the men snapped at Margaret as she reached the door. She paused, thought about offering a retort, but then decided it might be wiser to keep on walking. After all, she did not want to give these men any notion that their comments were having an effect on her.

She made her way up the small flight of steps and through the door situated to her left. Once inside the main hall she made her way to another door located once more to her left. She opened the door and entered.

Inside, the Round Room looked splendid. Seats had been laid out and at the far end, where another door was located, a table had been put in place. The table was covered with a white cloth and there was a jar of water and some glasses lying on a tray, placed upon it. Behind the table were four chairs, indicating that there would probably be three speakers tonight. The fourth chair would be for their President, Mrs Black.

There were a number of ladies already there, some had taken their seats and others were standing about. Margaret noticed Mrs Black standing to her left, three other women standing beside her and listening, intently, to her every word. Mrs Black never used her first name; it was as if she saw that as some way of keeping her anonymity. She was a woman well through her fifties, with grey hair tied up in a bun on the back of her head. She was small and petite of frame, but could hold her own in a discussion, or argument. She had been a widow for ten years and now spent most of her time championing the cause for women to at least have a greater say in the politics of the land, even if they were to be denied an actual vote.

Margaret turned and left the room again. She took off her coat as she walked round to the cloakroom. As she neared the small window, through which their clothing was passed, she noticed Sadie Ashton already there and talking to another, younger woman. Margaret assumed this must be another of Sadie's new recruits.

Sadie turned as Margaret approached. "Good evening, Margaret, might I introduce you to Ada Houston, this will be her first meeting."

Ada looked very young; in fact she was probably one of the many students from the university, who were showing an active interest in politics, especially when it came to the Suffragettes. The Aberdeen Women Liberal Association did not affiliate itself directly to the Suffragette Movement, but in having political views any woman was immediately throwing her weight behind the Movement. After all, what good were political views without the right to vote? Ada held out her hand and her face lit with a bright smile. Margaret thought her to be very pretty. They shook hands.

"Good evening, Ada and to you, Sadie. It looks like we'll get a good turn out tonight."

"I believe one of our speakers is very good," added Sadie, "though I have to admit to getting a little tired of doing little more than talking."

Margaret knew that Sadie was referring to the more militant side of the Suffragette Movement. There were a growing number or women who firmly believed that the only way to get their message across was through acts of violence and outright rebellion. It was felt that men would continue to do no more than make patronising comments towards them unless action was taken to force the establishment to change its ways.

There had already been one or two incidents in Aberdeen. There had been that incident, with the Reverend Webster the previous December when one of the local papers had reported that a spirit of revolt had now manifested itself in the Aberdeen Women Liberals due to them feeling that the adoption of tactics, similar to those of the suffragettes, was the only course that could effectively be followed.

In April 1908, Emily Davison, well-known nationally for now being a full-time member of the Suffragette Movement, had attacked a clergyman at Aberdeen Railway Station in the mistaken belief that he was the new Prime Minister, Mr Asquith. It had not been uncommon for Emily Davison to attack innocent men in her quest to get at the politicians of the day, for she had cared little for who her targets really were and more for the message she was getting across in gaining publicity for her actions.

These were the kind of actions supported by Sadie Ashton. She was the kind of woman who wanted to throw bricks through windows and generally disrupt the world in which the male dominated. She had no inclination to marry again and now concentrated on trying to make the world a better place in which women could live and prosper.

The three women went back through to the Round Room and found what they thought would be good seats. By eight o'clock everyone was in and the door closed. Mrs Black and the other three women standing beside her, made their way to the front and sat down behind the table. Mrs Black then checked a watch that she took from her bag and called the meeting to order. She then stood up and passed a few opening remarks before introducing the first of their guest speakers.

The first speaker turned out to be Miss Elspeth Gawthorpe, a well-known Suffragette, who had spoken at the university just the month before. Ada passed a comment to that effect before settling back and listening to what was about to be said. Miss Gawthorpe rejoiced in the fact that she had an audience actually prepared to listen to her. The university meeting had been gate-crashed by male undergraduates who had done everything in their power to cause maximum disruption. It had been some time before events had settled down enough to allow Miss Gawthorpe and her colleague that night, Miss Fraser, to actually say anything.

However, there were to be no such problems on this occasion. She spoke for twenty minutes and most of it was of a positive nature. She spoke of the change of Prime Minister in the April. Mr Campbell-Bannerman had resigned, through ill-health and Mr Asquith had now taken over. It had been noted that Mr Asquith had actively been against women getting the vote since 1882 and that there was little chance of him ever changing his views without more than a little persuasion. That, of course, meant militant action.

When Miss Gawthorpe stopped speaking and sat down there was a polite round of applause. Mrs Black then introduced the second of their speakers, a member of the Glasgow Women Liberal Association. She only spoke for a few moments and the third speaker, who was actually there to talk about medical matters as they related to women, took up no more than another ten minutes. Mrs Black then asked for questions and another thirty minutes went by as Miss Gawthorpe, mainly, dealt with the points that were raised. Mrs Black then brought the proceedings to a close and all the women began moving towards the cloakroom.

Margaret found herself standing with Ada and Sadie again as they waited for the queue to clear a little.

"That was all so exciting, wasn't it?" Ada announced, her eyes wide with joy.

"It's not enough though," Sadie added quickly.

Margaret looked concerned. "What do you mean, it's not enough?"

"This new Prime Minister won't listen to our arguments any more than the last one," Sadie continued. "He's entrenched in old ideas and there is little chance of him changing those ideas without something happening to make men, in general, change their views concerning us women."

"How, exactly, do we change how men think?" challenged Margaret.

Sadie thought for a moment. "I don't know exactly, but it has to start with us getting the public on our side. The more people who support our cause then the more pressure there will be for change. We need to get to a point where men will have no option other than to give us the vote."

Margaret thought for a moment. "But how do we get the public on our side?"

"By keeping our arguments in the public domain," Sadie replied. "We cannot afford to let anyone forget about us. Whatever it takes, we need to keep our argument on the front page of every paper and we need to ensure that every time Parliament meets, they will have to discuss some issue that concerns our cause."

"Whatever it takes?" asked Margaret.

Sadie nodded. "Basically, yes."

"The national Suffragette Movement seem to be having some success in getting their message across. Miss Gawthorpe said as much at the meeting tonight," Ada then added.

"We may be winning some minor victories," conceded Sadie, "but we are nowhere near winning the war."

"You make it all sound so violent," added Margaret.

"That's because it is," insisted Sadie. "Men will continue to ignore us unless we do something to shake them out of their cosy little world."

"I say again," said Margaret, "like what?"

Sadie sounded frustrated when she answered. "Oh, I don't know, but I am sure we could think of something if we all put our minds to it."

"Just be careful, Sadie, you don't want to end up behind bars," Margaret said, glancing at Ada, who seemed lost in her own little world. Margaret now worried that Sadie's words might be striking a chord with someone as young and impressionable as Ada.

The three women now moved forward and collected their coats. As they put them on, Ada spoke again.

"What is it that you do, Margaret?"

"Mainly charity work. That was where Sadie and I met."

"Are you married?"

Before Margaret could respond to the question, Sadie had spoken. "Margaret is not only married, Ada, but she is married to the enemy."

"Sadie!" remonstrated Margaret.

"Whatever do you mean?" added Ada.

"Margaret is married to a police officer, a senior police officer at that."

"Which has no effect on anything," Margaret then said, staring hard at Sadie who simply smiled.

"Does your husband agree with women getting the vote?" Ada then asked.

"My husband cares little for politics, Ada. He doesn't bother to vote himself and probably gives little thought to others voting, whether they be male or female."

Having buttoned their coats the three women made their way to the front door. It was now getting dark outside, though the light had still to fade completely. They stood outside, by the pillars that fronted the building and concluded their conversation. Margaret managed to steer the topic away from Jake and also away from militant action.

Agreeing to see Sadie on Friday, at another charity meeting, Margaret walked down the stone steps and turned left. Sadie and Ada were still talking and Margaret worried, as she walked home that Sadie might be spreading the sort of misinformed militancy that would do more harm, than good, to their cause.

***

FIVE

Thursday 04th June

The morning had started brightly enough and Jake had enjoyed the relatively short walk to his work. As he had walked to work, his mind had gone back over the night before. He had been getting ready for bed when Margaret had arrived back from her meeting. She had become strangely aroused by the sight of him standing naked in the bedroom and, quite unlike Margaret, she had then been the instigator of their love-making. It had been a very pleasurable experience and Jake had fallen asleep with his head on her breast and his arm around her waist.

Although he had enjoyed the experience immensely, Jake couldn't help wondering what had been the catalyst for her passion. Maybe there were just times when the human body craved love in its most basic form and last night had been one of those times for Margaret? Whatever the reason, it had put a smile on Jake's face and a spring in his step that morning

He had arrived at Lodge Walk at a little after seven o'clock in the morning. The Desk Sergeant, Roderick Wheatley, nodded a good morning as Jake went by and three young Constables, whom he met in the corridor, half-saluted their superior officer. Jake hated such things, but they tended to happen anyway.

Jake chose not to go directly to his office but, instead, went out the back door of the building, crossed the parade ground and entered the front door of the mortuary building. He followed the relatively short route to the room where he knew he would find Doctor Stephen. He found the Doctor already hard at work, though not on a body that was relevant to Jake.

"Morning, Inspector Fraser, what can I do for you today?" Doctor Stephen asked, only looking up briefly before returning to his work.

"Have you anything more to tell me about Edith McIntosh?" Jake then said.

Doctor Stephen stopped what he was doing and stood up straight. He seemed to be thinking for a moment, as if trying to bring Edith McIntosh to the forefront of his memory. Eventually he spoke.

"I can formally confirm that she was strangled and that the curtain tie was probably the weapon. She was attacked from behind and died sometime on Saturday evening. There was no indication of sexual interference and no other marks on her body. You'll have my report on your desk later today, assuming I don't get any more interruptions."

Jake noted the mild rebuke. "My thanks, Doctor," he then said and turned to leave the building. He went back across the parade ground and made his way to his office, where he sat down at his desk and opened the drawer to his right. He removed the material he had placed there, the night before and laid it all on the desk in front of him.

He then pulled a thick, blue coloured, file closer towards him and undid the string that kept it together. He opened the file and started to spread the contents across his desk. Every item had the name *Tom Fleming* written at the top with an address in 1898 to the right of it.

There were a variety of items covering interview statements, reports from the Police Doctor, background information on the victim and various, often scribbled, notes on the main suspect, Tom Fleming. There was a surprising amount of material and Jake knew he had much to get through that day.

Before reading any of the papers he looked at the front of the file again. The main investigating officer was noted as Inspector Ash and his main assistant had been, as Ash had said, Sergeant Gauld. Jake had vague memories of Gauld. He had been a tall, gruff spoken Yorkshireman, who had never stopped moaning about the weather in the north-east of Scotland. He ended up living for twenty years in Aberdeen and yet he had never accepted how cold it got in the winter. Many had since told Jake that the weather in Yorkshire was nothing to write home about and that Gauld's fixation with the north-east weather had no logical basis.

Jake sat back in his chair and thought about what Ash had said concerning his meeting with Arthur Fleming. Why had Arthur been so sure that his brother's conviction had been tainted in some way? Was it just the love of a brother getting in the way of logical thought? No one ever wants to believe that a member of their family could ever be a killer, but obviously every murderer had to have a family of some kind to call his, or her, own. Some poor, unfortunate mother had to be responsible for the birth of every murderer who walked the planet.

However, there was one inescapable fact: Arthur Fleming was no angel himself. He had no reason to look upon his brother with rose tinted spectacles if crime truly did run in the family. The fact, then, that Arthur had strongly defended his brother carried more weight than it may have done with others. Would that then, however, have driven Arthur to commit murder himself, especially as he was desperately trying to clear his brother's name of that very crime?

It was indeed a puzzle.

Jake sat forward again and picked up the sheet of paper with the victim's name at the top. As he read, Jake took notes of his own. Somehow he had to make sense of the case before he spoke to Arthur Fleming. If there was any doubt about the conviction then Jake needed to know about it before he spoke to the grieving brother. There had been something about Ash's manner that had worried Jake. It came across as if Ash, himself, might even be having doubts about that particular case. It hadn't felt as if Ash had been hiding anything, but there had definitely been something. Possibly it was the fact Ash now connected the meeting with Arthur Fleming and the death of Edith McIntosh. No one else had any reason to link the two and perhaps there was no link to be made. Arthur Fleming may simply have been sounding off.

Jake began to build a picture of what had happened ten years ago.

Jean Maxwell had celebrated her twentieth birthday in the May of 1898. Back then Jake had been a Sergeant, learning his trade and taking instruction from the likes of Inspector Ash. However, he had never worked on the Maxwell case and remembered nothing of what had happened at that time. He had been too busy dealing with other investigations to devote any time to the work of others.

Jean Maxwell had been a pretty, vivacious girl who had worked as a maid in one of the big houses along Queens Road. Her employer, Professor Clive Barclay, had worked at the university and had been, by all accounts, very good to his staff. Tom Fleming had worked in the garden at the house in Queens Road and had got to know Jean through the fact they had frequently come in to contact there.

On the third of June, 1898, Professor Barclay had returned from work to find the back door of his property wide open and some garden tools lying in the kitchen. There had also been mud on the floor leading upstairs, where he found Jean lying on the bed in the main bedroom. Her clothes had been in disarray and she had been strangled. On the bedside table were two, empty glasses and a half-finished bottle of wine. There was also a button lying on the floor of the bedroom quite close to the bed.

Ash had immediately suspected Tom Fleming as he had been known to have been working at the house that day and was nowhere to be seen when Barclay had got home. The fact there was mud on the floor and garden tools in the kitchen further convinced Ash that Fleming had to, at the very least, have been in the house.

Jake picked up some more papers and kept reading. Ash had sought out Tom Fleming and had eventually arrested him in the Saltoun Arms pub later that evening. Fleming had been taken to Lodge Walk, where he was interviewed by Ash and Gauld. Jake now picked up the record of that interview and read through it.

Fleming had denied, from the very first moment of the interview that he had had anything to do with Jean's death. He had become rather distraught at the news of her death and did confess to having feelings for the girl. Ash had taken this as being further motive for Fleming being in the house. The working theory swiftly became that Fleming had gone in to the house to share a drink with Jean and perhaps indulge in a little romance. With the house to themselves they had ventured upstairs to enjoy the luxury of the master's bedroom. Initially they had both had thoughts of romance but, for some reason, Jean had changed her mind once they had reached the bedroom and had suggested that Fleming leave. He had been too aroused by that time and had then tried to force himself upon her. She had made a noise of some kind and in trying to keep her quiet, he had strangled her.

It was certainly a strong theory, but there appeared to be no real evidence to back it up. The most damning piece of evidence had been the button, which was later proved to have come from Tom Fleming's working jacket.

Fleming had argued that he lost buttons all the time and that anyone might have picked one up almost anywhere. He further argued that he thought too much of Jean to ever force himself upon her. He said that he had worked in the garden all afternoon, leaving around five to go to the pub for a drink. At that point Jake checked the paperwork for any indication that the pub had been visited to confirm the time at which Tom Fleming had arrived. There was nothing.

Jake returned to the main account of what had happened. The Police Doctor had estimated the time of death as being around four that afternoon. As far as Ash was concerned only Fleming had been anywhere near the house at the time of the murder, therefore only Tom Fleming could have committed the crime.

Basically, Ash had decided, at a very early stage, that Fleming was his murderer and had stopped looking for anyone else from that moment. He seemed more intent on confirming his theory rather than looking for alternatives. The main problem with his theory, at least to the casual eye, was the total lack of firm evidence. However, even without that evidence, Tom Fleming was duly charged with the murder of Jean Maxwell and placed in a cell awaiting trial.

The court case had taken place two months later. Fleming had been represented by Logan McMaster, whom Jake knew to be a rather insignificant name in the legal circles of Aberdeen. McMaster still worked in the city but had progressed little in the ten years that had elapsed. McMaster had argued, rather badly if the court transcript was anything to go by, that Tom Fleming had been too busy working in the garden to notice anything that might have been going on in the house. He had further argued that anyone could have gone in through the front door while Fleming was working at the back.

Neither Fleming, nor McMaster, could explain how the button had turned up in the bedroom, nor could they explain how the mud had been brought in from the back garden. Fleming had said that the back door was still closed when he had left at five, but given that the crime appeared to have been committed by then, no one seemed moved to believe him. Fleming had further said that he, himself, had never been in the house, let alone any of his tools. He could not, therefore, explain how the tools had found their way in to the kitchen.

Fleming had further argued that, had he really been the killer, would he honestly have gone to the pub leaving all those clues behind? McMaster had added that, by doing so, his client was pointing a finger straight at himself and surely no killer would ever do that. Jake had to agree that it made no sense for Fleming to have murdered Jean and then to leave the mud, the tools, the glasses and the button lying around for anyone to find. However, Ash had paid little attention to such a defence and the jury were soon to follow suit.

Jake read what little had been written about Professor Barclay. He had lectured in Classics History at the University and had lived at his home in Queens Road since early April, 1897. He had employed Jean as soon as he arrived in Aberdeen and had always found her to be a loyal and efficient employee. The Professor had said at the trial that he had been aware of a flame being lit between Jean and Tom. He had said that the young couple, however, had never done anything untoward in his presence. He had also said that he had found it hard to believe that Jean would willingly take a man upstairs in the house, no matter how innocent the idea might have initially been.

In the absence of any other suspects, Tom Fleming had been found guilty and was sentenced to be hanged within the week. He had been twenty years of age when the noose broke his neck.

Jake sat back in his chair and rubbed his eyes. He took his watch from his pocket and checked the time. An hour and a half had passed since he had sat down. His notebook now contained a few ideas of his own and his mind was mulling over everything that he had learned.

Nothing, in what Jake had read, actively proved that Tom Fleming had had anything to do with Jean Maxwell's murder. In fact, there was no actual proof that Tom had ever been in the house, let alone romantically involved in the Master's bedroom. Basically anyone could have put some mud on the floor and dropped a button in the bedroom. As Fleming had argued, *anyone* could have entered through the front door while he was out the back. The same person could then have left the house as Barclay had found it, for the Professor did not get home until a full hour after Fleming said that he had left.

But if that were the case, then the killer would have to have remained in the house, with Jean's body, not knowing when Tom Fleming might leave, nor when Professor Barclay would get home. That seemed quite a risk in Jake's estimation. If you had just murdered a woman, in a fit of passion, why would you then wait around for the gardener to leave and then make the crime look like he had committed it? It didn't make much sense to Jake and further pointed the finger at Fleming. If he hadn't brought the mud in to the house then why would someone else seek to frame him?

Jake returned to Professor Barclay. He read what little had been written about the man, once again. Barclay had been thirty-two years old in 1898 and described as a mild-mannered man with little life outside of his work. Jean had been the only employee who had a room in the house. Jake pondered on whether there had been anything sexual between the Professor and his maid. Could the Professor have committed the crime? He had been the one to find the body, so he could also have been the one to have killed her. But why?

Jake went through to one of the rooms where a telephone had been positioned. He connected to the switchboard operator and asked to be put through to the University. Within no time at all he found himself speaking to a woman who informed him she worked in the office and yes, she could provide some information on Professor

Barclay. The information, however, had not amounted to very much. The Professor had left the University and the city, if the woman's memory was to be believed, a matter of weeks after Tom Fleming's trial. Jake found that a bit strange. What had made the Professor leave Aberdeen; he asked the woman that question.

"I really can't remember," she replied. "Perhaps you should speak to Professor Riley?"

"Who might Professor Riley be?" enquired Jake, by way of reply.

"He worked with Professor Barclay in the Classics Department. Professor Riley retired two years ago."

"Where might I find him?"

"He lives in Hamilton Place," replied the woman and she also provided Jake with the number. He wrote it down, thanked the woman for her help, then stood up from the desk at which he was sitting and returned to his own office. He put on his jacket and headed for the front door. He was about to leave through the door when his attention was drawn, once more, to the Desk Sergeant. Roderick Wheatley had been the main Desk Sergeant since the retirement of Bill Turnbull almost a year ago. Like Bill, Roderick had been chosen for his even temperament, which meant he did not get so worked up about things as some of the people who called at his desk.

When arguments could so easily have raged at that front door, Roderick had been able to keep everyone's feet on the floor and had, therefore, reached an amicable solution all the quicker. Roderick's other attribute was his memory. He had been a police officer for over twenty years and could sharply recall every case he had worked on. His memory had been invaluable to many of his colleagues as they now worked on modern cases.

"Roddy?"

"What can I do for you, Jake?"

"What do you remember about the Tom Fleming case?"

Wheatley fell silent for a moment as his mind recalled the case and sifted through the memories for anything that might be conceived as being useful.

"I remember it was the case that gave Inspector Ash a higher profile around here. It ultimately led to him being the first choice when the new Chief Inspector role came along, as you may, yourself, recall?"

Jake nodded. "Was there anything about the actual investigation itself that you can recall as being untoward?"

Wheatley looked concerned. "You don't think that Ash got it wrong do you, Jake?"

"Superintendent Ash has, himself, suggested that Tom Fleming's brother, Arthur, firmly believes in his brother's innocence and that he threatened a friend of the Superintendent very recently."

"Edith McIntosh?" added Wheatley.

Jake smiled. "Not much passes you by, does it, Roddy?"

"I keep my eyes and ears open, that's all, Jake. It can't be a surprise to anyone that Arthur would believe his brother to be innocent. No one wants to admit to having a murderer in the family."

"I agree, Roddy, but Arthur's a criminal himself and having another criminal in the family might not be so important to him."

Wheatley considered that for a moment. "You may well be right, sir, however there must have been enough evidence to satisfy a jury."

"I've read the case notes," said Jake. "There was evidence, but it was all pretty flimsy."

"Maybe it was the weight of evidence rather than the strength of it that got Tom Fleming convicted?"

Jake thought for a moment. "Perhaps; or maybe they really did get it wrong."

"If they did then it seems rather unlikely that the real killer will be found after all these years," suggested Wheatley.

"Unless the killer was under their nose the whole time," added Jake. "From what I've read there was no attempt to look beyond Tom Fleming for a suspect. No one even questioned the account given by Professor Barclay. It was basically his account of events that passed in to history as the sole account of what happened. What if the good Professor was lying?"

"They were bound to believe the word of a Professor ahead of a gardener, weren't they, sir?"

"I rather suspect they were," was Jake's final word as he made his way out the front door.

It was pleasant enough outside for Jake to take a stroll up to Hamilton Place. He arrived at the front door of Professor Riley's house and knocked as hard as he could. Sometimes, in these big houses, it was difficult to hear someone at the door. As it happened, the door opened quite quickly and a plain looking, young girl in a crisply laundered maid's uniform stood before Jake.

"Is Professor Riley at home?" he enquired.

"He is, sir."

"Might I be allowed in to see him?" Jake then said after it became apparent that the young girl wasn't going to say, or do, anything until he had spoken first. She hesitated, as if the request was going to pose her problems, but then she seemed to make a decision and she stepped back. Jake entered.

"In here, sir," the girl then said and led the way in to the front room. "If you would care to take a seat, I'll let the Professor know that you are here."

"Thank you," added Jake, sitting on the settee and looking around a room that was spotlessly clean and immaculately furnished. There was a painting, above the fireplace, of a proud looking man, bedecked in his professorial finery and Jake assumed that it might be Riley himself. When the door eventually opened and an elderly gentleman walked in, Jake was provided with that last piece of evidence that confirmed the man above the fireplace was indeed Riley.

"Mavis tells me you are a police officer, I do hope I've done nothing wrong?"

It had never ceased to amuse Jake when people always assumed *they* had done something wrong, because the police had called on them. Jake quickly assured the Professor that he was there purely for the purposes of gathering information and that the Professor had nothing to be concerned about. Relieved to hear that, the Professor then asked if Jake would like some tea, to which he replied that he would. Mavis was summoned and instructed to bring tea and some cakes.

"Now, what can I do for you, Inspector?" Riley then said as he finally sat down on a chair to Jake's left.

"I'm here about Professor Clive Barclay, I've been told that you knew him quite well?"

"My God, why would anyone still be talking about Clive after all this time? It must be ten years since he left Aberdeen."

"Suffice to say, Professor Riley that we are re-visiting the Jean Maxwell murder and trying to get to know Professor Barclay a bit better. As I am unable to speak to the man himself, I'm hoping his friends and colleagues can help."

"But surely, apart from renting the house in which Jean Maxwell was killed, Clive can have no other connection with the case?"

"He was Jean's employer and as such, I would have expected him to have been interviewed more thoroughly at the time of the murder," Jake then said. "As it was, apart from making a formal statement about how he had found her body, nothing more was really asked of him."

"I'm not sure I'll be much help to you, Inspector. I worked with Clive, but it might be stretching things a little to say that I *knew* him. To be honest, I don't think anyone really *knew* him, at least not in the workplace."

"Do you know why he left Aberdeen when he did?"

"He got another job. He had arrived in Aberdeen from Cambridge, in eighteen ninety-seven, but told me he had never really settled. He then said he'd accepted the offer of a job back in Cambridge, so he resigned from Aberdeen and left."

"A bit of a climb-down coming to Aberdeen from Cambridge, isn't it?" Jake asked, a tone of disbelief in his voice.

"He always claimed that the Aberdeen job had been a step up for him. I'm sure he had liked the work here, he just didn't like Aberdeen. He always said it was too cold."

"I used to know someone like that," added Jake, his mind thinking of Sergeant Gauld. "So, Professor Barclay was only in Aberdeen a matter of months?"

"Fourteen or fifteen as I recall."

"And he always lived in the house in Queens Road?"

"Yes. I believe he had known the owner, prior to coming to Aberdeen and they had come to some arrangement concerning the monthly rental."

"Do you happen to know who that owner was?"

Riley shook his head. "I'm afraid not. I expect, after all this time, the house could well be under different ownership anyway."

"What kind of man was Professor Barclay?"

Riley thought for a moment. "Quiet; reserved. He kept himself very much to himself most of the time."

Mavis came in at that moment, carrying a tray on which she had placed two cups, in their saucers, a pot of tea, a jug of milk and a bowl of sugar. There was also a plate with an assortment of cakes on it, lying beside the teapot. She crossed the floor and laid the tray down on a table that set equidistant between the Professor and the policeman. She then turned and left the room. Riley stood up and walked over to the table where he poured two cups of tea and offered one, along with a cake, to Jake. He accepted both with thanks. The Professor took his tea and cake back to his seat.

"Can you recall the day of the murder at all, Professor Riley?"

"There was nothing much to recall. I was never interviewed at the time, presumably because I had nothing to say on the subject."

"Was Professor Barclay at work on the day of the murder?"

"He was."

"All day?"

"Ah, now that I couldn't tell you, because I was not at work that afternoon. I had been given some time off do deal with a family matter."

"So, it's possible that Professor Barclay finished early as well?" prompted Jake.

"I remember he had a lecture at two on a Friday, but that he also liked to get finished as early as possible; it being the end of the working week."

"So him claiming not to have got home until nearer six would not have been normal for a Friday?"

"He certainly wouldn't have been at the university until that time, though he may have had other matters to attend to before going home."

"Would there have been any record of when he would have finished on that, or any other, day?"

Riley laughed. "We didn't keep time sheets, if that is what you mean, Inspector. Our time is our own; we decide when the working day begins and ends and for that we have to answer to no one. The only people who could accurately tell you when the lecture finished would be those students who had attended it, but I should imagine tracking them down after ten years might prove a little difficult."

Riley paused, taking time to eat some of his cake and sip a little tea.

"Am I to take it, from your line of inquiry, that you now believe Clive might have had something to do with that poor girl's death?" he then continued.

"Perhaps not directly," conceded Jake, "but he certainly should have been questioned in a lot more detail at the time. My main aim, at the moment, is to find conclusive proof that Tom Fleming murdered Jean Maxwell and speaking to Clive Barclay may go some way to providing me with that."

"But I seem to remember Tom Fleming was found guilty and hanged for his crime. There must have been conclusive proof at the time?" Riley added.

"There was certainly enough to satisfy a jury ten years ago, Professor Riley, but maybe just not quite enough to satisfy this Police Inspector today. Anyway, I've said too much already and would ask that you say nothing of this conversation to anyone else."

"Do not concern yourself, Inspector, I have no reason to discuss such matters with anyone else. However, you having doubts over the evidence provided does rather support my concerns about Clive Barclay at the time. It wasn't that I ever thought him to be a murderer, but I always did wonder what the real reason was for him coming to Aberdeen. Although he always claimed the Aberdeen job was, technically, a step up, I always agreed with your initial assessment that it was really a climb-down."

"You believe his reasons for coming to Aberdeen were never truthfully given?" Jake added.

"If I think about it, Inspector, I'd have to say that I always felt that Clive Barclay was running away from something when he came to Aberdeen. I have no idea what that might have been. Perhaps the way was cleared in the fourteen months that he was here, to allow him to return to Cambridge."

Jake took a note of the Professor's comments. He asked a few more, general questions to allow him time to finish his cake and tea. He then thanked the Professor for his help and was shown to the door. He handed the Professor a card.

"If you think of anything about Professor Barclay that you feel might be of help then please call at Lodge Walk and ask for me."

"I will, Inspector," Riley said as he opened the door to allow Jake to leave.

***

At the moment Jake was leaving Professor Riley's house, Superintendent Peter Ash was leaving Lodge Walk. He was a worried man and felt that he now needed time to think. He returned to the Prince of Wales and ordered a beer at the counter. He then took his drink over to a table that stood free from other customers. He sat down and took a long drink from his glass.

His mind was in turmoil. He had convinced himself that Arthur Fleming had taken Edith's life to get back at him over the conviction of Tom. It had always been a conviction achieved more by the way in which the case had been built rather than the evidence produced to support that case. Ash had taken the view, very early on, that Tom Fleming was his man and he had never really wavered from that viewpoint, even after all these years.

Ash drank some more beer then reached in to his pocket and took out a cigarette case. He took one cigarette out and placed it between his lips. He then took a silver, monogrammed vesta case from another pocket and striking one of the matches, lit the end of the cigarette. He exhaled the smoke and finished his beer. He then went to the counter and bought another before returning to his chair.

He wasn't sure what was annoying him the most; the fact that he might have got the Tom Fleming case wrong or the fact it might have led to Edith being killed. She had been a lovely friend, providing him with some much needed companionship and an ear when he had needed it. There had never been anything more in their relationship, but already he was missing her.

He thought back ten years again as he attacked his second beer and puffed hard on his cigarette. He had never considered there could be anyone else involved in Jean Maxwell's murder. Tom Fleming admitted to having feelings for the girl and he had been seen hanging around her on previous occasions. It seemed obvious that he had had his advances rebuffed and in a state of anger he'd strangled the poor girl. The mud inside the house had surely proved that.

He did have to admit, however, that he had often wondered what the young couple had been doing in the main bedroom when she had had a room of her own to which they could have gone. He had surmised that it was a case of the mice playing while the cat was away. In other words, Jean and Tom had played at being lord and lady of the manor by taking alcohol up to the main bedroom while the master was at work. For whatever reason, Jean had changed her mind once they got there, but Tom had continued to force himself upon her, leading to him strangling her and then running away.

As he sat there, running over the facts of the case in his mind, he couldn't help but think that he had messed up in some way. Looking back over those ten years seemed to sharpen his mind even more and the facts, as they had been discovered, now didn't appear to be facts at all.

Why would Tom Fleming, if he had indeed killed Jean Maxwell, run away leaving his tools in the kitchen and mud on the floor? He would have had time to tidy up had he chosen to do so, but sometimes panic takes over and rational thought simply flies out of the window. Why would he also leave the glasses by the bed? Now that he was really thinking about it, there were far more questions than he had ever sought to answer at the time.

He remembered interviewing Tom Fleming. The young man had broken down when told Jean was dead. He had pleaded innocence all along and yet no one came even close to believing him. He had said he'd spent the afternoon in the garden before going to the pub. He had left the tools *at* the back door, not inside the kitchen and he claimed, quite categorically, that he had never been inside the house. Ash remembered one particular comment from Tom Fleming.

"Why would I need to go in to the house when Jean could more easily come out in to the garden?"

It was a good question and Ash had chosen to ignore it. Along with so many other things that he ignored, simply because to question them meant boring holes in his precious theory. Looking back now it was obvious to him that someone else might have been involved. He'd never even checked on Professor Barclay; just taken everything the Professor had told him at face value. After all, what possible reason would a university Professor have for lying to the police?

Ash thought some more as he worked his way through five more beers. The clock on the wall showed the passage of time, but Ash was too far gone to be able to focus on the hands. He knew it had to be late as the light was fading outside and the landlord was no longer willing to serve him alcohol. He had been politely asked to go home, though it was with some reluctance that he eventually made his way to the door.

Outside there was a chill in the air. Ash paused in the street to light another cigarette. As he puffed thoughtfully, an idea entered his head. At first it seemed a strange idea and he was of a mind to ignore it. However, the idea took root in his mind and began to blossom in to a very good idea. In fact, it soon seemed like the best idea he had ever had and Ash smiled to himself as he set off along the street in the direction of the stone steps that would take him up on to Union Street.

He had no idea what time it was, but the streets of Aberdeen were quite quiet with mainly men wandering about. Ash went up on to Union Street and turned right, along past the graveyard. He was thinking, once more, about Edith McIntosh, only this time such thoughts made him feel very sad and a tear formed in the corner of his eye. Had Arthur Fleming really killed her to avenge his brother's hanging? Had Edith died because of him and the actions he had taken ten years ago?

It now seemed very likely, at least to him, that she had. Had he done his job properly all those years ago then perhaps both Edith and Tom Fleming would still be alive. Suddenly he felt a tremendous urge to be punished for what he had done.

He walked up Union Street; all the time the sadness was weighing heavier upon him. He arrived at Union Bridge. Recently widened and newly opened it was a marvel of modern engineering. Ash stopped on the bridge and looked out across the railway line and Union Terrace Gardens. The lights from His Majesty's Theatre twinkled back at him and he was suddenly gripped by a serenity that had not been there earlier in the evening when he had been mulling over the Jean Maxwell murder.

Maybe it was just the alcohol, but Peter Ash had never felt as relaxed and free from worry as he did at that very moment. Suddenly, everything fell in to place and there seemed only one course of action that he could take.

Without any further thought Peter Ash climbed on to the highly ornate balustrade and jumped.

***

SIX

Friday 05th June

The body was found at six o'clock the next morning. At first it was assumed that employees of the railway companies would deal with the investigation until the corpse was identified. Lodge Walk was notified and Chief Constable William Anderson said that he would take personal control of proceedings. The body of Superintendent Ash was removed to the mortuary at Lodge Walk and the Police Doctor asked to check the body for any sign of foul play. None was found.

Jake was in a state of shock as he went about his business that day. It was obvious to everyone that Peter Ash had committed suicide but Jake also had a pretty good idea as to why he had done it. Ash had been feeling guilty for his part in the Tom Fleming investigation and no doubt, he had also persuaded himself that Edith McIntosh's death was now linked to that investigation. Jake was now even more certain that even Peter Ash believed Tom Fleming to be innocent by the time he jumped off the bridge. However, he could still not see an obvious link to Edith McIntosh's murder and, annoyed though he might be, Jake did not see Arthur Fleming as a murderer; especially ten years after the original event.

Jake had two people to see that day. He would see Arthur Fleming later, but first he was making his way to Golden Square and to the office of Ward, Logan and Shinnie. Throughout the short walk, Jake could not stop thinking about Peter Ash, especially as he crossed the Union Bridge. He even found himself stopping for a moment and looking down on the track below.

It was a little before ten when Jake arrived at the granite building, set in to the corner of Golden Square to the right of where the Music Hall was situated. Jake went through the front door and found himself in a short corridor, off of which came three further doors. The one to his immediate left had glass in it and through this he could see a reception area. Jake entered that room and was greeted by a middle-aged woman with grey hair tied up on her head and a pair of spectacles hanging around her neck on the end of a cord. The spectacles sat on her ample bosom and her face was set in an expression of severity, which did little to make visitors feel welcome.

"May I help you?" she then enquired with an expression that seemed to say to Jake; *and you'll better have a good reason for being here.*

Jake showed the woman his identification. "I would like to see Mr Shinnie, please."

The woman did not respond at first, making Jake wonder if she had actually heard him. After a brief pause, however, she leapt in to action. She produced a large, bound book from beneath the counter and proceeded to open it at a page marked with a large bookmark. She then took the spectacles from their haven on her bosom and placed them back on her face. She looked down at the book, running her finger down to a line that seemed to be of greatest interest to her. She then glanced at the grandfather clock, which stood against the wall to her left.

"It would appear that Mr Shinnie does indeed have a few moments to spare before he will be required to go to court. If you would like to sit down, I will inform Mr Shinnie that you are here."

"Thank you," Jake said and went over to three chairs that were situated around a small table on which sat a copy of one of that morning's local newspapers. He knew the news of Peter Ash's death would not make the papers until the lunchtime editions, so he was not tempted to pick the paper up and read what they might have said about the Superintendent.

He did know, however, that the story would run for a few days as the journalists tried to get to the bottom of why a high ranking police officer should suddenly decide to kill himself. Of course, once they got wind, as they surely would, of the fact that Jake was re-investigating the Jean Maxwell murder then it would not be long before two and two would be added together and the correct result achieved. Peter Ash's name would, most surely, be dragged through the dirt and a good man's name tarnished forever.

It was not long before the door leading back to the corridor opened and a man came in to the room. He noticed Jake sitting at the table and turned to face him.

"Inspector Fraser?"

Jake stood up. "Yes."

"I'm Reginald Shinnie, would you care to follow me."

They went along the corridor to the door on the far right, which was currently lying open. Shinnie led the way in to the room and closed the door. He then waved an arm in the general direction of a chair that was positioned closest to them.

"Please have a seat, Inspector."

Shinnie made his way round the desk and sat down. Jake's first impressions of Shinnie were that he seemed to be a funny, little man, not at all what you might expect for a lawyer. He stood little more than five feet tall and he had slightly bulging eyes that, on occasions, gave the impression they were looking in different directions. His hair was longer than might have seemed fashionable and his manner carried a natural haughtiness that some would have found annoying. All in all he was not the type of man you might want defending you in court. In Jake's estimation, he had far too comical an appearance to ever be taken seriously.

"I'm here about Edith McIntosh," Jake began.

"Ah yes, poor Edith," Shinnie added, leaning forward in his chair and only just managing to lean on the desk. Jake wondered, for a second, if there might be a cushion on Shinnie's chair to help him reach his desk. The thought passed before a smile could form on Jake's face. "I still haven't come to terms with the cruelty some of my fellow human beings are capable of, Inspector."

"Quite," added Jake. "I was wondering, Mr Shinnie, if you would could tell me the contents of Miss McIntosh's Will and also whether, or not, you might have a note of anything Miss McIntosh might have had in her home that would have been of particular value."

"Edith had no family, so there seems little need for me to keep the Will under lock and key for much longer. It is some time since we drew it up and I have to confess that I don't recollect all the detail of it. If you would just give me a moment."

Shinnie stood up, though it might not at first have been that apparent as there wasn't that much more of him visible than when he had been sitting down. He made his way to the door and out in to the corridor. Jake waited patiently, looking around at the array of books on show. He was also surprised to see there wasn't a window to the office; perhaps that privilege was only accorded to Mr Ward and Mr Logan.

Shinnie returned, carrying a large, brown envelope, which looked even bigger in his small hands. He returned to his chair and sat down. He then opened the envelope and took out two sheets of paper. He scanned the contents first before actually saying anything.

"Ah yes, I remember now, we did make a change to the will at the beginning of the year. I can't imagine how I allowed that to slip my mind. Edith left her house and possessions to a man by the name of Peter Ash and she left all her money to the newly formed City Police Pipe Band."

Jake's jaw nearly hit the floor. "She left her house to Peter?"

"Do you know him?"

"I knew him, Mr Shinnie."

"You *knew* him?" queried the solicitor, picking up on the use of the past tense.

"He was my Superintendent and he died last night. He appears to have jumped from the Union Bridge."

Shinnie looked greatly perturbed. "Oh my, that's dreadful."

"And I don't think that Peter Ash ever thought his relationship with Edith McIntosh had been as close as to have her leave her house to him," Jake added.

"When someone has no family they often turn to a close friend when deciding who should benefit from their estate. Obviously Edith felt close enough to Peter Ash to want to make that change to her Will."

Jake looked confused. "So what happens to the house now?"

"It now legally becomes a part of Mr Ash's estate as Edith died before him. However, as Mr Ash did not know he owned the house, at the time of his death, then he would be unable to include the property in his own Will. You would have to see who his benefactors are and let them decide what ought to happen to the house now."

Jake wasn't sure that Ash would have any benefactors, but made a note to inform the Chief Constable whom, he felt sure, would have a copy of Ash's Will before long. If anyone was to benefit from Ash's death then they could now add a house to their good fortune.

"If we might set the Will to one side, for the moment Mr Shinnie, would you now be able to tell me if Miss McIntosh had anything of value in her home?"

Shinnie now turned to the second sheet of paper that he had taken from the envelope.

"Edith McIntosh inherited many things that her father had collected over the years, but none of those items were, as far as I am aware, deemed to be of any great value. There was an inventory drawn up around eighteen months ago and this is it," Shinnie concluded and handed the sheet of paper to Jake.

Jake ran an eye down the length of the page and then halfway down the other side. There were a variety of items listed with a nominal amount noted at the side. He noted immediately that there was no mention of miniature paintings.

"Who valued the items?" he then asked.

"I believe it was Adam Kerrigan; he works for the auctioneers, Gibson and Son."

Jake remembered that Gibson and Son had an outlet in Rose Street. "May I keep this for a little while?"

Shinnie looked less than impressed by that request. "If you give me a moment I will ask one of the ladies in the office to write a copy for you. I really would prefer to keep original documents within our possession."

Jake was more than happy with that arrangement and waited another ten minutes while the list was copied on to another sheet of paper. When he was given the copy he could not help but marvel at the neatness of the writing. It was one area of Jake's life that had never been too successful; no matter how hard he tried his handwriting simply refused to remain legible for the length of a whole paragraph.

Jake then thanked Shinnie for his time and for the copy of those items collected by Doctor McIntosh. He stood up and left the office.

***

On his way back to Lodge Walk, Jake stopped off at the tearoom, located within the premises of Sangster and Henderson. He sat at a table by the window, which afforded him a view of Union Street. He ordered tea and a scone from a plain looking waitress who seemed to have lost the ability to smile. As she turned to go and retrieve his order, Jake found it amusing that someone working in the public domain, could be so glum all the time. The waitress returned with the tea and scone and Jake settled back to enjoy a few moments to himself.

He found himself thinking about Peter Ash and his relationship with Edith McIntosh. Had there been more to it than Ash had admitted? Had Ash maybe known that the house would be left to him? Had he, therefore, had a hand in Edith McIntosh's death?

His train of thought went no further. It was all rubbish. There was no way that Peter Ash had had anything to do with Edith McIntosh's death, unless her murder *was* connected, in some way, to the Jean Maxwell case. Even with that thought now occupying his mind, Jake still felt there could be a number of reasons as to why Peter Ash killed himself. He would need to have that discussion with the Chief Constable on his return to the office.

Firstly, he had to finish his tea before going to see Logan McMaster.

***

Fifteen minutes later Jake was in the office of Logan McMaster. The great man had agreed to find five minutes of his precious time to see the Inspector and both men now sat in a cramped room, ventilated by a small window and with little space around them to swing the proverbial cat. Logan McMaster himself was a small, weedy looking man who greatly enjoyed the sound of his own voice. Unfortunately for him and that of his profession, much of what came out of Logan McMaster's mouth was of little interest to anyone else.

"My goodness me; Tom Fleming, that is going back a bit," McMaster added after Jake had told him the reason for his visit.

"What can you remember about the case, Mr McMaster?"

"I can remember that I lost, Inspector. It was one of my earliest cases and had I won that one, my legal career might have been a whole lot more successful."

"I've read the case notes and there didn't appear to be much in the way of evidence. Why do you think the jury decided to find him guilty?"

McMaster thought for a moment. "Firstly, let's not forget that Fleming *may* have been guilty all along. Personally I never believed that and I still don't to this day. Why then did the jury find him guilty? There's no doubt the investigating officer, Peter Ash, came across with confidence and he presented what little he had in a very strong and persuasive manner. I've always believed, however, that the major problem faced by Tom Fleming was that there was never anyone else in the frame. Fleming *was* the only man there that afternoon."

"What about Professor Barclay?" enquired Jake.

"He found the body so he could hardly have been there when the poor woman was killed," McMaster replied.

"You only had Professor Barclay's word for what happened that afternoon. Why was everyone so quick to believe him?"

"He was a university professor, Inspector," McMaster answered," what possible reason would he have had for lying?"

"If he had been the killer he would have had the perfect reason for lying," suggested Jake.

McMaster looked as if the idea was the most ludicrous thing he had ever heard. "And why would a university professor want to kill his maid?"

"I don't know, but it should have been considered at the time. As it was, Barclay told his story, everyone believed him and Tom Fleming went to the gallows as a result. Everything you argued at the trial was relevant and should have been considered a whole lot more than it was."

"I looked for a way out for Fleming, but I would never have considered Professor Barclay as being a possible murderer."

"In an effort to save my client I think I would have been tempted to suggest that the only other man, knowingly connected to the case, was more involved than he had cared to admit. It might just have given the jury something to think about."

McMaster's tone was one of outrage as he replied. He felt that his reputation as a lawyer was being questioned.

"But there was absolutely no evidence to indicate that Barclay had had anything to do with Jean Maxwell's death."

"There wasn't much more against Tom Fleming and yet they hanged him for it."

"You really believe the jury got it wrong, don't you?"

"I do and I believe that Peter Ash was thinking the same last night just before he killed himself."

***

It was another half an hour before Jake arrived back at Lodge Walk. Roderick Wheatley informed him, as he entered through the front door, that the Chief Constable wanted to see him. Jake was pleased to hear that as he, most certainly, wanted to see the Chief Constable.

He went to his office and collected some papers he thought might be necessary, then went upstairs to where the Chief Constable had his office.

Chief Constable William Anderson sat at his desk with a solemn expression on his face. He had been the Chief Constable of Aberdeen City Police since January of 1903 and had proved himself to be a fair-minded man who, on the whole, had the respect of his entire Force. Anderson had brought many changes to the City Police and most of them had been for the better. He invited Jake to take a seat before saying anything further.

"This is a terrible business with Superintendent Ash."

"It certainly is, sir," added Jake.

"There seems to be no other conclusion than that he jumped from the bridge," the Chief said. "Whatever could have affected his mind enough as to make him want to take his own life?"

"I believe I may have a suggestion."

"Which is?" prompted the Chief Constable.

"Superintendent Ash had come to the conclusion that actions he took ten years ago had led to the death of Miss Edith McIntosh this week."

"Why would he think two events, ten years apart, were connected in any way?"

"Ten years ago the then Inspector Ash investigated the murder of Jean Maxwell and decided that the murderer was Tom Fleming. Fleming was duly tried and found guilty. He was later hanged. Tom Fleming's brother, Arthur, bumped in to Superintendent Ash whilst he was in the company of Edith McIntosh and threats were made. The Superintendent was of the opinion that Arthur Fleming then killed Edith McIntosh in revenge for the Superintendent wrongly having Tom Fleming charged with the murder of Jean Maxwell."

The Chief looked even more serious. "Was Tom Fleming wrongly charged and convicted with that murder?"

"I've read through the case notes, sir and I have to say the evidence against Tom Fleming was hardly conclusive of his guilt."

"Do you think Ash got the wrong man?"

The question was blunt but it was the obvious question to ask, given what Jake had already discovered,

"Yes, sir, I believe he may have done."

"Do you also believe that Superintendent Ash may have come to that conclusion himself and that would be further reason for him taking his own life?"

"That is perfectly possible, sir," agreed Jake.

"Do you think it possible that this Arthur Fleming murdered Edith McIntosh?"

"I have yet to speak with Arthur Fleming, sir, but I'd be very surprised if he murdered anyone. Don't get me wrong, the man is no angel, but in trying to clear his brother's name I just can't see him committing murder himself."

"And what about the Jean Maxwell murder, have you any theories as to who might be the real killer?"

"Professor Barclay was Jean's employer and the man with the most opportunity to set a bogus crime scene. His account of events was never questioned and basically it was *only* his account that put the noose around Tom Fleming's neck. Peter Ash never really looked beyond Tom Fleming for a suspect."

"So do you think Barclay was the killer?" the Chief then asked.

"He could well have been, sir, but proving there had been another hand in the murder could prove difficult after all this time."

The Chief thought for a moment. "What do you want to do now, Jake?"

"I'd really like to speak to Clive Barclay, but I have no idea where he is. He left Aberdeen soon after Tom Fleming's trial and reportedly went back to Cambridge."

Anderson sat back in his chair and pondered for a few seconds. "Very well," he eventually said, "continue to investigate the Jean Maxwell murder alongside that of Edith McIntosh and keep me informed of anything you discover."

"There is something else," Jake then said, before the Chief could bring their meeting to a conclusion. "Edith McIntosh left her house and possessions to Peter Ash in her Will."

The Chief Constable looked as surprised by that news as Jake had felt himself. "But I thought they were just friends?"

"They were. She had no one else, sir. She left her money to the Police Pipe Band, which must have been something else that Peter had told her about."

"I find it difficult to believe that anyone would leave their house to a friend if that friend were not extremely close. I take it there is no likelihood of Ash being involved in Edith McIntosh's murder?"

"None, whatsoever, sir."

"Okay, Jake. I'll find out if Ash left a Will and if he did, we'll see who will now benefit from the ownership of Edith McIntosh's house. In the meantime, I'll let you get on."

Jake left the room and returned to his office. He now needed to speak to Arthur Fleming, but first he wanted to speak to someone in Cambridge with a view to finding out more about Professor Barclay.

Jake found a room with a phone in it and asked the operator to find the number for Cambridge University and to connect him to anyone connected with that establishment. A few moments went by before a voice spoke in his ear.

"To whom am I speaking?" Jake began.

"My name is Ariadne and I work for Professor Higgins."

The voice sounded young. "Good day to you, Ariadne, my name is Jake Fraser and I am an inspector with Aberdeen City Police in the north-east of Scotland. I am phoning your university in the hope that I might speak to someone about an employee by the name of Professor Clive Barclay."

"We do not have a Professor Barclay here at the moment," Ariadne replied. "I've been here for five years and I'm not aware of anyone of that name working here in that time. Which subject did he lecture in?"

"The classics, I believe," replied Jake. "I know he was working there around eleven or twelve years ago, is it possible that someone, still at the university, might remember him?"

"I really don't know. Can you afford to wait a little while I ask around?"

"Perhaps you could find someone, who might be able to help and get them to phone me here in Aberdeen?"

Ariadne agreed and Jake gave her the number she should ask for. They both put the phone down and Jake went back to his office. He had no idea how long it would take Ariadne to find someone, who might be able to help, but he hoped it would be sooner rather than later. Before he sat down again he decided to go back through to the front desk and ask Sergeant Wheatley to find an address for Arthur Fleming. He felt ready to speak to him now.

***

It was early evening. Cecil Bainbridge had finished for the day and was looking forward to dinner. Tonight, he hoped, would be a special dinner. He had organised a nice, quiet table in the far corner of the dining room, where hoped he and his guest would not be disturbed beyond staff coming and going with their food. It had been some time since Bainbridge had eaten in the company of a woman and he was looking forward to it immensely.

His guest was to be Lucy Gill. In the four days she had been at the hotel he had spoken to her on many occasions and now felt there was a connection between them. He had asked her, the previous evening, if she would like to have dinner with him and she had readily agreed. Cecil Bainbridge had never been totally at ease around women, but he felt different with Lucy and he had been delighted to be able to spend some time with her over a nice meal.

Bainbridge was already at the table waiting when Lucy arrived. She was looking particularly attractive, dressed in a dark blue dress and with her hair tied up. He stood up as she arrived at the table. He took her hand and kissed the back of it. Lucy smiled and he thought she looked even more attractive as a result. This woman was not far off Bainbridge's own age and yet she still had a sexual magnetism that he found intoxicating. He held the seat back for her and she sat down. Bainbridge then returned to his own chair.

He began by ordering an expensive bottle of wine, which he hoped would impress his guest. He had no idea why, but he desperately wanted this woman to like him. He looked around the dining room, hoping that everyone was noticing him sitting there in the company of an attractive woman. Bainbridge knew that he was seen as a figure of fun by many of the staff; well he would show them, they would see him in a different light tonight.

The wine was brought and poured. Bainbridge lifted his glass and Lucy followed suit.

"To a lovely meal and entertaining company," he said.

Lucy clinked her glass of off his. "Cheers," she said. They drank, then put their glasses down again.

"Tell me a little about yourself, Miss Gill," Bainbridge then said.

Lucy looked almost coy as she played with her glass as it lay on the table. "There isn't a lot to tell, Mr Bainbridge....," she began.

"Oh, please, call me Cecil."

Lucy smiled again. "In that case, you must call me Lucy."

Bainbridge grinned. He felt the ice was now well and truly broken with this woman and the night could only get better. Lucy Gill continued with her life story, at least the one she wanted Cecil Bainbridge to hear.

"I was born in Edinburgh to parents who were financially comfortable without being rich. I lived there until I was twenty-five and then began touring Scotland, picking up work when I needed it. My parents had both died by that time and my only living relative was my uncle, who lived in Peterhead. Unfortunately, for Uncle Mac, he died four years ago, leaving me to inherit a sizeable sum of money, which now allows me to live my life pretty much as I choose to. I also inherited Uncle Mac's mansion, but I only live there occasionally. To be honest, I find the Peterhead area a cold and unwelcoming place. How about you, Cecil, tell me a little about yourself."

Bainbridge was halfway through his own life story when the soup arrived. Nothing more was said until they had eaten. As the plates were taken away, Bainbridge returned to his story and Lucy sat listening attentively. It had been a technique she had learned over the years. She now had the ability to look interested while listening to even the most boring of people. Not that Bainbridge was the worst, by any means.

"So you never married, Cecil?" she finally said as Bainbridge concluded his story by informing Lucy that he had been at the Palace Hotel for quite a few years and was now seriously contemplating moving on.

"I never found a woman who would have me," Bainbridge replied with a smile. Lucy laughed and adjusted the napkin lying on her lap. She paused for a moment before saying anything more. Everything about Lucy Gill's life depended on timing. She had to come across as a believable character to the people she swindled. If they didn't believe in her then they would never invest in the little deals she would eventually offer them.

"I'm guessing that you, too, will be financially comfortable, Cecil," she eventually said.

Bainbridge did not take the question as an intrusion in to his personal affairs. This woman was simply interested in him; that was all. He looked around the dining room noting, from a management perspective that the room was filling up nicely and also that no one seemed to be paying the slightest bit of attention to them. He leaned forward, however and lowered his voice a little.

"I do have a little money set aside for a rainy day, one cannot be too careful when it comes to personal finance."

"How true," Lucy said, sipping some more of her wine. She knew it was an expensive variety and would, therefore, be stronger. The last thing she could afford to do was get even slightly drunk. Lucy's entire existence depended on her keeping a clear head when discussing business. "I just knew you would be a man who is careful with his money, Cecil, I bet you keep a record of everything in a little book somewhere?"

Bainbridge smiled. "You already seem to know me so well, Lucy."

They were once more interrupted by the arrival of their main course. They had both chosen pork, served in a gravy with vegetables on the side. Again they both fell silent as the meat was eaten. Bainbridge ordered another bottle of wine. Lucy had tried to dissuade him from doing so, but he had insisted and she had, somewhat grudgingly it seemed to Bainbridge, agreed in the end. The truth of the matter was that Lucy wanted Bainbridge to be affected by the alcohol without actually getting drunk. It was essential that they both had their wits about them when she introduced the subject of share certificates. Once she had him hooked then they could finish a second bottle of wine.

The main course was eaten and the plates taken away. Lucy kept Bainbridge talking so that he forgot about drinking his wine. They would have coffee at some point, but there seemed no hurry as they sat talking and laughing at and about nothing in particular. To a casual eye observing them it was nothing more than two people getting to know each other. A friendship was, perhaps, forming amidst the chat and the laughter.

Coffee was eventually brought and Cecil Bainbridge lit a cigar as he stirred two spoons full of sugar in to the dark liquid. He never took milk.

"Have you decided when you'll be leaving Aberdeen?" Bainbridge then asked.

Lucy decided now was the time to introduce the sole reason she had accepted Bainbridge's invitation to have dinner with him.

"I will only be here for maybe two more days. I am tying up some business, within the next forty-eight hours and then I will be on my way."

Bainbridge sat forward, his curiosity piqued.

"What exactly is your business, Lucy?"

Lucy did not answer immediately. As ever, it was about timing. She sipped at her coffee and kept Bainbridge dangling for a little while longer. Eventually she spoke.

"I make money for other people."

At the mention of money, Bainbridge's expression changed; it happened every time. He was now even more interested in what Lucy had to say. As soon as someone was offered the chance to make easy money, they were on their way to being hooked.

"And how exactly do you do that, Lucy?"

Lucy again paused. She did not want to rush this; she did not want to sound as if she had said these things many times over, even if she had. She wanted Cecil Bainbridge to feel as if he were being offered something special; as if he wouldn't be getting such a good deal had he not got to know Lucy first. Eventually, Lucy was ready to continue.

"Cecil, have you ever heard of the Broxburn Oil Company?"

"I can't say that I have."

Excellent, thought Lucy.

"The Broxburn Oil Company was established in eighteen seventy-seven and then, around seventeen years ago, they expanded, even going as far as to create a company village. It is a major and very profitable concern, Cecil. They employ around seventeen hundred people and process hundreds of tons of shale each day."

Bainbridge was growing impatient. "This is all very interesting, Lucy, but what has that to do with you making money for others?"

Lucy knew that the question Bainbridge really wanted to ask was, "*How do I make that money?*"

Lucy now took the time to look around, as if checking for prying eyes or ears. She then picked up her bag and took some paper from it. She handed one sheet to Bainbridge and allowed him a moment to study what he had just been given.

"Are these shares in the company?" he finally asked.

"It is indeed and it has already provided me with a healthy dividend. Payment, which goes in to my bank account every three months."

"How much is that dividend, if you don't mind me asking?"

Of course Lucy didn't mind him asking. The more information she could provide for him the more chance there was of him parting with some of his money. Obviously the more he thought he would get back, the more he would invest in the first place. Lucy told him how much he ought to receive as dividend on his shares. Bainbridge looked suitably impressed.

"Since I bought my shares, I have become close friends with one of the directors of the company and he provided me with the chance to start up a little business of my own."

Bainbridge's face changed expression at the mention of Lucy having a close, male friend. Lucy touched the back of Bainbridge's hand as she spoke next.

"Don't worry, Cecil, there is nothing romantic in my friendship with this director. It is purely driven by business."

Bainbridge smiled again. Lucy was rapidly getting the impression that she could ask this man to do anything for her and he'd do it. He wasn't just being driven by greed, he actually seemed to have fallen for her. Part of Lucy was pleased to know that even at her advancing years she could still turn a head it seemed.

"And what is that business, Lucy?" Bainbridge then asked.

Lucy realised that she was still touching the back of Bainbridge's hand and she now removed her hand and sat back in her chair.

"I find new investors for his company and in return he pays me a small fee."

"So you could get me shares in this company as well?" Bainbridge then asked, his eyes wide with excitement.

Lucy knew she had him hooked, but it was still necessary to make things anything but straightforward. She sat forward a little again.

"I could get you shares, Cecil, but there is a slight problem."

"What might that be?" Bainbridge now asked, his manner becoming increasingly impatient. He just wanted to get to the bit where he could make some easy money.

"The price of each share is about to go up, so for you to get them at their current price I'd have to have your payment with the company by Tuesday at the latest, which would mean you going to your bank on Monday. I don't feel that gives you enough time to consider whether, or not, you want to buy the shares."

"What will the price go up to?" Bainbridge then asked.

Lucy fed him some figures and a story about the shares only being made available to companies after Tuesday. She was basically telling Bainbridge that this was a once in a lifetime opportunity and he needed to make his mind up quickly. However, she would fully understand if he wanted to pass on the offer. The more she made it sound as if she was trying to talk him out of doing something, the more she was actually talking him *in* to doing it. She knew she was now in the process of reeling this man in, his lip well and truly hooked on her line.

Bainbridge thought for a moment before speaking again.

"Is the dividend payment guaranteed to be as high for some time to come?"

"As long as the company maintains its current strong trading position your return can only increase. That is the beauty of shares, Cecil, you make money as long as the company is making money. If I tell you that the Broxburn Oil Company produces and sells up to sixteen tons of candles per day, you can see that through that outlet alone, your investment is safe."

Bainbridge ordered more coffee and lit a cigarette to go with it. Lucy declined anything more and sat back to give Bainbridge more time to think.

"If I missed this opportunity, when would you next be in Aberdeen?" Bainbridge then asked. Lucy thought for a moment.

"I really don't know. Another six months at least, though it could be a lot longer and remember, the price of the shares could well go up again by then."

"In that case, Lucy, you must count me in," Bainbridge finally announced.

Lucy smiled. "Excellent, Cecil. How much would you like to invest in the company?"

"From what you said, if I were to invest five pounds I'd be getting roughly three pounds per quarter by way of a dividend, is that correct?"

"It is indeed, Cecil. That's one pound per month for doing nothing."

Bainbridge had already started to think about what he could do with the extra money. He had also decided that if he invested more money in the Broxburn Oil Company then his dividend would be higher. For an initial outlay he could then sit back and watch the money pour in. He knew how much he had saved over the years and was now prepared to withdraw some of that in the name of making a profit over time.

"I want to invest ten pounds, Lucy," Bainbridge eventually said.

Lucy nearly fell off her chair. She hoped that her shock had not been obvious to Bainbridge. Ten pounds, she'd never managed to swindle anyone of that much money before. She'd be able to live for a long time on money like that. She pulled herself together and managed a smile.

"You won't regret that decision," she then said and patted the back of his hand again. Bainbridge fluffed up like a peacock and grinned.

"I am so glad that I met you, Lucy Gill," he then said.

You won't be for much longer, thought Lucy.

"Will you be able to get me the money on Monday?" was what she actually said.

"I'll go to the bank as soon as it opens. I presume you won't mind signing a receipt for the money, it is rather a lot?"

"I will sign anything you want," Lucy added. *For it will be worthless.*

Lucy provided a little more background to the shares deal and by the time she was finished, Bainbridge had also finished his coffee. Lucy then said that she was tired and that she thought she would retire. Bainbridge asked if he could walk her to her room and she accepted. At the door, she thanked Bainbridge for the evening and the meal. She also thanked him for his investment and arranged to see him when she went down for breakfast the following morning. She then gave him a kiss on the cheek and opened the door to her room.

Bainbridge stood in the corridor for a few moments longer. His hand came up and touched the spot where Lucy's lips had landed. He smiled to himself. He felt so sure that this was to be the start of something pleasant, something very pleasant indeed.

***

SEVEN

Monday 08th April – Morning

True to his word, Cecil Bainbridge went to the bank for opening time. The bank manager seemed perturbed at the thought of any customer taking as much as ten pounds out of his bank. He acted as if the money had been his own. However, eventually the transaction was completed and Cecil Bainbridge was able to make his way back to the hotel to meet with Lucy.

It was mid-morning before he saw her. He gave her the money and she signed a receipt for it. Bainbridge asked Lucy to have dinner with him again that evening and she accepted, fully in the knowledge that she would be long gone by then. She allowed Bainbridge to kiss the back of her hand and she almost felt sorry for the man as she watched him walk away for what she knew, would be the last time.

***

It was a little after one when Cecil Bainbridge left his office with the intention of having some lunch. He wondered if Lucy might consider joining him. He asked the young man on the reception desk if he knew if Miss Gill was in the hotel.

"No, Mr Bainbridge, she went out around an hour ago. She left her key, saying she was going for a short walk and that she would be back later."

"Very good," added Bainbridge and he made his way through to the kitchen area where he would have something to eat. As he sat chewing on a piece of meat and drinking a cup of tea his mind drifted to happy thoughts about Lucy Gill. He didn't like to use the word *love* after such a short time in her company, but he had to admit to himself that Lucy had made quite an impression on him. He smiled at the thought of all the money he would make from his shares in the Broxburn Oil Company and pondered on whether he might be buying an engagement ring with some of it, some day.

Bainbridge was finishing his lunch when one of the staff came hurrying in to the kitchen and made their way over to where the manager was sitting.

"Yes, what is it?" Bainbridge asked, sounding annoyed at being disturbed.

"You'd better come at once, Mr Bainbridge," the young man said, "we believe Miss Gill has left without paying her bill."

The words cut through Cecil Bainbridge like a sword made of ice. He felt chilled to the bone but tried to put a brave face on things. He forced a smile.

"Whatever do you mean, she's only gone for a walk."

"I don't think so, Mr Bainbridge," the young man insisted.

Bainbridge wiped the corners of his mouth and stood up. "Very well."

The two men made their way through the reception area and up to Lucy Gill's room, where they were met by one of the young women who cleaned the rooms. She, too, had an expression of concern upon her face and Bainbridge now began to feel really worried about what might have happened to his ten pounds.

The door was opened and all three entered the room. Bainbridge looked around. The bed had been made and the room looked tidier than it should when someone was still officially occupying it.

"There were some clothes lying on the floor," the young woman began to explain, "so I decided to hang them up. When I opened the wardrobe there was nothing in it. The few good dresses that Miss Gill had are gone. You also need to look in her travelling case."

Bainbridge followed the woman's gaze to the large case that Lucy Gill had arrived with. He made his way over to it and pulled the lid open. He looked in horror at the stones and papers that were inside, along with a rather dirty and tattered dress. He looked up at the other two and then back to the case. It was now obvious that he had been conned by a woman he had never known. He had handed over half of his life's savings to a woman whose name he now didn't even know.

Bainbridge hurried from the room and made his way down to reception. He asked the young man who had seen Lucy Gill leave if she had been carrying anything.

"I believe she did have a bag with her, yes," the young man replied brightly. Given the fact that Lucy Gill had not only conned Bainbridge, but had not paid her hotel bill either, he did not appreciate the brightness of the young man's tone.

"And she definitely said she'd be back?" he then added.

"Just going out for a walk was what she said," said the young man.

Bainbridge could only hope that that turned out to be true. He went back to his office but couldn't concentrate on anything for thinking about his ten pounds.

***

By four o'clock Cecil Bainbridge knew for certain that Lucy Gill, or whatever her real name might be, would not be coming back. She was long gone, probably on a train to somewhere as far away from Aberdeen as possible.

How could he have been so stupid? It was said there was no fool like an old fool and Cecil Bainbridge certainly felt very foolish now. He put on his coat and informed the young man on reception that he was going out for some air.

As it was he walked the short distance to Lodge Walk and visited the police office. Sergeant Wheatley took some notes and then asked Mr Bainbridge to wait in one of the interview rooms. He then spoke to Jake, who suggested that Sergeant Mathieson might deal with it. Jake further suggested that Sergeant Wheatley should find a particular photograph before Mathieson spoke to Bainbridge.

"Do you think it's her again?" Wheatley had said.

"It sounds like it to me, wouldn't you agree, Roddy?"

"It's certainly the kind of swindle she'd get up to," agreed Wheatley who went off to find the photograph before asking Sergeant Mathieson to have a word with Bainbridge.

By the time Mathieson arrived in the interview room, Bainbridge had been waiting nearly fifteen minutes and was beginning to work himself in to a lather. He was angry, more at himself than anything else but ready, none the less, to spark off at anything or anyone.

Mathieson sat down and laid his open notebook on the table in front of him. Bainbridge looked up, a thin film of sweat on his forehead and a look on his face that left Mathieson in no doubt that murder would be committed if Mr Cecil Bainbridge were to be able to locate the woman he had known as Lucy Gill.

"Would this be the woman who ran off without paying her hotel bill?" Mathieson then asked as he slid the photograph he had received from Wheatley across the table.

Bainbridge looked down at the woman looking back up at him. She didn't look so glamorous and she certainly didn't look so attractive, but it was definitely the same person.

"Yes, that's her. Who is she really?"

"We know her as Margaret Isabella Reid, the Press know her as 'The Buchan Heiress.' The woman has been through more names than I've had hot dinners."

"Is she a professional confidence trickster?"

"She is indeed, Mr Bainbridge so don't feel too bad; she's been swindling half of Scotland for the last twenty years."

"Can you find her, she swindled money from me as well as not paying the hotel bill?" Bainbridge then asked, almost pleaded at Mathieson.

"We might be able to find her, but I would be very surprised if you'll see your money again. How much did you give her?"

Bainbridge looked down at the table, looking somewhat sheepish. "Ten pounds," he eventually said. "She said she could get me shares in some company but I had to pay her quickly as the price of the shares was about to go up."

"Firstly, let's get some details," Mathieson then said and he got Bainbridge to talk him through exactly what had happened in the time that 'The Buchan Heiress' had been in the hotel. He also got Bainbridge to provide a description of how the woman now looked as the photograph was now nearly ten years old. "And she had some kind of certificate with her?" Mathieson then asked when he got to the point where she had hooked and then reeled in Cecil Bainbridge.

"She has paperwork that all looks very authentic. I'm sure I wouldn't be alone in being fooled by it."

"The shares idea is a new one on me," Mathieson admitted. "Margaret usually just gets her lodgings for nothing and then moves on. Maybe she's getting grander ideas as she gets older."

"I don't really care what her ideas might be as long as you catch her and lock her up. The woman is a menace to society."

"She's a pest, I'll agree with you there, sir. We lock her up and when she's released she just goes back to the world she knows best. She must be in her forties now so you'd think she'd see the light and settle down to a normal life."

"I had actually thought she might have chosen to settle down with me," Bainbridge said, a look of sadness crossing his face.

"You said Margaret left a large case; was there anything in it?"

Bainbridge told Mathieson of the rubbish he had found in the cases. The woman was most certainly travelling light and the case had merely been part of her story. Again, Bainbridge questioned himself as to how he could have been so stupid.

"Have you touched the room at all?" Mathieson then asked.

"It has been tidied and the bed made."

"There may not be much to find in that case, but I'll come back with you and have a look around."

"Very good, Sergeant."

***

It was early evening when Jake made his way to a flat in The Green. He had been told that Arthur Fleming would be back in Aberdeen that day and that he ought to be at home by late afternoon. He was.

Fleming opened the door on Jake's third time of knocking. He did not seem too happy at being wakened and he became even more unhappy when he found out that Jake was a police officer. Rather reluctantly he invited Jake in to what was a cramped and cluttered space. There were two rooms, neither of them large and both of them swamped with items ranging from newspapers to half-eaten plates of food. There was an unhealthy smell to both the flat and the block in which it was situated. Jake made a mental note not to stay any longer than he had to.

They went in to the room that passed for a kitchen and living room. Fleming sat down at a small, wooden table and lit a cigarette. For once Jake didn't mind someone smoking, it took away some of the more offensive aromas that had been playing around his nose.

"Is this about Superintendent Ash?" Fleming then enquired. He said Ash's name like he was describing dog shit.

"In a way. He said you bumped in to him?"

"Literally. I hoped I'd never see the bastard again and then I go and walk in to him when I wasn't actually looking where I was going."

"He said you were quite threatening towards him," Jake added.

"That man sent my brother to the gallows for a crime he did not commit, how am I supposed to feel about him?"

"Why are you so sure that your brother was innocent?"

"Tom loved Jean; he would never have harmed her."

"I've come across many cases where men loved women but they still ended up harming them in some way. Alcohol is usually the cause."

"You mean the alcohol in the glass by the bed?" Fleming retorted. Jake nodded. "They said at the trial that the contents of those glasses was wine. My brother was hard pushed to drink beer, there is no way he'd have gone anywhere near a glass of wine. Anyway, where the hell was he supposed to have got the wine from?"

"The trial was told that Jean must have taken the wine from the kitchen," Jake then said.

"Professor Barclay said at the trial that Jean had been a loyal employee. Loyal employees do not steal wine from their employers, especially when they can't afford to replace what they've taken. Jean would have known that Barclay would have found out about the wine and she would have been dismissed on the spot. Can you imagine how near to impossible it is for someone to get a job in service without good references? What chance then for someone with no reference at all?"

Jake thought for a moment. It all made sense and it had all been swept under the carpet ten years ago because Ash had been so sure he had his man.

"Did you say all this at the time?"

"Too, bloody, right I did, but no one was listening, least of all Peter Ash. Once he had decided that Tom did it, he stopped doing his job. He drew up his report showing how the meagre evidence he had, fitted the crime and if there were any problems he skirted around them and moved on. By the time it got to court no one else cared what happened to Tom Fleming. By that time they were all rejoicing in the fact that Jean Maxwell would finally get justice. Well justice didn't do my brother any good, did it?"

"Superintendent Ash said you threatened the lady he was with," Jake added.

"What?" snapped Fleming, not fully understanding what Jake was asking.

"The night you bumped in to him, he said you threatened the lady he was with," Jake repeated by way of explanation.

Fleming leapt to his feet. "In that case, Superintendent Ash is a bloody liar. I made some comments in his direction that was all."

"He said you were looking at the lady when you said you'd make Ash suffer. Are you telling me that wasn't true?"

"That's exactly what I'm telling you. Look, I was mad with Ash and I said a lot of things in the heat of the moment. I'd never have done anything; I've been inside often enough and I don't want to go back again. Anyway, if Ash has a problem with me why isn't he here, dealing with it himself?"

"Because Superintendent Ash is dead."

Fleming looked genuinely shocked. "Dead? How the hell can he be dead?"

"I think guilt may have killed him," replied Jake and Fleming's expression now turned to one of confusion.

"I don't understand."

"Peter Ash went on to the Union Bridge last night and jumped to his death. I think even he had decided that your brother was innocent and he couldn't live with the guilt that that brought to him."

Arthur Fleming slumped back in to his chair and reached for his cigarettes again. "You believe Tom was innocent as well, don't you?"

Jake nodded. "There was very little against him in the first place, but yes, I think he was innocent."

"Do you have some idea who did do it?"

"No firm ideas. It's a bit difficult solving a case that's ten years old. I can only work on what was said at the time. Did you ever suspect someone in particular when you were so vehemently defending your brother?"

"I always assumed it was Professor Barclay. He had a thing for Jean and he would have had the money and the position to buy off any attempt to incriminate him. I mean, let's face it, the Professor could let himself in to the house, he could take and open the wine and he was a man; no man responds well to sexual rejection."

"I don't think anyone was paid off," Jake said quickly.

"No one needed to be paid off," Fleming added. "There was never anyone other than Tom suspected of committing the crime. Barclay just had to tell his story, repeat it in court and then sit back and watch my brother swing for a crime he never committed. I mean when it comes to the word of a university Professor against that of a semi-literate gardener, who is going to be believed?"

Jake considered the matter for a moment. "There is little doubt that the investigation into Jean Maxwell's murder was nothing like as thorough as it should have been. That still doesn't mean, of course, that Professor Barclay was the murderer. However, at the very least, he ought to have been questioned in more depth at the time. I agree that his word appears to have been accepted without question. All that I can do now, Mr Fleming, is give you my word that I will do all that I can to find the real murderer in this case. It can't bring your brother back but it might at least give rest to his spirit."

"Thank you, Inspector," said Arthur Fleming and those first two words were said with meaning.

Jake left the flat and made his way out on to The Green. He took a few breaths of air to clean his nose and lungs of the smell and fog he'd been standing in for the last few moments. Even though it was quite late, Jake decided that he would still go back to the office.

***

By the time Jake got back to Lodge Walk, Sergeant Mathieson had made it back from the Palace Hotel. He walked along the corridor, with Jake and entered his office with him. Jake closed the door and both men sat down.

"I take it, it was 'The Buchan Heiress' who was at the Palace Hotel?" Jake said.

"It was. She got five night's free lodgings and meals plus ten pounds from the manager, Cecil Bainbridge."

Jake looked puzzled. "What was the ten pounds for?"

"Shares in the Broxburn Oil Company, apparently sir."

Jake laughed. "Really?"

"The company does exist and her ladyship was her usual persuasive self. She also had a certificate to show Mr Bainbridge so someone must have printed that for her."

"She's getting sophisticated if she's at the stage of forging share certificates. Mind you it wouldn't be too difficult to do, I'm sure that you, like me, wouldn't know what a legitimate share certificate looked like if you found one in your soup."

Mathieson nodded his agreement and smiled. "I'll notify the other Forces that we are looking for her but it could be a little while before she surfaces again. Anyway, how are you doing with the Edith McIntosh murder?"

"I'm a bit side-tracked at the moment. The death of Superintendent Ash has brought to light the possibility that he put the wrong man to the gallows ten years ago. I rather feel compelled to try and find the real killer."

"What was the case, sir?"

"The murder of Jean Maxwell."

"Oh, yes, I remember that. I had just joined the Force and thought it all very exciting to be rubbing shoulders with men who could solve such crimes. I longed for the day when that would be me, but now I'm there I realise there's nothing exciting about what we do after all."

"Perhaps not exciting, but there should always be a satisfaction in the fact we catch bad people and let the courts do the rest. The only problem, in the Jean Maxwell case, seems to be that the wrong person was brought in front of the court and the legal system did little to save him. I'm beginning to think that there might be too much emphasis put on the opinion of the investigating officer; the court simply accepts all that is presented before it and then dishes out a punishment. There were holes in that case from the very beginning and yet no one seems to have even considered the possibility that Tom Fleming wasn't their man."

"Is that why Superintendent Ash killed himself?" Mathieson then asked.

"It was probably one of the reasons, but he was a man in turmoil during those last hours of his life. Perhaps the Jean Maxwell case resurfacing made him re-evaluate other events in his life; we'll never know now."

"Is there anything I can do to help, sir?"

"There is, actually," Jake replied. He opened the drawer of his desk and took out the sheet of paper on which the items, declared to be in Edith McIntosh's house, were listed. Jake handed the paper to Mathieson.

"Go to the auctioneers Gibson and Son and ask to see Adam Kerrigan. Ask Mr Kerrigan to go with you to Edith McIntosh's house and to help you check the list against the contents of the house, just in case there are other items missing. Also ask him to draw up another list of those items which do not appear to be on the original list and provide us with an idea of value."

"I'll go and see Kerrigan this afternoon and hopefully do the house visit at the same time," Mathieson then said, folding up the sheet of paper and putting it in the inside pocket of his jacket. He then left the room and Jake turned back to the sea of paper forming on his desk. In usual Jake form, he put the paper in to tidy piles but never actually got around to clearing any of it.

***

EIGHT

Monday 08th June – Afternoon

Margaret arrived at the meeting at exactly two o'clock. Throughout her entire life she had demanded punctuality from herself and nothing annoyed her more than being late for an appointment. Similarly, she did not take too kindly to other people turning up late. Today's meeting concerned helping raise money for the Aberdeen Industrial Association Girls' School, which was situated on Whitehall Road.

The meeting was held in the lounge of Mrs Cornelia Bulwer's home in Blenheim Place, just one street away from the school. Mrs Bulwer had had eight children of her own and now that they were of an age to fend for themselves she had turned her attention and her time, to trying to help children far less fortunate than her own. She had managed to gather a small, like-minded, group of women who were happy to give their time and energy to raising money that could then be donated to the school. Being women themselves, it had seemed appropriate that they should help a school for girls.

Industrial Schools had been introduced, during the course of the previous century, to try and deal with the problem of child vagrancy. Much of the power given over to the police and other authorities had been more about punishment than a genuine attempt to improve the life of the child. Industrial Schools were created to offer a home and an education for vagrant children or those who had been neglected by their parents.

As well as basic classroom education the girls of the Industrial School, on Whitehall Road, were also occupied in the work created by the building in which they were housed. Girls received training in general cooking and laundry work. They also did needlework, dress-making and machining. Margaret had even noted, on one account that she had recently read, that the girls also received one hour per week of free gymnastics and marching. She had felt sure, with much cynicism, that any girl would be better set up in life if she had the ability to march.

There were currently 65 girls living in the School and though the majority of the funding for its upkeep came from more formal organisations, there was still a place for private donation and it was through this avenue that the Ladies' Group sought to offer money raised from various events organised throughout the year. Now that that year was reaching its halfway point, Mrs Bulwer had arranged for a meeting to be held so they could discuss how much money had been raised to date and what more might be done in the second half of 1908.

By the time Prudence, Mrs Bulwer's irreplaceable housekeeper, had brought in the tea and cakes, there were six women, in total, sitting in the room. They all still wore their hats and there was an air of formality even though the meeting, itself, was to be conducted informally. Some general chat took place before Cornelia Bulwer called the meeting to order and a more formal discussion commenced.

The meeting was reminded that any money raised throughout 1908 would be donated to the School through the Annual General Meeting of its subscribers, which usually took place in January. Mrs Bulwer always attended, usually with one other member of their group. Margaret had said she would not attend the AGM as the Chief Constable and sometimes the Chief Constable's wife were always in attendance and she did not want to place her husband in an awkward position. This had been noted and accepted by the Group.

Sadie Ashton was another member of the Group. She sat across from Margaret, her hair piled beneath her hat and her eyes firmly fixed on Cornelia Bulwer. Margaret knew that Sadie's reasons for being there were slightly different from the others. The Ladies' Group was basically driven by a desire to help unfortunate girls have a better chance of making something of themselves. The limit of that desire usually amounted to some girls finding employment in domestic service.

Sadie Ashton did not see domestic service as being any life for a young girl and she would have advocated, had she chosen to make her thoughts more vocal, to provide a system whereby girls could have all the same options as the boys. Why shouldn't girls aspire to university and to good jobs in the same way as boys? Just because a girl had a bad start in life why should that prevent her from bettering herself as she grew older? As usual, there was always a more militant undercurrent to anything that Sadie Ashton set out to do.

However, little of that would have been evident to anyone watching her in the room at that moment. She sat so prim and proper, listening intently to every word Cornelia Bulwer said and responding accordingly.

"I have been informed by the Superintendent of the School, Miss Melvin," Cornelia was saying, "that they have placed thirty-three girls in to employment in the last three years. Girls are generally encouraged to give themselves to domestic service......"

Margaret noticed Sadie flinch at that point.

".....and to give them an incentive there is now a scheme, funded by the kind donation of a man by the name of Frederick Wright, whereby any girl who remains a complete year in her first situation in domestic service and shows due obedience to her employer will be liable to receive a gratuity of ten shillings."

There was a ripple of applause from the small group of women, though Margaret noticed that Sadie did not enter into their show of appreciation. Instead Sadie had reached for a second cake and returned her gaze towards Mrs Bulwer.

The rest of the meeting was taken up with a discussion on how best they might raise money over the second half of the year. They had already raised eleven pounds and were hopefully of achieving something similar in the remainder of the year. They had given the AGM, at the beginning of 1908, twenty pounds out of a total of thirty-three pounds and two shillings donated in total. At the mention of the money already raised there was another, impromptu, round of applause and this time Sadie Ashton did join in.

Nearly an hour and a half went by before all business had been discussed and the ladies were ready to leave. Margaret put her coat on and left with Sadie. Little was said as they walked through to Fountainhall Road, where they intended catching the tram in to Union Street.

***

It was just before four when Jake was informed there was a phone call for him. Someone on the phone from Cambridge University, the Constable who delivered the message believed the man on the phone to be a Professor MacLeod. Jake made his way to the room where the phone was located and sat down at the table. He took out his notebook, in case there were any relevant notes to be taken and then picked up the phone.

The connection was terrible and both men were required to talk louder than they might have preferred, simply to be heard.

"You wanted to know about Clive Barclay, I believe?" Professor MacLeod had then said after they had gone beyond the need for introductions.

"Yes, Professor MacLeod, some new information has come to light regarding the death of Professor Barclay's maid ten years ago and I was hoping to find Professor Barclay so that I, or one of my police colleagues, might talk to him."

"Are you of the opinion that Professor Barclay works here in Cambridge?"

"He told his colleagues at Aberdeen University that he was returning to Cambridge just after the trial. I take it he has moved on again."

"He never came back here," said MacLeod. "I haven't seen, nor heard, of Barclay since he left here to go to Aberdeen and that must be getting on for twelve years now. I have to say, I would have been very surprised if he had decided to come back to Cambridge."

"Why would that be, Professor?" enquired Jake.

"Too many bad memories for him. You do know why he left Cambridge in the first place?"

"No, I don't."

"His wife was killed in an accident in their home. She fell down the stairs after having a reaction to some pills she was taking for a sleep disorder."

Jake made a note of that and then wrote to the side **COINCIDENCE?** and underlined the word twice.

"What kind of man was Professor Barclay?" he then asked.

"A bit of a queer fish if I'm being honest. He was good at his job but saw himself as God's gift to women. If a woman came anywhere near him he seemed to change in to this person who went out of his way to impress them. He liked to be in the company of women, though I don't believe for one moment that he actually did anything to dishonour the marriage vows he had taken with Netty. He was very distressed by her death and that was why he decided to put as many miles between himself and his memories as possible."

"Did Professor Barclay have a maid at his home in Cambridge?"

"Of course. He was very fond of her; Rose I think her name was. You said something earlier about investigating the death of his maid in Aberdeen; don't tell me he left Aberdeen because of a death there as well?"

"Do we put it down to bad luck, or something more sinister?" Jake then said. It was more in the way of thinking out aloud until he realised to whom he was speaking. He really shouldn't have been making comments of that nature to a complete stranger. To his surprise, however, Professor MacLeod actually responded.

"Although I said I never thought Barclay would have done anything to dishonour his wife, there was some gossip around the University around the time Netty died to the effect that they were not as close as they had once been. Now, I stress it was never anything more than gossip, but it may have some bearing on the picture you are building of Professor Barclay."

"I presume that no one else at the University might know where Professor Barclay is these days?" Jake then asked.

"I shouldn't think so, but I will ask around and if I learn anything I'll phone you."

"Thank you, Professor MacLeod, you've been very helpful."

The phones were put down and Jake returned to his office. His mind was mulling over what had just been discussed and he now felt, more than ever, that Barclay needed to be found and interviewed. Was it possible that he had killed his wife as well as Jean Maxwell? Maybe he had some rather warped feelings towards the maids he employed? Maybe he was somewhere in the country already treating another maid in a highly inappropriate manner?

Jake prepared a notice, which he asked to be sent out to all the main Forces with a request that they pass it on to their local, smaller Forces. He wanted everyone to be on the look-out for Professor Barclay and he asked only that they notify him if the Professor was found and that nothing was to be done that might, in any way, alert him that the police were interested in his whereabouts.

***

Sergeant Mathieson was sitting in the small, administrative office of Gibson and Son. He was in the company of an attractive young woman with smiling eyes and the cheerful countenance of someone intent on living life to the full, no matter what constraints might be placed along the way. Mathieson's chair was behind the main door in to the office and there was another door behind and to the right of the young woman. She looked at the time on the clock beside her.

"He shouldn't be long, I really don't know what's keeping him."

Mathieson smiled. "That's okay."

He'd said it was okay, but inside he felt the complete opposite. He had been waiting nearly half an hour and was beginning to get more than a little annoyed, even though he had no intention of letting the young woman know that; after all, it wasn't her fault. In fact, if truth be told, Sergeant Mathieson was rather enjoying sitting with the young lady; he found himself wondering if she might be stepping out with a young man. It had been many months since Mathieson had stepped out with anyone.

"Have you worked here for long?" he then heard himself saying.

The woman smiled. "Two years."

"Enjoying the work?"

"Most days. How about you, I'm sure being a police officer must be very exciting?"

"The complete opposite most days. There is an awful lot of routine involved in what I do. We also see some sights that no one should have to see."

The young woman flinched. "Oh yes, I hadn't thought about that."

She momentarily returned to her work, but then she looked up again, her eyes wide with wonder and interest.

"Is someone here under suspicion?" she asked and Mathieson smiled.

"No, this is purely part of that routine I mentioned."

"Oh," added the young woman, sounding quite disappointed to hear that. She went back to doing her work, but Mathieson could tell that she was still mulling over how exciting, in her own mind at least, his job had to be.

Mathieson checked the time again and his temper rose a little further. The young woman picked up on his change of expression and stood up.

"I'll go and see what Mr Kerrigan is doing," she said and made her way to the door. Mathieson mouthed her a *thank you* as she opened the door and left the room. When she came back she was in the company of a tall, thin, young man with curly hair and a pitted complexion. His suit had been well worn though his shoes looked new and still retained a shine.

"My sincere apologies, Sergeant," Kerrigan said, as the young woman returned to her desk, "but I got tied up in some work for Mr Gibson."

"That's okay," said Mathieson, though he didn't actually mean it. It was anything but okay to keep someone waiting for as long as he had and had it not been for the company he was enjoying, he might have said more to Young Kerrigan. "This shouldn't take long, Mr Kerrigan, but might we go somewhere to talk?"

"Of course; there's a room at the back of the building, which is rarely used by anyone else."

Both men were soon seated in the room at the back. Sergeant Mathieson produced the sheet of paper he had been given by Jake and showed it to Kerrigan.

"I believe you produced this list of items during a visit to a Miss Edith McIntosh's house some time ago, sir, would that be correct?"

Kerrigan looked at the paper. "I really don't remember; it's certainly not my handwriting."

"It wouldn't be, sir, this is a copy provided by Miss McIntosh's solicitor, Mr Shinnie. It was Mr Shinnie who informed us of your involvement in producing the list with a view to attributing a value to everything."

"Well if Mr Shinnie says it was me, then it must have been," Kerrigan then said. Mathieson had been trying to age him, as they sat together in the room, but the best he could do was narrow it down to somewhere between thirty and forty.

"You may not be aware, Mr Kerrigan, but Miss McIntosh was murdered last week in her own home."

"My God," was all Kerrigan could say.

"The motive for her murder appears to be burglary."

"Items off this list, do you mean?" Kerrigan added.

"We do want to know if any of those items are missing, yes sir," replied Mathieson. "To that end I would like you to accompany me to Miss McIntosh's house and to check that list against the items still there."

"I would be delighted to help, Sergeant, but I would obviously have to clear it with Mr Gibson first."

"I understand, sir. I'd be more than happy to ask, on your behalf, if you think Mr Gibson might respond better to a direct police enquiry."

"I'll come back for you, if I need you Sergeant," Kerrigan said and he stood up and headed for the door. He was back within minutes, accompanied by a man whom Mathieson assumed was Mr Gibson. A short conversation ensued, in which Mathieson once more explained why he would like Mr Kerrigan present when the items in the house were checked. Mr Gibson fully understood but explained that Mr Kerrigan had duties that day, which could not be changed. It was quickly agreed that the two men would meet on Wednesday and it was further agreed that they would meet at the house. Mathieson left a note of the address, even though Mr Gibson had said they would have had it on file already.

Mathieson then began to make his way to the front door but something made him pause once he got there. It was a mad impulse, but he felt compelled to go through with it. He opened the door to the front office and received a lovely smile from the young woman whom he'd been speaking to earlier.

"Do you get any time off at lunchtime?" he asked.

The young woman looked a little confused. *Was this part of the police inquiry?*

"I get half an hour," she replied.

"Would you care to spend that half hour in my company someday soon?" Mathieson then asked.

He noticed her face go red and he fully expected her to politely decline the offer. As it was she said she'd be delighted and they agreed to meet on Friday. Mathieson said that he would collect her from work. They were both smiling broadly as he turned to leave the building.

***

NINE

Tuesday 09th June

Inspector Samuel Biddlecombe arrived at his office in the main building occupied by the Cambridge Borough Police. He was thirty years of age, five years under the average age of the men in his Force and newly promoted to the rank of Inspector. There were some, in the area, who had questioned his promotion. He was seen, by those same people, to be over promoted and only to have been given the rank of Inspector because his wife was the daughter of a Chief Constable, all be it from another borough.

Biddlecombe liked to believe he had been promoted on merit, but if Sybil's father being a Chief Constable had, in any way, helped, then so be it. Either way, he was an Inspector at the relatively young age of thirty and no one could now take that away from him.

He had arrived on a warm, sunny morning; the kind of morning when people would have been more inclined to take a picnic to a park somewhere than go in to an office and try to do some work. Biddlecombe had kissed his wife goodbye that morning and enjoyed his stroll to the office, purchasing a newspaper *en route* and generally taking his time. Consequently he had arrived at his desk a few minutes later than schedule, but no one had commented and he now took off his jacket and sat down at his desk.

Lying on the desk were items of morning mail that had been deemed relevant to his area of work. There were also messages and requests that had been received from other Forces. Biddlecombe's desk had become the place where people left things that they didn't, themselves, want to deal with. He didn't really mind as it gave him something to do and also gave him a sense of importance that he was carrying out duties on behalf of the Force, rather than just for himself.

Biddlecombe took out his pipe and lit it. He puffed contentedly as he began his journey through the papers lying in front of him. He created separate piles, as he went along, but one item caught his attention more than anything else. It was a request from Aberdeen. Biddlecombe tried to remember where Aberdeen was and came to the conclusion it was somewhere above Edinburgh on the map. He read the request and then read it again.

He had been a few months away from joining the police at the time of Professor Barclay's wife's accident, but he remembered the incident because his family home was only a few streets from where the accident had taken place. The death of a young woman, in such tragic circumstances, was not something to be easily forgotten. His first reaction to the information sent from Aberdeen had been the same as Jake Fraser's; no police officer took kindly to coincidence, particularly where crime was involved.

He pushed back his chair and stood up. He took the short journey to the main staircase and climbed to the second floor. He then followed the corridor until he reached the third door on his right. He went in.

The room was large, with a counter placed near to the door allowing the rest of the room to be taken up by rows and rows of cabinets. Here was housed the work of the Cambridge Borough Police, going back over thirty years. Somewhere, in one of these cabinets, would be the notes relevant to Mrs Barclay's death. Biddlecombe knew that the contents would not amount to much as it was highly likely that only a few people would have been questioned at the time of Mrs Barclay's accident. The police tended to pay little attention to accidents.

An elderly gentleman, wearing dark trousers, a white shirt and dark braces, came to the counter. Biddlecombe knew this to be Ron Yardley, an ex-police officer who had been persuaded to remain, in a civilian role, when the time to leave the police had come round. It had been felt that Ron's personal knowledge, as well as his ability to keep records in such a tidy order, would be invaluable to the workings of the Force.

"What can I do for you, Sam?" Ron asked as he leaned on the counter.

"Need to have a look at a file from eighteen ninety-six concerning the accidental death of the wife of Professor Clive Barclay."

Ron's eyebrows rose slightly. "Someone finally asking questions about that?" he said and this, in turn piqued Sam Biddlecombe's interest even further.

"Why do you say that, Ron?"

"No specific reason. However, I do remember the incident and I also remember thinking, at the time that everything seemed just a bit too neat and tidy, if you get my meaning."

"In what way?"

"Professor Barclay's account of events was never really questioned, as I recall. His was the only account after all and no one seemed moved to do anything other than agree with it."

"Was he alone in the house at the time of his wife's death?"

"I'm pretty sure there was a maid as well; in fact it may well have been the maid who found the poor woman at the bottom of the stair."

"Did you do any work on that particular investigation?"

"There wasn't an investigation to work on. Inspector Lovering visited the house, had a look around, asked a few questions and then decided it was definitely an accident and left it to the Coroner to investigate further. The inquest was little more than a formality. Barclay stood up and with tears forming in his eyes, informed everyone that his wife had been taking tablets to help her sleep for some time and that she must have been under the influence of those tablets when she lost her balance and fell down the stairs. A local doctor then confirmed that there had been evidence of Mrs Barclay taking tablets to help her sleep and he further said there were no marks on the body to indicate any form of violence having come her way prior to her fall. Little else was said and a verdict of accidental death was passed. Bill Jones was on duty that day at the Coroner's Office and I always remember him saying, when he got back to the mess room, that he thought there had been more to the case than had met the eye. He spoke about how Barclay was smiling as he left the building, as if he felt he'd just got away with something. Anyway, who's asking about Barclay now?"

"An Inspector Fraser from Aberdeen City Police. Apparently a maid was murdered in Professor Barclay's house in Aberdeen, back in eighteen ninety-eight and the Aberdeen Police now have reason to believe that the good Professor might have been more involved than had appeared the case at the time of the crime. After what you have just said, I'm already inclined to agree with them. Could you look out the file for me, please Ron? Could you also give the last address we had for Bill Jones and ex-Inspector Lovering?"

Ron went off for a few moments and then returned with the necessary file and addresses. Sam accepted both with thanks and then made his way back to his office. He was delighted to have some proper work to get involved with and had no intention of passing on this particular inquiry.

Once back at his desk Biddlecombe placed the file in his top drawer and then went to make himself a cup of tea. It was rather frowned upon, drinking tea at your desk but, along with smoking his pipe, it helped him to think. Biddlecombe could feel in his bones that there was more to be learned about Professor Barclay and he was already looking forward to getting started. He found a room, near the canteen, where he could get hot water. He had his own tea and pot so the water was all that was necessary, along with a strainer, of course, as he hated that last mouthful of tea always being full of leaves.

Five minutes later, Biddlecombe was seated at his desk, lit pipe in his mouth, steaming cup of tea to his right and the file, concerning the death of Professor Barclay's wife, open in front of him. Biddlecombe laid his notebook to his right and began to read through what little had been left by the investigating officer.

On the morning of Saturday, 3rd October, 1896, the police were called to the residence of Professor Clive Barclay and his wife, Netty. The maid, Rose Sim, had found Mrs Barclay lying at the bottom of the stairs when she had got up to get the house warmed that morning. Rose had then roused the Professor and he had told her to call the police.

Inspector Lovering had arrived and conducted a brief inspection of the body before releasing it to the Police Surgeon. Lovering had then interviewed Professor Barclay who had actually said very little. He had known nothing of his wife's whereabouts until Rose woke him that morning with the news. He had confessed to the fact that he and his wife were no longer sharing the marital bed and that was why he could not tell Lovering when his wife might have risen and gone for a walk through the house. The last he had seen of his wife had been mid-evening, the night before.

Barclay had gone to his Club around eight o'clock and had not got home until nearer midnight. He had gone straight to bed at that time, assuming his wife was already in her own bed. Biddlecombe checked another piece of paper. The Club had confirmed the times given by Barclay and the cab driver, who had taken Barclay from the Club to his home, was able to confirm that he dropped the Professor off at just after midnight. He had definitely then seen the Professor go in to his house.

Biddlecombe made his first note. *Barclay home at midnight. Mrs Barclay found dead at the bottom of the stair at 6am.*

He then looked at the report from the Police Surgeon. He had estimated Mrs Barclay had probably been dead for around four hours. Her neck had been broken in the fall and there were no other injuries found on the body, other than those that would naturally have occurred as she rolled down the stairs. The general consensus was that Mrs Barclay had died in an unfortunate accident and it was officially dropped from being a police matter.

Biddlecombe added another note. *Barclay home at midnight. Mrs Barclay dead by two. What happened in those two hours?*

The local Coroner had been handed the case to investigate and he had asked for a second doctor to inspect the body, just in case something had been missed. The second report supported the findings of the Police Surgeon and the inquest went through the motions before declaring Accidental Death. There was nothing extra to be learned from the inquest.

Mrs Barclay's body was released for the funeral and the formal paperwork filed away for posterity.

Not that there was much for Biddlecombe to gain from reading any of the material in the file. Barclay had given an account of what might have happened, everyone agreed, case closed. No questions had been asked of the Professor regarding his relationship with his wife, at the time of her death, or perhaps his relationship with someone else, given the fact that he and his wife no longer slept together. In view of what went on to happen in Aberdeen, it now seemed fitting to try and find Rose Sim and determine what more she might have known.

Biddlecombe made a note to do some research on where Rose might now be, should she still be alive and then stood up and put his jacket on. He checked his pipe was no longer burning and put it in his pocket. He put his notebook in his inside pocket and left the room. He went out the back door of the building and across to a bicycle shed, where he kept a bicycle for the purposes of making relatively short journeys around the area of the office. Today he was intent on seeing Bill Jones and ex-Inspector Lovering. Fortunately, for Biddlecombe, the two men lived less than a mile and a half from each other.

Bill Jones was his first port of call. Sam Biddlecombe had not known either man that well, but obviously he was more acquaint with Bill as he had never risen above the rank of Constable. Bill lived, with his wife and the last two of his six children, in three rooms on the second floor of a building that had clearly seen better days. He had moved there on leaving the police, as that had meant him having to give up his police house as well. He now lived in the only premises that he could afford.

Bill was pleased to see Sam. They may not have known each other that well, but a visit from an old colleague was always welcome. It brought back memories of better days and it also, just for a few moments, brought some meaning to Bill's life, which he now felt was drifting, rather aimlessly, towards its conclusion. He showed Sam in to the back room, his wife and children leaving them to talk. Bill then offered Sam a cup of tea, which he accepted. The two men then sat on threadbare chairs and drank their tea from cracked cups.

"What can I do for you, sir?" Bill had then asked.

"I want you to cast your mind back a few years, Bill, to a Coroner's Inquest that dealt with the accidental death of the wife of a university professor by the name of Barclay."

Jones did not have to think for very long. "Oh yes, sir, I remember that one well."

"Ron Yardley remembered you saying at the time that you thought Professor Barclay knew more than he had said, can you remember why you felt that way?"

"It was the look on Barclay's face that I'll never forget. He seemed to be smiling, or perhaps I should describe it more as a smirk, all the time that the evidence was being presented. It seemed to me that he had the look of a man who felt he was getting away with something."

"Did he attend the inquest alone?"

"No, as I recall, he came each day with his maid. I can't remember her name, but she was needed, on the first day, to give evidence. He gave evidence on the second day and on day three it was all over; accidental death."

"Do you recall ever noticing any sign of intimacy between Barclay and the maid; her name was Rose, by the way."

Bill thought for a moment. He had a long way to go back and many, more recent memories, to move before he could reach those that he needed at that moment. There was nothing obvious forthcoming and he said that to Biddlecombe.

"Did you ever have cause to cross paths with Professor Barclay either before or after that inquest?"

"No, sir. I'm pretty sure that Barclay left Cambridge a matter of months after the inquest, in fact he may have moved to Scotland."

Sam smiled. "You have as good a memory as Ron, Bill. Barclay moved to Aberdeen where, in just over a year, his maid was murdered in the house and Barclay was on the move again."

"Murdered?" repeated Bill.

"Yes and a local Police Inspector, along now with myself, believe that the wrong man went to the gallows. I think it is time that Professor Barclay answered some questions that ought to have been asked of him years ago."

"Where is he now?"

"That we do not know at present, but someone, somewhere, must know and we'll catch him some day, unless the Grim Reaper has taken him for his own."

Sam finished his tea and thanked Bill for his help. He then left the building and set off towards the area where Lovering lived. It did not take him long, through relatively quiet streets to find the property. Lovering lived in a terraced house, nicely appointed from the outside and set in a street where it was obvious his neighbours had more money available to them than poor Bill Jones.

Lovering answered the door almost immediately and was as pleased as Bill Jones was, to see Sam. They were soon sitting in a lounge but, on this occasion, Sam refused the offer of tea. He basically went over the same ground with Lovering, only this time it was from the point of view of the investigating officer and as Sam was effectively re-investigating the case he needed to tread carefully and not upset, or annoy, the ex-Inspector. The last thing Sam wanted was for his ex-colleague to refuse to help.

As it was Lovering remembered the case fairly clearly and was happy to talk about it. After they had spoken in more general terms, Sam eventually moved the conversation in to areas where he now thought Lovering was more likely to get angry.

"Did you ever, at any time, think that Mrs Barclay's death might have been anything other than accidental?"

"Murder, you mean?" Lovering almost snapped back, his tone heavy with disbelief.

"Would murder have been possible?" Biddlecombe asked again.

"I suppose it might have been," answered Lovering, his voice still carrying an edge to it, "but it wasn't. The woman fell down the stairs and broke her neck. There was no evidence of her being pushed and anyway, Professor Barclay gained nothing from his wife's death."

"Apart from freedom, perhaps?" added Biddlecombe.

Lovering looked at Sam and seemed to calm down a little. He thought some more in silence before speaking again.

"Do you now have reason to question the findings of all those years ago?"

"Professor Barclay moved to Aberdeen. A matter of months later, his maid was murdered in the house and a man arrested, convicted and hanged for the crime. Inspector Fraser, of Aberdeen City Police, now believes that Professor Barclay probably had more to do with the crime than was ever thought at the time. I agree with him and I also believe that Professor Barclay might have had more to do with his wife's death as well. In both cases everyone was very quick to accept the word of a university professor, as if it were an impossibility for them to lie. In both cases I believe there weren't enough questions asked, especially of the Professor."

"History may have given you a reason for questioning the Professor's word, but there was no reason at the time to believe that events could have occurred in any way, other than that described by the Professor."

"Did you ever think to ask him about his relationship with his wife?" Biddlecombe suggested.

"What had that to do with anything?" Lovering replied.

"At the time of her death it was obvious that Professor Barclay and his wife were not as close as they might have been. He admitted to them sleeping in separate rooms and it might have been an idea to have probed that relationship a little further."

"To what end?" asked Lovering in a tone that made it known to Biddlecombe that he took offence to having his investigative methods questioned, even after all these years.

"If Professor Barclay's marriage was all but over then he may have been looking for a way to gain his freedom without the scandal and cost of a divorce."

"But why would he want to go to all that trouble?"

"Perhaps he liked to have relationships with his maids?" Biddlecombe suggested. "That may have been why the maid in Aberdeen was murdered; perhaps she hadn't complied with his wishes."

Lovering scoffed. "Barclay wouldn't have needed to go to all that bother. His wife knew her place; she needed his position to give her life any true meaning and she would never have said, or done anything against him, purely over some dalliance with a maid."

"But what if that dalliance had become something more?"

"Love? With a maid?"

"It is a strong motive for murder," insisted Biddlecombe.

Lovering paused for a moment, allowing what had already been said to fully sink in.

"Perhaps if Aberdeen had happened first, then I would have felt a need to dig deeper. However, my case came first and as I've already said, nothing ever came to light to cast doubt on the word of Professor Barclay. If you look at the evidence you will see that everyone believed it was a simple case of accidental death."

Biddlecombe wasn't sure who Lovering was now trying to persuade most, himself or his guest.

"Did you ever see, or hear from, Professor Barclay after the inquest?"

"No. I think he left Cambridge soon after."

"And was that not suspicious in itself?" Biddlecombe added.

"Not particularly. If your wife had just died in the house, would you not want to get away as quickly as possible, were you able to do so?"

"Did Rose go with him?"

"I have no idea. Look, Sam, I investigated the case and accepted the verdict. I still don't accept, that given what I knew then, I did anything wrong."

"No one is saying you did anything wrong but you must admit that you perhaps did not conduct the investigation as thoroughly as it might have been."

Lovering though for a moment longer. He shook his head, he was clearly not even willing to admit that. Biddlecombe did not push his argument but decided to leave. Once out in the street he took stock of what he had learned through speaking to his ex-colleagues. He felt an even stronger need to find Professor Barclay and also to determine what might have happened to Rose. He climbed back on to his bicycle and returned to the office.

Once back at base, Sam Biddlecombe wrote a brief report of what he had done, to date, with regard to Netty Barclay's accidental death. Using two sheets of carbon paper, he produced two further copies of his report, one of which he filed with his own papers and the other he put in an envelope and along with a letter of explanation, set it aside to post to Inspector Jake Fraser, of the Aberdeen City Police.

Sam Biddlecombe then left the office once more and caught the tram that would take him closest to where Professor Barclay had lived at the time of his wife's death. Once there he knocked on the doors of the houses on either side of the property but found, to his annoyance, that both houses were now occupied by people who were not there when Netty Barclay met her end.

He widened his area of enquiry and finally came across Miss Redmond, who lived a little further down the road. Miss Redmond was in her early sixties but her mind was still sharp and her memory even better. She had invited Inspector Biddlecombe in to her home and offered him tea and cake, which he accepted with some relish.

Once seated in the parlour, Miss Redmond began to talk about Professor Barclay.

"He was a strange man. He came across as being very polite, always raising his hat to a passing lady, but there was just something about him that I never really liked. My sister was still alive at that time and she always used to say there was something suspicious about Barclay. She always thought he was hiding something and wasn't in the least bit surprised when poor Netty was found dead."

"Did you know Netty Barclay?" Biddlecombe then asked through a mouthful of beautifully baked cake.

"I don't think anyone really knew Netty. She rarely left the house and when she did she always had a frightened look about her. She was a mousey, little character and to be honest, not the type of woman you would expected Barclay to have married in the first place. She wasn't worth a lot of money, was she?"

The final question was asked in a tone of someone seeking to inject some excitement in to an otherwise drab conversation. Biddlecombe smiled.

"Not as far as I know. Did you ever think that Barclay might have been mistreating her?"

"I don't remember thinking that at the time, but over the years, when I've thought back on it, I have often wondered if there might not have been some form of cruelty going on behind the front door of that house."

"Do you remember their maid, Rose?"

Miss Redmond nodded. "Ah yes, Rose; there was something strange there as well."

"What do you mean?"

"She was very young and very pretty, but not very bright. Netty did once tell me that Rose wasn't very good at her job, but that Clive wouldn't hear of having her replaced. I don't like to say this, Inspector, but I fear there might have been something intimate between Professor Barclay and Rose. In fact, it may well have been that intimacy that led to poor Netty's demise."

"Was there ever any visual sign of intimacy between the Professor and Rose; perhaps after the inquest?"

"Oh, there would never have been anything obvious, Inspector. Had Barclay had any feelings for Rose then he would have kept them in check until the front door had been firmly closed."

"Can you remember if Rose left at the same time as Professor Barclay?"

"I seem to remember Rose leaving around two days before the Professor went off to some new job. I saw her leave the house with her bags and setting off along the street. Professor Barclay was standing at the door watching her, but she never turned round and I got the impression she was not happy to be moving on."

"But you never knew where she went?"

Miss Redmond shook her head. "No, I'm sorry."

"Can you remember what Rose looked like?"

"As I said, she was very pretty. The girl turned men's heads as she walked down the street. She had dark, curly hair and if I remember rightly, blue eyes. She would have been around five feet tall and always dressed well when not in uniform. I always had the impression that that girl was never short of money, which would have been rare for a maid."

"Did you ever see her with men friends?"

"I rarely saw the girl when she wasn't working."

"Have you ever seen Professor Barclay back in Cambridge since he left to go to Aberdeen?"

"Oh, I don't think he would ever come back here," Miss Redmond said, quite emphatically. "Whatever happened behind the doors of that house, Professor Barclay always knew a whole lot more than he was ever going to say, I'm sure of that."

"So you wouldn't have expected him to come back to Cambridge, at least not until much of the dust had settled?"

"I'm sure, over the passage of time, more than I have started to ask questions that Professor Barclay would rather not have to answer. I don't think he'd want to put himself in the position where neighbours were questioning his every action as they'd heard stories of his wife's demise."

Biddlecombe could see sense in that statement. He enjoyed another piece of cake and another cup of tea. He had asked a few, rather meaningless, questions to fill the time it took for him to finish. He then thanked Miss Redmond for her help and was shown to the door.

Back at his office he added another half sheet of paper to what was already in the envelope destined for Jake Fraser's desk. He then sealed the envelope and took it to the mail room.

***

TEN

Wednesday 10th June

Sergeant Mathieson arrived at Edith McIntosh's house at nine o'clock in the morning. It was cloudy and threatening rain, so Mathieson was quite pleased to have a job that would keep him indoors for part of the day. Kerrigan was already standing at the front gate when Mathieson arrived. They exchanged pleasantries and then walked up the short path to the front door. Mathieson unlocked it and both men entered.

Kerrigan shivered as he stood in the hallway. Mathieson noted the involuntary action and enquired if Kerrigan was okay with being in a house where a murder had been so recently committed.

"Yes, I'm fine," came the reply, though it did not carry much conviction. "Where do you want to start?"

"Perhaps we might follow the same route you took when you first drew up the inventory of items for Miss McIntosh?" Mathieson suggested and Kerrigan agreed that that was probably their best approach to the job in hand.

They started downstairs where most of the items, on the list, were situated. Kerrigan called out what he was picking up and Mathieson placed a tick beside it on the list. Where they found something not on the list, Mathieson added it on the other side of the paper and Kerrigan provided a rough estimate as to what the item might make at auction.

"When did you first prepare this list?" Mathieson asked as they reached the last of the items in the first room.

Kerrigan thought for a moment. "I believe the list was first drawn up by Gibson and Son around six years ago. Doctor McIntosh had asked for a record of his purchases for insurance purposes. However, the list you now hold in your hand was done by myself about eighteen months ago."

"Why the new list?"

"Miss McIntosh simply wanted an up to date list."

"Because she had bought a lot of new items?" Mathieson suggested.

"Nothing much was added, as I recall."

"Was there anything missing from the first list?" Mathieson then asked.

"A few items. I seem to remember Miss McIntosh saying that her father had sold some items just prior to his death."

"You don't happen to remember what those items were, do you?" Mathieson then asked, though it was more in hope than anything else.

"Sorry," Kerrigan replied. "However, if you check the original list against mine then you'll know what had been sold."

"Of course," Mathieson said, feeling a little stupid that he hadn't thought of that.

"And most of these items are worth something, are they?" Mathieson then asked, showing his complete ignorance in such matters.

Kerrigan smiled. "Everything has a value, Sergeant, but some of these items are worth pennies while others are worth pounds."

"And you can tell the difference?" added Mathieson.

"I'm far from an expert in all matters, Sergeant, but I do have an eye for certain items, which is why I work for Gibson and Son in the first place. There would be little point in being employed by an auctioneer if I were not able to accurately value items, which might be brought in."

Mathieson could see the sense in that. "So what is your area of expertise, Mr Kerrigan?"

"Mainly Japanese and Chinese art and pottery, though we don't see a lot of that around here."

"I shouldn't imagine," added Mathieson as they moved to the next room.

They made their way round the other rooms downstairs before making their way upstairs and starting in the study. Mathieson obviously did not make it know to Kerrigan that this was the room in which the body had been found.

After checking the few items that were on the list, Kerrigan turned to leave the room. Mathieson stopped him at the door.

"Have you ever been aware of Doctor McIntosh having a collection of miniature paintings?" he asked.

Kerrigan answered immediately. "I've never heard mention of anything like that. Why, did he have such a collection?"

"We believe he did have such a collection, but it's possible the collection was sold before his death. Perhaps they'll be on the list drawn up six years ago?"

Kerrigan looked unsure. "I don't remember everything that was on that last, Sergeant, but I'm pretty sure there was no mention of miniature paintings. I think I would have remembered that."

"Oh well, I don't expect we'll ever know the story behind that particular collection," Mathieson concluded and they left the room.

By lunchtime they had completed a check of the list. Eight items had been added and seven items were missing, either sold or stolen. Kerrigan was able to tell Mathieson that the items missing from the list were not worth very much, so Mathieson assumed that theft had not been the reason for their disappearance, especially as so many other items, of greater value, were still in the house.

Mathieson told Kerrigan that he could return to his work and then went on one last tour of the property. He concluded his tour in what had been Doctor McIntosh's bedroom. It was still laid out as if the Doctor was coming home that night. The bed was made and the cupboards and wardrobe still full of his clothes. Mathieson took his time to look around.

Eventually he arrived at the bedside cabinet, which lay to the right of the bed. Lying on top of the cabinet was a book and a pair of spectacles. In the top drawer he found a copy of the bible and in the second drawer there was some papers, though none of them were of any interest to Mathieson. He closed the door and then returned to the top drawer. This time he removed the drawer completely and to his great surprise he found two sheets of paper pinned to the bottom of it.

Mathieson removed the sheets of paper and studied them more closely. He had found another list of items. This time, he assumed, the list had been completed by Doctor McIntosh himself and it covered his collection of miniature paintings. Each painting was listed along with a brief description of it and an estimation of its value. Each painting was worth a lot of money, making the complete collection well worth stealing.

Mathieson replaced the drawer and as he did so, his eye was caught by a small book lying towards the back. He took it out and found it to be a diary, again completed in what he assumed was Doctor McIntosh's hand. He put both the diary and the sheets of paper in to his pocket and then left the room.

He went downstairs and closed all the doors to each room. He then went out through the front door and locked it behind him. He felt sure that he had much to discuss with Inspector Fraser when they both finally got together later that day.

***

The second post had arrived in the late morning and Jake found a pile of envelopes on his desk when he returned from having a swift cup of tea and a pie for his lunch at one of the many cafes on Union Street. He sat down at his desk and quickly sifted through the envelopes, his eye being caught by one having a Cambridge postmark. He quickly opened the envelope and took out the contents. He read Biddlecombe's report and accompanying notes, with interest and then sat back in his chair to digest what he had now learned.

Biddlecombe had pretty much convinced Jake of the fact that Professor Barclay had been, in some way, involved in his wife's death. He was now totally convinced that the Professor had also had some part to play in Jean Maxwell's death as well. Two deaths against him; there would surely be more if he were to dig a bit deeper. Taking a note of the description of Rose Sim that he had got from Biddlecombe, Jake put his jacket on again and left the office.

Jake returned to Arthur Fleming's property on The Green. He found Arthur at home, looking every bit as unwashed as before and clearly down on his luck. Arthur let Jake in and led him to the room they had occupied on his last visit.

"Did you ever meet Jean Maxwell?" Jake asked, coming straight to the point.

"I met her once."

"Can you remember what she looked like?"

"Pretty. Very pretty in fact. Tom was infatuated by her."

"Colour of hair?"

"Dark brown I think."

"How tall was she?"

"I can't remember, but I don't think she'd have been that tall; I mean, women aren't, are they?"

"Was she local to Aberdeen?"

"Definitely not. Tom used to call her his English Maid."

"Did she and Tom spend much time together?" Jake then asked.

"She would sometimes bring him a glass of water on a hot day, or they might chat for a little while if she was out hanging up the washing. It was all very innocent, Inspector, which is why I always knew there was never anything in that story of them drinking wine and having sex in the middle of the day. Neither Tom, nor Jean, would have thought of doing that; at least, not with each other."

"Well, thanks for your continuing help, Mr Fleming," Jake concluded and started to make his way to the door.

"I didn't think I was being helpful," Arthur said as he hurried to catch up.

"No, believe me, what you've told me just now has been immensely helpful."

Jake opened the door and left. He made his way down to The Green and from there, walked back to the office. By the time he had taken off his jacket and sat down at his desk he had Sergeant Mathieson sitting beside him with a grin, the width of Union Street, on his face.

"What are you looking so pleased about?" Jake enquired.

"I found this in Doctor McIntosh's bedroom," Mathieson answered handing the diary and sheets of paper to Jake. Jake felt a mixture of pleasure that the items had now been found but annoyance that he and others had missed them in the first place. He sat back and looked at the sheets of paper first.

"The miniature paintings," he then said, by way of a statement. "At least we now know they definitely existed."

"Doctor McIntosh was known to have sold some items just prior to his death, so it is perfectly possible that the miniatures were sold then."

"Which means burglary may not be the motive for Miss McIntosh's murder," Jake added.

"Possibly not," agreed Mathieson.

Jake read through the list. There were fifteen of them in total and they were all worth a lot of money. Each painting was of a female in an either naked, or semi-naked pose and he could well imagine many men would be keen to purchase them, were they ever to come on the market. The list was not dated but at least it provided Jake with some idea of what he was now looking for.

Jake then cast an eye over the diary. There were only a few entries in the book, but they all referred to a woman by the name of Mildred. Beside each entry was also the amount of money which the Doctor had paid to Mildred for her services. The sums of money were not small and Jake deduced that either Mildred had been exceptional in the service she had provided, or else Doctor McIntosh was being as kind to her as Jake had been to Alice.

"So, we now know what we are looking for, but we can no longer be sure that they were stolen in the first place," Jake then surmised.

"That appears to be the case, yes sir. I'll go back to Gibson and Sons and see if they can provide me with a copy of the list that was drawn up six years ago while Doctor McIntosh was still alive. If the miniatures are on that list then we'll know they were sold prior to his death."

"Very good," Jake added. "Also, see if you can locate this Mildred. She must be a local prostitute, so I assume someone will know who she is."

***

At the very moment that Jake was providing Mathieson with his latest instructions, Inspector Frederick Swanson, of the Edinburgh City Police was reading through a file he had had brought to his office after reading the message from Aberdeen City Police with regard to Professor Barclay and the murder of Jean Maxwell.

Frederick Swanson was forty-eight years of age and had been a police officer for twenty-five years. He was a short, heavy built man with greying hair that always looked like it could do with trimming. He also had the bushiest eyebrows in the whole of Edinburgh City Police and they seemed to sit atop his eyes like a couple of ferrets guarding a food cache.

Swanson had been reminded of a murder, which had taken place in Edinburgh in 1903. A maid had been found murdered by the master of the house on his return from work. It transpired he had worked at the university, though the man's name was not given as Professor Barclay, merely *Mr* Barclay.

Swanson read some more. Mr Barclay had worked in the administration office of the university, having started there in 1902. He had come home from work on the night of Thursday, the Fifth of November, 1903, to find his maid, Anna Trotter, lying dead in her room. He had been at a party to celebrate Guy Fawkes' Day and had not got home until nearer midnight.

The police had been called and Inspector Riddle had taken charge of the investigation. The medical report revealed that Miss Trotter had been strangled, though there was no evidence of sexual interference. Glasses had been found in her room and it had been assumed, from that, that she had had company whilst the master was away. It had further been assumed that this mysterious guest had to be the killer.

The investigation had lasted for three months but no one had ever been caught. A note at the end of one of the pages informed Swanson that Mr Barclay had since left Edinburgh and was believed to have gone back South. Swanson finished reading the contents of the file and then stood up from his desk, put on his jacket and set off to see someone at the university.

***

Jake was now sitting in his office on his own. The afternoon had disappeared and he was now harbouring thoughts of going home. He had not spent as much time with

Margaret, recently, as he would have hoped and there was nothing on his desk that could not wait until the next day. However, even though he wanted to leave, there was something keeping him in that seat at his desk.

His mind was trying to work two investigations at the same time, which was not proving that easy. Regarding the murder of Edith McIntosh there was still some debate as to what the motive had been for her murder. If the miniature paintings had already been sold then there appeared to be nothing else, of any value, missing from the house. The more he thought about it, the more he convinced himself that those miniatures had to be the reason for the burglary. He made a note to ask Sergeant Mathieson to visit the local antiques outlets, just in case someone had attempted to sell the stolen goods already.

Whilst Jake had some idea where he was going with the Edith McIntosh murder, things weren't so clear with the activities of Professor Barclay. Jake's latest theory was that Jean Maxwell and Rose Sim were one and the same person. Jake felt sure that Rose had travelled to Aberdeen with Professor Barclay and that they had been living together whilst maintaining the pretence of being maid and employer. Something had then changed, probably Rose showing too much interest in Tom Fleming and Barclay had decided to put an end to it all in the only way he knew; murder.

His plan had been to kill Rose and point the finger at Tom. That way he removed them both from the scene and allowed him to move on, yet again. The motive was sound but, of course, there wasn't a shred of evidence to support it. Jake knew that he would have to dig a lot deeper, hopefully with the assistance of Sam Biddlecombe, before he got anywhere near building a case against Professor Clive Barclay.

Eventually, Jake threw his pencil down on the desk and decided it really was time to go home.

***

Inspector Swanson returned from the university and sat at his desk to mull over what he had learned. The *Mr* Barclay referred to in his notes had turned out to be *Clive* Barclay after all. Why then had he chosen to work in Edinburgh University in a clerical capacity when he was a Professor capable of tutoring?

Swanson had met with the Head of the Department under which Barclay had worked. The gentleman had been of the opinion that Barclay had been a good worker, but that he had always had a feeling that Barclay had been capable of so much more. He had come to Edinburgh, he had said, from Aberdeen and had produced references from both Aberdeen and Cambridge, confirming he had worked, in a clerical capacity, in both establishments and that he had carried out those duties to the satisfaction of his employer.

Swanson could only assume the references had been fraudulently created as Barclay had been a Professor and unlikely to have made a habit of working in a clerical and therefore lesser paid role. On the other hand, maybe he had taken lesser jobs when not wishing to attract attention to himself.

Swanson had also asked if anyone at the University had thought it strange that a clerical member of their staff could afford to rent a large house and employ a maid and a housekeeper, as Barclay had done. The reply was simple; Barclay had said that he had private money and that he had only taken the job to fill some time, rather than necessarily assist him in paying his bills.

On the question of why he had left Edinburgh, the reply was again very simple. Barclay told them that he had applied for, successfully, a role back in Cambridge. He had made that announcement while the police had still been investigating the maid's murder. Barclay had finally left Edinburgh once the police had given him permission to do so. Yet again, no one had ever really considered the possibility that Barclay might have been involved in the crime. It seemed that wherever he went and whatever story he told, he was instantly believed and immediately removed from the investigation. Whatever else, Swanson now thought about Professor Barclay, he couldn't help but admit that the man must have been very plausible in everything he said.

Swanson left his office and walked the relatively short distance to the office of the Chief Constable. Chief Constable Roderick Ross had been in post since 1900, having previously been the Chief Constable in Bradford. Ross had been thirty-four years of age when he had taken up post in Edinburgh and was viewed, by many of his staff, as being a hard taskmaster. He had even been sued, in 1906, by an ex-officer whom Ross had sacked due to the officer, it had been claimed, failing to protect the Chief Constable's good name amidst an abundance of rumours circulating in the area.

Swanson did not like the Chief and he always felt the feeling was mutual. Swanson, therefore, was of the opinion that he had probably gone as far as he could under the leadership of Ross. The two men sat in the office that day and spoke of nothing other than the work being carried out by Swanson with regard to Clive Barclay.

"So, sir, as a result of what I now know about Clive Barclay and the fact that he has questions to answer in other Forces as well, I would respectfully ask that I be allowed to travel up to Aberdeen and speak, face to face, with the Inspector who is already investigating Barclay for a murder committed there around ten years ago."

Chief Constable Ross had considered the matter for a moment. "I agree that a trip to Aberdeen might be helpful to both Forces. However, if you are going there I would ask that you speak with Sergeant Fullerton first. He is working on a case that also has connections to Aberdeen so it would seem prudent for you to, as it were, kill two birds with the one stone."

"Very good, sir, I'll speak with Fullerton tomorrow and arrange to go to Aberdeen on Friday."

Swanson had then returned to his office to make the necessary preparations, which would include him making a rare telephone call to Inspector Fraser in Aberdeen.

***

Margaret had surpassed herself again in the culinary department. The evening meal she had placed before Jake had been perfection on a plate and he had eaten every scrap of it with relish. Margaret never ceased to be amazed by the speed in which Jake could eat his way through a plate of food. He always said he didn't like it to get cold, but Margaret knew that there was no chance of that happening such was the speed with which everything disappeared.

After the meal they sat through in the lounge, drinking tea and enjoying each other's company.

"Have you any more meetings this week?" Jake had enquired.

"No formal meetings, though I am seeing Sadie for lunch on Tuesday."

"You seem quite close to Sadie these days," Jake then observed.

"Not close. We are friends, but there is something about Sadie that I find more than a little unsettling."

Jake looked concerned. "What might that be?"

"I can't put my finger on it. She is nice enough to myself and everyone else, with whom she comes in to contact, but there is just something about her that leaves me feeling more than a little unsettled. I fear she might be capable of anything if she put her mind to it."

"You mean something criminal?" suggested Jake.

"Perhaps. As I said, I can't put my finger on it; there's just a something about her."

Jake thought about checking out Sadie Ashton at the first opportunity. Verbally he changed the subject and then they decided to play cards before going to bed. It was something they did quite a lot, even though Margaret tended to win. Jake always argued that he spent all day concentrating so it was difficult to keep mentally agile at night. Margaret responded that he was simply rubbish at playing cards and it had nothing to do with the lack of an agile mind.

After another serious defeat at the hands of his wife, Jake and Margaret then went to bed. There was no love-making that night, though they did lie in each other's arms for a little while before both drifting off in to a deep and pleasurable sleep.

***

ELEVEN

Friday 12th June

Thursday had been a day of gathering some more information for Jake. Mid-morning he had been told that someone was on the telephone for him and he was surprised to hear that that someone was an Inspector from Edinburgh with more news of dead maids connected to Clive Barclay. Swanson hadn't said very much, saving the main discussion until the next day when he would be in Aberdeen. He also mentioned the fact he had information on another matter and when he said what it was, Jake said he'd have his Sergeant sit in on their meeting. They had then agreed to meet just before lunchtime the following day.

Just after lunchtime Mathieson had come in to Jake's office to tell him that he had found Doctor McIntosh's lady friend, Mildred, and he now had her in the interview room. Jake went through with Mathieson to interview the woman. He found someone who had probably been quite pretty at one time in her life, but who was now looking rather haggard and hard-faced due to the life that she had been forced to live. She was well-dressed and clean, however, and Jake could not help but think that this woman still had some pride in her appearance. True to her profession she wore a dress that plunged at the front to offer Jake and Mathieson a view that they found difficult to ignore.

Mildred's second name was also McIntosh, but she quickly added that that was pure coincidence and that there had never been anything permanent between her and the Doctor. Jake asked if she would like some tea and she said that she would. She also added that something to eat wouldn't go amiss either. Jake smiled and then sent Mathieson to get a pie and a cup of tea from somewhere. Mathieson looked less than enthused until he realised that he could delegate the order to someone else and then get back for the rest of the interview.

Mildred didn't have much to say. She had had, in her words, a special relationship with the Doctor and at times he had no longer felt like a client. Jake was reminded of Alice, once again and the relationship he had with her over a period of time. Mildred was older than Alice had been, but he could well understand Doctor McIntosh wishing to ensure that Mildred's life was made a little better for knowing him.

"How old are you Mildred?" Jake then asked.

"Thirty-eight."

"And the age difference between yourself and Doctor McIntosh was never a problem?"

Mildred laughed. "He was a client. As long as he paid me he could have been dead for all I'd have cared. As it was, the Doctor paid for time to do things other than have sex. He told me that he no longer had the urge, but that he liked the company of women and that was really all he wanted from me."

"Did he ever mention having a collection of pictures?" Jake then said.

"You mean his dirty pictures? He used to speak about them, yes."

"Did he ever show them to you?"

Mildred laughed again. "Good God, no. He did tell me once though that these," and with that she glanced down at her breasts with some pride, "were as nice as them that was in his pictures. "

"So you didn't always meet the Doctor for sex?" Jake then asked, by way of clarifying their relationship.

"We had sex sometimes but on other occasions he would just sit and talk to me. Occasionally he'd ask me to take my clothes off and then do nothing more than look at me. I may not have much of a face these days, but the body is still good."

At that moment the door opened and a young constable came in with the tea and pie. He placed them on the table in front of Jake who immediately pushed both items across to Mildred. Her face lit up and she attacked the pie with much enthusiasm. The constable left the room and Sergeant Mathieson made a face as he watched the gravy start to run down Mildred's face. It was not a pretty sight.

"Did you know where Doctor McIntosh kept his miniature pictures?" Jake eventually asked once he felt Mildred had eaten most of the pie. She wiped her face with the back of her hand.

"He never said."

"And did he ever mention selling them?"

"He never said," Mildred said again, as more gravy ran down her chin.

"Do you know if Miss Edith McIntosh knew about the paintings?" Jake then asked.

Mildred stopped eating and laughed. "I shouldn't have thought so. Those pictures were not for the eyes of a lady from what I could gather."

"Did you often go to the Doctor's home?" added Jake.

"Usually."

"And was Edith there at the time?"

"I expect so, though I never saw her. We were always in Doctor McIntosh's bedroom and from there I never saw nor heard anyone else."

"Okay, Mildred, you've been very helpful."

Jake waited until Mildred had finished her food and then let her go on her way.

Jake returned to his desk but he had only been there five minutes when the Chief Constable had asked to see him. He was still clearing all the issues that had arisen with the suicide of the Superintendent. The main problem was that of Peter Ash's estate. Ash's Will had left all his possessions to a distant cousin, there being no one else close to him. The matter was now in the hands of a local solicitor who was having problems finding the cousin. Until he could be found and the matter of Edith McIntosh's house discussed, nothing much could be done with regard to Edith's estate.

After they had discussed the Superintendent's estate, the Chief then turned the conversation to matters a little closer to home. With the Superintendent's death it meant there was a vacancy in the chain of command. The Chief knew that a permanent solution would take a little time, but there was still a need for something temporary to be put in place. The current Chief Inspector would step up and the Chief wanted Jake to fill the post of Chief Inspector.

"Thank you for thinking of me, sir, but might I have a little time to consider the offer before I give you my answer?" Jake had then said.

The Chief had found Jake's request a little surprising but had agreed to give him the weekend to think things over. He asked for an answer on the Monday and Jake said that he would get one.

And so it was that at seven o'clock that Friday morning Jake was sitting at his desk still pondering on the answer he would give the Chief. He had spoken to Margaret, the night before and she'd been so proud of him and couldn't understand why he was stalling on giving the Chief Constable an answer. If truth be known, Jake didn't really know why he was stalling either.

He was certainly concerned that taking the role of Chief Inspector might take him away from what he was best at doing; namely investigating and solving serious crimes. He also worried that life might become little more than a sea of paper and a multitude of petty decisions. He was aware that the Chief, himself, still got involved in some investigations but, in the main, they were usually left to the Inspectors.

He decided to turn his mind to work-related matters and forget about possible promotions, at least for a little while.

***

Before sitting down to discuss business, Jake took Frederick Swanson to the Empress Café for something to eat. Swanson had been travelling all morning from Edinburgh and hadn't had time to eat anything before arriving in Aberdeen. They talked about things in general over a plate of stew and a mug of coffee. They may have been detectives by profession, but both men were struggling to detect much meat in their stew. There was plenty gravy and vegetables, but not much else. However, it tasted okay and at least it filled a gap.

Back at Lodge Walk, Jake asked Mathieson to join them and the three men settled down, in Jake's office, to talk about current investigations. Swanson opened proceeding by taking some papers from his briefcase and handing them to Sergeant Mathieson.

"I believe you have had a visit from 'The Buchan Heiress," Swanson then said. "She's been pretty active of late, including duping a Doctor in Edinburgh in to allowing her to live with his family for a week. She even had the audacity to invite the Doctor and his family to come up to Turriff and live with her at her mansion. She let them get on the train and then disappeared."

Jake was smiling. "I know she's a habitual criminal, but you have to admire the nerve of the woman. I swear she could sell a coal fire to someone living in an igloo."

Swanson did not see the humour in their conversation. "The Buchan Heiress" was, at worst fraudulently acquiring money from people and at best, a total pest to the police as they seemed to be forever looking for her.

"Sergeant Fullerton has been dealing with the annoying woman in Edinburgh and he wanted you to see those papers. He would also appreciate you letting him have anything that you might have on her previous escapades. Maybe if we all work a little closer then we'll catch this woman with enough reason to keep her in prison longer than the usual six months that she seems to get."

"Do you have any idea where she might be just now?" Mathieson then asked.

"We haven't heard anything about her for a few weeks. You've had her in Aberdeen since she was last in Edinburgh. I'm guessing she'll be in Dundee or Glasgow, if her past movements are anything to go by. Anyway, I'd be obliged if you could post a report down to Fullerton, bringing him up to date with your own investigation."

"I'll deal with it as soon as we are finished here," Mathieson then said.

"Excellent. Now let's move on to Professor Clive Barclay. What a nasty piece of work he appears to be."

"If he really has been responsible for the three deaths that we know about, then it begs the question; how many more might there be?"

"My thoughts exactly," agreed Swanson, "which is why I thought a chat was in order. The more Forces we have looking for this gentleman then the more chance we have of catching him."

"Agreed," said Jake. "We have to assume that wherever he is, he'll still retain a connection with a university. It seems to be the world in which he is most confident."

"We need to put out a new request, to all Forces within a university catchment area, to be on the look-out for Barclay. We also need to ensure that if anyone finds him, they don't give the game away and allow him to make good an escape. We need this man in custody and we also need you and I to be part of any interrogation that might take place."

"Inspector Biddlecombe, in Cambridge, knows a fair bit about Barclay as well," Jake added.

"Then we keep him informed of our actions as well," said Swanson. Jake studied the Edinburgh Inspector for a moment. The man looked to be around Jake's age, perhaps slightly older, but it was difficult to look at him without being distracted by those eyebrows. Jake had seen a drawing once of the character Mr Hyde, from Robert Louis Stevenson's story of Doctor Jekyll and Mr Hyde and he had been illustrated with eyebrows as fierce as those above Swanson's eyes. Fortunately the rest of the man's appearance was not so frightening.

The three police officers then drew up a record of everything they knew about Professor Barclay. They started in October, 1896, with the death of Mrs Barclay in Cambridge. They noted the death as accidental, but placed a large question mark to the side. The next event was in June, 1898, when Jean Maxwell was murdered in Aberdeen. They noted that Tom Fleming was found guilty of the crime and hanged soon after. Another huge question mark was placed to the side of this as well. Finally they wrote down details of events in Edinburgh in November, 1903. Anna Trotter had been found murdered, but no one had ever been caught.

The similarities between the crimes scenes of Jean Maxwell and Anna Trotter were inescapable. However, even if there hadn't been other issues to attract the attention of the police the mere fact that Clive Barclay had been present at them all was enough to confirm, at least as far as Jake and Frederick Swanson were concerned, that Barclay had to be a murderer who had killed more than once.

"It's interesting," Swanson then said, as he looked down at the notes they had made," that Barclay never seems to stay anywhere for very long. He came to Aberdeen in eighteen ninety-seven and then leaves after a murder in eighteen ninety-eight. He arrived in Edinburgh in nineteen hundred and two and left after another murder, this time in nineteen hundred and three. If he had killed elsewhere then he may not have been very long in moving on from there as well."

"He's obviously never been that concerned about leaving a footprint in time, wherever he has gone," Jake then commented. "Apart from becoming *Mister* Barclay, in Edinburgh, he's never made any real attempt to hide his identity. It's as if he feels confident that we will never piece the jigsaw together and actually catch him."

"He's like so many people who kill more than once," added Swanson, "they start to get over confident and then they believe that they are beyond the law. He probably thinks he *can't* be caught now."

"It may well be that his over confidence will ultimately be his undoing," said Jake. "However, the main problem for us, at the moment, is that we have no idea where Barclay is as of today and more importantly, we have no idea where he has been these last five years. It's possible he could have killed twice in that time."

"Or be dead himself," suggested Mathieson. Jake nodded in agreement with that comment, but Swanson seemed to be thinking about something else.

"There was also a five year gap between the murders of Jean Maxwell and Anna Trotter. If he has taken to murdering on a five year cycle then he'd be due another victim this year."

"If he's that orderly," countered Jake. "I'm guessing the man kills when he feels the need to do so. I believe he killed his wife so that he could be with Rose Sim. I further believe that Rose then came to Aberdeen and became Jean Maxwell. Once Jean Maxwell began to show too much interest in Tom Fleming, Barclay killed her, waited to see Fleming hang and then moved on. Why he would want to kill Anna Trotter, I don't know. Maybe he just liked killing by that time."

"Or maybe he just has a thing about maids," Swanson added. "Are you sure about Rose Sim being Jean Maxwell?"

"Not sure, but it would make sense and it does provide a motive for the first two crimes."

"Okay, I'll dig deeper in to the Anna Trotter murder. There wasn't a great deal of information gathered at the time and I'm not sure what I might learn now after five years have elapsed."

"And in the meantime, we'll maybe learn more from another Force, for I feel totally sure the good Professor has more crimes to answer for, if we only knew about them."

Each officer retained a copy of the notes that had been taken. Jake accompanied Swanson back to the railway station and saw him on to the first train back to Edinburgh. They had exchanged telephone numbers so that, if required, they could discuss the case without the need for train journeys. Mathieson had gone off to prepare some material for Sergeant Fullerton and there was genuine air of co-operation as they concluded another working day and set off for home.

***

TWELVE

Sunday 14th June

It had not been a nice day in Aberdeen. The sky had remained cloudy but the breeze had kept the temperatures a lot lower than would have been preferred in the middle of June. The people of Aberdeen had gone about their business as usual. Disappointment may have sat heavily upon them, with regard to the weather, but no one in the north-east of Scotland ever lets a dull day hold them back from getting out and about.

One such Aberdonian out, making the best of a bad day, was Archibald Diamond. Diamond was a teacher at Aberdeen Grammar School and already looking forward to the summer break. He liked his job but he enjoyed his holidays even more. He had been a teacher at the Grammar School for ten years, having gone there straight from university. His main subject was Mathematics, but he also turned his hand to teaching science subjects when required.

Diamond had walked down Union Street and then turned in to Union Terrace. He had taken the first steps down in to the Gardens and found a seat to sit on that was situated in the sporadic sunshine and protected from the breeze. He sat and watched the world pass him by, noting that some of the men nodded in his direction. Mr Diamond had refrained from nodding back.

Women had never held the same attraction for him. He had enjoyed being with boys most of his life and now found a relaxed pleasure in male company that never seemed to be there when women were present. It was this pleasure that had driven him to the world of education and a chance to teach at a boys' school. Not that he would ever have allowed his sexuality to interfere with his desire to be a good teacher.

After an hour in the fresh air, he made his way out of the Gardens and walked back to Union Street. He crossed the road and went in to the Palace Hotel, where he ordered Afternoon Tea and sat by a window while he ate and drank what was brought to him. The hotel had been busy and he spent another hour watching everyone coming and going and generally relaxing. After a busy week at the school it was nice to now sit and do nothing for a while.

It was late afternoon when Archibald Diamond decided to go home. He lived in a flat on Union Grove. He had been there for seven years and enjoyed the environment, especially for its close proximity to Union Street and the school.

He made his way up the stair to the door of his flat and let himself in. It was neat and tidy for Archibald Diamond did not like clutter of any kind. Not that he could take all the credit for the flat being so tidy; some had to be given to his cleaner, Mrs Mills. She visited twice a week and always left the place spotless.

He had been brought up by a strict mother who had always kept the family home neat and tidy. It had, perhaps, been the strictness of his mother that had first turned young Archibald away from women. He had grown up to hate his mother and with his father being killed in an accident at sea, when Archibald was only five, there had been no male presence to give the growing boy a balanced view of family life.

Archibald had thrown himself in to his own education and now he threw himself in to the education of others. He took his job very seriously and always sought the best for his pupils. They, no doubt, saw him as a hard taskmaster, but he convinced himself that he only did it for their own good. Life held nothing for a young boy without a good education.

The afternoon passed in to evening and Diamond sat in his lounge and ate a light meal, washing it down with a bottle of beer. He felt at one with life and the prospect of a summer break on the horizon, made him feel even better. At seven he went for a brief stroll before returning to his flat at a quarter to eight. On his return he had paused in the doorway, sensing that something wasn't quite right and yet not knowing what that might be.

He even called out because he had an overwhelming sensation that someone was in the flat. Obviously there was no response; after all it was highly unlikely that a burglar would call back. He closed the door and hung up his coat. He then made his way through to the lounge, where he poured himself a drink.

Diamond had then sat on the settee, sipping his drink. For the first time, since he had moved to that flat, he had a sense of unease. He stood up and was just about to do a quick tour of the flat when he heard a knock at the door. He put his drink down and went in to the hall. He paused at the door for a moment. It was quite late for visitors and he briefly thought about not opening the door at all. After a few seconds of thought he unlocked the door and opened it.

"Oh, it's you," he said in a somewhat surprised tone. "I wasn't expecting to see you this weekend."

"I had a change of mind," the young man, standing in doorway, said. "You are pleased to see me?"

Diamond took a moment to respond, but eventually he smiled and stepped back. "Of course I am, do come in."

***

THIRTEEN

<u>Monday 15th June</u>

Mrs Mills sang to herself as she made her way along Union Grove, stopping outside the property she visited every Monday and Thursday, wind, rain or shine. She carried her bag, the one in which she kept her cleaning materials and she kept on singing, even though the weather was, once more, on the depressing side.

She climbed the stairs to Mr Diamond's flat and unlocked the door with the key he had given her on the day he had employed her. He had been a trusting man, Mr Diamond and she would never have done anything to betray that trust. She opened the door and went in. She knew it would be empty as Mr Diamond would be at his work. Mrs Mills had never had much of an education and she felt happy for those boys who would now benefit from Mr Diamond's knowledge. She wondered what it would have been like to have had a better education. What would it have been like to be able to count, for example?

Mrs Mills closed the door and then paused. Mr Diamond was a creature of habit and he always closed all the interior doors before leaving the flat. Today, the door to the lounge was open. She called out, thinking that Mr Diamond might have taken a day off work due to illness of some kind. There was no reply. Mrs Mills took off her hat and placed it on the table by the door. She then started to unbutton her coat as she took some tentative steps towards the lounge door.

She called out again. There was no reply.

Mrs Mills then pushed the lounge door open a little further and stepped through. She stopped immediately, her eyes almost failing to comprehend what they were seeing. The furniture was in disarray and there was blood everywhere. Lying on his back on the carpet, his face battered almost beyond recognition, was, Mrs Mills assumed, Mr Diamond.

Mrs Mills let out a scream of horror but did not wait to find out if Mr Diamond was alive or dead, she simply turned and went back out of the flat, intent on finding a policeman as quickly as possible.

***

Jake was at Archibald Diamond's flat within half an hour of being told that a body had been found. It was, by then, almost the middle of the morning.

Sergeant Mathieson had, once more, arrived ahead of him and was now standing in the lounge, alongside Doctor Stephen when Jake walked in. The room was still a mess. Furniture had been overturned and blood covered both furniture items and the carpet. Lying, at Doctor Stephen's feet, was the body of a man. His face was barely recognisable as being human. Jake took a step nearer and noted that the man was wearing a robe and possibly nothing else.

"What do we have?" he then asked, looking around the rest of the room.

"The body of one Archibald Diamond, sir," Mathieson then said. "He was a teacher of mathematics at the Grammar School."

"Another Grammar School teacher?" Jake said, but more by way of thinking aloud than expecting an answer. He looked across at Doctor Stephen, "What can you add, Doctor?"

Doctor Stephen stepped over the body and moved a little closer to Jake. "He was killed some time last night. As you can see he was the victim of a vicious attack. I'm sure he was dead long before his attacker stopped hitting him. Quite honestly any one of the blows that were rained down on him could have killed him. There was a lot of anger behind this attack."

"Is that the weapon?" Jake then asked, nodding in the direction of a statue lying on the mat.

"It is. I'll get it checked for fingerprints but there's a lot blood on it, so we struggle to get a good impression."

"Are we looking for a different killer?" Jake then asked.

"The two murders couldn't be more different, that's for sure. Miss McIntosh was strangled by someone who appears to have been quite cold and calculating, whereas this murder is the work of a madman."

"Who found the body?" Jake now asked.

"Mr Archibald's cleaner, Mrs Mills. She is in the kitchen with one of our constables. I gave her a cup of tea as she was quite upset."

"Very thoughtful of you," Jake said looking across at his Sergeant. "Would you visit all the neighbours and find out if they heard or saw anything. I can't believe all this was achieved without making some noise."

"Very good, sir," Mathieson replied and headed for the door.

"I'll tell you something else, Inspector," Doctor Stephen added. "The killer must have had blood on him after an attack like this."

Jake nodded his agreement. He then went through to the kitchen where he found Mrs Mills sitting at the table, nursing what remained of her cup of tea and staring at the wall in front of her. The constable left the room as Jake entered.

Mrs Mills was a round woman, wearing a blue dress and white apron. She had obviously been crying, though had stopped by the time Jake arrived. He sat down beside her.

"It must have been a terrible shock, Mrs Mills?" he said.

The woman's eyes never left whatever spot on the wall they were staring at. "Who would want to kill Mr Diamond?" she said quietly.

"That is what we intend finding out," replied Jake. "How long have you cleaned for Mr Diamond?"

"It must be coming up for five years."

"Did you see much of him in that time?"

"Very little. He was always at work and during the holidays he made a point of being out and about."

"Do you know if he had many friends?"

"No. I got the impression he was a solitary man. Everything he ever spoke about doing was always on his own."

"No lady friends?"

Mrs Mills' eyes finally moved away from the wall. She turned her head and looked at Jake for a moment before responding to his question.

"I don't think he liked the company of women very much," she then said and returned her attention to the wall.

Jake pondered on that comment for a moment before he realised what Mrs Mills might have been trying to tell him. He chose not to pursue that subject for the moment.

"Was the front door unlocked when you arrived this morning?"

"No, I unlocked it with my key when I arrived."

So the door was locked, thought Jake. *That either meant the thief already had a key or he had taken Mr Diamond's key when he had left.*

"Do you know where Mr Diamond kept his key?"

"There is a dish in the hall. He usually put it there when he was at home."

Jake went out in to the hall and looked for the dish. He found it and was not at all surprised to see that the key was missing. It was fairly obvious as to how the killer made good his escape, but how had he got in in the first place? Jake returned to the kitchen and sat down again.

"Have you had a chance to look around the flat in case anything has been stolen?" Jake then enquired.

"I went for the police and then I've sat here ever since," Mrs Mills replied. "I'm certainly not going back in to that room," she then said and her head nodded in the direction of where Mr Diamond still lay.

"I fully understand, Mrs Mills, however I really would appreciate you checking the other rooms, just in case something might be missing."

Mrs Mills finished the last of her tea. "Only if you come with me," she then said. Jake agreed and they made their way out of the kitchen.

The flat consisted of a lounge, a bedroom, a kitchen and another, smaller room, which Mr Diamond had apparently used as a study. The toilet was on the landing. They went to the study first. Mrs Mills looked around and seemed happy that nothing had been disturbed. From there they made their way to the bedroom. It was obvious, even to Jake, that someone had been in there as clothes were strewn around the floor and the wardrobe door still hung open.

Jake's first thought was that Mr Diamond had been interrupted whilst getting dressed. However, that made little sense as he knew Mr Diamond had died the previous evening. Mrs Mills immediately started tutting and made to pick up some of the clothes. Jake stopped her.

"Please, Mrs Mills, you must leave everything as it is. This is now a crime scene and it may well be the case that there could be something in this room that may yet prove useful to the investigation."

"But Mr Diamond would never leave a room looking like this," Mrs Mills said. "He was a very tidy man and he would have been appalled to know that we found this room in such a mess."

"Would you know if any clothes were missing?" Jake then asked.

"Probably not," relied Mrs Mills, making her way over to the wardrobe. She cast an eye along the line of clothes hanging within it. She then turned to Jake. "His coat is missing, unless it's lying somewhere through with him."

Jake made a note of that fact and then thanked Mrs Mills for her time. He went to find a constable who could arrange to take Mrs Mills home. He then returned to the lounge where Doctor Stephen was once more on his knees studying the body.

"Discovered anything else, Doctor?" asked Jake.

"Nothing much."

"Then feel free to take him back to the mortuary and have a closer look," added Jake, turning to have another wander through the property.

He went back in to the bedroom and started to pick up some of the clothes that were lying around. Given that the killer would have had blood on him, had he taken Mr Diamond's coat to cover the evidence?

Jake stood for a few more moments pondering on the events that may have taken place the previous night. If Mr Diamond was only wearing a robe then, presumably, he had been getting ready for bed. Had he then heard a noise and gone to investigate, disturbing a burglar in the process? Even if that had been the case, why would any burglar feel the need to attack Mr Diamond with such ferocity?

Not a great deal about the crime scene made much sense to Jake. It was a scene of such violence that he questioned whether it really could be connected to the murder of Miss McIntosh. Perhaps it really was nothing more than coincidence that two Grammar School teachers had been murdered, in their homes, so closely together. Jake gave a little more thought to the possibility of coincidence and dismissed it at once. Although there may not have been an obvious link between the two murders, none the less, Jake was of the opinion that a link had to be there somewhere.

The question Jake now asked himself was; were they looking for a burglar who murdered, or a murderer who covered his tracks by appearing to be a burglar?

Jake finally decided there was little more to be gained by standing in the bedroom, staring at clothes strewn around the floor. He left the room and made his way to the door. He then turned back and went in to the lounge where Doctor Stephen was packing his bag.

"I'm off to the Grammar School; I'll see you back at the mortuary later."

"I may not have much more to tell you," Doctor Stephen said.

"We can talk anyway," added Jake and he then turned and left the flat.

***

It was an hour later before Jake was seated in Morland Simpson's office once more. The Rector looked irritated to have been interrupted, yet again, at work. However, after Jake had explained why he was there, Morland Simpson seemed to change altogether. He was distressed to hear that a second of his teachers had been murdered and horrified to think others may yet be in danger.

"Should we all be afraid for our safety?" he had then asked.

"At this moment in time, sir, I really don't know. I still believe the motive behind these attacks has been burglary. Miss Grainger may also have been a victim and yet she was not attacked."

"Why would that be?" asked Morland Simpson.

"We can only assume that she was just lucky that the thief was finished with his business and away before she got home."

"Is there anything that the rest of us can do?"

"I suggest that you warn all your staff who live alone, to be more vigilante around their homes, just in case this burglar still has other targets in mind."

Morland Simpson nodded. "Of course, Inspector, I shall see to it personally that everyone is spoken to, before the end of the day."

"My thanks for that sir. Now, might it be possible for me to talk to any member of staff who may have known Mr Diamond quite well?"

Morland Simpson thought for a moment. "It may be best if you were to speak to the other members of our Mathematics Department."

Jake agreed and was shown to a room beside the Public Office where he was asked to wait. He was then told that the teachers in question would be told to go through, one at a time, to see the Inspector.

Five minutes later and the door opened. A young man, wearing a gown and mortarboard entered. He was tall and his most prominent feature was a very long and pointed nose. When he spoke, he spoke with a clipped tone that sounded almost military in its delivery. Jake's instant opinion was that this man was accustomed to talking uninterrupted and he dreaded to think what would have happened to any boy caught not listening.

"I don't have much time," the man said, as he sat down and took off the mortarboard. "However, the Rector said you wanted to see me."

"He didn't tell you why?" Jake then said with some surprise.

"No he did not."

"Had you noticed that Mr Diamond had not turned up to work this morning?" Jake then asked.

"I hadn't actually. I've had classes all morning."

"Might I ask your name?"

The man seemed unwilling to give out information of that kind. Jake noted the silence and offered an explanation for his request.

"Mr Diamond was violently attacked in his home at the weekend and is dead, I'm very sorry to say."

The man's face paled visibly. "My God," was all he said.

"So as these questions are part of a murder enquiry I need the name, age and address of everyone I interview for the report that I must write."

"Of course," the man then said. He gave his name as being Patrick Baxter and he was thirty-three years old. His address was in Rosemount. He was also visibly shocked with the news that had just been given to him. He then went on to say that he had been a teacher at the Grammar School for seven years and in that time had come to know Archibald Diamond quite well, though never as more than a colleague rather than a close friend.

"We didn't socialise or anything," Baxter added.

"What can you tell me about Mr Diamond?" Jake then asked.

"He was amusing and conscientious. He put in far more hours at the school than anyone else in the Mathematics Department."

"Were you aware of him collecting anything that may have been of value?"

Baxter thought for a moment. "I don't remember Archibald ever talking about such matters. Do you have a particular reason for asking?"

"The motive for the attacks on both Miss McIntosh and Mr Archibald appears to be burglary. Now we know what was stolen from Miss McIntosh but we have no idea what, if anything, was taken from Mr Archibald."

"But surely no one breaks in to a house and then leaves without taking anything," Baxter said.

"They would if what they went for wasn't there," replied Jake. "That was why I wondered if Mr Diamond had ever spoken about owning something of great value. If he had done and someone else had heard about it, then there is your motive for breaking in to Mr Diamond's home."

"I'm sorry, Inspector, I never heard Archibald talk much about his personal life, let alone anything specific about items of value."

Baxter then produced a packet of cigarettes from a pocket beneath his cloak. He found matches in another pocket and proceeded to light a cigarette and inhale heavily.

"The Rector frowns on his staff smoking, but there really is a time and a place for everything. Do you believe we are all now in danger of some kind?"

"As I said to the Rector, I really don't know. I have asked him to warn all staff, who live on their own, to be more vigilant around their property. We are still, essentially, looking for a burglar so it is mainly having property stolen that should worry other members of staff."

"Could it be an ex-pupil with a grudge?" Baxter then suggested.

"It could be," agreed Jake, "or there could be a member of staff who is passing on information to the burglar."

Baxter exhaled a cloud of smoke and made a noise of disgust. "I can't believe that, Inspector. Surely there's no one on the teaching staff who would stoop so low."

"You'd be surprised who might turn to crime if they felt the return was worth it."

"But not a teacher," Baxter added in a tone that seemed to say *they have to be above reproach.*

"Were you aware of Mr Diamond and Miss McIntosh being friends outside of work?" Jake then enquired.

"I shouldn't have thought so," answered Baxter. "The teachers of the Lower School don't usually mix with those of us in the main building and anyway, Archibald was more of a man's person, if you get my meaning."

"Was Mr Diamond well liked around the school?"

"Not by the pupils, but then are any of us?" Baxter responded.

"How about his colleagues?"

Baxter gave that a little more thought. "I don't think he was actively disliked by anyone, though I know of one or two who were less than enamoured by Archibald's penchant for male company. Mr Jenkins, in particular found that rather difficult to accept."

"Mr Jenkins?"

"Yes, he teaches English, though rather badly because he is Welsh," Baxter added with a smile.

"And he didn't like Mr Diamond?" prompted Jake.

"As I said, Inspector, Mr Diamond preferred the company of other men and I don't think Mr Jenkins took kindly to that notion."

"There have been veiled hints from more than one person, concerning Mr Diamond's sexuality. Was everyone aware that he was a homosexual?"

"Not everyone, but certainly most of the male staff were aware. It's not exactly natural, but each to their own, that's what I say."

"And Mr Jenkins was more open in his disapproval?" Jake asked.

"Mr Jenkins did not like the idea of any man being a homosexual, but I hardly think that led to him visiting Archibald and killing him. Mr Jenkins dealt with the issue by simply ignoring it. The two men were civil to each other, while at work, but would have had nothing to do with each other outside of these walls."

Jake kept Baxter talking until he had finished his cigarette and then let him leave. Jake then went to the window and opened it. He ushered some of the smoke out and hoped that none of the pupils were noticing. He then returned to his chair and waited for the next teacher to come through.

The next time the door opened a young man, looking young enough to almost still be at school himself, came in to the room. This turned out to be Benjamin Parsons, the final member of the Mathematics Department. Parsons was actually thirty years of age and had been teaching at the Grammar School for the last three years. His face was marked from a lifetime of acne and he wore his hair short to scalp so that he looked almost bald from a distance. The overall image was quite intimidating and Jake could imagine many pupils living in fear of this man.

Parsons reacted in much the same way as Baxter when given the news about Diamond. He did not, fortunately for Jake, reach for his cigarettes, however. Jake asked Parsons essentially the same questions. The young man, having been at the school for such a short time, spoke of Diamond as being a helpful colleague but beyond that he could offer little to help to Jake. Jake asked if Parsons knew about Mr Jenkins not liking Diamond. He said that he was aware of that but, like Baxter, did not see a little disagreement on sexuality as being a suitable motive for such a violent attack.

Jake decided to speak to Mr Jenkins anyway. For that to be arranged he had to go back to the Rector and ask his permission. Again, Morland Simpson responded with anger rather than a genuine desire to help. However, he did ask a young woman in the general office to go and get Mr Jenkins. If he was teaching then he was to arrange for someone to watch over his class and to come at once. She was to only tell him that the Rector wished to see him; Simpson did not want word of a police officer visiting the school getting home to any of the parents.

Ten minutes later, Jake was back in the same room with Gareth Jenkins. The English Teacher came across as a timid character, possibly lacking in self-confidence and definitely not carrying any authority in his demeanour. Jake could imagine more classes walking all over this teacher and making his life hell in the process. Jenkins wore glasses and his eyes flicked about, nervously, from behind them. He sat on the chair opposite Jake and kept his hands clasped together on his lap. He looked more like a naughty schoolboy hauled in front of the Rector than a teacher with a responsibility for the education of so many boys starting out in the world.

Jake informed Mr Jenkins of Mr Diamond's murder, but did not get quite the same reaction as he had had from the other two teachers. Mr Jenkins looked shocked, but not upset.

"Maybe one of his men friends attacked him; I hear they can be quite violent towards each other when the mood takes them?" Jenkins then said with a sneer in his tone.

"You didn't like Mr Diamond, did you?" Jake then pressed.

"I didn't like the fact he enjoyed the company of men. It isn't natural and he certainly wasn't the type of man we should have had around adolescent boys."

"Were you aware of any issues with the boys?" Jake then asked.

"Well, of course not. The man may have had strange sexual preferences, but he wasn't stupid. He would never have done anything around the school to draw attention to himself or to put his job in jeopardy."

"So how did you all know that Mr Diamond was what he was?" Jake said.

"You could just tell by his demeanour and the fact he never spoke to having any female friends. His world and his interests were entirely male orientated."

"Or maybe he was just shy around women and preferred the company of men," Jake added.

Jenkins sat in silence for a moment. Jake could tell that the man was debating with himself; there was more to tell, it was just a matter of him deciding whether, or not, to tell a police officer.

"Archibald Diamond was, most certainly, not shy, Inspector and I know about his sexuality because I saw something, with my own eyes that confirmed my suspicions."

"I'm listening," added Jake.

"I saw Diamond coming out of one of the public toilets that are noted for being frequented by men of a certain sexual persuasion. He was in the company of another man who was still in the process of buttoning up his waistcoat. It seemed obvious to me that whatever was going on within the confines of that toilet, was not even remotely natural."

Jake nearly smiled. It was probably true that Archibald Diamond was a homosexual, but if the only evidence against him was that he left a public toilet in the company of a man doing up his waistcoat, then it wasn't the most damning evidence. Jake could see there was little to be gained by speaking to Jenkins any longer. He let him go and then returned to the Rector's office to inform him that he was now leaving and to thank him, once again, for all his help, even though he hadn't actually offered any.

Jake left the school and headed back to Lodge Walk.

***

In the afternoon Jake visited the Chief Constable to update him on how the investigations were going. Chief Constable Anderson liked to feel a part of his Force in every way possible and demanded, of his Inspectors, that he be kept up to date through regular meetings.

"We now have a second murder involving a Grammar School teacher, sir," Jake began, "but it may still be pure coincidence. The murders are of an entirely different nature and we may be looking for two killers."

"Why would anyone want to murder schoolteachers?" the Chief then asked.

"The motive for the killer being in these people's homes is definitely burglary, but why he then chooses to kill is something I haven't come to grips with yet."

"Clearly he is being disturbed by the owner returning home," added the Chief.

"That would seem to be the case, sir, but it still doesn't explain why he chooses to kill rather than simply flee the scene. Most burglars have a natural desire to steal but I haven't come across many who would commit murder quite so easily. Both Miss McIntosh and Mr Diamond could have been easily overpowered. All the burglar had to do was tie them up or even just shut them in a room long enough for him to make good his escape. There seems no obvious reason as to why he would kill these people as a first option."

"In that case he must have been recognised," the Chief then suggested. "Does that mean you are looking for a fellow teacher perhaps?"

"The burglar being recognised would be a strong motive for murder, but I struggle to believe that a teacher at the Grammar School would have the talent, or the inclination, to turn to burglary in his spare time."

"A pupil maybe?" the Chief then said.

"Perhaps, but this burglar seems to possess information about his victims that would be difficult, if not impossible, for a pupil to gather."

"What kind of information?" asked the Chief.

"I'm sure the burglar knew when the property would be empty and I'm still of the opinion that the burglar either has a key to the property or the ability to pick locks without leaving much evidence of him being there. We're looking for an expert locksmith, which is another reason for ruling out the pupils."

"Do we know of any other teachers who may already have been visited by this burglar?"

"One of the other teachers, a Miss Grainger, told me that she had suspected someone might have been in her flat whilst she was out a few weeks ago."

"And that was before Miss McIntosh?"

"Yes. If she was visited by our burglar then I can only assume the crook was finished with his business and away before she returned. That being the case she may well be very lucky to still be alive."

"So he has struck three times and on two of those occasion he was moved to murder?" the Chief added, more by way of thinking aloud.

"It would appear so, sir," agreed Jake.

"You've certainly got yourself quite a mystery there, Jake," the Chief Constable then said. "Is there anything that links Miss McIntosh and Mr Diamond, but doesn't link with Miss Grainger? In other words, would the burglar have had a reason to kill the first two that did not exist with Miss Grainger?"

Jake thought for a moment more before speaking again. "Not that I am aware of at the moment. The plain fact, sir, is that nothing makes much sense. I'm sure that burglary is the motive and yet nothing was taken from Miss Grainger and I'm pretty sure nothing was taken from Mr Diamond either. To be honest I can't even be sure that anything was taken from Miss McIntosh. We know that her father's collection of miniature paintings is no longer in the house but we don't know, for certain, that they were stolen. Miss McIntosh may have sold them after her father's death."

The Chief Constable looked perplexed. "In which case this may not be about burglary at all, it may simply be someone with a grudge against Grammar School teachers?"

"No, sir, strange as it may seem at the moment, I firmly believe burglary is the driving force behind what's happened."

"And there's no other motive for the murders of Miss McIntosh and Mr Diamond?"

"Not that we can find, sir. They both teach at the Grammar School, but they weren't friends outside of work and don't appear to have anything in common."

"So it may just be pure coincidence after all?"

"You know I don't like coincidence, sir, but on this occasion that may well be all it is."

"You mentioned a miniature painting collection; what was the subject of the paintings?" the Chief then enquired.

"Naked women, sir. The Doctor kept them locked away in a cupboard in his study. As we found the body of Miss McIntosh in the same room we immediately assumed she'd disturbed someone who was already there. As far as I can see the only reason for searching that room would be to find the collection of miniatures."

"So the burglar may be someone who had been to the house before; someone who knew about the collection?"

"And someone who was, in turn, known to Miss McIntosh, which was why she had to be silenced. It's the only theory that really covers everything with any success."

"The theory covers Miss McIntosh's murder, but why would anyone then go on to kill Mr Diamond?"

Jake shook his head. "Still working on that, sir."

The Chief paused for a moment. "It still looks to me that someone else at that school is involved in some way," he eventually said.

"I agree, sir. At the very least I feel sure that someone at the school is passing information about their colleagues to the burglar."

"Sadly for you, Jake, without a clear lead in this case there seems little chance of you ever catching the killer," added the Chief.

"Indeed, sir."

"Well keep at it, Jake. If anyone can get to the bottom of this, you can. Now, what about Professor Barclay?"

Jake updated the Chief on his meeting with Swanson and the fact that the Aberdeen and Edinburgh police Forces were now working so closely together on the matter. He also said that they working together on 'The Buchan Heiress' as well.

"That woman is a menace," the Chief said, at the mention of her nickname. "We need to put her away for a long time and stop all this nonsense of six months here and there. We'll keep Mathieson on this, it'll do him good to have a case of his own."

Jake nodded. The Chief then fell silent for a moment or two, before changing the subject.

"Can I please now have your decision on whether you wish to be our temporary Chief Inspector, Jake?"

Jake knew what Margaret wanted him to say. He still had one concern.

"Would I be allowed to continue with active investigations, sir?" he asked.

The Chief Constable smiled. "Of course you would, Jake. Look, I'm seriously thinking of giving the Chief Inspector more authority in dealing with the serious crimes that befall our area. I believe that murder and rape, for example, might benefit from the input of a more senior officer. If you take this role, Jake, you will have the opportunity to prove that the Chief Inspector can investigate crimes as well as deal with the more mundane actions, such as supporting the Inspectors and completing the necessary paperwork arising from staffing issues."

Jake pondered some more.

"In that case, sir, I'd be delighted to fill the role until you decide on a more permanent solution."

The Chief stood up. "Excellent." He offered his hand and Jake stood up to accept the handshake. Both men were smiling and Jake felt that the Chief looked genuinely pleased with his decision. He knew that Margaret would be delighted and he looked forward to bathing in her smile later.

"When will I start, sir?" Jake then asked as the handshake was completed and the Chief had sat down again.

"Shall we say next Monday?"

"Next Monday will be fine, sir," Jake concluded and then turned to leave the room. He had just reached the door when the Chief spoke again.

"Are you remembering there is a service for Peter at Queen's Cross Church tomorrow?"

Peter Ash had not had a formal funeral. His body had been taken to Glasgow where it had been cremated, an act which some people thought to be barbaric and ought to be illegal. However, it was not possible for someone who had committed suicide to be buried in consecrated ground and the decision was taken that if he couldn't be buried properly then he wouldn't be buried at all. Glasgow had had a crematorium since 1895 and the number of cremations continued to rise year on year, even though those numbers were still quite low. In the first ten years a mere one hundred and ninety-one had taken place.

Instead of a funeral, the Chief Constable had organised a memorial service at which friends and colleagues could gather to remember the life of Peter Ash. The Reverend John Steele had agreed to hold the service as long as there had been no mention of the manner in which Peter Ash had died.

Jake turned. "Yes, sir, I was remembering and I will be there."

The Chief simply nodded and Jake turned and left the office.

***

Jake arrived home that evening with beer and stout. He poured a glass of each and presented the stout to Margaret. At first she wondered why alcohol had been presented to her, but then the penny dropped and a smile as wide as the River Dee spread across her face.

"You've accepted," she said.

"I've accepted," Jake added and they clinked glasses before taking a drink.

They then sat and talked until the meal was ready. After they had eaten and enjoyed a little more alcohol, they sat together, talking about the future until late before tiredness forced them off to bed.

***

FOURTEEN

Tuesday 16th June

Mathieson came in to Jake's office at just before eight in the morning. Word had filtered out that Jake was to become the new temporary Chief Inspector and Mathieson wanted to be the first to congratulate him. Jake waved the congratulations away and passed a comment along the lines of not being sure if it was the right decision. Mathieson assured him that he would make a great Chief Inspector and that, if nothing else, he should be pleased with the extra money for a while.

They then got down to business. Mathieson had spoken to all the neighbours around where Archibald Diamond had lived. No one had paid much attention to him though some did speak about the number of men who had come and gone to the flat. One also spoke of a man calling on Diamond at around mid-evening on the Sunday.

"That must have been around the time of the attack?" added Jake.

"Perhaps, sir. However, the description is pretty vague and I doubt if it will help us much."

"But this man has to know something that could be of use to us," insisted Jake. "If he didn't actually carry out the attack then he might have seen, or heard, something that could bring us a little closer to our murderer."

"I don't disagree, sir, but the description that I was given could apply to half the men of Aberdeen. Apart from him however the neighbours did not report much. Essentially, Diamond seems to have kept himself to himself, sir."

"But Doctor Stephen reckoned there had to have been noise created by the attack. Did no one hear anything?"

"If they did, they're not saying."

"So it would seem," agreed Jake. "Are you remembering we have Peter Ash's memorial service this afternoon?"

"I am, sir. Meanwhile I'll get on with checking the lodgings of Aberdeen in case the 'Heiress' had come back."

The two men parted with a smile. Jake spent a few moments clearing the last of the paperwork from the previous day. He knew that the amount of paper he would have to deal with would increase immensely from the following week, but he also knew that he would just have to grin and bear it. Mathieson had been right, the extra money would come in handy; it always did.

***

Margaret sat in the tearoom of Watt and Grant and waited for Sadie Ashton to arrive. It was always the same when they arranged to go anywhere together; Sadie was always late. They had arranged to meet at midday and it was now nearly fifteen minutes past. Margaret had ordered a pot of tea so her time was not entirely wasted.

Five minutes later and Sadie Ashton was finally seen making her way through the tables towards Margaret. When she arrived she went through her well-rehearsed act of apology, blaming everything but herself for her time-keeping. Margaret, as always, said it really didn't matter and Sadie sat herself down at the table and began looking at the menu. Once they had ordered Margaret opened their conversation.

"How was your weekend?"

She was referring to the fact that Sadie had been in London over the weekend attending a Suffragette march that had been arranged for the Saturday. Sadie's eyes widened with excitement as she leaned forward and began to talk about her time down South.

"It was amazing, Margaret, you really should have been there. There were thousands of women present in the march and we had some very well-known speakers, including Mrs Pankhurst herself. It was a truly moving experience, Margaret, having so many women gathered together with one common cause in mind. When you see such a turn out it makes you even more convinced that we are doing the right thing."

"Was there any trouble?" Margaret asked as a waitress brought another pot of tea for Sadie.

"Not really. The police were there in numbers and there were one or two men who shouted obscene comments in our direction, but in the main it went off quite peacefully."

Sadie poured a cup of tea and added sugar and milk before stirring it thoroughly. She then looked up at Margaret.

"Mrs Pankhurst remains very militant in her views."

"I'm sure she does," agreed Margaret.

Sadie stared at Margaret, in silence, for a moment longer. She then spoke.

"Would you be any more militant if you weren't married to a police officer?"

Margaret put her cup back in its saucer. "Sadie, whatever my opinion it has nothing to do with Jake. I could never agree that violence has a place in any argument. As soon as you cross that line you risk losing public sympathy and without the public sympathy for our cause we'd have nothing."

"I'm not advocating violence, as such," conceded Sadie, "but surely the occasional wake-up call is required to ensure that one side of an argument is never forgotten."

"How would you define a wake-up call?" Margaret asked.

Sadie smiled and leaned forward a little further. "A few broken windows here and there, perhaps or maybe even the occasional policeman's hat knocked off."

Margaret smiled. "Now you are making fun of me."

Sadie reached across the table and put her hand on Margaret's arm. "I'm not making fun, Margaret, I'm being deathly serious. All we have to do is ensure that no one forgets about us, or the message we carry. We can achieve that through the most mundane of actions, but we must accept that there has to be times when we resort to any methods necessary to ensure our message receives front page news."

Margaret was about to speak when the waitress returned with their main meal. It was chicken for Margaret and ham for Sadie. They also requested another pot of tea, only this time they would share one. Once the waitress had left them alone again, Margaret spoke.

"There is a very thin line between making a statement that might be acknowledged and doing something that will lose you the argument forever. If any of our members end up getting arrested then we've crossed that line I referred to earlier. Seeing a procession of women going to court, even for minor offences, will soon alienate the public and along the way alienate other women who may have thought about joining us. We need to build our numbers for the more women who are arguing alongside us then the more noise we make in the ears of those men who would try to ignore us. We win our argument through sheer volume of noise and to achieve that we need as many women as possible to be with us on the road ahead."

Sadie smiled again. "We need to find you a soapbox for you Margaret; that was a very impressive little speech."

Margaret smiled. "You see, I do feel passionately about our cause, I just don't see the need to resort to violence to further that cause."

Sadie chewed on a forkful of ham. "I understand your feelings, Margaret, but the truth is that, occasionally, mere words are not enough. Mrs Pankhurst has been fighting for votes for women for many years now. She gets publicity when she speaks and for that she is truly grateful. However, we get more column inches in the papers when our members do something a little more dramatic. I'm not advocating that we hurt anyone, but I do believe that we need to do more, at times, than simply talk."

"I guess we just have to agree to disagree on this, Sadie," Margaret then said and Sadie accepted the situation with another smile.

The two women ate some more food. Margaret looked around the tea-room. It was nearly all women and she wondered how many of them actually cared whether they got the vote or not. Here they were, enjoying a lunch with their friends and discussing anything from the weather to the latest fashion. Amidst all that normality was there any place for arguing about the vote?

"Do you really think the bulk of women in this room actually care if they get the vote, or not?" Margaret then asked Sadie.

"I do. We women are forced to live in a man's world where men have become cosy and complacent, especially when it comes to the immediate world around them. They find themselves a nice, little wife and then sit back, happy to let her do all the household chores and be at his beck and call every minute they are together. We are expected to provide food and comfort and in return what do we get, a roof over our heads and an allowance, if we are very lucky. The Suffragette Movement, to most men, is nothing more than a circus act. It is there to be viewed for a little while and then move on. It is there to be replaced, some day, by a new act; but it is, most certainly, only there to entertain and serves no purpose in actually changing anything. Men can never see the day when women will have an equal say in who governs this country. Men will never accept that a woman can have a political mind of her own, for if they accept that then they are taking the first step towards letting women out of the kitchen and nothing scares a man more than a woman who isn't in the kitchen."

"An interesting analogy," Margaret added as she ate some more of her food and poured another cup of tea.

"It's not just an analogy, Margaret, it's a statement of fact. Once we free our minds of being in that kitchen we start to control our own destiny. Just think about it, Margaret; if men didn't have us women around to cook for them and to mend their clothes and often as not, look after their pay packet each week, just where would they be?"

"Jake managed alright before he met me," countered Margaret.

"Obviously some men can look after themselves, but I argue those numbers are pretty low. Most men are spoiled by their mothers so they then seek a wife who can replace mother in the cooking and mending departments. However, they also want a wife so that they can find sexual satisfaction in life and have someone to look after any children, born from those sexual moments. We women are an essential part in that as well remember. If we even denied men their sexual favours, just think what an effect that would have."

"Any woman denying a man his conjugal rights is likely to find herself on the wrong end of a violent attack. I hear what you are saying, Sadie, but in the real world too many women are actually scared of their husbands and would never dream of doing anything to annoy him, in any way. You have some noble ideas but too few women could actually associate themselves with those ideas."

"But if we could at least give those women hope that one day things would get better, then surely that alone is worth fighting for?" Sadie added with passion in her voice.

Margaret put her cutlery down and looked sternly at Sadie. "We have a long road to walk, Sadie, to even get most women up to the standard of life that we enjoy. Too many women have not had the education that we have had. Too many women simply cannot think for themselves; they've been brought up to believe that without a man in their lives they are nothing. They have been brought up to believe that their place on this earth *is* to cook and bear children and that only happens after they have found themselves a husband. Women like that care not for your ideology, Sadie and they care even less about being able to vote. To many of those women, the vote is nothing more than a mark on a piece of paper; it doesn't actually amount to anything."

Sadie was silent for a moment as she digested what Margaret had just said. "In that case," she eventually added, "we need to re-educate those poor women and prove to them that life does not have to be spent running after a man."

"But many women are happy to run after a man," Margaret insisted.

"Are you?"

"I don't have any problems with Jake because he understands how I want to live my life. Jake doesn't expect anything of me simply because I am his wife."

"He'll expect sex," Sadie said, rather bluntly.

Margaret could feel her face redden. She looked around to make sure no one was hearing what they were talking about and then, lowering her voice further, she responded.

"Jake does not *expect* sex, it arises because we love each other and wish to share that love on a physical level at times. A good marriage will always have sex within it, but that does not necessarily mean the man is always the dominating factor. Some men are happy to have sex when it is offered rather than force themselves upon their wives."

"*Some* men, perhaps," agreed Sadie, "but *most* men want things their way and they are the men whose outdated opinions need to be changed."

Margaret scoffed. "You will never do that, Sadie. That type of man will never change; at least not in our life time. I believe that our argument will carry on for years to come and we may never see the day when all women will have the right to vote."

"Which is why we need to be more militant," Sadie added. "We need to make sure that our argument is acted upon sooner rather than later or we will, as you suggest, still be debating the subject for many years to come."

"I thought we'd agreed to disagree on the subject of militancy, Sadie, "Margaret then concluded as she finished her meal and placed her cutlery carefully on the plate. Sadie finished her meal as well and sat back from the table.

"Very well, Margaret, you will hear no more talk of militant action from me. When is our next Liberal Group meeting?" she then asked.

"End of the month. We have a meeting with Cornelia next week and then the Liberal meeting will be the week after."

Sadie Ashton took a small notebook from her bag and wrote something in to it. She then put the book away and placed her bag back at her feet. She looked around the room, looking at each woman as Margaret had done earlier.

"Do you really believe that most women don't care about what we are doing?"

"For generations many women have been living subservient lives, it may take further generations to bring about any change to that."

"Not if I can help it," said Sadie Ashton. It was little more than the sound of someone thinking aloud, but Margaret heard it and she felt that even in that short sentence there was still an undercurrent of menace, which she did not like to hear.

***

The turnout at Queen's Cross Church had been high. Words of praise were said for the life of Peter Ash, but no mention made of his death and how it had come about. The Chief Constable, himself, had said a few words about how much he was feeling the loss of such a valued officer. Without family to attend, his friends and colleagues made up the numbers filling the aisles.

Jake walked away from the church, telling those around him that he needed time to think. He began walking back towards the city centre. When he reached the grassed area in front of Queen's Terrace, he chose to have a seat and watch the world pass him by for a few moments. He couldn't stop thinking about Peter Ash and what he must have been thinking the day they hanged Tom Fleming. It started Jake thinking about all the men he had effectively sent to the gallows. He felt sure that they were all sound convictions; had Ash felt the same way about Tom Fleming, or had he always known he probably got the wrong man?

The sun appeared from behind a cloud and cast some heat on Jake as he sat taking the air. One or two people went by, but no one paid any attention to the man sitting on the bench, apparently lost in his own thoughts. Half an hour past before Jake decided he had better get back to the office.

***

Inspector Samuel Biddlecombe was feeling happy for the first time in days. He had spent all of his time at work looking for a new lead on Professor Clive Barclay. Every time Barclay left somewhere he said he was going back to Cambridge and yet there was no evidence, of any kind, to prove that he was currently in Cambridge. Biddlecombe was aware of the work carried out by Jake and Swanson and also the fact they had put out a general request to all Forces, working within the catchment areas of universities, to look out for Barclay.

There had been nothing so far, but it was, of course, still early days. However, Biddlecombe had not been of a mind to sit back and wait for information to come to him. He had always been more pro-active than that, so he had decided to go back to the university and seek out someone who may have known Barclay on a more personal level. After passing through a few possibilities he had arrived at a woman who, although no longer working for the university, was known to a current employee and had been working for Barclay during his time at Cambridge. The current employee had been able to give Biddlecombe an address for the woman and it was with growing excitement that he had made his way to her home in the early evening.

Mrs Hughes, as she was now known, lived with her husband of the last three years, in a house situated only a few miles from the university. She no longer went out to work, being happy, Biddlecombe had been told, to stay at home and provide food for her husband.

Biddlecombe knocked on the door and stood back to await someone to open it. A few minutes passed before the door opened and an attractive woman, wearing a crimson dress with a white apron, stood before him. He introduced himself and showed her his identification card.

"Might you be Mrs Hughes?" he then enquired.

"I am," the woman replied with some uncertainty as to where all this was leading.

"I wondered if I might ask you a few questions about Professor Barclay, I believe you knew him when you were both at Cambridge?"

"Professor Barclay?" the woman repeated with a tone of surprise. "That was over ten years ago."

"I appreciate it was some time ago, but I'd still really like to speak to you about it. Might I come in?"

"My husband isn't home yet," Mrs Hughes said, as if that seemed to make some difference.

"It is you that I've come to see," Biddlecombe stressed and after another moment of thought, Mrs Hughes finally let him in to the house.

She led Biddlecombe through to a room at the back of the house and offered him a seat. She then sat down herself, but continued to play, rather nervously, with her apron.

"I believe you knew Professor Barclay quite well? Biddlecombe had then begun.

Mrs Hughes seemed reluctant to respond at first, her eyes glancing towards the door as if she were expecting someone to walk through at any moment. Biddlecombe began to think that this woman might be a little afraid of her husband. He patiently waited for her to respond, which she eventually did.

"I knew him, I'm not so sure that I would say I knew him well."

"You must have been very young?"

"I was seventeen when I started working at the university, but it would have been around two years after that before I got to know the Professor."

"And how did you get to know him?" added Biddlecombe.

"He was intent on writing a book at that time and he asked me to type up his notes for him. I thought it was all very exciting and agreed immediately."

"What kind of man was he?"

"Very polite."

"Did you see the Professor outside of the university?" Biddlecombe then said.

"We did have dinner a couple of times, but that was only to discuss the typing of his manuscript; there was never anything inappropriate, he was a married man after all."

"Did he ever speak about his wife?"

"Not really. I got the impression that they weren't very close."

"But Professor Barclay never did anything to cause you concern?" probed Biddlecombe.

"Look, Inspector, why exactly are you here, after all this time, asking questions about Professor Barclay?"

Biddlecombe chose to ignore the question for the moment. "Were you still working for the Professor at the time that his wife died?"

"Yes."

"Did he ever talk to you about his wife's death?"

"You still haven't answered my question, Inspector," Mrs Hughes eventually said.

Biddlecombe now knew that it he didn't give some explanation for him being there, it was highly unlikely that Mrs Hughes would tell him anything of value.

"Some new evidence has come to light that casts doubt on how Mrs Barclay may have died. I believe that Professor Barclay knew more about his wife's death than ever came to light at the time."

Mrs Hughes looked surprised. "But the coroner ruled accidental death, didn't he?"

"That was how it appeared at the time, but it may no longer be so straightforward now."

Mrs Hughes sat in silence for a moment. She eventually spoke.

"Do you now believe that Professor Barclay may have killed his wife?"

"We're not at the stage of saying that, just at the moment, but there certainly seems a need for us to have a word with the Professor about what really happened that night his wife died."

"Even though I was very young, Inspector, I did always think that the Professor enjoyed the company of younger women and that being married was never seen as being a barrier to his actions."

"Did he ever speak about a woman by the name of Rose?"

"His maid?"

"Oh, you knew who she was."

"He certainly spoke about Rose when he was at work. He used to say his life would have been a mess without Rose there to tidy up after him."

"So, you remember Professor Barclay talking about Rose and yet he never spoke about his wife?"

Mrs Hughes thought for a moment. "Now that I think about it, he never spoke about his wife at all. It was as if she never existed."

"But he never tried anything inappropriate with you?" Biddlecombe then enquired.

"He was always the perfect gentleman towards me, which is why we have kept in contact since."

Biddlecombe couldn't believe his ears. "You're in contact with Professor Barclay?"

"Oh yes, I get a Christmas card from him. He always puts a note in with it, telling me what he's doing these days."

"And you had one last Christmas?" Biddlecombe asked, hardly able to contain his excitement.

"Yes."

"Do you still have it?"

"Of course."

"Might I be able to see it?"

"It's personal, Inspector, I didn't even let my husband see it."

"This could well be a murder inquiry, Mrs Hughes and that Christmas card could be a vital piece of evidence. I implore you to let me see it."

Mrs Hughes seemed to debate with herself before standing up and leaving the room. She was quickly back, holding an envelope in her hand, which she gave to the Inspector.

"Has he always sent you a card at Christmas?" Biddlecombe asked before actually opening the envelope.

"When he first left Cambridge we'd write letters but that quickly developed in to exchanging cards at Christmas and we've just kept up the habit."

Biddlecombe's excitement level rose a notch. "You mean, you have an address for him?"

"I have an address that was correct as of Christmas, assuming my card actually reached its destination."

"May I have a note of that address?"

"If it will help your investigation, though I seriously doubt the notion that Clive could be a murderer."

Suddenly it was *Clive* now. Biddlecombe began to think that Mrs Hughes wasn't being entirely honest with him when she spoke about her relationship with the Professor. Maybe it wasn't just maids who caught his eye, maybe it was young girls in general? Mrs Hughes left the room again but soon returned with a piece of paper on which she had written an address. It may now be six months old, but it was the nearest, to date, that Biddlecombe had come to Professor Barclay.

He read the writing on the paper. So, Professor Clive Barclay had been in London in December of 1907.

"He gets around," Biddlecombe commented.

"He doesn't like to settle in one place for any length of time."

No, that's because he keeps murdering people, thought Biddlecombe, but he omitted to make that thought audible. At that moment they heard the sound of someone coming in the front door. Biddlecombe noticed the look of fear that passed across Mrs Hughes face. He stood up as the door to the room opened and a large man, wearing a pin-stripe suit and dark hat, came in to the room. He stopped immediately when he saw Biddlecombe standing beside his wife.

"And who the hell are you?" he snapped.

Biddlecombe took out his identification card. "I'm Inspector Biddlecombe from the local constabulary."

"Why are you here?" the man then asked, his eyes flicking between Biddlecombe and his wife, as if he didn't care who answered the question. It was Biddlecombe.

"There's been some break-ins in this area, so we've been going around warning residents and collecting information, wherever possible."

"And that takes an Inspector, does it?" Hughes then said with some suspicion. His eyes moved back to his wife and Biddlecombe found the man's demeanour very threatening.

"We take break-ins very seriously, Mr.....eh, Hughes?"

Hughes still stared at his wife. Biddlecombe did not like what he was seeing, especially the fact that Mrs Hughes was now recoiling, as if she were expecting the back of her husband's hand.

"Well you can just leave now," Hughes said, holding the door open.

Biddlecombe held his ground for a moment. "Mrs Hughes, might you leave us for a moment, I'd like a word with your husband."

Mrs Hughes stood still for a moment, her eyes never leaving her husband.

"About what?" Hughes then snapped again at the Inspector.

Biddlecombe calmly turned to Mrs Hughes and once more asked her to leave the room, which she eventually did. As soon as they were alone, Biddlecombe grabbed Hughes and pushed him back against the door. Biddlecombe's arm came up across Hughes' throat and he drew closer so that their faces were a matter of inches apart.

"I don't know you, Mr Hughes, but I already know that I don't like you. You strike me as being a bit of bully, especially towards that lovely wife of yours. Well listen and listen carefully, you rank piece of shit; if I hear of anything and I mean *anything* happening to your wife, then I will be back here faster than you can fart and when I do come back I guarantee that I will rip your miserable little body apart and cast you to the wind. Do I make myself clear?"

Hughes was trying to answer the question, but Biddlecombe was still squashing his windpipe. Eventually the pressure was released enough for him to nod and make a noise, which seemed to be one of agreement. Biddlecombe took his arm down and began to step up.

"What is it to you?" Hughes then sneered. "Fancy her or something?"

Biddlecombe launched himself at Hughes again and this time the pressure on the man's windpipe was almost fatal. By the time he released the pressure Hughes could only slide to the floor, gasping for breath. As he sat on the floor, Biddlecombe stood over him.

"Remember, if you do *anything* to your wife then I swear to God I won't be so nice to you the next time we meet. Good day, Mr Hughes."

Biddlecombe went out the door and along the hall towards the front door. As he reached the door, Mrs Hughes came out of a room to his right. She looked terrified. Biddlecombe took a card from his pocket and offered it to Mrs Hughes.

"If that husband of yours as much as looks at you the wrong way, you come and tell me, okay?"

Mrs Hughes looked down at the card and nodded quietly. Biddlecombe then opened the door and left. Mrs Hughes stood for a moment and then, for the first time in the last three years, she actually began to think that life might start to get better.

Outside, on the pavement, Inspector Samuel Biddlecombe knew that he had just crossed a line but, by God, he'd enjoyed it.

***

FIFTEEN

Thursday 18th June

Jake was back at his desk. He had missed Wednesday thanks to a stomach upset that he had assumed had come from something he had eaten. He had spent the day being sick and trying to sleep it off in his bed. Margaret had been the perfect nurse, offering him words of comfort when needed and providing a nice serving of soup once he began to feel like eating again. In those few hours of suffering he had come to love his wife even more.

Now back at his desk, Jake set about catching up on what had happened the day before. He found a message that had been left by Inspector Biddlecombe. There was a possible useful address in London that he was following up on. Maybe, just maybe, they'd soon have Barclay in custody.

There were a few other items of information, but nearly all of it referred more to Jake's new position as Chief Inspector and as that didn't start for a few days he immediately pushed it all to the side. He was sitting back and thinking about getting himself a mug of tea when Mathieson came in to the room. He was looking quite excited.

"I was checking out the local outlets for anyone who might be able to help with the miniatures that went missing from Edith McIntosh's house and came across, late yesterday afternoon, an antiques shop in the Castlegate who may have bought one of the items. I need to check it against the descriptions left by Doctor McIntosh and you still have that."

"Does the shop still have the item in question?" Jake asked.

"They do."

"Do you know what time they'll be open today?"

"Ten o'clock."

"We'll both go round at ten and check what they have," Jake then said.

"Very good, sir," added Mathieson, who then turned and left the room.

***

Inspector Biddlecombe had been cleared by the Chief Constable to take a little trip to London. He had arranged to meet Inspector Snow at King's Cross Station and they would both then travel to the address Biddlecombe had been given for Barclay. The journey to London was around an hour and a half and Biddlecombe had set off early that morning to ensure he would be in London for around nine.

Inspector Snow was a young man who looked as if he may have had a little too much to drink the night before. His eyes were sunken and red and his attire had the look of having been picked up and thrown on that morning rather than being removed from a wardrobe full of clean and pressed clothing.

They two men journeyed in a police vehicle that was driven by its own engine. Biddlecombe had found it all rather exciting and wondered when the day might come when Cambridge Police would be driving around in such machines.

The address they had was only a few miles from the station and it did not take them long to get there. It was a large house, set back from the road and with a high, stone wall protecting it from public view. The police officers got out of the car and walked up the curving driveway to the house. Snow rattled the ornate door knocker and stepped back to await someone opening the door. When the door did finally open a woman, who looked to be in her late thirties, maybe early forties, enquired what the visitors might want.

Snow showed his identification and asked if they might speak with the master of the house. They were informed that the master was at home and invited to enter the house. They were then taken in to a sitting room and told to sit down whilst the master was fetched. The woman then left the room, moving with a serene grace that made it look as if she might be on wheels rather than legs.

Moments passed before the door opened again and a man entered. He was dressed in a black suit, with a matching waistcoat. His hair was as black as his suit and cut quite close to his head. He was in his thirties and greeted the police officers with a smile and the offer of a handshake. He also provided his name, which was Francis Middleton.

"Now, what might I do for you?" he then said as they all sat down.

Biddlecombe took control of the interview and Snow seemed content to sit back and rest his hangover.

"I have been given this address as being the residence of a Mr Clive Barclay around Christmas time of last year. Would that be correct?"

"Clive *Barclay*?" Middleton asked in response.

"Yes."

Middleton shook his head. "There has never been a man of that name living here, though we did have a Clive *Nelson* here around Christmas."

"I take it that Mr Nelson has since moved on?" Biddlecombe then asked.

"He left here in February. It was such a shame, he was an excellent handyman."

Biddlecombe looked a little confused. "Did you say that Mr Nelson was a *handyman*?"

"Yes."

"Did you employ him in that capacity?"

"It didn't start out that way. Mr Nelson took a room with us and asked if there were any jobs around the house that he might do. It developed from there and soon we were actively paying for his services. It didn't last that long, however as he decided to move on in February, as I said."

"Do you know where he was going?"

Nelson thought for a moment. "He had been speaking about going to Scotland; Edinburgh I think. I gave him a good reference, along with the last of the money due to him and off he went."

"Did he have any close friends while he was here?" Biddlecombe then asked.

"He was very friendly with Olive but, apart from that he pretty much kept himself to himself and stayed in his room."

"Is Olive your maid?" Biddlecombe then said.

Nelson looked quite surprised by the question. "She was, as a matter of fact."

"Was?" added Biddlecombe.

"Yes, she left us a week or so before Clive did."

Biddlecombe glanced at Snow, who seemed lost in thoughts of his own and didn't appear to even be listening to what Middleton was saying.

"Where did she go, Mr Middleton?"

"I don't actually know. She simply wasn't here one morning. Her bag and what few possessions she had were gone as well, so we were left to assume that she had chosen to move on without telling us."

"Had you given her a reference?"

"That's the weird thing, I hadn't and you wouldn't expect a maid to get a new post without one, would you?"

"No you wouldn't," agreed Biddlecombe. "Have you replaced her?"

"Of course."

"Was Olive's room cleaned out before the new maid arrived?"

"Not really, though I'm sure Ann will have cleaned it thoroughly by now."

"Might I see the room anyway?" Biddlecombe then asked.

Middleton muttered something about it all being very strange, but led the way, none the less, up to the maid's room. Ann was busy working elsewhere in the house as Biddlecombe entered the room and had a quick look around. There was little to be seen, but he checked in the drawers and under the bed, just in case Olive had left something behind. There was nothing.

Biddlecombe re-joined Snow and Middleton in the sitting room. "When you said that Nelson was friends with Olive, did you get the impression that something of a romantic nature may have been forming between them?"

Middleton was instantly outraged at such a suggestion. "I would never have allowed such a relationship to form under my roof, Inspector."

"Very good, sir. Well, thank you for your time and the information," Biddlecombe then said and made his way to the front door. Snow fell in to step behind him. Once they were outside Snow turned to Biddlecombe.

"Didn't learn much then?"

"On the contrary," replied Biddlecombe, "I may have learned a lot."

Snow had a look of utter confusion on his face as got in to the back of the car with Biddlecombe and the driver asked where they wanted him to take them. Biddlecombe asked to be taken back to King's Cross.

***

In Aberdeen the sun had broken through and the air was beginning to heat up ever so slightly. Jake and Mathieson left Lodge Walk and strolled the short distance to the Castlegate where they went in to the small, antiques outlet of Mordecai Abraham.

Mr Abraham had long, white hair and a large, hooked nose that seemed to dominate his face. He hunched over the counter and rubbed his hands together as he greeted his two visitors. His friendly smile faded quickly when they told him who they were, though he did acknowledge that he remembered Mathieson from the day before.

Grudgingly, he went through to the back and then reappeared with the miniature in question. Jake checked it against those described by Doctor McIntosh. There was a match. The painting was of a naked woman, sitting on a sofa and looking straight at the artist. Her hands were in her lap, covering her pubic area and she had a warm, inviting smile on her beautiful face. It was well painted and Jake could understand why it would be worth so much money.

"Who brought this to you?" Jake then asked.

"A young woman."

Jake looked at Mathieson with a slightly confused expression on his face. "A woman?"

"Yes. Pretty little thing with blonde hair and way too much make-up."

"When was this?"

Abraham took a book from under the counter and laid it on top of the counter. He then opened it at a certain point and looked down a list of written entries.

"Monday, the eighth."

"Do you take a note of names when you buy items?"

"I do; she gave the name Emily Palmerston."

Jake did not believe, for one moment that that had really been the young woman's name. He vaguely remembered that Lord Palmerston's wife had been called Emily, so that was probably where she had got the idea from. Jake was also pretty sure that they were not looking for a blonde either. In other words, nothing that Abraham could tell him would be of much use to the investigation.

"We're going to have to retain this, Mr Abraham as it is evidence in a police inquiry."

Abraham looked distraught. "But I paid her two pounds for that item; it's mine now."

"It's stolen, Mr Abraham," was all that Jake said.

Jake wrapped the miniature in his handkerchief then placed it in his pocket. Mr Abraham watched him with a heavy heart for he feared that the two pounds he had paid, which he had thought at the time to be a bargain, was now looking like money down the drain rather than the investment he hoped it would be.

"It goes without saying, Mr Abraham," Jake then said, "that if the young lady returns with some more miniatures I want you to let us know immediately. If you could stall the young woman and maybe get her to come back at an agreed time, then that would be even better."

"I'll see what I can do," Mr Abraham said, but he really had no intention of doing anything of the sort.

Jake and Mathieson left the shop and made their way back to Lodge Walk. Mathieson was speaking as they walked.

"At least this proves that the miniatures *were* stolen and that Miss McIntosh hadn't got rid of them after her father's death."

"So it would seem, which gives us our motive back again," Jake added.

As they walked Jake considered where they were with the case. He wasn't sure how helpful retrieving the miniature would be, but he lived in hope that the young woman would surface again and when she did, they would be ready for her.

***

That afternoon Jake had a call from Inspector Biddlecombe. The line was atrocious and they were shouting that loud at times that many of their colleagues had wondered why they had bothered with the phones, surely they'd be able to hear each other anyway?

"I think Barclay may be back in Edinburgh and he may be calling himself Clive Nelson now," Biddlecombe had said after explaining to whom he had been speaking. "He left London in February, so I suppose there is every chance he may even have moved on again."

"He usually puts mileage between himself and his last residence after he's done something," Jake then said.

"By 'done something,'" Biddlecombe added," I take it you mean killed someone?"

"That is usually the case," agreed Jake.

"Which brings me to the most worrying thing that I heard from Mr Middleton. Their maid, Olive, appeared to have left them a week or so before Barclay left. Strangely, the maid packed her bag in the night and left. She didn't get a reference and she didn't tell anyone that she was leaving. I can't help but think she may have become another of his victims."

"Only a body has never been found," added Jake.

"No, but I am going to ask Inspector Snow, who accompanied me this morning to investigate the matter further. I will ask him to check any bodies that may have been found recently. I'll also ask him to return to the Middleton household and speak to them all again, only this time as part of a murder investigation. Olive may yet turn up, but I'm not expecting it."

"I would agree," said Jake. "I'll get in touch with Inspector Swanson, in Edinburgh and let him know that we think Barclay may be back in his area. You said you thought he might be calling himself Clive Nelson, was that correct?"

"That was the name he used in London. He worked there as a handyman, so perhaps he's given up his connections to universities."

"He'll know we'll be looking there," said Jake. "Anyway, thanks Inspector Biddlecombe for all your help and I'll keep you abreast of any developments."

"If we are now to work so closely together, the very least we can do is use our first names. I'm Sam."

"Jake."

"Speak to you again soon, Jake," concluded Biddlecombe and the phone line was cut.

Jake immediately asked to be connected to Edinburgh and he provided the number he was seeking. A little time passed before a voice spoke in Jake's ear. He asked to speak to Inspector Swanson and then waited a few moments until he arrived at the phone. The connection was slightly better, but not much.

Jake explained the situation to Swanson who seemed less than overjoyed to possibly having Barclay back in his area. He noted the new name and the possible line of employment, thanked Jake for the information and then put the phone down.

Jake then decided to pay a visit to the mortuary and see if Doctor Stephen had anything else to tell him following the murder of Archibald Diamond. Jake found the Doctor in a bad mood. He had tickets for the theatre but was now in danger of missing the performance if he couldn't get his paperwork completed. He was, therefore, less than pleased to see Inspector Fraser walk through the door of his office.

"I haven't finished with Archibald Diamond yet," Doctor Stephen said, as if that might have been enough to cause the Inspector to leave immediately. It did not have the desired effect.

"But you still have something you could tell me," Jake said, hopefully.

The Doctor laid his pen down on his desk and sat back in his chair. "Archibald Diamond died from a series of blows to the head. The murder weapon was a bronze statue of a man. There were no fingerprints on the statue that we could use, so I am assuming the attacker was wearing gloves. Diamond died on the Sunday evening, possibly between about seven and eleven, though I'm guessing nearer to eleven as he appeared to be ready for bed. He was the victim of a sustained and violent attack. As I said at the time, there was lot of hate in the attack; Diamond was dead long before the attacker stopped hitting him."

"So, if it is the same killer then the motivation for the two attacks must have been different?" Jake asked.

"I'm not so sure this is the same killer, Inspector Fraser. The hatred that came out of him in the attack on Diamond just doesn't appear to be present in the murder of Edith McIntosh."

"It is highly likely that Archibald Diamond was a homosexual, Doctor Stephen, so perhaps the hatred that came out whilst attacking him was because our burglar has a hatred for homosexuals and he already knew about Mr Diamond."

"It would certainly explain the hatred," the Doctor conceded, "but if someone went to the flat for the purposes of robbery then why turn that in to some act of mindless violence? This has to be like Edith McIntosh in the sense that the burglar could have escaped the property and not had to commit murder at all."

"Unless this is actually about the murders and it's the robberies that are the red herrings?" mused Jake.

"It would make more sense from the evidence we've gathered already," agreed the Doctor.

"In which case, why was Miss Grainger left alone?" was Jake's last thought before he thanked the Doctor and made his way back to his office.

***

The evening in Edinburgh was a glorious one with blue skies, sunshine and still a residue of heat from the day. Doctor Thelonious Watt came down for dinner at a little before eight. His wife, Caroline, was already sitting in the lounge along with his eighteen year old daughter, Mary. Watt poured himself a sherry, but did not offer one to his wife or his daughter; he did not approve of women drinking alcohol.

They were chatting amicably amongst themselves when the door opened and their guest walked in. Lucy Gill was wearing a new dress. It was the deepest blue and cut low at the front. She knew that the Doctor liked her very much and she was intent on maintaining his interest. If that meant showing a little more flesh than usual, then so be it. She knew she had made the right impression when the Doctor's eyes lit up and disappeared down the front of her dress.

"Ah, Lucy, right on time," said the Doctor.

Mrs Watt and her daughter looked at Lucy with a slightly less approving expression. They couldn't understand why this woman was living with them; it wasn't as if any of them actually knew who she was. She had arrived in Doctor Watt's life via a friend who had referred her after being told by Lucy that she was feeling unwell and was worried that it might the same illness as had befallen her mother. Lucy had further explained that, due to her mother's untimely death, she had inherited a large mansion in the north-east of Scotland and was now awaiting a substantial sum of money to be paid in to a bank account that had been opened in her name. In the meantime she was short of somewhere to stay and not feeling very well at the same time.

Doctor Watt had not only examined her and put her mind at rest that there did not appear to be anything seriously wrong with her, but had insisted that, for the duration of her time in Edinburgh, she should stay with him and his family. Lucy had feigned her surprise at being asked to stay with the Doctor, but she had soon come around to agreeing with his request and had moved in three days ago.

She had suggested she would be leaving on the Saturday and Mrs Watt, for once had quietly rejoiced when she had heard that. Lucy had said that her money should be through by then and that she would get them something by way of her thanks, before she left.

"Is that a new dress?" Caroline Watt has asked as Lucy had made her way in to the room.

"It is," answered Lucy, without adding the fact that she had stolen it that afternoon from a store on George Street. In Lucy's mind it was more of a swap than actual theft as she had left the dress she had been wearing in the changing area. She had gone to try it on and while no one was watching, calmly put her coat on and walked out of the shop. Before anyone had noticed, she was lost in the afternoon crowd.

"Has your money come through in that case?" Caroline then asked.

"It has actually," Lucy replied with the usual sweetness to her tone that always seemed to be there. It was another factor that Caroline Watt just couldn't stand.

"In that case, I take it you will definitely be leaving on Saturday?"

"I have to leave on Saturday, Caroline, as I now have been granted formal access to the family mansion in the north-east."

"Perhaps we could visit you some time?" Caroline said next and received a withering look from her husband who clearly felt she had asked enough.

Lucy, as ever, took any interrogation in her stride. "That would be lovely, though perhaps you might allow me a week or two to prepare for visitors?"

"Oh, I wouldn't dream of arriving before you had settled in," added Caroline, whose tone betrayed the fact that she didn't believe a word that came out of Lucy Gill's mouth.

Lucy smiled sweetly and then accompanied the family through to the dining room where she enjoyed yet another fabulous meal. The only thing that was missing was a nice glass of wine. Had she known the Doctor did not agree with women drinking alcohol then she would have found somewhere else to live whilst she was in Edinburgh.

Lucy ate her meal that evening debating with herself as to whether, or not, she should take anything else from the doctor before she left. Part of her was of the opinion that free lodgings and food for the best part of five days was more than enough. However, the other part of her looked around the home and saw many items that she could sell for, what to Lucy, would be a small fortune.

She had used this ruse before, some eleven years ago and on that occasion had managed to persuade the Doctor and his family to pack their bags and come with her to her mansion. On the route to the station she had doubled back and had managed to remove a few items from the house before the Doctor had realised the error of his ways and come back to the house. Lucy had heard, sometime later, that the Doctor was at Montrose before deciding that all was not well with his mysterious lodger.

Lucy wondered if she might possibly get away with the same ruse again. She looked at the others sitting round the table. Caroline Watt was not a nice person and she clearly had not fallen for Lucy's charm. The daughter, Mary, was not very bright, but she was exceedingly pretty and Lucy felt sure that the girl would find herself a nice husband one day and settle down to producing children.

Having children had never been on Lucy's agenda. She had lived her life purely for herself. She had no desire to settle down with a man and she had never had any desire to have children. There was not an ounce of maternal instinct in her; she even found it difficult to be nice to other people's children. It had been a good philosophy to live by as now, as she got older, she had no one dependant on her. Lucy Gill, or whatever else she chose to call herself, had only her own needs to satisfy and they were simple in the extreme.

Lucy's eyes alighted on the Doctor. He was a nice man. He obviously saw the best in everyone and had set out to do as much for Lucy as he could. He had asked her no awkward questions and had expected nothing of her whilst she was under his roof. The more she thought about it, the more she decided that she had taken enough from the man and that she would leave quietly on Saturday without further ado. As if reading Lucy's mind and being aware of her last few thoughts, Mary Watt then spoke.

"Have you ever married?"

The question had taken Lucy by surprise, not by its content, but by the fact it proved Mary Watt actually had a voice; it hadn't been used much in the last few days.

"Mary, don't be so personal," Doctor Watt snapped at his daughter, who immediately recoiled back in to her shell.

Lucy smiled. "I don't mind answering the question, Doctor Watt; after all, it's perfectly innocent. Yes, Mary, I was married, but my husband was in the army and he was killed in action."

"Oh, really," added Caroline Watt, "and where was he serving at the time?"

Lucy had the answer off pat. She had used it so many times before that she almost believed it herself. She spoke slowly and confidently and added the odd bit of emotion where she felt it might be most effective. By the time she was finished she was only just holding back the tears and Mary Watt was quick to apologise for upsetting her. Lucy told her not to worry and returned to her food.

After dinner Lucy returned to her room. She checked the paperwork for the oil shares swindle and decided that it was beginning to look a little overused. She really needed a new idea, but she had little time to think of something and then acquire the necessary paperwork to support it. It was so easy to play on other people's greed for money, but she knew that the older her props looked, the less likely anyone was to believe in them.

Lucy went to sleep that night with thoughts of new swindles still rolling around inside her head.

***

SIXTEEN

Friday 19th June

On the Friday Jake had a fairly quiet time. He had no cause to leave the office and nothing new, of any consequence came his way. The same could not be said for Inspectors Snow and Swanson.

In London, Inspector Snow had started treating Olive's disappearance as something far more sinister. Enquiries had been carried out around the Middleton household as to whether anyone had actually seen Olive leaving. The police found no one who had seen anything, other than one neighbour who claimed to have seen Olive in the company of a man, earlier in the evening on which she was supposed to have left. The description of the man had been of little help to the inquiry.

However, given Clive Barclay's history, Snow was now of the opinion that he, almost definitely, had had something to do with Olive's disappearance. Snow had returned to the Middleton household and once more spoken to Francis Middleton, who was outraged to be told that the police now thought Olive might be dead.

"Don't be stupid, man," Middleton had erupted, "Olive won't be dead; she'll just have gone off with some young man who filled her head with thoughts of love. She was a very impressionable, young woman."

"When did you last see Olive?" Snow had asked choosing, for the moment, to ignore Middleton's assessment of the situation.

Middleton took his time to think. It had all happened four months ago and he hadn't thought much of it at the time, other than the fact Olive had not asked for a reference. To now have to dredge up something pertinent from his memory was proving more difficult than even he might have thought.

"Let me see, Clive Nelson left on the fifteenth of February. I remember that because it was my wife's birthday and we went out for a celebratory dinner. When we got back, Clive had gone. I suppose, in that case, Olive must have left us maybe three days before that."

Snow wrote a spread of dates in his notebook. If Olive was known to be missing on the twelfth, then maybe something had actually happened to her on the eleventh? Of course, it was still possible that nothing had happened to her at all.

"Had you noticed any change in Olive just before she left?"

"What do you mean by change?" Middleton asked, still sounding less than willing to be of any great help to the police.

"You said you thought she might have had her head filled with thoughts of love," Snow suggested. "Had her manner changed in any way at all?"

"I really didn't notice anything, but then she was the maid and you don't tend to pay much attention to them unless they do something wrong, do you?"

Condescending bastard, thought Snow, but he kept that to himself.

"Would your wife remember anything?" Snow then said.

"I shouldn't think so."

"Have you spoken to her since I was last here with Inspector Biddlecombe?"

"Of course I have spoken to my wife, but not about Olive, I didn't think it was necessary. I didn't want to upset her."

"But why would your wife have got upset by Olive leaving you?" Snow then asked.

"You've just said that Olive may be dead, that would be upsetting enough."

"Only you didn't know that Olive might be dead when you spoke to your wife. Is there any other reason why you would not talk to your wife about Olive?"

Middleton puffed out his chest. "What exactly are you suggesting, Inspector?"

"I'm suggesting nothing, Mr Middleton, I'm merely trying to ascertain why you do not feel it necessary to seek your wife's views on Olive's disappearance."

Middleton's expression remained stern and it was a few moments before he eventually agreed to go and speak to his wife. He refused to let Snow see her on the grounds that she might find it too distressing. He further informed Snow that his wife was of a nervous disposition and easily upset. Snow could well understand that being married to a man like Francis Middleton was likely to upset anyone, nervous disposition or not.

Snow was left sitting on his own for the best part of forty-five minutes before the door opened and Middleton returned. He crossed the room and sat down again. His expression was just as stern as when he had left.

"My wife did remember Olive acted a bit strange in the last few days before she left. She seemed nervous though gave no explanation when challenged about her demeanour."

"And how was Clive Nelson? Snow then enquired.

"Same as ever, pleasant, talkative and a good worker."

"And you never saw him looking to spend time with Olive when they were not working?"

"There isn't that much time outside of work, Inspector and they would never have had the same half day off."

"Were their rooms close?" Snow then asked and got the same outraged eruption as Biddlecombe had got for suggesting any impropriety under the Middleton roof. Snow let Middleton calm down again and then calmly said, "That still doesn't answer my question."

"They were next door to each other on the top floor," Middleton eventually said.

"So, had something being going on between them, you'd be the last to know about it, wouldn't you?" Snow added, enjoying the fact that Middleton was now physically squirming in his chair.

"I suppose," he conceded with some reluctance.

"So why would Olive have been more nervous in the last few days of her employment?" Snow then asked.

"I really don't know. Mind you, Olive had also been rather sickly in those last few weeks that she was here."

"Sickly?"

"Yes, vomiting at odd times of the day. She said it had to have been something that she had eaten but as she ate pretty much what we did, I found that difficult to believe. I remember my wife asked Olive one day if she might be pregnant, which I thought was a damned cheek seeing as the girl didn't even have a man in her life."

"Did Olive answer the question?" Snow then enquired.

"No, she just ran from the room crying, which is what I would have expected. The girl must have been mortified to be asked such a question."

Snow noted in his book that Olive may well have been pregnant and that immediately offered him a motive for Barclay wanting her dead, presuming he was the father. Snow was also finding it difficult to believe that Francis Middleton could be so naïve. He honestly seemed to think it impossible for Olive to get pregnant simply because she was a maid working in a busy house. Snow was more inclined to believe, now knowing the specific liking that Barclay had for maids, that Olive had informed Barclay that she thought she was pregnant and had paid with her life for imparting such information.

"What kind of jobs did Mr Nelson do around the house?" Snow then asked.

"Anything and everything. He also worked in the garden; the man wasn't bothered where the next job came from. As I said, he really was an excellent worker."

"Might I see some of the work he did in the garden?" Snow added, beginning to think that poor Olive may be buried out there.

Middleton had not read anything in to Snow's question and led the way out of the room and ultimately out in to the garden. Snow asked if he might be left alone to have a look around and Middleton returned to the house. It was a large garden with three trees at the bottom where the fence separated their land from their immediate neighbours. It was a well-tended garden and Snow took his time walking round.

Towards the end of the garden, between the trees and the fence, Snow found a piece of ground that looked as if it had been dug over more recently than the area around it. Snow stood beside that spot and looked back towards the house. It was well protected from view and Snow's stomach tightened at the thought of why this area may have been dug over.

He continued round the garden and came upon a small shed situated more to the side of the house. The door wasn't locked so he opened it and went in. He found a spade propped up in the corner, so he picked it up and made his way to the bottom of the garden. He took his jacket off and hung it on the lower branch of one of the trees. He was just about to start digging when a voice spoke from behind him.

"Who are you and what are you doing?"

Snow turned around to find a scruffy looking gentleman, with a cigarette stuck in the corner of his mouth, looking back at him with an element of suspicion.

"I'm a police officer; Inspector Snow to be precise."

"And what's a police officer doing in this garden with a spade?"

"Digging, if you'd be so kind as to let me get on with it."

"Do you want me to go to the police office and get on with some of your work, seeing as you've seen fit to come here and do some of mine?" the man then quipped.

"Very funny," said Snow, leaning on the spade for a moment. "May I ask whom you might be?"

"The gardener around here, Ivan Saunders."

"Did you take over from Clive Nelson, Mr Saunders?"

"I did."

"And did you dig over this particular piece of ground?"

Saunders looked down at the slightly looser area of ground. "No, I wasn't even aware there had been anything done down here, I've concentrated on the area nearer to the house since I started."

"In that case I must ask you to leave while I get on with some digging," Snow then said.

Saunders looked confused. "Expecting to find anything?"

Snow smiled. "I fear that there may be a body buried here and I need to test my theory. To that end, I must insist that you leave me alone."

Saunders shrugged, took a drag on his cigarette and then removed it from his mouth while he exhaled the smoke.

"If you need a hand, give me a shout," he then said and walked away.

Snow turned back to the job in hand. He was not looking forward to what he might find and he still hoped that he was wrong. He put the spade in to the ground and carefully started to dig where the earth was already loose. He had not been required to dig very deep before he was able to confirm his theory.

***

Jake was sitting in the Empress Café enjoying a spot of lunch. He had been busy that morning completing two other cases that he had been working on for a few weeks and the paperwork for those cases was now ready for the court. It meant he could now return his attention to the murders of Edith McIntosh and Archibald Diamond. Not that there was much to return to, if he were being brutally honest with himself.

Jake took a piece of paper from his pocket and what was left of an oft sharpened pencil. He took a bite of his pie and gave some thought to the double murder. He made a few notes to himself.

He was happy to stay with the theory that Edith McIntosh had been murdered for her father's miniature collection. With the young woman surfacing to sell one of the paintings, it confirmed that they had been stolen and that they were, probably, still in the Aberdeen area. The first two questions, which Jake noted, were who was this mystery woman and how had she acquired the miniatures?

The burglary theory was not so strong with Archibald Diamond. Nothing appeared to have been stolen and the manner in which he had been killed showed a level of violence seen nowhere else. Being killed for his sexuality made more sense. Jake wrote down; *Who was the mystery visitor that evening? Is he our killer?*

Then there was Miss Grainger and her apparent visitor. Had she been the first to be burgled and if so, why had nothing been stolen there either? Was the thief merely taking pot luck with his visits and he'd struck it lucky with Miss McIntosh? Jake's pencil hovered over the paper for a moment and then he wrote; *Was Miss Grainger a trial run of some kind? Could it honestly be a teacher colleague who is carrying out these crimes?*

Jake ate some more pie and gave the puzzle a little more thought. If Miss McIntosh's miniatures had been the sole reason for the burglaries then were the visits to Miss Grainger and Mr Diamond simply a smoke screen for the main job? And, if so, why then kill Mr Diamond?

Jake wrote: *Are we looking for a burglar who murders or a murderer who steals?*

Jake allowed his thoughts to roam for a while. The café was starting to get busy and he wondered how long it would be before someone would be asking to share his table. He didn't want murder notes lying around at a time like that, so he pushed the piece of paper back in his pocket along with the pencil.

Jake finished his pie and drank the last of his tea. He was finding this case very baffling indeed. A thought then struck him. What if the murder of Edith McIntosh had been out of necessity because she could identify the burglar, but the murder of Archibald Diamond had been simply provide the police with a false lead? What if there was no actual connection between the two incidents other than a very clever killer now trying to throw the police off his scent? Maybe the stealing of the miniatures was all that this case was about and everything else was a smoke screen?

Jake decided he needed to follow the stolen goods and not be distracted by anything else.

He stood up from the table and then headed back to the office.

***

Inspector Swanson had arranged to have the weekend off. It was rare for him to do such a thing, for he seldom had a reason not to be at the office. Swanson had devoted his life to his job and had never found the time for relationships. He had few friends and tended to pass the time of day by being at work, rather than wasting it on idle socialising. This had led to others taking more time off as they knew good old Frederick would be there to cover for them.

This weekend would be different. Frederick Swanson's sister was visiting Edinburgh, from her home in Cornwall and he had taken two days off in which to see her. They had not seen each other for five years and were both looking forward to spending some time with each and catching up on any news. Swanson's sister was eight years his junior and they had never been that close throughout their lives. However, when they did meet they usually had fun as they had shared interests in many things.

Before the weekend could begin, however, Swanson had much to do in his quest to find Clive Barclay. He had asked for uniformed officers to check all lodgings in Edinburgh and also to check with any lawyers, or agents, with responsibility for renting properties. They were looking either for Clive Nelson, or Clive Barclay but were also to note anyone by the name of Clive, just in case he had chosen to change his surname again.

Swanson realised he might end up with many more names than was necessary but it seemed the only logical place to begin. He also contacted the university, just in case Barclay returned in a capacity more suited to his qualifications. Swanson did not think, for one moment, that he would, but again he needed to try and cover all possibilities. Now that Barclay was aware of the police being on to him, it was more likely that he would keep changing his name. If he were to also change his first name then they might never find him, at least not before he was free to kill again.

Having now felt that he had done as much as he could, Frederick Swanson put on his coat, wished those around him a pleasant weekend and went home.

***

SEVENTEEN

Monday 22nd June

Jake arrived at the office early. It had been the usual start to the day, dull and threatening rain. The temperature was also disappointingly low as it had been the day before when Jake and Margaret had gone to the Duthie Park for a stroll around. Even though the weather had not been particularly nice there had been a number of other people taking the air and the experience had not been entirely unpleasant. Jake enjoyed being out with Margaret. She was a handsome woman and he still found it difficult to believe, on occasions, that she had fallen in love with someone like him.

This was to be his first day as Chief Inspector Fraser, though he was intent on changing as little as possible. He would not seek to be called Chief Inspector and he would try, as much as possible, to be the same Jake in front of the men as he had always been.

He had hardly had time to sit down when Sergeant Mathieson came in to the room. He was clutching a sheet of paper, which Jake recognised as a formal report of an incident. He wondered if this might be connected to the Grammar School investigation, but he was to quickly learn that something else had happened, over the weekend, to further take up their time.

"Good morning, *Chief* Inspector," Mathieson said with a hint of a smile, "something else that requires our attention."

"What is it?"

Mathieson chose not to directly answer the question but, to instead, hand the report over to Jake. Jake took his time to read through it.

Officers had been called to the Bon Accord Club, in Bon Accord Crescent, on Sunday morning. Four windows had been broken the night before and a printed sheet of paper pushed through the letterbox. The printed sheet of paper was attached to the formal report, compiled by Constable Fettes. Jake read through that as well.

Sometime between midnight on Saturday and ten o'clock on Sunday morning, four windows had been broken in the property occupied by the Bon Accord Club. The windows had been broken by stones being thrown from the pavement. The printed sheet of paper, which had been pushed through the letter-box, stated that no property should ever be for the purposes of men only and that the time had come for women to rise up and be heard. The statement was attributed to an organisation going by the name of The Aberdeen Voice for Women and there was a large AVW stamped in red in the bottom corner, as if to give the organisation further credence.

"I've never heard of The Aberdeen Voice for Women," Jake eventually said, placing the report on his desk.

"Neither has anyone else sir, but if their actions on Saturday are to be an indication of their intentions then I'm guessing we're going to hear a lot more about them in the days ahead."

Jake nodded. "The printing looks to be quite professional. Have a walk round some of the main printers and see if anyone can put a name to whomever ordered and presumably, paid for them."

"Will do," added Mathieson and he left the room.

Jake then turned his attention to the usual mound of paper that tended to occupy his desk on a Monday morning. He could never believe how much seemed to happen on a Sunday when he wasn't there. The Sabbath was supposed to be a day of rest, but it seemed obvious that criminals did not abide by that philosophy.

Near the top of the pile was a message from Inspector Biddlecombe. He had received word from London that the body of the missing maid, Olive, had been found buried in the garden and that they were now, formally, adding her murder to the growing list of Barclay's victims. Biddlecombe had further stressed the need to catch Barclay as quickly as possible, before he could kill again. Jake did not disagree with the sentiment but still felt it might be easier said than done.

Once he had cleared the new paperwork Jake then put his coat on and left the building. He made his way up to the premises of Gibson and Son and asked if he could speak to Mr Kerrigan. It transpired that Kerrigan was out at a house doing some valuation work, so Jake asked if the young girl in the office could ask Mr Kerrigan to go down to Lodge Walk on his return. She said that she would.

As Jake turned to make his way out of the office the door opened and a man, matching Jake's height, came in to the room. His hair was thinning and his face bore a rather weary countenance as if he carried the problems of the world upon his shoulders. He was in his late forties and carried some papers, which he was looking down at as he entered the room.

"Ah, Mr Gibson," the young girl said to him, "this is Inspector Fraser. He'd like Mr Kerrigan to go down to Lodge Walk when he returns."

Gibson turned to look at Jake. "We've already helped your Sergeant," he then said, as if that cleared them from any other involvement with the police.

Jake thanked him for their help to date but explained that new information had come to light and he hoped that Mr Kerrigan might be able to help. Gibson asked if there was anything that he might do, so Jake eventually agreed to going through to Gibson's office with the intention of speaking about the miniature paintings.

The office was quite spacious though cluttered with all manner of items, ranging from the nude statue of a woman standing in the corner to a stuffed fox standing in the other. Paper lay on top of Gibson's desk, but the mess did not seem to bother him. He invited Jake to have a seat then went around the desk and sat down on a large and well-padded chair.

"We have found notes, which had been kept by Doctor McIntosh, in which he records, in some detail, a series of miniature paintings, which he had collected over the years. Would you know why these miniature weren't included in your firm's inventory of items owned by Doctor McIntosh?"

"If they weren't on the list then we were obviously never shown them."

"But I thought your list was drawn up for insurance purposes?" Jake then asked.

"It was."

"And yet items of value were not included?"

"As I said, Inspector, the family must have chosen not to show the paintings to us. They, no doubt, had their reasons."

"No doubt," added Jake.

Gibson sat forward in his chair. "Do you have these paintings, Inspector, because if you do I'd be delighted to value them for you," Gibson then said.

"No, Mr Gibson, I don't have the paintings. All we know is that Doctor McIntosh collected them and they're not in the house now."

"Do you know the nature of the paintings?"

"Women in a state of undress, so not the kind of thing Miss McIntosh might have approved of."

"So you won't know exactly what each painting looks like?" Gibson said.

"Only what the Doctor wrote about them," answered Jake, not wishing to tell anyone, for the moment, that he actually possessed one of them.

"Does he put an age on them?"

"I believe they were all painted from the middle of the eighteenth century up until the middle of the nineteenth century. Doctor McIntosh collected them during the last quarter of the last century."

"Did he put a price against them?"

"He did, but I wish to keep that to myself for the moment," replied Jake.

"Of course, Inspector, I had not meant to pry."

"Assuming that these miniatures are of good quality, would you see a market for someone wishing to sell them?"

"There is always a market for naked, or scantily clad, women, Inspector. Men will never tire of looking at the feminine form."

"So it might be possible to sell them to a private collector who would ask no questions?" suggested Jake.

"I should have thought that anyone with stolen goods would try to sell them on privately. There are too many records kept in shops and auctioneers, so getting caught becomes that little more likely."

"Does your company deal with miniatures of that kind?" Jake then asked.

"If we were to be selling something of that nature then it would only be by private auction. Items like that can only exist in a man's world, Inspector."

"Have you sold items like that in the past?"

"We have sold the occasional nude, yes, but always to an invited audience."

"So you have some idea of the men who might already have collections in which these miniatures might sit quite nicely?" Jake then suggested.

"I might have an idea of who would be interested, but client confidentiality prohibits me from giving out their names."

"I understand, Mr Gibson. We can only hope that none of the men you are protecting ultimately end up connected to the murders I'm investigating."

Gibson's face turned red and he looked away. His eyes eventually made their way back to look at Jake. He paused for a moment, apparently weighing something up and then spoke again.

"Very well, Inspector, I'll give you one name, but only because he is another dealer and probably has no personal involvement in any of this. He does, however, do quite a lot of work in areas where the materials for sale may not be to everyone's liking, if you get my meaning?"

"I understand, Mr Gibson; now what is the gentleman's name?"

"Robert Jamieson, he has a shop on Holburn Street just before you get to Willowbank Road."

Jake wrote the name in to his book and then stood up. He thanked Gibson for his help, asked that Kerrigan still come to see him at Lodge Walk and then turned and left. As he was at the top end of Union Street, Jake decided to walk round to Jamieson's shop on Holburn Street.

The shop was big with big items filling up the space. Everything looked expensive, though most of it wasn't to Jake's taste anyway, so he felt no desire to buy anything as he stood at the end of the shop waiting for Mr Jamieson to come down from his office. When he did arrive he eyed Jake with some suspicion. Jake also took time to form a judgement of Mr Jamieson, simply from his demeanour and general appearance.

Robert Jamieson was dressed in a morning suit with a flower in his lapel. His hair was long, sitting on the collar of his shirt and looking as if it could do with a good clean. He was clean-shaven and had a slight twitch beneath his right eye, which Jake would have imagined wasn't the best image to have for someone involved in retail.

"Yes, Inspector, what might I do for you today?"

"Could we go somewhere a little more private?" Jake then suggested.

Jamieson looked annoyed at the suggestion but eventually suggested that they go through the back. This idea led them to a room full of furniture, which Jamieson explained was awaiting being priced. They chose a chair each and sat down. Jake's was extremely comfortable and he did think, just for a moment that it might be worth buying. He quickly dismissed the notion as it was blatantly obvious that Jamieson's prices would be well outside the pocket of an acting Chief Inspector.

"I'm investigating two murders, Mr Jamieson. We believe that the reason behind at least one of those murders was burglary. A series of miniature paintings were stolen. These paintings were of naked women and the collection was put together by a man by the name of Doctor McIntosh. He kept a record of all the pictures but also, as luck would have it, we have, in our possession, one of the paintings."

Jake took the miniature from his pocket. He was taking a risk showing this to Jamieson because it was still possible that he might be involved in trying to sell the stolen items. Jake uncovered the painting and handed it across to Jamieson who looked instantly impressed.

"My, my Inspector but this is the work of a true artist. It is absolutely exquisite."

"So it's worth a lot of money?"

"At the right auction, or to the right collector, this item alone would fetch maybe six or seven pounds."

Jake could now see why Mordecai Abraham had been so annoyed at having to give up the item he'd bought from the blonde woman. He had just been denied a straight five pound profit on re-selling it. He quickly did a little mental arithmetic and deduced that there had been around seventy to eighty pounds worth of miniatures in Doctor McIntosh's cupboard; a small fortune to any criminal. He wondered why one had been sold for two pounds when even to a complete novice it was obvious that these paintings were worth so much more than that. Maybe whoever had stolen them hadn't considered the difficulties in trying to sell them on, or maybe they were just desperate for money?

Jamieson, rather grudgingly, gave the miniature back to Jake who immediately wrapped it in his handkerchief again and put it back in his pocket.

"Have you ever sold something like that?" he then asked.

Jamieson knew that he had to be careful in what he said. "I have sold items of that nature though not, sadly, of that quality. I cannot believe that the collector of those pieces bought any of them in Aberdeen."

"So you would be better to sell them outside Aberdeen as well?" Jake then enquired.

"Quite definitely, Inspector. Items of that quality need to be sold in London where there is real money being spent. Aberdeen doesn't really appreciate quality as a city, so it is left up to one or two collectors, who do have an eye for the best things in life, to fly the flag for the rest of us."

"It goes without saying, Mr Jamieson that if someone does approach you trying to sell a miniature of the kind I have just shown you, that you will contact the police immediately."

"I will do my duty as a good citizen, Inspector, though it will break my heart not to be able to possess something of such quality."

Jake left Jamieson's shop and made his way back to Lodge Walk. He had only been back five minutes when he was told that Mr Kerrigan was at the front counter. Moments later both men were seated in the interview room and Jake got the impression that Mr Kerrigan was acting rather nervously.

"Is there something wrong?" he asked.

Kerrigan tried to look relaxed. "No, why do you ask?"

"You just looked nervous."

"I've always associated the police with doing something wrong and even though I haven't done anything wrong, I still find that being here strangely brings on a feeling of guilt, none the less."

Jake smiled. "As far as I know, Mr Kerrigan, there is no reason for you to feel guilty. I simply want to ask you a few more questions about the items that you listed in the McIntosh household and also talk about some other items, which you didn't have on the list."

McIntosh now looked puzzled rather than nervous. "I'm not sure what you mean by items that I did not have on the list. I listed everything that Miss McIntosh asked me to list."

"Did Miss McIntosh ever refer to items that her late father might have collected?"

"Not that I recall."

"On your tour of the house were you made aware of a room, which Doctor McIntosh had used for his own purposes?"

"No."

Jake took the miniature from his pocket. He uncovered it and handed it to Kerrigan whose eyes lit up.

"So you've never seen anything like this before?" Jake asked.

"I most certainly have not," Kerrigan replied. "This is perfection, so there is no way that I would forget seeing something of this obvious quality. Did this come out of the McIntosh household?"

"We have reason to believe so, yes," Jake replied, taking the miniature back.

"Well I definitely didn't see anything like that," added Kerrigan. "It must be worth a small fortune as well, so it really should have been on my list."

"And Miss McIntosh definitely never mentioned the existence of miniatures such as that?"

"Definitely not, but then paintings such as that are hardly something that a lady would wish to discuss."

Perhaps, though Jake, *but someone must have known about the existence of the miniatures, otherwise they'd still be there.*

Jake asked a few more general questions before agreeing to Mr Kerrigan returning to his work. Jake went back to his desk with a nagging feeling that he wasn't getting anywhere very fast. As he sat, alone, in his room he kept wondering how anyone else had found out about those miniatures if Edith McIntosh had not been in the habit of speaking about them? His mind drifted back to Mildred McIntosh. Jake was the last person who would have wanted to wrongly accuse a prostitute, simply because of the unfortunate way she was forced to live her life, but he did start wondering if Mildred might have said something, either to a client or to someone else whilst in a state of drunkenness.

Jake decided to ask Mathieson to find Mildred again so he made a point of seeking him out, later in the day, after Mathieson had returned from his tour of the printers. Before discussing Mildred, Jake asked if Mathieson had learned anything from the printers.

"Not a great deal, but I haven't got round them all yet. I should get finished tomorrow."

"Okay, well keep me informed of developments and while you are out there could you try to find Mildred McIntosh again."

Mathieson was grinning as soon as Jake had finished asking the question. "Finding Mildred will be easy, sir, she's in the cells sleeping off God only knows what."

"When was she arrested?"

"Early this morning. Constables found her asleep on Market Street with her dress hitched up and her legs wide apart. Even drunk she managed to offer them a good time for a penny."

Jake was now smiling. "I'll go and see how she's doing."

He made his way to the cells and asked the Duty Sergeant if Mildred was likely to be in the land of the living yet.

"She was blind drunk when they brought her in, but she ought to be a little more human by now. I was intent on giving her a cup of tea and throwing her out soon, there's no way I'm wasting court time on her."

"Get the tea ready and I'll take it in with me," Jake added and the Sergeant went off to boil the kettle.

When Jake entered the cell Mildred McIntosh was awake and sitting up. Fortunately, for Jake, her dress was not around her waist and she was just sitting, quietly staring at the wall. Her eyes adjusted to the man coming through the door of her cell. She even managed a smile.

"Inspector," she said, trying to sit up, "if you just give me a minute to make myself a little more presentable."

She picked up a bag that had been dumped on the floor and from it she produced a brush, which she then proceeded to pull through her long and straggly hair. Jake crossed the floor and put the tea on a small table to Mildred's right. She finished with her hair, slightly adjusted the bodice of her dress and then smiled again.

"There, that's better, now what can I do for you Inspector in return for this lovely cup of tea that you've brought me?"

"I'm back about Doctor McIntosh's miniature paintings, Mildred. Do you think he would have spoken openly to others about them?"

"Oh, no, he wouldn't have talked about them with others. I remember Doctor McIntosh saying someone would nick them if they became public knowledge."

"Did you ever speak about them with someone other than Doctor McIntosh himself?"

"I never really spoke about them; after all, they were nothing to do with me."

"You see, people are telling me that Edith McIntosh didn't speak about them and you're telling me that Doctor McIntosh didn't talk about them and yet someone knew they were there because someone did nick them."

"And you think that's me?" added Mildred in a matter-of-fact tone rather than a highly offended one.

"Actually, Mildred, I don't think it was you, but I was hoping you might have had some idea as to who else could have known about them."

Mildred drank her tea and seemed to be thinking, though in Mildred's case that wasn't always so easy to judge. Eventually she answered Jake, which proved that she really had been thinking after all.

"Doctor McIntosh did say that he was going to get his collection valued."

"When?"

"A couple of years before he died."

"And did he get them valued?"

"Don't know."

"Did he ever mention the name of a company in connection with a valuation?"

"No, but then, even if he had I'd probably not remember now. A couple of nights on the booze and everything becomes a bit of a blur."

Jake put his hand in his pocket and took out a penny, which he gave to Mildred. "Treat yourself to a proper meal, Mildred and try to steer clear of the drink for a little while. Your clients will think more of you if you're conscious while they're doing it with you."

"D'you think so, Inspector?" Mildred added, as if she wasn't entirely convinced herself.

Jake left the cell laughing and told the Sergeant to let her out once she'd finished her tea.

Back at his desk Jake was left wondering if Doctor McIntosh maybe had had the collection valued at some point and that was the person passing on information to the thief. The problem with that theory was that Mildred had said Doctor McIntosh had spoken about a possible valuation years before his death. Had anyone learned anything at that time, why would they then wait years to use the information?

Keeping everything in the here and now, Jake kept coming back to the Grammar School. It still made more sense for the information to be coming out of the school, which meant that someone had got close enough to Miss McIntosh to get her talking about items of value that may have been in her possession. Jake decided to return to the Grammar School and speak to some of the teachers who had worked with Edith McIntosh. Maybe they had been aware of the collection?

However, that would wait for another day.

***

The man and woman met briefly at the Union Street end of Rose Street. It was almost as if they had bumped in to each other as the man raised his hat and appeared to apologise for his actions. Anyone passing would have paid little attention to the event, which was exactly what the man and woman wanted.

Before moving on, however, the man pushed a piece of paper in to the woman's bag. The woman was not to read the contents of the paper until she got home. When she did, she grew more and more concerned about how close the police might be getting.

They knew that they had to keep calm, but with the police now holding details of the miniatures it was going to make it impossible to move any of them on within Aberdeen, unless she could find someone prepared to buy them privately.

The woman sat down and pondered on the predicament she now found herself in. She needed a solution and she needed one quickly.

***

EIGHTEEN

Tuesday 23rd June

Frederick Swanson came up trumps on a wet and depressing Tuesday morning. Clive Barclay had, indeed, made contact with the university, though not with a notion of gaining employment, but more with a hope of getting a loan of some money. He had visited the university the day before and spoken to some old colleagues. No one had been particularly pleased to see him and no one had agreed to lend him any money. The university could not say exactly where Barclay was lodging, but at least it proved he *was* in Edinburgh. The university colleagues, who had spoken to him, also confirmed that Barclay was looking scruffy and not like himself.

Frederick Swanson increased the number of officers checking out lodgings within the city centre. He didn't believe that Barclay would go outside of the city centre and it was now perfectly possible that he might leave again, having come up short with his attempts at getting money. Swanson was of a mind, however, that Barclay was probably getting desperate for money and desperate men often do desperate things, which immediately gives them away. Swanson ordered his officers to check the cheap and nasty residences as he was very much of a mind that Barclay would not be able to afford much in the way of a roof over his head.

Just before lunchtime two constables arrived back at the building in which Frederick Swanson had his office, accompanied by a man they had just arrested. They had found him, fast asleep on a lice-infested bed, in a room in a house that hadn't been cleaned in months. They had found him because he had still been using the name Clive Nelson. Having already been paid for the room, the fat woman at the front door, who also looked like she hadn't been cleaned in months, had no problems in pointing the police officers at the relevant room.

It was obvious to everyone that Professor Clive Barclay had fallen a long way.

Barclay was put in a cell and then washed thoroughly. He was given some clothes to wear and a meal to eat. By the time they had done all that, Frederick Swanson had been in touch with Jake, in Aberdeen and had arranged that they would both conduct the interview with Barclay as soon as Jake got to Edinburgh.

Jake had not even waited for the Chief Constable's blessing before hurrying to the station and jumping on the first train bound for Edinburgh. He had also despatched a constable to tell Margaret what was happening and not to expect him home that night.

It was nearly six o'clock in the evening before Jake arrived at the police office where Barclay was being held. Swanson shook his hand at the door and led him to one of the interview rooms after asking a constable to go down to the cells and bring Barclay to them. He also despatched another officer to the university with instructions to come back with someone who could positively identify Clive Barclay.

A few moments later all three men were sitting in the interview room and two constables were outside, standing at the door. Even after a wash, Clive Barclay was looking in a bad way. For a man in his early forties he looked a whole lot older. His hair was longer and unkempt and his eyes sunken in to his face. He sat in silence, staring at the wall beyond where Jake and Swanson were sitting. Jake opened the proceedings.

"Will you just confirm, for the record, that you are Professor Clive Barclay?"

Barclay said nothing, but continued to stare at the wall. Jake took the silence to be a statement in the affirmative and moved on.

"We've been tracking you around the country, Mr Barclay and we've noted that you don't like being in any one place for long, why is that?"

Barclay still said nothing. His eyes never left the wall he was staring at. Jake kept on speaking.

"Did you know a maid by the name of Olive before you left London in February, Mr Barclay?"

There was a flicker of movement to Barclay's eyes, but he still said nothing. Jake did not wait for anything to be said.

"I'll re-phrase that, Mr Barclay and say that you *did* know a maid by the name of Olive and that we now have the evidence to prove that you murdered her."

This time the reaction from Barclay was much more noticeable and just for a second, or two, his eyes moved towards Jake and then away again. It was obvious to Jake that Barclay was now frantically trying to work out if these police officers did actually know anything, or whether they were just fishing for him to say something that might force him in to incriminating himself.

"We found her body, Mr Barclay. We found Olive's body and we can now formally add her murder to an ever growing list of previous murders that you have committed. We know that you killed Jean Maxwell in Aberdeen in eighteen ninety-eight, though Jean Maxwell's real name had probably been Rose Sim."

Those words drew the biggest reaction from Barclay. His eyes stared at Jake for a few seconds and both Jake and Swanson thought they were actually about to illicit some form of statement from the Professor. As it was, he pulled back at the last moment and reverted to staring at the wall. Even whilst maintaining his silence the Professor had still, in actual fact, shown he knew more than he was saying by the manner in which he reacted.

"We further believe, Mr Barclay, that you also killed your wife, probably due to your affair with Rose Sim. Rose moved to Aberdeen with you and adopted the name of Jean Maxwell. All went well until Jean started to show some affection towards Tom Fleming. You couldn't live with that, could you, so you killed Jean and made it look as if Tom had done it. He went to the gallows and you went to Cambridge."

Barclay remained silent. At that moment there was a knock at the door and a constable took a step in to the room and asked if he might have a word with Inspector Swanson. Swanson left the room, but returned moments later accompanied by a smartly dressed gentleman, wearing a coat, hat and carrying a rolled up umbrella.

"Barclay, what the hell have you done to end up in here?" he said and the man sitting opposite Jake spun round and then turned back again. Swanson took the other gentleman out of the room, he had already done what he would have been asked to do and that was identify Clive Barclay. Swanson soon returned and sat down again. This time it was Swanson who spoke first.

"Okay, Professor Barclay, let us now start from a point where we know you definitely *are* Clive Barclay and that you have been in Aberdeen, Edinburgh, Cambridge and London where it is now our firm belief that you committed murder on more than one occasion. Have you anything to say for yourself before we start formally charging you?"

Silence hung in the room for a little while longer before Barclay finally turned his eyes, first to Swanson and then to Jake. Eventually he spoke and when he did it was in the tone of the learned man that he was; a deep and mellifluous tone.

"You cannot charge me without evidence. As I haven't done anything wrong, there can't possibly be any evidence."

"Do you now admit that you were in London around Christmas time?" Jake then asked.

"I was."

"Living in the Middleton household, doing odd jobs for them?"

"Yes."

"So you'll have known the maid, Olive?"

"I knew her as a colleague."

"So you didn't get her pregnant?" Jake then said.

Barclay's eyes flickered slightly but, in the main, he held himself together. "No, I did not get her pregnant."

"Why did she leave the household then?"

"I don't know."

"Just coincidence that she left a few days before you did?" added Jake.

"Must have been."

"Why did you choose to leave?"

"Felt like a change of scene."

"But you were making money with the Middletons and now you are reduced to begging in Edinburgh. Seems a strange move to me," added Jake.

"Sometimes you just get that urge to move on," Barclay insisted.

"Especially if you've just murdered someone," said Jake bluntly.

Barclay stared hard at Jake. "I haven't murdered anyone and even if I had you couldn't prove a thing."

Jake now leaned forward.

"Okay, this is what we know already, Professor Barclay. In eighteen ninety-six, in Cambridge, you told the police that you awoke one morning to find your wife lying at the bottom of the stairs, dead. You claimed she had been taking medicine to help her sleep and that they must have affected her balance. No one questioned you very thoroughly at the time, seemingly happy to accept your account of events. You sat through the Coroner's inquest and were very happy to accept the verdict of accidental death because you were one of only two people who knew that not to be the case. Your maid, Rose Sim, also knew what had really happened to your wife. She sat with you, through the inquest, no doubt providing you with moral support and perhaps a whole lot more."

"What the hell are you insinuating?" Barclay snapped.

Jake ignored the question and kept on talking.

"After the inquest verdict, Rose left your house a few days before you did. You then moved to Aberdeen where, in eighteen ninety-eight, you claimed that you had come home from work to find your maid lying dead in your bed. The maid was known as Jean Maxwell by that time, but I'm willing to bet that she was really Rose Sim for I'm pretty certain that you were having a sexual relationship with her and had been doing so since before your wife's death."

Barclay was about to say something else but Jake held up his hand and silenced him.

"Please, let me continue," he said and Barclay sat back in his chair with a look of silent disgust. "You told the police you'd found the maid in your bed and that the glasses by the bedside proved that she must have had a gentleman friend with her and that this gentleman friend had to be her killer. Thanks, in no small measure to the evidence that you had planted, the finger was immediately pointed at the gardener, Tom Fleming. Yet again and quite amazingly, no one saw fit to question your account of what had happened and unfortunately, the investigating officer did little more than proceed to fit any evidence he did have, to that account. No one seems to have even bothered finding other suspects. So, Tom Fleming hangs and you, again, move on. In nineteen hundred and three, in Edinburgh, you again claim to have come home from work to find your maid dead in bed. You tell a similar story of glasses being left by the bed and some unknown male friend being responsible for the murder. The police, on that occasion, never did find any credible suspects, but again they seemed happy to accept your account of events. Now, this year in London, the maid, Olive goes missing shortly before you, yourself, decide to move on. Olive's body is found buried in the back garden of the house in which you carried out handyman jobs and gardening. One suspicious death and three murders, in four different locations and the only thing linking them all is your presence. Now, *Mr* Barclay, you are either incredibly unlucky to have had so many maids murdered whilst in your employment, or you are a cold-blooded killer. Now I know which one of those two my money is on."

"Circumstantial at best," Barclay said and looked away again. "You've said yourself that no one thought it necessary to question me at the time, so why are you doing so now?"

"For one thing it is only now that we have been able to piece together the chain of events and the part you played in them. Until then your accounts of these deaths had all been heard in isolation, so each investigating officer assumed that their death was the only one in which you had been present. We now know that there is a list of deaths, throughout the country, linked to you. Now, I ask again, do you have anything to say for yourself?"

Barclay pondered for a moment and then sat forward. "Any chance of a cigarette?"

"No," Jake replied quickly. "You can have a cigarette while you write your confession."

Barclay smiled. "You can't get a confession out of an innocent man, Inspector. At best you have suspicions galore, but not a scrap of evidence that even links me to these events."

"Don't be too quick to assume that the passage of time has, in some way, covered your tracks. We have a witness who will state in court that Tom Fleming was not a great one for alcohol and when he did drink it was always beer. Basically, from what we've been told, Tom would never had considered drinking wine and it also seems highly unlikely that a maid would risk losing her job by stealing a bottle of wine from her employer. After all, it's not as if you wouldn't have noticed the bottle was missing. I'm more inclined to believe that Jean, no let's call her Rose because that's who she really was, was dead in your bed because you had been there with her. You had had one last moment of intimacy with her prior to killing her. You had decided to kill her because you knew she was starting to have feelings for Tom, the gardener and you didn't like that. You decided to kill Rose and make it look as if Tom had done it. You planted a little evidence here and a little evidence there and then carried out your usual, well-rehearsed, statement to the police."

"I'm hearing plenty theory, Inspector, but no mention of anything that actually passes as evidence," Barclay insisted.

Jake smiled. "Ah, but I was keeping the best until last, Mr Barclay. Are you aware of the technique by which fingerprints can be taken from suspects and matched against evidence gathered at a crime scene?"

"I know all about fingerprints, Inspector, but fail to see what that has to do with anything you've said to me here today."

"The investigating officer, back in ninety-eight, maybe didn't ask all the questions that he should have, but he did do one thing that has turned out to be very beneficial to this inquiry."

Barclay looked a little concerned and Jake could tell that he was beginning to break down the wall that Barclay had built around himself.

"There's nothing he could have done ten years ago that would matter today," Barclay said, but Jake sensed in the man's tone that he was starting to get worried.

"Ten years ago, Professor Barclay, the investigating officer picked up the two glasses from the bedside table and placed them in a bag. No one else has touched those glasses and they have lain in a cupboard in the Police Office in Aberdeen ever since. Obviously fingerprints could not be checked in eighteen ninety-eight, but they can now."

Barclay no longer looked so smug. "There's no way that fingerprints could be checked after all these years," he said.

"Oh, but they can," added Jake. "We'll take your fingerprints in a moment and then have them checked against those that are on the glasses. I'm willing to bet every penny I have that only your prints will be on both of those glasses because I doubt if your lady friend ever touched them. I think she was already dead before you set the scene and those lovely fingerprints of yours is what will prove me right and put a noose around your neck."

"I don't believe you," Barclay added, though his expression told a different story.

"Just give me a minute," Jake then said and he left the room. He was away for a little while, but when he did return he was carrying a sheet of paper. "I took this with me from Aberdeen as I had a feeling I would need it."

As Jake finished speaking he slid the sheet of paper across the desk and invited Barclay to read it. It was part of the inventory of the evidence that had been gathered at the time Jean Maxwell had been murdered. It was clear for him and anyone else to see that amongst the items gathered were two glasses. To the right of the note about the glasses was a handwritten extra, which simply said *"No lip rouge on the glasses even though Jean was wearing rouge on her lips when she died. How could that be?"*

Barclay finished reading the paper and the blood visibly drained from his face. That look of confidence had gone completely and he even took the time to read the paper again, as if, perhaps, trying to find a way out within its prose. There wasn't one. He had never thought about the lip rouge and he knew how damning fingerprints could now be. Jake read his expression and pressed home his advantage.

"The fingerprints will be enough to get that guilty verdict in court, Mr Barclay, but I thought you'd also like to see that the question of the lip rouge rather blows a hole in your account of events. I'm told, by a number of lady friends that it is impossible to drink from a glass without some of their lip rouge transferring to that glass. How then had Rose managed to drink her wine without leaving any rouge marks on her glass?"

Barclay looked a broken man. His self-confidence had disappeared and he fell silent as he thought through how best to get himself out of this predicament. Jake continued to speak.

"I don't really need to prove anything else, Mr Barclay, because your conviction for the murder of Rose Sim will be enough to send you to the gallows. However, I *want* to prove you did the other murders and to that end, I and my fellow Inspectors will continue to gather evidence until we have more than enough to put a noose around your neck many times over. It really is such a pity that you can only hang once. Now, *Mr* Barclay, what do you have to say for yourself?"

Barclay remained silent for a few moments longer and then his whole demeanour changed. He sat upright in his chair and once more his face carried an expression of smugness. He even smiled.

"Very well, Inspector, it seems that I under-estimated you and that you do appear to have some evidence. What a pity."

"Do I get that confession now?" Jake then asked.

"Do I get my cigarette?" Barclay replied.

"You'll get that cigarette."

"Then you'll get your confession. However, before I say another word I want you to agree to transfer me to Cambridge for trial."

"I hardly think you are in a position to debate where justice will take its course, Mr Barclay. At the moment Aberdeen has jurisdiction as we have the strongest case. If you wish to change that, in any way, then you will have to make a full confession. It will then be up to others to decide where you are ultimately tried."

"I killed twice in Cambridge," Barclay then announced. "I never killed more than once anywhere else. Does that give Cambridge jurisdiction now?"

Both Inspectors picked up on the fact that Barclay had already confessed to a crime of which they knew nothing. How many more women had this man killed?

"Look, Mr Barclay," Jake then said," it seems that you have many murders to tell us about and I rather think you want to tell us now. You don't want to go to court for one crime when there are so many more for which you want to take credit. You want the world to know how clever you have been over the years, so when you eventually stand up in court, wherever that might be, you'll make the headlines around the country as one of Britain's most prolific murderers. So, we'll get you some paper and a pen and you can write down all that you've done. Only then can anyone decide where best to put you on trial."

Barclay smiled again. "Very well, Inspector, get me that paper and a cigarette and I'll list my most defining moments."

The grin on Barclay's face sent a shiver through Jake's body. This man was positively enjoying his moment of glory. For the moment he could say no more to Barclay, he just had to get out of the room. He stood up and made his way to the door with Swanson at his side. As they left the room a constable went in to keep an eye on the prisoner.

"You never said you had glasses with fingerprints on them," Swanson said as they made their way back to his office.

"That's because we don't," added Jake and it took a moment before Swanson understood what he was saying.

"You mean you were bluffing?"

Jake paused for a moment and then smiled.

"I suppose I must have been."

Swanson laughed. "Remind me never to play poker against you, Jake Fraser."

They sat down in Swanson's office. "I quickly realised that we really didn't have any actual evidence to hold against him, so I decided to invent some and see where it took us."

"So where did the inventory come from?

"The typewriter in your office. I had just finished what I thought was a rather authentic looking document when I had that flash of inspiration about the lip rouge. It crossed my mind that if Jean had never touched the glasses then there wouldn't have been lip rouge on them and there should have been."

"But how do you know she'd have been wearing lip rouge?"

"I didn't, but even ten years ago, a woman meeting with her lover would have wanted to look her best. Now obviously there wouldn't have been the same options back then, but I guessed that Barclay wouldn't have known that either."

"You're a crafty bugger, Jake Fraser," Swanson said and they both laughed. "Do you think they'll move him down to Cambridge for trial?"

"I shouldn't think so; there really is no need as his confession will give you all that you'll require to put him on trial here. We know he committed murder in this city and when he confesses to it, the noose can be placed around his neck."

"Happy days then," added Swanson with a grin.

He went off to arrange for a constable to take paper and a pen in to Clive Barclay. Jake remained in Swanson's office. On Swanson's return it was agreed that the paperwork, for the other murders, would be sent to Edinburgh for inclusion in their court presentation. Some of it was circumstantial, but the sheer weight of evidence was what would convict Barclay, even if they hadn't persuaded him to confess.

Clive Barclay eventually confessed to ten murders in total. Once he had started writing about himself and what he had done he had found it impossible to stop. He actually enjoyed telling everyone what he had done. Once he had finished and signed his statement, the papers were taken through to Swanson's office where the two Inspectors cast an eye over the detail of what Barclay had written.

Now that they knew *what* he had done, Swanson and Jake returned to the interview room to try and ascertain the *why* of what he had done. They both sat in silence as Barclay began to explain his actions.

"I had a privileged upbringing. We always had maids and I used to think, when I was young, that there could be no woman as beautiful as some of the maids who worked for my father. When I was fifteen I convinced myself that I was in love with our maid and one night I tried to get in to her bed. She laughed at me. She told me not to be silly and that being the son of the master did not give me any right to expect sexual favours from her. I lay in my own bed for three nights crying at the thought of how I'd been rejected and I vowed to gain my revenge one day. I killed her three months later by pushing her in front of a tram. No one saw me do it and after I had killed once, I realised how easy it was going to be to kill again."

"Have you ever actually loved anyone in your life, Mr Barclay?" Swanson then asked.

"I loved my mother and I really did think I loved that first maid. Apart from those two, the part that women have played in my life has pretty much been at my direction. There was never any requirement for me to love them, they simply served a purpose until I decided they were no longer needed. Maids became an easy option as they could hardly complain about anything that the master did."

Jakes anger boiled over. "You really are a complete shit, aren't you Mr Barclay? I hope you're arrival in Hell is a swift one and that you suffer for all eternity for the crimes that you have committed."

Barclay smiled and once more Jake's blood ran cold.

"I was never going to heaven, Inspector. I read my bible when I was young and to me, heaven was always a place where I'd be bored. You see, I've always had what others might describe as a nasty streak running through me, so the Gates of Heaven were always destined to remain closed for me. That being the case it made sense to enjoy myself and if Hell is my final destination then so be it."

"So murder has been your idea of enjoying yourself?" Swanson added with some disgust in his tone.

Barclay took a moment to reply. "No, I would argue that the maids provided my enjoyment; having to kill them was just an unfortunate turn of events."

"Tell me," Jake then said, "I was right to assume that Jean Maxwell really was Rose Sim?"

"Yes she was. Rose, bless her, really loved me. She never quite understood how employers and employees are supposed to get on. She was very free with her favours and as long as they were coming in my direction I was more than happy having her in my life and my bed. However, once she started fraternising with that Tom Fleming then I knew it was time to move on."

"What had your wife done to make you want to move on from her?" Jake then asked.

"Ah yes, poor Netty. I suppose she didn't do anything, that was her problem, she *never* did anything. She denied me my conjugal rights so I turned to Rose for a little comfort and quickly realised that Rose offered me all that I needed and having a wife was suddenly nothing more than a distraction. I crushed some of Netty's tablets and put them in her bedtime drink. She really did go for a walk around the house that night, so it very easy to give her a little nudge once she reached the top of the stairs. It was a beautiful sight seeing her tumble down that stair and then lie so wonderfully still at the bottom."

"Did Rose witness what happened?"

"Good grief, no. I never work when there are witnesses around. No, what Rose said at the inquest was all true."

"Do you have any conscience at all?" Swanson then asked.

Barclay smiled again. "None whatsoever. In fact if I could do it all over again I do believe I would."

Barclay filled in a little more detail to the crimes he had committed and an hour later Jake and Swanson finally left the room. Two constables stepped in to the room to keep an eye on Barclay. Swanson and Jake went back to his office and Swanson produced a bottle of beer from one of his desk drawers.

"He's quite insane," Swanson announced, holding up the bottle by way of asking Jake if he wanted some. Jake nodded and Swanson produced a couple of glasses from the same drawer.

"And yet he knew exactly what he was doing," added Jake. "Every crime was expertly planned to always make it look as if he were the innocent party. Had we not started to piece together the sheer number of crimes committed by this man, then he would most certainly still be out there looking for his next victim."

Swanson poured the beer and handed a glass to Jake. "Let us drink to the success of buying that man a one way ticket to Hell."

"I'll drink to that," said Jake and both men drank some of the beer.

"Do you want to tell Inspector Biddlecombe, or will I?" Swanson then said.

"I'll need to get back to Aberdeen, so I'll leave it to you to tell Biddlecombe. He has played a major part in this success as well."

"Yes, it can't be often that a murder has been solved by the direct input of three Inspectors in three, entirely different Forces."

And with that both men sat down to finish their glass of beer and discuss matters that did not require a Detective's mind. It had been a new experience for them all to work so closely with officers from a different part of the country and it had been an experience that they had all enjoyed.

It would be half an hour later that Jake finally left Swanson's office and began his journey back to Aberdeen. This particular investigation had come to an end and a man would go to the gallows for his crimes. Jake had every right to feel satisfied as he made his way to the station.

***

NINETEEN

Wednesday 24th June

Margaret and Jake had breakfast together. Jake had been late in getting back from Edinburgh and had slipped in to bed without waking Margaret. He had slipped an arm around her waist and lost himself in the warmth of her body.

Jake told Margaret about the arrest in Edinburgh and how that was one more madman off the streets. Margaret smiled with pride as she listened to what Jake had to say. Margaret had boiled a couple of eggs and they had bread and tea along with them. As Jake put his coat on and prepared to leave he turned to Margaret.

"Have you ever heard of an organisation known as the Aberdeen Voice for Women?"

Margaret thought for a moment. "Not that I can recall. Why?"

"Some windows were smashed at the weekend and they seem to be taking the credit for it," explained Jake.

"And you think it might be some of our more militant ladies?" Margaret then asked.

"Not at all; I've never heard of them and I just wondered if you might have heard the name mentioned at some of your meetings."

"Well I haven't," Margaret said again and Jake decided not to say anymore as he felt whatever he might say would probably be taken up the wrong way by his wife and he really didn't want to annoy her.

Jake kissed Margaret and wished her a good day. He then left the house and made his way down to street level. Margaret, on the other hand, hurried to get dressed. She was going to see Sadie Ashton and ask what she might know about the Aberdeen Voice for Women.

When Jake arrived at work he was immediately met by Sergeant Mathieson who seemed slightly agitated.

"They've struck again," he said before Jake even had time to take his coat off.

"Who have?"

"The Aberdeen Voice for Women activists."

"What have they done this time?"

"Smashed the front window of Councillor Manning's home and left this in his letter-box."

Mathieson handed a sheet of paper to Jake on which had been printed the following statement:

It is time for women to have a say in the government of this country. It is time for women's views to be heard.

The Aberdeen Voice for Women   AVW

Jake finished reading the paper and looked up. "I take it Councillor Manning is not very happy?"

"Councillor Manning was not chosen at random, sir. He is one of the most vocal members of the current Council and constantly speaks out against the actions of Mrs Pankhurst and her followers. If this AVW is a branch of the Suffragette Movement then Councillor Manning, for one, will want all-out war against them."

"Okay, leave it with me. I'll go and see him later today and give him the chance to let off some steam for a while. In the meantime, step up the patrols around other Council Members, especially those who are known to actively support Manning's views."

"Very good, sir."

Jake then sat down and took stock of what the day might hold for him. He had paperwork to complete and send to Frederick Swanson concerning the Clive Barclay case. He needed to visit the Grammar School and speak to some of the teachers who would have worked with Edith McIntosh and he still needed to find a positive link between the murders of Edith McIntosh and Archibald Diamond. It would be a busy day indeed.

But before he did anything further he made himself a cup of tea and worked through the morning mail.

It was, therefore, after ten when he left Lodge Walk and enjoyed a casual stroll up to the Grammar School. He made contact with the Rector again and found him a little more sociable. He arranged for Jake to be taken over to the Lower School and for three teachers to be asked to have a word with them. They would be notified as to when to leave their class.

Jake sat in a small room that was being used to store books. There was a small table and two, wooden chairs. They weren't very comfortable but they served the purpose of giving them somewhere to sit away from prying eyes.

The first teacher to be asked to see Jake was Miss Grainger. She remembered Jake from his first visit and was quick to say that she doubted if she would be able to tell him much more.

"You said, the last time we spoke, that you were quite good friends with Edith McIntosh but I never actually asked if you had been to her house at any time?"

"I was there on a couple of occasions."

"Were you aware of Miss McIntosh's father's collection of miniatures?"

"No. As I said, I was at the house a couple of times but only for an evening of chat and that was usually about our shared interests."

"Like Gilbert and Sullivan?" suggested Jake.

Miss Grainger smiled. "Yes, interests like that."

"Going back to the suspected break-in at your home, Miss Grainger; if nothing was stolen why did you think someone had been in your home?"

"As I said before, Inspector, it was just a feeling. Call it a sixth sense, but I came home that night to a distinct feeling that someone had been there in my absence."

"And had they been in your home then they would have had to have had a key to get in; am I right?"

"I suppose so," Miss Grainger said.

"Any yet you never gave your key to anyone else?" Jake added.

"No."

"So how would they have acquired a copy of your key?"

Miss Grainger thought for a moment. "I really don't know, Inspector. Look," she then added quickly," I may have been completely wrong that night. I only mentioned it after what had happened to poor Edith; I rather wish I hadn't now."

"On the contrary, Miss Grainger, the thief visiting you may well be the biggest clue we have in this whole, sorry affair."

Miss Grainger did not enquire as to how that might be. In fact she said nothing more and Jake decided that there was probably nothing more to learn from her so he asked her to bring one of the other teachers to him. Moments later he was sitting opposite Maud Schivas, a tall, almost manly woman, who exuded a strong *don't mess with me* attitude.

"I started here the same day as Edith," Maud began, "but we never became friends."

"Were you ever at her house?"

"I was there once. We had had a Christmas night out and a few of us went back to Edith's for a sherry and a laugh. She had a good sense of humour, Edith and was always ready for a laugh."

"Were you aware of any items in her house that may have been worth a lot of money?"

"I noticed that her house was full of items but they meant nothing to me. I'm not a things person, Inspector; a vase is a vase, that's all."

"Did Edith ever speak to you about her father's collection?"

"Not specifically. I believe she did say, one day, that her father had left her a collection that was worth a considerable amount of money and that someday she might get around to selling it."

"But you didn't know what that collection actually was?"

"I don't believe she ever said."

"And did she ever mention selling that collection?"

"Not to me."

"Okay, thank you very much, Miss Schivas."

The third teacher to come through to see Jake was very young. She had only recently arrived at the school but had been placed under Miss McIntosh's guidance for her first year. She had taken the death of Miss McIntosh very badly as, although they were not close friends, they had been close colleagues in school.

Prunella Holmes was very pretty and Jake noted she had blonde hair. Her face was lightly touched with make-up and she wore a black dress that followed the curves of her body most effectively.

"She was a lovely woman," Prunella had said, "I can't imagine anyone wanting to kill her."

"Did she speak about much outside of work?"

"Not much. I always thought she was quite a private person."

"Were you ever at her home?"

"Oh, no, there would never have been any reason for me to do that."

"Did Miss McIntosh ever talk to you about anything that her father may have collected?"

"She did make me blush one day when she said that her father had collected items that were not really suitable for ladies. She did not, thankfully, elaborate on that comment."

"Were you aware of Miss McIntosh having many friends outside of work?"

"She was seeing a gentleman friend just before her death, but I don't think it was in a romantic way."

"Would that have been Peter Ash?" Jake then asked.

"Yes, that's the gentleman. I think Edith really liked him and it was nice to see her happy."

"In the short time that you have been here, Miss Holmes, have you been aware of anyone hanging around the school or acting in a threatening manner?"

Miss Holmes shook her head. "Not that I've noticed. You don't think someone is angry with the school, do you?"

"At this precise moment, Miss Holmes, I'm not sure what to think but, no, I'm fairly sure that other teachers are not in any danger."

"But Miss McIntosh and then Mr Diamond, surely two murders cannot be put down to pure coincidence?"

"Oh, I don't believe it is coincidence, Miss Holmes, I just haven't worked out a connection between Mr Diamond and Miss McIntosh, other than the fact they both worked at the same school. Anyway, my thanks for your help."

Miss Holmes left the room and Jake sat thinking for a few moments. It seemed as if Edith McIntosh may have spoken about her father's collection without ever actually explaining what it was. If she had really been that offended by it then maybe she had sold it at the earliest opportunity. Even if she hadn't, there still seemed no reason for anyone else finding out about the collection and it's potential worth.

But even if someone had found out about it and passed that information on to a third party, how would they then have known where to find the miniatures? Surely Miss McIntosh would never have been in the habit of giving out that much detail and if the intruder had not known exactly where to look then he had to have been in the house for quite a while, to allow him to search it properly. Had he killed Miss McIntosh and then began his search? Was that why he killed her so that he could take all the time in the world to search for the miniatures?

As usual, the theory was sound for Miss McIntosh, but nothing fitted so neatly for Mr Diamond's murder. No matter how much thought Jake gave to the case he could not come up with a motive that fitted the two murders. He was giving himself a headache thinking about the murders so decided to switch off for a little while. He stood up and left the school, letting the office know as he went.

***

Margaret had taken the tram as close as she could to Sadie Ashton's house, before walking the short distance that remained and knocking on the door. Sadie's housekeeper opened the door and invited Margaret in to the house. She then left Margaret sitting in the lounge while she went to notify Mrs Ashton of her visitor.

Sadie came in to the room moments later. She smiled broadly, clearly pleased to see Margaret.

"Has there been some change to tomorrow's meeting?" she asked as she sat down beside Margaret on the settee.

"No, nothing like that," Margaret replied, suddenly feeling a little awkward being there.

"So, do what do I owe the pleasure of this visit?" Sadie then said.

Margaret thought for a moment. Now that she had Sadie in her presence she couldn't actually think how best to phrase what she wanted to say, without causing offence to her friend. She couldn't come straight out and accuse Sadie of militant action when she had no proof, as yet, of who might be involved in the breaking of windows around Aberdeen. She eventually decided to keep her comments, at least initially, as general as possible.

"Do you think it is possible that we may have other, more militant, Suffragette supporters within the city?"

"I'm sure we have, Margaret, but you didn't come rushing over here today to throw general statements at me. What is it you really want to ask?"

Margaret could feel her face redden. "I'm not here to accuse you of anything, Sadie, but I don't mind admitting that I did think of you when I heard that some windows had been broken over the weekend."

"Where were these windows?" Sadie asked.

Margaret knew that she shouldn't really be sharing this information with anyone else, but she had dug her own hole, for the moment and needed to continue with the conversation for a little longer.

"At a Gentlemen's Club, I believe."

Sadie smiled. "I believe I did suggest that a few windows needed to be broken, Margaret, but what I omitted to say was that those windows would never have been in a Gentlemen's Club, they would have been far more important windows than that."

"So you don't know who was behind the action?" added Margaret.

"No, I don't."

"Have you ever heard of the Aberdeen Voice for Women?" Margaret then asked.

Sadie shook her head immediately. "No, should I have?"

"Apparently they are trying to take the credit for smashing the windows," said Margaret, hoping that no one else, especially Jake, would ever find out what they were discussing.

"Then perhaps we really do have new players in the game?" Sadie suggested.

"New players who believe that smashing windows is the way to win their argument?"

"Irrespective of their methods, Margaret, new players are always welcome. I don't know about you, but it fills my heart with joy at the fact that fellow believers continue to increase in number with each passing month. If men can't see that the tide is turning against them, then they must be blind."

"Men may see the tide turning, Sadie, but they won't even begin to support our cause if they feel threatened by it. Smashing windows is no way to make anyone's presence known."

"But it *did* make their presence known Margaret and that is my point. Whether you like the idea, or not, militant action does get you publicity."

Although other issues were discussed over a cup of tea when Margaret left Sadie's home, a little while later, those were the words that kept rolling around in her mind.

***

It was early evening when Jake arrived at the home of Councillor Manning. He had meant to be there earlier, but had decided to call on Arthur Fleming first. Jake had felt it necessary to tell Fleming that the real murderer of Jean Maxwell had now been caught and that the name of Tom Fleming was now clear. Arthur acknowledged that the news would not bring his brother back, but at least he could now claim his brother's body and have him properly buried in consecrated ground. Arthur had thanked Jake for at least giving him the chance to put his brother's soul to rest.

Jake had then moved on to Councillor Manning whose house, on Queen's Road, was set back from the street with a curved driveway and a large covered doorway. There were no outward signs of damage and Jake was left to assume that workmen had already been out to replace the broken panes. Jake knocked on the door and waited for someone to come.

Five minutes later and Jake was in the sitting-room, sitting on a soft and comfortable settee and sipping at a cup of tea, which had been offered to him. Councillor Manning was sitting across from Jake in a large chair, which he claimed had been specifically designed for him and him alone. Manning held a large glass, full of whisky, in one hand and a cigarette in the other. He was a fat man, pompous in his attitude to everything and the type of man who, generally, gave Councils a bad name.

"So, Inspector, have you caught the women responsible for breaking my windows?" Manning had asked, after they were seated.

"I'm afraid we haven't, Councillor. There is very little to go on and had it not been for the leaflet laying claim to breaking your windows, we'd be none the wiser as to who might have done it."

"But they did lay claim, which must make life easier for you," insisted Manning.

"Just because someone lays claim to a certain action doesn't actually mean that they did it, Councillor."

Manning dragged hard on his cigarette and loudly exhaled smoke towards the ceiling. "What the hell do you mean by that? Who would take the trouble to print off a leaflet claiming to be representing some militant women's group and then not actually take part themselves in any action that might follow?"

"Someone trying to undermine the views that these women are trying to put forward?" suggested Jake. "If you disagree with the Suffragette Movement then what better way to garner public opinion against them than to make it look as if they were undertaking a wave of violence."

"You can't seriously believe that, Inspector?"

"I have to keep an open mind until the evidence says otherwise," Jake replied. He really didn't like this man and if someone was intent on breaking all his windows, every night, Jake wasn't sure that he'd get too excited about finding them. As it was he had to at least appear to be going through the correct motions. "Did you see, or hear anything last night?" he then asked.

"My wife and I sleep at the back of the house so, no, we didn't hear anything."

"Is there any chance that your staff might have heard something?"

"We do not have live-in staff, Inspector, so it was only my wife and I who were at home when this happened."

"So it was the breaking glass that woke you?" Jake enquired.

"Actually we didn't realise the windows were broken until early this morning when my wife got up to get herself a glass of water. She woke me at that time and we contacted the police. A couple of uniformed officers called but they couldn't do very much."

"How long have you been a Councillor?" Jake then asked.

"Eight years."

"And in that time, I believe you have spoken out quite strongly against women's rights?"

"I speak my mind, yes," replied Manning, in a tone that said *but that's what I'm supposed to do, isn't it?*

"So you don't believe that women should have a say in politics?"

Manning looked surprised to even be asked the question. "But, of course, I don't believe that women should have a say in politics. How can they have a say in something they could never understand?"

"How do you know that women don't understand politics, Councillor Manning, have you asked any of them?"

Manning wasn't sure if he liked this police officer's manner, but he did not go as far as to say so. Instead he continued to play his part in their conversation.

"I don't need to speak to any of them, it's obvious that women could never understand the complexities of politics. Politics was created for men and that's how it ought to remain, as far as I am concerned. There simply is no need for women to get involved in the making of decisions, which men are already perfectly able to make."

Jake thought about Margaret and knew, that in their household, he would never dream of making a decision on Margaret's behalf, unless she had specifically asked him to do so. As Jake heard what was tumbling from Councillor Manning's mouth he could begin to see why Margaret and her friends were so annoyed at the lack of interest being shown in the their argument to be given the vote.

"It is possible," Jake then said, "that your views have annoyed a number of people during your time on the Council. That being the case the list of culprits, who could have broken your windows, may go beyond a group of women."

"But they've told you they did it," added Councillor Manning with increasing frustration.

"That's assuming the Aberdeen Voice for Women actually exists," countered Jake. "I have to tell you, Councillor that neither I nor any of my colleagues have ever heard of them."

"Which doesn't, in itself, mean that they don't exist, Inspector."

"Very true, Councillor, but until we know a whole lot more about them I'm not prepared to blame them for anything, just at the moment. However, should we prove, a little way down the line that the Aberdeen Voice for Women was responsible for the breaking of your windows then I assure you, Councillor, the full weight of the law will be thrown at them."

Councillor Manning looked at Jake for a moment. "I do believe you are having fun at my expense, Inspector and I'm not at all sure I like that."

"It's a few broken windows, Councillor, even if we catch the culprits there really isn't an awful lot that we can do, beyond ensuring they reimburse you for any costs that you may have incurred as a result of their actions."

"It sounds to me, Inspector, that you have every sympathy with these women. That perhaps makes it impossible for you to investigate this incident impartially?"

"Whatever I may, or may not, think, Councillor, nothing will get in the way of me investigating this incident. Keeping an open mind is not a crime in itself and I find it necessary, whilst doing my job, not to be led down one particular road when there may be others worthy of investigation."

"Have it your way," Manning snapped back, "but you've got what is tantamount to a confession and yet you still say it may be someone else."

"I simply say that I have never heard of the Aberdeen Voice for Women, Councillor and that until I know more about them and what they might stand for, I shall continue to keep an open mind."

Jake did not tarry much longer in the Councillor's house. He finished his tea and was on his way again. He walked home, enjoying the evening air and allowing his mind to clear of the day's work before facing Margaret. He always tried very hard to shield her from his work, even if that work was beginning to get closer to her own world of ideas and beliefs.

Jake was fairly sure that Margaret would never stoop as far as to smash windows or throw eggs at Councillors, but that did not deny her the right to support the actions of those who did. Jake had never had a personal cause that came anywhere near women seeking the vote, so he really could not fully understand what they were going through.

He pushed those final thoughts from his mind as he climbed the stairs and opened the door to their home.

***

TWENTY

Friday 26th June

Councillor Manning arrive at the Town House in the middle of the morning. He was attending a meeting of the Planning Committee and keen to get the day's business over and done with so that he could enjoy the weekend ahead. He had promised his wife a trip to Dundee so that they could visit their son. They had tickets for the train that afternoon and he hoped that the meeting would not take very long.

As he approached the door to the Town House he noticed a small crowd had gathered and he hurried his stride to get through the door before anyone could accost him. As it was, no one in the crowd seemed interested in getting too close to him. However, someone, somewhere in the middle of the crowd, chose to launch two eggs in his direction. Such was his intent to hurry through the front door of the Town House that Manning saw neither of the missiles coming.

The first hit him square on the head and the second landed on his back, spreading yoke across his hair and suit. He turned to remonstrate with the small crowd, which he now noticed were all women, but they had already started to disperse, clearly happy that their work that day was done. Manning hurried inside and made his way to the toilets where he attempted to wash the egg from his hair and face. He had just taken off his jacket when the door opened and Councillor Brady came in.

"In the name of heaven, Walter, whatever has happened to you?"

"Those bloody women and their call for the vote," Manning replied. "I can't imagine what they intend to achieve throwing eggs at Councillors."

Councillor Brady tried to hide his amusement as he attempted make the necessary noises of sympathy towards his council colleague. "Is this the same lot who broke your windows?"

"It's bound to be, isn't it? Well maybe the police will take this a little more seriously than they did the windows. This is a direct assault on my person and that must merit charges being brought."

"Do you know who threw the eggs?" Brady then asked.

"Not exactly, they were hidden in a crowd."

"So how will the police bring charges if *you* don't even know who did it?"

"It is for the police to discover who did it," Manning added. "I can only tell them what I know and they can take it from there."

"I wish you well, my friend," was Councillor Brady's last words before he made his way in to one of the cubicles.

***

Lucy Gill arrived on the early afternoon train from Glasgow. When she had left the Watt household, the previous Saturday, she had made her way to Glasgow to make contact with a man she often used to produce documents for her that looked both authentic and valuable. For a small cost she could acquire paperwork that might lead to her making a serious amount of money. All she needed were the ideas.

Lucy felt good to be back in Aberdeen. There was nowhere that she really called home, but she always thought that Aberdeen came the closest. Not that she had any intention of setting up a permanent home in Aberdeen; too many people might recognise her. She now stood on the platform, once more playing the part of a new arrival in town. Again she was immediately joined by two porters, keen to help her. There was no doubt her advancing years had not caused her to lose any of her appeal to men. She met both porters with her best smile but declined their offers of help. She only had a small bag and could manage herself. Both men looked disappointed that their services were not required.

Lucy left the station and walked down Guild Street to the end of Market Street. She paused again, deciding whether she should remain in the city centre, or whether she should go over in to Torry and find a small guest-house in which to lie low for a day or two. The idea of a guest-house appealed to her, but the desire to have some real comfort around her won the mental argument, so she made her way up Market Street and booked in to the Douglas Hotel.

She had to choose her lodgings carefully these days. It was a matter of remembering all the places she had run from and making sure she didn't make the mistake of going back. She only hoped, now she was back in Aberdeen that she did not bump in to Bainbridge, or anyone else she had conned over the years, whilst walking on Union Street, or visiting the shops.

Having booked in, Lucy made her way up to her room and placed her bag on the floor. She checked the view from her window, which amounted to nothing of any interest and then sat on the bed. It was comfortable and inviting and she thought about having a sleep but was concerned that if she did she might miss dinner and her stomach was already complaining.

She stood up and crossed to where she had left her bag. She picked it up and placed it on the bed. She opened it and removed what little in the way of clothing had been folded inside. She either hung those items in the wardrobe or placed them in the top drawer of the chest of drawers that lay under the window. She also took a book from her bag and placed it on the bedside table. She then put the bag back on the floor and lay back on the bed.

Her mind wandered back over days gone by. Her life had never been anything other than one endless journey around Scotland, hopefully keeping one step ahead of the police and hopefully always making enough money along the way to make that life as comfortable as possible. In the beginning it had been fun, but now it was tiring and now it was becoming little more than a chore. Lucy Gill needed to be Margaret Reid again, only this time for good. Somehow, Margaret had to re-establish her true identity and she could only achieve that by making enough from one last swindle to allow her to settle down somewhere.

That was why she was back in Aberdeen. That one last confidence trick that would bring in some serious money and allow her to live the rest of her life without constantly looking over her shoulder. That one last job would be another sale of fraudulent shares certificates, only this time the company did not actually exist and Lucy could only hope that no one looked any further than the writing on the paper.

Lucy had identified the man from whom she hoped to extract a large sum of money, but the final thoughts, regarding her latest plan, began to drift off in to the distance as she fell in to a deep sleep, the type of which she had not experienced in a long time.

***

Jake and Margaret arrived at the Queen's Rooms at half past seven. Jake had booked a table the day before without telling Margaret; he had wanted it to be a surprise. He had deliberately acted vague about their wedding anniversary so that everything, on the day, would be a nice surprise for her. He had only told her that morning that they were going out, though he had made no mention of their anniversary. As he had made his way to work he could imagine Margaret fuming around the flat, thinking her husband had forgotten what day it was.

As they sat down at their table, Jake took a box from his pocket and handed it across to Margaret. She looked at it and then up at Jake, noticing his eyes were smiling. He was enjoying this moment.

"What is it?" she eventually asked.

"Open it and see. I warn you now, future anniversaries won't always be as good in terms of what I buy you."

Margaret now smiled and opened the box. Inside was a necklace, a beautiful, silver necklace, which she felt sure would have cost Jake far more than he could probably afford.

"I wanted to mark the first anniversary with something special," he said, reaching across and taking Margaret's hand. "You make my life so special nowadays that I can't imagine how I survived before I met you."

"You managed," Margaret quipped, taking the necklace out and urging Jake to help her put it on. Once it was on and sitting properly, Margaret announced that she would not take it off, possibly for some time. Jake sat down again as Margaret took something from her bag and handed it to him.

"I'm afraid what I bought for you isn't anything like as good. I should never have doubted you remembering the date and wishing to mark it in some way."

Jake opened the bag he had been presented with and took out a book. It had been one that he had mentioned a few months back and he was delighted to receive it, even if he wasn't exactly sure as to when he would find the time to read it. He stood up and walked around the table so that he could take Margaret's hand and kiss the back of it. He had decided that kissing her full on the lips may not have been totally acceptable in a public place. She inclined her head slightly and smiled as he returned to his seat and started to read the menu.

Margaret always enjoyed coming to the Queen's Rooms. It had been one of the first places that Jake had taken her after they had met and each time they had returned since, they had always tried to make it feel like it was the first time all over again. They tried to maintain the romance of the moment for, in doing so, they felt they might retain the romance in their relationship.

They ordered their food and Jake chose a bottle of wine to accompany their food. It was unusual for them to be so extravagant, but Jake felt a wedding anniversary was the perfect time to be extravagant and he had already decided that the boat would be well and truly pushed out in the course of the evening. After the meal had been completed they ordered coffee and held hands across the table as they drank it. The restaurant management realised that they were witnessing a special occasion at table four and offered them a liqueur with the last of their coffee, which they both accepted.

By the time they left the restaurant they were both feeling the effects of the alcohol. Neither was prone to drinking much and by their own standards the night had produced a heady mix. The clung to each other as they made the relatively short journey home. Whether it was the effects of the alcohol, or simply the romance of the evening, but they could not wait to fall in to bed.

It was very late before either of them felt the need for sleep.

***

<u>TWENTY-ONE</u>

Sunday 28th June

Jake and Margaret were sitting at the kitchen table. A pot of tea lay between them and having just finished a freshly boiled egg, they were now enjoying the toast Margaret had made to go with them. Jake was casting an eye through the local newspaper, from the day before and Margaret was reading a book. They were enjoying the peace and quiet though, unknown to them, that was about to be shattered

Jake heard the knocking at the door first. He glanced across at Margaret with a look of annoyance and then looked at the clock lying beside him on the table; it was just after ten o'clock.

"Who can that be?" Jake said, rather sharply.

Margaret remained as calm as ever. "I suggest that you go to the door and find out."

Jake folded the paper and threw it down on the table. He then pushed his chair back and left the room. Whoever was at the door was still knocking and Jake could sense an urgency that convinced, even before he opened the door, that the caller was bringing him news from his work.

Jake opened the door and Sergeant Mathieson was standing on the landing. He looked apologetic and was soon backing that up in words.

"I'm so sorry to bother you, sir, but we have someone at Lodge Walk and I rather thought you'd want to be the one to interview her."

Jake looked a trifle confused. "Who might that be?"

"A Miss Prunella Holmes, she's a teacher at……"

"The Grammar School," Jake added, "yes I know, I've already spoken to her. What has happened to Miss Holmes?"

"She's been burgled, sir, and the fact you have spoken to her already explains why she wants to speak to you now," Mathieson then said.

Jake thought for a moment. "You'd better come in, Sergeant, I need to change my clothes before I go anywhere."

Jake led Mathieson through to the kitchen where Margaret greeted him with a smile and the offer of a cup of tea. Mathieson glanced at Jake, as if seeking his permission before answering.

"I'll be a little while, Sergeant, so sit yourself down and enjoy your tea and my wife's company."

"Thank you, sir," said Mathieson, pulling a chair back from the table and sitting down. Jake left the room and went through to the bedroom where he quickly washed and changed in to his work clothes. By the time he returned to the kitchen, Mathieson and Margaret were deep in conversation and Mathieson's teacup was half empty.

Jake gave Margaret a kiss on her cheek and informed her that he' be back as quickly as he could. Mathieson then gulped down the last of his tea and the two men set off for Lodge Walk. The walk down Schoolhill had been quite pleasurable as the sky was covered in only light cloud and the sunshine was getting through to warm the air.

It did not take long for the two men to cover the distance between Rosemount Viaduct and Lodge Walk. They went straight to the interview room, where Mathieson had left Miss Holmes and found her finishing off a cup of tea that had been provided for her by the Desk Sergeant.

Jake and Mathieson sat down. Miss Holmes was looking as pretty as ever, dressed in her Sunday best and with just a hint of make-up on her face. Jake was the one to speak first.

"Good morning, Miss Holmes, I had not expected to see you again so soon."

"And in somewhat distressing circumstances."

"Indeed. My Sergeant informs me that you have been burgled, Miss Holmes, would you be kind enough as to tell us what happened?"

"I was out at the theatre last night, Inspector and did not get home until after eleven. As soon as I entered my flat I sensed that something wasn't quite right. I know that I had closed all the internal doors, prior to leaving and yet one of them was slightly ajar on my return. I called out, but there was no one there. I walked around the flat and checked for evidence of someone else being there. I found nothing, though two, small ornaments do appear to be missing."

"Are these ornaments worth much?"

"I shouldn't think so, they were bought during visits to Glasgow and I certainly didn't pay much for them."

"Was the door to your flat forced?" Jake then asked.

"No."

"So someone had a key?" Jake then suggested.

"If they have then I don't know how that can be. I've never given a key to my flat to anyone else."

"And you say there were no other signs that anyone had been in your property apart from the two items that are missing?"

"That is correct."

"Where is it that you live, Miss Holmes?"

"On Esslemont Avenue, directly across the street from the school. I took the flat for the very reason that it was so close to my work."

"Have you ever had anything like this happen to you before?"

"Never."

"Have you noticed anyone hanging around your property in recent days?"

"No."

"Has anyone at work been asking you questions about your domestic situation?"

Miss Holmes looked shocked. "Surely this can have nothing to do with my colleagues at work? Are we not the victims in all this?"

"A growing number of you are the victims, but the fact that the burglar appears to have a means of access to your houses and also some knowledge of your domestic habits, leads me to deduce that someone, close to you all, has to be working with the burglar. Someone is passing him information and may even be gaining access to your house keys. Only in the school do you all come together in one place. It is the only time that someone could be getting close enough to you to gain information."

"Apart from poor Miss McIntosh and Mr Diamond, I wasn't aware of anyone else being targeted, if that is the correct word."

"Miss Grainger reported the fact that someone had been in her home while she had been out one night. As nothing was taken from her home she did not tell the police until after Miss McIntosh had been murdered. However, if Miss Grainger was the first victim then it further adds fuel to the fire of our theory that we have a burglar on the loose, but one who is more than willing to turn to violence to maintain his freedom and his anonymity."

"Miss Grainger has never mentioned anything at work about being burgled."

"As I said, she could not be sure that someone had actually been in her home, but her senses indicated that that may have been the case. However, my main concern in all this is the fact that doors never seem to be forced. It seems as if the burglars have keys to the properties and if that really is the case then that means someone, very close to all the Grammar School teachers, is gaining access to your keys with a view to having them copied."

Miss Holmes suddenly looked distressed. She had not stopped to consider the facts of the matter, she had simply assumed she had been the victim of a random act of violence and that that would be the end of the matter. The thought, however, that someone might have a key to her property and might then return at some later date, had distressed her enormously.

"You don't think he'll come back, do you?" she then asked.

"I shouldn't think so," Jake replied in as comforting a tone as he could muster. "The burglar has seen what you have in your home, Miss Holmes and obviously decided that only those two items, of which you speak, were worthy of his attention. There would now be no reason for him to call back at your flat, however, as an improvement on your personal security, I would suggest that you have the lock changed to your front door."

"I will arrange for that immediately, Inspector."

Sergeant Mathieson spent a little more time taking detailed notes from Miss Holmes before arranging for a constable to accompany her home and to check her flat before leaving again.

Mathieson then joined Jake in his office.

"Well, sir, what do you make of that?"

"Pretty much what I said through there; it now seems clear that someone who knows these teachers quite well, is passing information to the burglar. Armed with a key and knowledge that the house ought to be empty, the burglar knows, even before he gets there that the robbery is going to be relatively straightforward."

"Perhaps we're looking for a locksmith?" Mathieson suggested.

"We may indeed, but we are also looking for someone at that school who is working with the criminal. These are not truly random choices. These are people living alone and who are, generally, out at the time the burglar first calls."

"But who could that be?"

"I have no idea who it might be and just at the moment, little notion as to how we will even begin to identify the culprit. There is something else that's been bothering me," Jake then said.

"What would that be, sir?"

"I still can't help wondering why Edith McIntosh and Archibald Diamond needed to die."

"I thought we'd already decided that they must have disturbed the burglar and he'd panicked," added Mathieson.

"This seems to be a burglar with relevant information concerning his targets. He has access to their properties and he knows they'll be out. Why, then, would he twice be caught in the act by these people coming home?"

"He took longer to do the job than he thought?" suggested Mathieson.

"But there was no job at Mr Diamond's. He could have been in and out in a matter of moments and yet he was still there when Mr Diamond got home. It's as if he wants them to come back so that he can kill them."

"So we're back to looking for a murderer who steals to cover his true motive for the crimes?" added Mathieson.

"But then there's the little matter of Miss Grainger and Miss Holmes. They both were visited by, what I assume, was the same burglar and yet nothing further happened to them."

Mathieson looked crestfallen. "It's all a bit of a mess, isn't it, sir? By the way," he then added quickly, "did you notice Miss Holmes had blonde hair?"

Jake smiled. "I'm paid to detect, Sergeant, so yes I did notice the colour of her hair."

"Could she be the mystery blonde who sold the miniature?"

"And if she were, why would she now be reporting a crime on her own home?"

"Another smokescreen, perhaps? What better way to throw us off the scent than to imply that you, too, are a victim when in fact you are the perpetrator?"

Jake pondered for a moment. "Perhaps, though I find it hard to believe that Miss Holmes could be a criminal."

"I agree, sir, but someone at that school has to be a criminal, if our theory is correct."

"Agreed, Sergeant, though we're no nearer to identifying that criminal than we were the day Miss McIntosh was murdered. Do you happen to know if the Chief Constable is in today?"

"Actually he is, sir. I believe I heard someone say he had come in to clear some paperwork, which was required by another Force."

"In that case, I'll see if he can spare me a few moments," concluded Jake as he left the room.

The Chief Constable was sitting at his desk, the surface of which was covered with paper from corner to corner. The Chief had a look on his face that seemed to indicate to Jake that he was not at all sorry to have been interrupted. He invited Jake to sit down and then sat back to hear what his Acting Chief Inspector had to tell him.

"Another Grammar School teacher has been burgled, sir. We now have, what appears to be four burglaries and two murders and the only solid lead is that they are all connected to the Grammar School."

"We'll come back to that in a moment, Jake," the Chief then said, "but first let me congratulate you on the good work that you and Mathieson have done with regard to catching Clive Barclay."

Jake smiled. "Thank you, sir, although it was anything but down to Mathieson and I that Barclay has now been caught and will, most certainly, hang. The investigation was a good example of co-operation across Forces, sir. I wish we always had that level of help during a murder inquiry."

"Well, at least we can lay claim to one success," the Chief added and then seemed to lose himself in deep thought for a few seconds. "Now, take me through the Edith McIntosh inquiry again, starting from the very beginning."

Jake then proceeded to talk the Chief Constable through the case, starting with the attempted burglary at Miss Grainger's home. He continued to cover what had then happened to Miss McIntosh, Mr Diamond and Miss Holmes.

"And in all the cases the burglar got in to the property either with a key or with a professional knowledge of locks?" asked the Chief.

"Yes, sir."

"But only Miss McIntosh and Miss Holmes had anything stolen?"

"Yes, sir."

"Then that has to be the only reason for everything that has happened. Someone set out to steal from Miss McIntosh and in the process was forced, for whatever reason, in to killing her. Everything else that has happened since has been to try to steer us away from that main event."

"But if we follow that theory, sir, then we can't explain why Miss Grainger was visited *before* Miss McIntosh."

The Chief thought for a moment. "Miss Grainger always said that she *thought* someone had been in her home. What if she had never been visited at all and it really all had been in her mind. That makes Miss McIntosh the first victim and everything else can more easily be explained."

Jake gave that some thought. "It would make more sense if that were the case."

"But however we look at this case there seems one inescapable fact and that is someone at the school is working with the burglar. You need to find that someone and then you'll find your killer."

"Our burglar has professional knowledge, sir, so I'll put the word out on the street and see what comes back. Someone might know who's active at the moment," added Jake.

"Always a good place to start, Chief Inspector," concluded the Chief Constable.

Jake left the room and made his way back to his office. He wasted little time in tidying up what little mess he had made and leaving the building. He hurried home, wishing to enjoy what was left of the day with Margaret.

***

Jake changed in to something a little less formal and they went back outside in to the warm sunshine. They decided to walk to the Victoria Park and sit in the sun for a little while.

Rosemount was busy with fellow Aberdonians, keen to take the air and get some exercise in the process. They cut through and walked up Esslemont Avenue, crossing at the top and continuing down Watson Street. From there they could enter the park, which they found to be very busy with families, sitting on the grass and enjoying the afternoon warmth.

Jake and Margaret were fortunate to arrive at one of the seats just as another couple were leaving. They sat down and watched the activity that was going on all around them. Dogs barked and children laughed and let out whoops of excitement. Margaret watched it all with a broad grin.

"What a lovely day to be out," she said.

"What a lovely way to forget the job I do," added Jake and Margaret gave his hand a squeeze. She could never fully understand how her husband dealt with the sights he was forced to see in the course of a day's employment. She had no idea how he managed to deal with those sights, but she did what she could to offer her support and could only hope that that helped him.

On the other side of the road lay the Westburn Park, though being more modern, it did not have the look of the Victoria Park, with its trees and ornate fountain. Jake could see that a group of scruffy looking boys were playing football across in the Westburn Park, something they would not have been allowed to do where Jake and Margaret were sitting. *Something for everyone,* thought Jake as he sat in quiet contemplation, enjoying the day.

Even though he had told Margaret that sitting there helped him forget the job he did, he still could not fully switch off and his mind continued to mull over certain issues relevant to the Edith McIntosh murder. He decided to go out again, in the evening and have a word with someone who was usually able to gather information from sources that Jake was never likely to reach.

They sat for about an hour and then stood up and started to make their way home. Once there, Margaret disappeared in to the kitchen to cook some steak and kidney that she had bought. While it was cooking they sat in the lounge and drank some sherry. After they had eaten their meal Margaret returned to the lounge and Jake made his apologies before going out for a little while.

He knew that Margaret was less than pleased with him, but he also knew that he needed to get the word on to the street about the Grammar School burglaries as soon as possible.

Jake made his way to a small hotel that lay just off the Castlegate. It was a family run affair and attracted a clientele that probably would not have been given a room anywhere else. They also had a small bar, at the back of the building, which tended to serve alcohol when it wasn't always legal to do so. As a result they attracted even more drifters who often dropped in for a drink, rather than be booking a room.

Jake was well known to the owners of the hotel, so when he walked through the front door no one raced to get out the back and make good their escape. They knew that their minor misdemeanours would not be of interest to this particular police officer and that his visit would have more to do with gathering information than actually arresting anyone.

Jake walked through the reception area to the bar at the back. He stood in the doorway and surveyed the occupants of the room. It was a small room and there were far more people drinking than there should be. Some glanced in Jake's direction but, generally, everyone carried on drinking and talking, oblivious to the fact there was police officer in their midst.

Jake finally spotted the face he was looking for. It was a dirty face, which was pretty much in keeping with the rest of the man. As Jake made his way nearer, he noticed the dirty face turn in his direction and recognition light up in the man's eyes.

"A word," Jake said over the last of the bodies that lay between him and the bar.

The man at the bar said something to the barman and then started to move in Jake's direction. They both then left the bar area and went outside. The man with the dirty face was known, to almost everyone, as Stinky. He was called that for obvious reasons as he rarely washed and only changed his clothes when he absolutely had to. As they stepped on to the pavement, Stinky took half a cigarette from one pocket and a match from the other. He struck the match on the wall and lit the end of the cigarette.

"What can I do for you, Inspector?" he then said, as a trickle of smoke came down both nostrils.

"What can you tell me about a series of burglaries that have taken place recently?"

Stinky took another drag on the cigarette. "Mr Fraser, there's been a lot of burglaries in Aberdeen, there always is, so you'll need to give me a lot more than that if you want me to help."

"These burglaries are connected to teachers at the Grammar School."

"Ah, yes, two of those teachers were murdered I believe?"

"They were. We know that miniature paintings, worth a lot of money, were taken from the home of one of the murdered teachers and we also know that someone tried to sell one of those miniatures here in Aberdeen. What we don't know, however, is who the burglar might be. He is clearly a professional at his trade and I wondered if you'd heard anything."

Stinky puffed on the cigarette and then dropped what was left of it on the pavement before standing on it. He seemed to be thinking for a moment, but when he spoke it was not to say what Jake was hoping to hear.

"I need another fag," was what he said as he disappeared back in to the hotel.

It was another ten minutes before Stinky reappeared. He was already smoking as he came out of the door and he moved a little closer to Jake.

"I've not heard anything beyond the fact the jobs were being done. It's certainly not one of the known lads around town, I can tell you that."

"Someone from outside Aberdeen?" suggested Jake.

"I'm not saying that, I'm just saying it's not one of the name's you might expect."

"We have a new player in the game?" Jake then said.

"That's the way it looks to me," added Stinky.

"Keep your ear to the ground," Jake then said, pushing some coins in to Stinky's hand, "and let me know if you hear anything. In the meantime, don't get too drunk with what I've just given you."

Stinky smiled, though his mouth showed far more gum than teeth. He liked Jake Fraser; for a police officer he was an honourable man. Jake turned and walked back in to the Castlegate. Stinky returned to his place at the bar; he now had more than enough money to finance a session that might help him forget just how bad life could be for him.

"Keep them coming until this runs out," he announced to the man behind the bar as he slapped some money on the counter.

"What you do, Stinky, rob a bank?" the man said.

"Yeah, something like that," grinned Stinky as he started drinking the first of many pints of beer.

***

TWENTY-TWO

Monday 29th June

Jake went to the Grammar School first thing that morning. Once again the Rector was less than enamoured to see Jake until he explained why he was there. At that point the Rector had slumped in to his chair with a look of utter dejection.

"What is happening, Inspector?" he then said. "I see no sense in choosing teachers to burgle."

"I know you won't want to hear me say this, sir, but it seems ever more likely that teachers are being burgled because another teacher is providing the thief with valuable information as well as, possibly, the house keys."

Morland Simpson looked even more outraged. It was beyond his comprehension that any of his teachers could be involved in anything even remotely criminal. They were all professionals with a reputation to maintain.

"You say this information had to have come from a teacher, but could it not, just as easily, have come from a pupil?" the Rector then suggested.

Jake shook his head. "I don't believe that a pupil would know the plans of the teachers. These burglaries have taken place when the occupant of the property has been out and entry has been gained, I am sure, by means of a key. No pupil could get close enough to a teacher to acquire their house keys and yet that is what must have happened before the thief could possess a copy of those keys."

Morland Simpson thought some more and eventually nodded. "I can see your point, Inspector, though I find it difficult to believe. Assuming that we do have a criminal in our midst, is there anything the school can do to help you catch him or her?"

"Firstly, don't say anything to anyone about us suspecting as teacher. We don't want to scare them off, just at the moment. However, it would be very helpful if you could think of any of your staff who might be experiencing financial difficulties? I'm thinking we're looking for someone who needs money fast, particularly as they have already tried to sell one of the items stolen from Miss McIntosh."

Morland Simpson thought some more. "Unfortunately, Inspector, as I told you the first time you called, I really do not know my staff on a personal level and even if I did, I feel sure that they would not wish me, of all people, to know about any financial problems they might be having."

Jake could see the sense in that comment. "Are many of your staff new to their posts?" he then asked.

Morland Simpson told Jake that only three teachers were new to their posts and Miss Holmes had been one of them. He went on to say that he had no reason to doubt the integrity of any of his staff and that no one, in particular, sprang to mind when pondering on the possibility of one of them now being crooked.

Jake decided there was little point in saying much more to the Rector. He stood up to leave, but turned back as he reached the door.

"Might I ask that you warn any of your staff who live on their own, to be more vigilant around their home, just in case the burglar chooses them next."

"Of course, Inspector, I will speak to them all personally."

"And also suggest, as diplomatically as possible that they think twice about the information they share around the school."

The Rector nodded again.

"Thank you," Jake then said and left the room.

An hour later, back at Lodge Walk, Jake had been sitting at his desk signing off some incident reports when the Desk Sergeant had popped his head around the door. He informed Jake that a young man was asking to speak to the officer investigating the murder of Archibald Diamond.

"I'll be along in a minute," Jake said.

A few minutes later, when Jake entered the interview room, he found a very young looking, very nervous, young man who was smoking a cigarette and tapping the top of the table at which he sat. He looked up as Jake entered, but said nothing. Instead he crushed the last of his cigarette in to an ashtray and picked up his cigarette case. He proceeded to light another one and inhale hard. Jake sat down.

"You asked to see me?" he then asked.

"Are you investigating the murder of Archibald Diamond?"

"I am. My name is Inspector Jake Fraser. Who might you be, sir?" Jake then asked.

The man seemed to be deciding whether, or not, to give a name, but then seemed to decide that he would.

"Ian Lord."

"And do you have information concerning the attack on Mr Diamond?"

"I believe I may have," Mr Lord said, though Jake still sensed the man was being very reticent in his response. There was another silence, which led to Jake prompting him, once more, for an answer.

"And that information is what exactly?"

"I didn't do it," Lord then announced.

Jake was rather taken aback. "I hadn't thought, for one moment, that you had, Mr Lord. However, I feel there is something you have come here to tell me, so please take your time and tell me what it is."

Once more Lord went quiet. He dragged hard on his cigarette and appeared to be wrestling with himself as to what he should do next. Jake was happy to sit and wait. Eventually Lord spoke again.

"I was at Archibald's flat on the evening he would have been attacked."

"Inside the flat?" Jake prompted.

"Yes."

"What time would that have been?"

"I arrived around eight in the evening."

"How long were you there?" Jake then enquired.

"About an hour."

"Why were you there?"

That was the question that appeared to cause Mr Lord the most difficulty when it came to providing an answer. He sat for what seemed like an eternity, his fingers tapping all the more on the table and his face contorted in an expression of inner turmoil. He finished his cigarette and squashed it in to the ashtray along with the others. Jake half expected him to light another, but he didn't. Instead he sat forward in his chair and his voice lowered as he spoke.

"Archibald and I shared a particular interest."

"A particular interest?" Jake repeated.

"We prefer the company of other men, if you get my meaning?" Lord then said.

"And you were together for an hour?"

"About that, yes."

"Was anyone else there at the time?" Jake asked.

"No."

"Did you get the impression that Mr Diamond was expecting someone else to visit him?"

"He didn't give me that impression, no. That was why I decided to come and see you, just in case you had my description and thought that I might have been his attacker."

"I'm very pleased you did come forward, Mr Lord. Is there anything else that you can tell me?"

"Archibald and I hadn't known each other for long, so I never really got to know the man properly. I can't tell you anything about him, if that was what you wanted to know."

"Were you at Mr Diamond's flat a lot?"

"A couple of times before that night."

"Was Mr Diamond pleased to see you that night, when you called?"

"He certainly seemed to be. A little surprised, perhaps, but not upset."

"And there was no indication that someone might already have been there?" added Jake.

"Definitely not. Mr Diamond was alone, I'm sure of that."

"Do you know if Mr Diamond had any other gentlemen friends who were prone to calling on him at home?"

"Mr Diamond was not promiscuous, Inspector, if he was with me then he was with no one else."

"And you felt that he was *with you*, Mr Lord?"

"Very much so. We may not have known each other for very long but we were already very close."

"If you don't mind me saying this, Mr Lord, but wasn't Mr Diamond a good bit older than you?"

"Age plays no part in a relationship, Inspector, if the two parties are comfortable with each other. Are you going to arrest me now?" Lord then asked.

Jake considered the question for a moment. "No, Mr Lord, I won't be arresting you. You have helped me with my inquiries and for that I am grateful."

Lord put his cigarette case in to his pocket and stood up. "Thank you for being so understanding, Inspector."

"Not at all, Mr Lord," concluded Jake, also standing up. He led the way from the room and accompanied Lord to the front door. He headed back to his office, though en route he was stopped by the Desk Sergeant.

"Sorry to bother you sir, but I have a Chief Inspector Will, whose based at Inverurie, wanting to have a word with you on the telephone."

"About what?" asked Jake.

"Apparently you have a discussion with him once a fortnight and today's the day," the Desk Sergeant explained.

"Well, today isn't going to be the day, Sergeant; I have far too much to do. Tell Chief Inspector Will that I'll phone him when I have a moment."

"Very good, sir," concluded the Desk Sergeant who then set off along the corridor.

Jake returned to his office and gave some thought to what Mr Lord had just told him. Obviously Lord had been the young man seen on the landing. Jake was happy to accept that Lord was unlikely to be the murderer, but at least he now had a clearer idea of the timescale of events as they had unfolded that night. Someone else had to have called on Archibald Diamond after nine o'clock, which meant that Diamond would have been at home when the visitor arrived.

How could that have been a burglar? Unless the burglar *had* been in the house when Diamond had returned from his walk. That being the case, was he then trapped in the house while Diamond and Mr Lord had their assignation? Had the burglar witnessed what had happened and had that then been the reason for the burglar killing Mr Diamond? Was it an outpouring of anger at having to watch two men having sexual relations with each other?

Jake knew many men who might have killed in circumstances like that.

Were that the reason for Diamond's death then it explained why there had been so much violence shown towards him. It also explained why the burglar had felt the need to kill again. The motivation for him killing Mr Diamond was totally different from that of Miss McIntosh. Jake felt sure he was definitely just looking for one person.

He sat forward once more and turned his attention to the paperwork that lay before him.

***

Lucy Gill was now ready to put what she hoped would be her final plan in to operation. The man she needed to meet was called Anthony Wilson. He was in his fifties and keen to find himself a second wife. Lucy had actually seriously thought, at one time, that marrying Wilson might actually be the easier route to take. After all, the man had money and a nice house on Holburn Street. He was still a fine looking man and might have made an excellent husband had it not been for the fact he was man of deep, religious beliefs and an intense hatred of alcohol and anyone who chose to drink it.

There was no way that Lucy could spend the rest of her life without the prospect of a drink now and again. Anthony, therefore, had to be no more to her than another victim.

Wilson had invested a large sum of money in The Forsyth Temperance Hotel, on Union Street. As a result of that investment he tended to spend every lunchtime in the dining room enjoying someone else's cooking. He had also become a close friend of the manageress, Miss Jack, though there had never been any sign of their relationship blossoming and of Miss Jack contemplating becoming Mrs Wilson.

Lucy had met Wilson twice before, on visits to Aberdeen and she already knew that the man had more than a passing interest in her. She had felt, after their last meeting that she was definitely on that list of possible wives. Although not keen to marry the man, she had every intention of using the interest he had in her to her own advantage.

She made her way to the top of Market Street and crossed Union Street when there was a slight break in the amount of vehicles passing. The Forsyth Hotel was a little way along on the right.

It was not a hotel that Margaret Reid, or Lucy Gill, would normally visit. Any establishment that felt alcohol was a sin was not a place suitable to the likes of Lucy Gill. However, she had visited a few times in the past, building a character and knowing that one day, it might be of use to her. Today was that day.

Lucy entered through the small, front door and climbed the stairs. The reception area was well decorated and exuded a welcoming atmosphere to the new arrival. Behind the counter was a young woman, wearing a white blouse and black skirt. Beside her stood another woman, one whom Lucy recognised at once.

"Miss Jack, it has been some time since we last met," Lucy announced with a smile.

"Well, well, Lucy Gill. What brings you to Aberdeen?"

"A little business, as usual," Lucy replied brightly, her eyes already looking around her.

"Do you need a room?"

"Bit short of cash at the moment, so I've already taken a room in a bed and breakfast in Torry."

"Are you here for lunch?" Miss Jack then asked. She was a serious looking woman in her late thirties, but Lucy knew that beneath that serious façade was a woman with a sense of humour and a desire to enjoy life as much as she could.

"I was hoping to have something to eat while I was here."

"And were you hoping to see Anthony at the same time?" Miss Jack then asked. Lucy adopted the expression of someone whose plans had just been discovered. She smiled and looked almost embarrassed.

"Does he still have lunch here every day?" she then asked.

"He does indeed," replied Miss Jack, glancing at the clock above her head. "He should be here just after mid-day."

"Then I shall find a table and wait for him," Lucy added with a smiled. She made her way through to the dining room and sat at a table that afforded a view down on to Union Street. She asked for a pot of tea and sat back, awaiting Anthony Wilson's arrival.

***

TWENTY-THREE

Tuesday 30th June

Before Jake did anything more on the Tuesday morning, he found a telephone and made a call to Chief Inspector Will, who seemed delighted to hear from him. They discussed some cases that had crossed boundaries and they chatted about more general matters. Will then congratulated Jake on his temporary promotion and they agreed to speak again in two weeks' time. As Jake put the phone down he had actually felt like a proper Chief Inspector just for a moment or two.

He went back to his desk and sat down. He read through some papers and signed a few others. He also had two reports to read, which he found to have been badly written and totally lacking in substance. He scribbled at the top of both, *Please write these again and the next time actually add some relevant information,* then tossed the papers in to a basket where he knew someone would collect them later and disperse them to the appropriate people.

Having finished that, Jake went for a walk. He wanted some time to think and he also wanted a cup of tea and something to eat. He had got out of bed a little later than usual and had not had time for breakfast.

As he made his way in to the café he noticed Alan MacBride already sitting at one of the tables. Jake walked over to him.

"Morning, Alan," he said, "mind if I join you?"

"Have you finally got a story for me?" MacBride asked.

"Mind if I join you?" Jake said again.

MacBride waved a hand at the spare seat opposite him. "Feel free."

Jake sat down and a young waitress was across immediately. He ordered some bacon and eggs and a pot of tea.

"Intent on being here for a while?" MacBride then asked with a smile.

"Just hungry, that's all."

"So, what happened to my Grammar School murder story?" the journalist then said.

"I told you that you would be the first to hear if I had anything to say on that matter," Jake replied, looking around the other clientele of the café.

MacBride sat forward. "I hear the murders might be connected to a series of burglaries that have been carried out in the city?"

"Now where did you hear that, Alan?"

MacBride smiled. "I'm a journalist, I'm paid to keep my ear to the ground."

"Well you'll get nothing more from me on the subject of burglaries," Jake added. "As soon as I have something…..," Jake began.

"I'll be the first to know," interrupted MacBride. "Yes, I know where I stand in the pecking order."

"Have I ever let you down with a story in the past?" Jake then said.

"No."

"There you go. As soon as we get somewhere with the investigation in to these murders then I'll be in touch."

"What about the attacks on Councillor Manning?" MacBride then asked, deciding that he might get more of a story out of that.

"What about them?" replied Jake as the waitress arrived at the table with his pot of tea.

"I'm led to believe he's under attack from a bunch of women."

"And no doubt it was Councillor Manning himself who led you to believe that," added Jake pouring his first cup of tea.

"Are you condoning the actions of these women?" MacBride asked, sensing a story really was developing.

"No, Alan, I am not condoning anyone's actions, I am merely trying to keep Councillor Manning's opinions in perspective. After all, everyone knows how outspoken he has been against women seeking the vote. He has made a lot of enemies and until we know exactly who may behind these current incidents, I'm not prepared to make any comment."

"What do you know about the Aberdeen Voice for Women organisation?"

"Not a lot beyond the fact that we've seen the same leaflets as you have. We have an active murder inquiry taking precedence at the moment, so we haven't had much time to look in to the activities of a women's organisation."

"Councillor Manning wasn't happy to be getting eggs thrown at him."

"I'm sure he wasn't, it's a devil of a job to get the stain out of your suit."

"These women need to be stopped," MacBride then said, taking a drink of tea from his cup and watching Jake take a drink from his own cup.

"Are we still talking about the Aberdeen Voice for Women?" added Jake.

"They're obviously militants; they'll kill someone someday, you mark my words."

"As far as I am aware, Alan, no one has ever been killed by a flying egg," Jake said.

"It may have been an egg the other day, but who's to say what they might throw the next time," MacBride added.

Jake smiled. "Alan; Councillor Manning has been the only target to date and until we know a whole lot more about the Aberdeen Voice for Women, I am saying no more."

"But, surely these militant women cannot be allowed to attack any of our councillors?" MacBride suggested.

"The arrival of these leaflets was the first anyone knew about the Aberdeen Voice for Women. So far they have broken a few windows in Bon Accord Crescent and at Councillor Manning's home. Someone then decided to throw a couple of eggs at Councillor Manning. Those incidents hardly amount to the most militant of actions; even you should see that, Alan."

The waitress returned with Jake's bacon and eggs. He started to eat what was on the plate and MacBride chose to remain quiet while he did. When Jake was nearly finished with the bacon and eggs, MacBride began to talk again.

"It's still a public attack on one of our councillors," insisted MacBride.

Jake put his knife and fork down for a moment. "Let me ask you something, how popular would you say Councillor Manning is?"

MacBride sat back for a moment, as if taken aback by the question. "He's not the most popular, I'll grant you that" he then admitted.

"There you go then," added Jake, "he has many enemies and it is yet to be proved that some of those enemies are militant ladies?"

"They've left leaflets; they've admitted smashing his windows at least."

"Anyone could have had those leaflets printed. Until we know that it was definitely a group of women I, for one, am keeping an open mind."

"But they attacked the windows of that Club as well."

"Indeed someone did," agreed Jake, "but until we know a lot more than we do, I'm not making any accusations and I'm certainly not making any assumptions either."

McBride finished his tea. "Going back to the Grammar School murder, is there anything we can tell our readers to allay their fears of this maniac striking again?"

"Just tell your readers that the police are doing all that they can to catch this man, but we have to accept that some cases take longer to solve than others."

MacBride looked less than inspired by such a reply, but he had known Jake Fraser long enough and if Jake said there was no story then there was story. MacBride also knew better than to push the Inspector any further.

"I'll leave you to enjoy the rest of your tea," he then said and stood up.

Jake held up his hand. "Okay, Alan, sit down again and I'll give you a story that you *can* write."

Jake proceeded to give MacBride enough detail concerning the Barclay investigation to fill a few column inches of his newspaper. MacBride wrote everything down, thanked Jake for his time and then left.

Jake poured some more tea and sat back in his chair. His thoughts turned back to Councillor Manning. He felt the Councillor brought much upon himself. However, the first question that needed answering was what exactly was the Aberdeen Voice for Women? Jake not only needed to know who and what they were, but also if they had any connections to the ladies with whom Margaret socialised.

Jake did not want to have to put Margaret in a difficult position but if it transpired that she knew some of the members of the Aberdeen Voice for Women then he would be forced to ask her questions that he'd rather not ask. Jake drank some more of his tea and hoped that that day would never come.

***

The evening brought a light rain to Aberdeen and Margaret kept her umbrella up as she walked around to the Music Hall. When she arrived she put her coat, hat and umbrella in to the cloakroom and stood, for a moment, in the hall. Sadie Ashton came in just after her. Margaret noted that Ada and another young woman were in Sadie's company. They came over to Margaret.

"Good evening, Margaret," said Sadie, "are you ready for some healthy debate?"

"I'm always ready for healthy debate, Sadie," replied Margaret with a smile. "Good evening, Ada."

"Good evening, Margaret, this is Maud, she's here for the first time."

Maud was a fair-haired, mousey looking young woman with a pixie-like countenance and a thin frame. She said hello to Margaret and smiled. Margaret said hello back and the four women then made their way through to the round room again, where the chairs had been laid out for a large attendance.

Once everyone was seated, Mrs Black stood up. She was dressed in a deep purple dress that looked almost black in some lights. Some of those attending thought that Mrs Black might have been in mourning for something as her stern expression seemed to support the colour of her dress.

"Welcome ladies," she said, "may I start tonight by talking about something, which has saddened me greatly. I have been told that Councillor Manning recently had his windows smashed and he, himself, was hit by an egg as he entered the Council Chambers. Now I am assuming that no one in this room was responsible for either of those attacks as it, in no way, champions our cause. I am all for keeping our message in the public eye, but attacking a man who is simply standing for the good of his constituents, serves no purpose, no purpose at all."

"Mrs Black?" Sadie Ashton then said as she stood up. Mrs Black, rather reluctantly turned to acknowledge another speaker in the room.

"Yes."

"Whether, or not, anyone in this room actually threw that egg at Councillor Manning I, for one, applaud their actions. Councillor Manning is the kind of man who brings out the worst in me. He talks to women as if they were second class citizens with no brain of their own. He talks to us as if we could not possibly understand the complicated world in which he lives and he talks as if he would never support women being given the vote. He, therefore, sets himself up as a target by expressing such unacceptable views."

There was a ripple of applause in the room, informing Mrs Black immediately that Sadie had support in the room for her comments. Sadie paused and Mrs Black realised she was now expected to react in some way to the suggestion that Councillor Manning had deserved everything that had come his way.

"If we condone the throwing of an egg at a Councillor, Mrs Ashton, then at what level of violence do we say enough is enough?"

"The truthful answer to that question, Mrs Black, is that I don't know."

There was a gasp in the room. Sadie continued.

"But what I do know is that we will never win our argument if we do not, at times, resort to measures, which might be viewed by others as being extreme. Men like Councillor Manning need to realise that women ought to have the same rights as men. He needs to realise that his opinion is not the only one that ought to be heard when discussing women's rights. If the occasional egg is required to remind him of our existence and of our cause, then so be it."

Another ripple of applause, only this time a little louder. Margaret looked around the room, surprised at some of the women who seemed to be supporting Sadie's argument.

Mrs Black looked flustered for a moment. "I can't believe that this group would wish to discuss the taking of militant action. Surely that is something best left to those far closer to Parliament than we are."

Sadie looked around the room then spoke again.

"I am not necessarily advocating militant action, Mrs Black, but I do want to elicit some response from the ladies here tonight as to how they feel we should best proceed with pushing our message out to the people of Aberdeen. I, for one, do not believe that women will ever be given their due rights without a fight and in all fights there have to be casualties."

There was another murmur of agreement at that point, which Mrs Black picked up on immediately. She paused again, realising that she was being backed in to a corner; one that she would rather not enter. Eventually she said the only thing she thought she could say.

"How does everyone else feel about Mrs Ashton's suggestion?"

Ada and Maud immediately jumped to their feet and expressed total support for Sadie. Margaret couldn't help thinking that it had all been rehearsed and poor Mrs Black was being railroaded by these women. Ada and Maud sat down again, but a few others now voiced support and Mrs Black knew that she would have to, at least, allow a discussion on the subject of how militant the group was prepared to be.

"Very well, it seems that a debate is necessary. In that case, Mrs Ashton, perhaps you would like to come out front and give us a full account of where you stand on the subject of militant action."

Mrs Black sat down again and Sadie made her way to the front. Margaret noted an expression of triumph on her face and got the distinct impression that Mrs Black's time as Chairwoman might almost be up.

Sadie stood at the front for a moment, gathering her thoughts before eventually starting to speak.

"Ladies, I believe that we all have the same aim in life; I believe that we all come together at these meetings not only to voice our support for the Liberal Party but also to express our support for women's rights. Ultimately, we all want the same thing, we want to be given the vote so that we can help decide the future governments of this country. It is a noble cause but it is one that has the sternest wall to break through, if we are to ever achieve our goal. That wall, ladies, is the mass of male opinion."

Some women nodded at that point. Margaret noticed that Ada and Maud were almost applauding as they listened to what Sadie had to say. Both women had also sat forward in their seats; they were soaking up every word. Sadie continued.

"Men have been voicing their opinions for centuries and appear to have reached a point where they simply refuse to believe that we women might have an opinion of our own. We are never asked for an opinion on anything other than what we might have for dinner or, perhaps, which new dress we should buy. In a man's world we are nothing more than window dressing; we are there purely for their needs and nothing else. Well I feel the time is rapidly approaching where those ideas need to be challenged; the time is coming when a woman will reserve the right to not only have an opinion of her own, but to have that opinion heard and acted upon."

A ripple of applause passed through the room. Margaret could now see that more women were paying close attention to Sadie's words; there was no denying, she was certainly in control of her audience now.

"Ladies, it saddens me to say this, but men are really only interested in us when we are in the kitchen or the bedroom."

Mrs Black tutted loudly and one or two of the older ladies looked offended by the mere mention of the bedroom. Margaret found it mildly amusing that some of the ladies might be in agreement to the odd egg being thrown, but were still mortally offended at the mention of anything even remotely close to sex.

"Mrs Ashton, what may go on in the privacy of people's bedrooms has no place in this discussion," rebuked Mrs Black.

Sadie smiled. "My apologies if I have offended anyone of a sensitive disposition, but my point still stands. Men do not take us seriously and remember, it will be men who ultimately vote on whether or not women receive greater rights in the future. They will only vote in our favour if they fully understand that we are capable of having an opinion on such important matters as who might govern the country. We can make them understand through debate and discussion, but there will be some men who won't want to have that debate or discussion. They will need to be forced to listen to what we have to say and to gain their attention we may need to take action that none of us would normally choose other than in these extreme circumstances. Ladies, I am not standing here advocating that we throw bricks through the window of every man in Aberdeen, all I am asking is that we at least agree to consider such action if those circumstances dictate."

"And who will decide if the circumstances dictate, Mrs Ashton?" asked Mrs Black, her stern expression looking even more pronounced.

"We should decide by a democratic vote," replied Sadie. "Should anyone feel that circumstance were right for militant action then they would have to persuade the attendees at our meetings before such action could be undertaken."

"But surely any such action would be pointless?" Mrs Black added quickly.

"Perhaps, Mrs Black," conceded Sadie, "but let me ask you this; how many people know about our meeting here tonight?"

It took a moment before Mrs Black realised the question had not been rhetorical.

"My friends and family know, so I should imagine that will be the same for everyone else here tonight."

"Okay," Sadie then said, "let me say that each person in this room has twenty people who know they are here. That amounts to one thousand people who at least know we are probably discussing women's rights. Someone threw an egg at Councillor Manning and the local newspapers printed the story. Suddenly thousands more Aberdonians are aware that there is a group of women fighting for their rights. Now it may not ultimately affect what they think of our cause, but they certainly know about it and surely that is a small victory in itself."

Mrs Black now stood up, obviously feeling that she now had to defend her point of view.

"Some people are of the mind that any publicity is good publicity, but I strongly contend that that is not the case. If ordinary citizens read about egg throwing and window breaking they will associate those actions with criminals, not with people who are trying to argue for a constitutional change in this country. We need to garner public support and I do not believe you will do that through militant action."

"Mrs Pankhurst clearly does not agree," Sadie then said.

"And Mrs Pankhurst is welcome to her opinion, as are you, Mrs Ashton. However, I believe that any action taken so far away from the House of Commons is unlikely to make that much of a difference nationally. Mrs Pankhurst, on the other hand, can get her message delivered straight to the Prime Minister's door, should she wish to do so."

"But, in our own way, we can still ensure that our message remains in the public domain and sometimes, the only way you can do that is to take action destined to gain publicity rather than to necessarily move our argument forward in any positive manner. This is going to be a long fight and if we are not careful we will lose the argument through apathy."

Nearly half the room applauded at that stage. Mrs Black no longer looked very sure as to how she should proceed.

"How does everyone else feel about what Mrs Ashton has said?"

Ada leapt to her feet. "I support Mrs Ashton one hundred per cent. I have youth on my side but, no disrespect, I do not want to be the age of some of the women in this room and still be fighting for my rights. I want a say in how I live my life and I'm not prepared to wait years to get it."

An elderly lady at the front did not leap to her feet but held up her umbrella instead. The room fell silent to allow her to speak.

"A noble sentiment, my dear and I hope with all my heart that you have your right to vote before you reach my age. However, violence, of any kind, gets us nowhere. If we become more militant then we invite the police to take action and once we have crossed that line there is no going back. How can we continue to argue our case if half our members are in prison at any given time."

"I don't mind going to prison," shouted Ada.

The elderly lady smiled. "My dear, you would not last five minutes in prison. You are too accustomed to the finer things in life."

Many of the women in the room laughed and Ada fell quiet again, suitably chastised. Mrs Black was next to speak.

"Perhaps, ladies, we are getting ahead of ourselves here, anyway. These meetings are to show our allegiance to the Liberal Party, they are not, in themselves, a place to discuss Suffragette issues. If that is indeed what you want to discuss then perhaps you have to seek another platform from which to do so."

Sadie Ashton turned to look at the ladies gathered before her. She looked at a number of faces, noting that many of them seemed inspired by what she had said.

"Very well," she then said, "I offer those who wish to do more to get our message across, the opportunity to do just that, by whatever means is deemed necessary. I suggest that we form a separate group, as yet unnamed and that we seek out the members of the Aberdeen Voice for Women Group so that we may offer any help and support that they may feel they need. How many ladies here would wish to be part of that new group?"

Around twenty hands went up and Mrs Black looked as if she had taken that as a personal insult. Sadie looked triumphant and Margaret looked disappointed. She had not wanted militancy to come anywhere near her little world and she now needed to distance herself from anything that Sadie Ashton might be planning.

"Before I sit down," Sadie then said, "could I just ask that those ladies, who put their hand up, please give your name and address to me at the end of the night so that I might contact you once we have organised a meeting date and time for our new group."

Sadie then sat down again. It took Mrs Black a little while to compose herself. The purpose of the meeting had been all but declared void by Sadie Ashton's actions, but as there were still many there who were not of a mind to agree with Mrs Ashton, Mrs Black decided to continue.

The meeting lasted another forty-five minutes and the proceedings were brought to a conclusion. Margaret went to the cloakroom to collect her coat and Sadie, Ada and Maud all arrived at the same time. Margaret came straight to the point.

"Are you all members of the Aberdeen Voice for Women?"

"I'm certainly not," replied Sadie, "but if I can find who is behind it then I'm sure I'll be joining."

Margaret noted that Ada and Maud did not say anything. They put on their coats with a look of excitement on their young faces.

Ah, the problems of youth, thought Margaret, *they have more tomorrows ahead of them than most and yet everything has to happen today, there is no thought of waiting until any of those tomorrows come along.*

"Can we still be friends, Margaret?" Sadie then said as she was buttoning up her coat.

"As long, it seems, as we keep politics out of it."

"But we really agree on the major issues," insisted Sadie. "We both want the vote for women, it's just that your way of getting there is slightly different from mine. No matter who may be right, the end product will benefit us both."

"I do not disagree, but I cannot put my name to anything even remotely illegal."

"Ah, yes, the husband would not approve, eh?" mocked Sadie.

Margaret became instantly annoyed. Her tone was sharp. "*I* would not approve," she said, "*this* has nothing to do with Jake."

"I apologise," Sadie said immediately. "We may not agree on everything, Margaret, but I really do value your opinion and hope that we can still meet for tea on occasions?"

"That would be lovely. Shall we agree to meet sometime next week?" Margaret then said.

Sadie thought for a moment. "Shall we meet on Tuesday of next week at Watt and Grant's?"

"Ten o'clock?"

"Excellent. I look forward to it."

Sadie Ashton and her two, new-found friends, then set off for the front door. Margaret was still arranging her umbrella when Mrs Black came up to her side. Her eyes were still following Sadie.

"I fear we have a dangerous one in our midst," she said quietly.

"She has some unique ideas, I'll grant her that," added Margaret.

"It puts you in an awkward position, does it not?"

Margaret smiled. "I'm accustomed to sitting on the fence, Mrs Black. I've been there long enough to have splinters in my bottom."

Mrs Black did not get offended at a lady mentioning her bottom. Instead she saw the humour in what Margaret had said and supported it with a smile. She then spoke.

"Will we see you at the next Liberal meeting, Mrs Fraser?"

"Of course, Mrs Black, I'm not quite ready to run off and buy half a dozen eggs in time for the next Council meeting."

Again Mrs Black smiled and Margaret made her way to the front door. The rain was heavier and she put up her umbrella before walking down the stone steps and turning left towards Golden Square.

Margaret was home within ten minutes. Jake was sitting at the kitchen table finishing a plate of cold meat and bread that had been left for him in the larder. He stood up and kissed Margaret as she entered the room.

"Good meeting?" he asked, as he returned to his food.

Margaret unbuttoned her coat. "Interesting. Sadie Ashton eventually nailed her colours to the mast tonight."

"Mrs Militant is now officially on the loose, eh?" Jake quipped.

Margaret laughed. "She's certainly intent on joining this Aberdeen Voice for Women if she can find them."

"You mean she doesn't know who they are?" Jake asked with disbelief in his tone.

"Apparently not."

"That does surprise me," said Jake.

"I have to confess, it surprises me as well," added Margaret as she took her coat off and went through to the bedroom to hang it in the wardrobe. By the time she got back to the kitchen Jake had poured a cup of tea for her. She sat down at the table.

"What kind of day did you have?" she then asked.

"The usual; the getting nowhere fast sort of day. I had Alan MacBride nipping my head this morning over the attacks on Councillor Manning. MacBride has already decided there is a group of mad women loose in Aberdeen intent on killing someone someday, if that will help get their message across."

Margaret smiled again. "I don't think anyone is intent on murder, but there is a growing air of discontent that may yet lead to laws being broken. I suspect you may have some busy days ahead of you."

Jake put his hand over Margaret's and squeezed gently. "Don't let me stand in the way of your personal beliefs and desires. I know I said I didn't want to have to arrest you some day, but that doesn't mean you can't stand up and be counted with any group you wish. I respect your views and I respect how you will air them."

Margaret stood up and walked round the table. She kissed the husband whom she loved so much and when she spoke again there was a twinkle in her eye.

"Are you tired?"

Jake picked up on her meaning at once. "Not *that* tired, no."

"Good, then after we've finished our tea, I suggest we go to bed."

Jake thought that that was a perfectly wonderful suggestion.

***

TWENTY-FOUR

Thursday 02nd July

On the Thursday, Jake finally got a slight break in the Grammar School murder inquiry. A man appeared at Lodge Walk in the afternoon. He wished to see Sergeant Mathieson and when he said who he was, Mathieson made sure that Jake was present when he spoke to the gentleman.

The man's name was Perceval Stanton and he ran another of the antique retail outlets in Aberdeen. He was an aristocratic looking gentleman with greying hair and heavy whiskers either side of his face. He looked to be in his fifties and he spoke with the tone of someone who had been well educated. Sergeant Mathieson introduced Jake to Mr Stanton and it was Stanton who spoke first.

"Sergeant Mathieson asked to be notified if anyone tried to sell me well-painted miniatures of naked women. Well, a young woman tried to do just that at lunchtime today. I'm sure it was one of the paintings you had on your list, Sergeant."

"What did you do, Mr Stanton?" Jake then asked.

"There wasn't much that I could do, Inspector. The woman did not look the type to tarry any longer in my shop than was absolutely necessary. When I told her that the miniature was too expensive for me, she turned and left."

"Was there anything about her that was memorable in anyway?" Jake then enquired.

"She was very attractive, but that wasn't what made her memorable; no, the most memorable thing about the young lady was that she was, most definitely, in disguise."

"Are you sure?" Mathieson then added.

"Oh yes, Sergeant, quite sure. She was wearing a blonde wig and theatrical make-up. I believe she was trying to make herself look older than she actually is."

"How old do you think she is?" said Jake.

"Thirty-something, perhaps. With the make-up and wig she was trying to pass herself off as someone in her late forties."

Jake sat forward. "Can you tell us anything else about her?"

"She was well spoken; obviously she had had a good education. She's around five feet four, or five, in height and she has brown eyes. I'm afraid I don't remember any more than that."

Jake was smiling. "I think you've remembered enough as it is, Mr Stanton. Do you think the young woman will come back to your shop?"

"I shouldn't think so, she now knows I'm not prepared to pay the kind of money she is probably expecting."

"How much do you think the miniature would be worth?" Jake said.

"I should imagine anything between two and five pounds, depending on where you sold it. A private buyer might even pay more as it really was of the most exquisite craftsmanship."

"Did the woman appear nervous to you?" Jake then asked.

"Oh yes, she isn't accustomed to doing something illegal, I'm sure of that."

"And did she appear to be alone, or was someone waiting outside the shop?"

"I didn't notice anyone else."

"Well, thank you very much for your help, Mr Stanton; if you remember anything else please call on us again."

"If anything else does spring to mind I shall seek out Sergeant Mathieson at once," Stanton added and then stood up to leave the room.

Mathieson showed Mr Stanton to the front door and then made his way to Jake's office, where he found his Chief Inspector already sitting at his desk.

"Well, that was all very interesting, wasn't it?" Jake said. "We now know that we're probably not looking for a blonde woman at all and that there is still at least some of the stolen miniatures in Aberdeen. I must say, she's taking a risk trying to sell them locally."

"All very interesting, I agree sir, but it doesn't actually get us any nearer to identifying her, does it?"

"We know her height now and the fact she has brown eyes," Jake added. "Neither of those can be changed with make-up and a wig."

Mathieson nodded. "Very true, sir. So what do we do now?"

"If she visited Mr Stanton today then there is every chance she visited other outlets at the same time. I suggest, Sergeant that you go round them all just in case some other shop owner can add to what Mr Stanton told us."

"I'll deal with that right away, sir," concluded Mathieson as he stood up and left the room.

Jake cleared some more papers from his desk, now wearing his Chief Inspector hat and then turned his attention back to the Grammar School related crimes. He took out a sheet of paper and laid it down in front of him. He began to write:

Edith McIntosh – definitely robbed of her father's collection of miniatures. This has to be the motive for someone being in Miss McIntosh's house. We still have to assume that the burglar resorted to murder as a means of escape from the house.

Could a woman have strangled Edith McIntosh? Strangling is more a man's method of killing, so is the woman with the wig nothing more than an accomplice to the killer, or did she play more of a part than that?

Maybe the woman learned of the collection and then told a male friend? What if the male friend was knowledgeable about antiques and knew the value of what was being stolen? Might Mr Kerrigan be involved in any of this, after all he was in the house pricing everything else and we only have his word that he didn't know about the miniature collection.

Archibald Diamond – why was he murdered? Was the burglar in Diamond's house and witnessed what unfolded with Mr Lord? Or was it another acquaintance of Mr Diamond's who murdered him in a fit of jealous rage? In other words, does his death have no bearing on who killed Miss McIntosh? It does not appear as if anything was actually stolen from Mr Diamond so perhaps there was no burglar.

Juliet Grainger and Prunella Holmes – Where do they fit in to all this? Miss Grainger was first but can't even be sure she was burgled. Miss Holmes had someone in her house and a couple of items were taken. Are these visits purely random after all, or is there some other reason for him visiting these teachers? Beyond being the victims of a burglar they maybe play no further part in this mystery.

Which brings me back to the one question that most needs answering; why was Edith McIntosh murdered? If burglary was the motive then the burglar could have been in and out of the house without Miss McIntosh knowing. Even if she had returned while he was still in the house he could have made good his escape without her even knowing. Why then did he feel the need to kill her?

There can only be one reason. Miss McIntosh not only saw him, but she recognised him as well. The burglar, for some unknown reason, had to have been a part of Miss McIntosh's life and she had to be silenced before she could tell anyone who he was.

However, if that were indeed the case, why continue with the other burglaries, surely the risk level rose by continuing to rob Grammar School teachers.

Or could it be possible that the other burglaries were merely carried out to cover the fact that stealing Miss McIntosh's miniatures was always the only true part of their plan? Could everything else be a smokescreen? Perhaps, but surely no one would kill another human being simply to put the police off their scent?

Jake stopped writing and sat back. Was that really what all this was about? Someone found out about Miss McIntosh's collection and set out to steal it. As they were known to her they had to kill her before making off with the miniatures. Knowing that the police would throw all their resources in to finding a killer, a plan was hatched to make it look more like a burglar was on the loose.

It all sounded very feasible, but for one rather important fact. Miss Grainger had been visited by the burglar before Miss McIntosh. That meant that she was the starting point in the puzzle, which further meant a more random approach by the burglar than Jake's new theory would allow.

Apart from the slight problem with Miss Grainger, Jake decided that it still made more sense to make Miss McIntosh the real reason for all that had happened. She was the only one to have definitely been robbed but, if she had known her robber, then who could it have been? How many men would Miss McIntosh have known who would have been able to gain personal information about her? Jake doubted if anyone would have fallen in to that category, which brought him back to the mystery blonde. She was obviously connected to the burglar in some way and had to be the one gathering information on her colleagues; which meant she definitely had to be working at the Grammar School.

So who was the criminal in their midst? How best could she be identified? Just for the moment, Jake hadn't the faintest idea.

What he did know, however, was that the burglar knew how to go about his business and yet was not known to the other criminal element of Aberdeen. That being the case he either had to be a new player in the game, or someone who had recently arrived in Aberdeen. Either way, there was every chance that the man had a good knowledge of what might sell easiest and for the best money.

Jake felt it was still possible that Mr Kerrigan knew more than he had been saying, so he decided to go and speak to him one more time.

***

They found a small room at the end of the corridor from Mr Gibson's office. Adam Kerrigan looked as nervous as he had done at Lodge Walk. He offered Jake a seat and then sat down himself. Kerrigan's nervousness was the main reason for Jake coming straight to the point. He really did not want to make this young man suffer any more than he was.

"Do you know any of the teachers at the Grammar School?"

"No."

"You didn't, by any chance, attend the Grammar School as a pupil?"

Mr Kerrigan laughed. "I was never that privileged."

"Beyond valuing her household items, had you known Miss McIntosh in any other capacity?"

"No."

"And you definitely didn't know about her miniature collection?"

Kerrigan started to get annoyed. He could sense that he was being accused of something without those words actually being said.

"Look, I've told you all that I know about Edith McIntosh. I was asked to value her items for insurance purposes, which I did. In that time there was never any mention of miniature paintings and the first I knew about them was when you showed me one at the police office."

Jake nodded and thought for a moment. He decided on a change of questions.

"Are you in a relationship at the moment, Mr Kerrigan?"

Kerrigan looked somewhat taken aback at the intrusion in to his privacy. He took a moment to answer.

"I really don't think that's any of your business, Inspector."

"In a murder inquiry, Mr Kerrigan, everything becomes my business. Now, would you please answer the question?"

Kerrigan took a little while to respond yet again. Eventually he sighed deeply and spoke.

"Well seeing as you insist on me answering your question, Inspector, no; I am not currently in a relationship."

"When were you last in a relationship?"

"Oh, for goodness sake!" Kerrigan snapped. "Inspector, I have not enjoyed feminine company for over two years, something of which I am neither proud, nor wish to make public. I also fail to see what my private life has to do with the death of Edith McIntosh."

"I'm simply trying to fit all the pieces of a very complicated puzzle together, Mr Kerrigan and although it may not seem so to you, the answers you are giving are helping me find a solution. Now, returning to Miss McIntosh, were you ever aware of her using other companies with regard to valuing her precious items?"

"She certainly never said anything about getting a second valuation."

"Has anyone else in this company dealt with Miss McIntosh?"

"I don't think so. She did speak to Mr Gibson once, but that was very briefly here in the office and I don't believe he ever spoke to her again."

Jake thought for a moment. He was happy to accept that Mr Kerrigan was telling him the truth and it now seemed highly unlikely that he was connected either to burglaries, or mystery blondes. Jake then asked if he might have a moment with Mr Gibson. Mr Kerrigan went away to get him and Jake looked around the small room as he waited for them to come back. When they did, Gibson suggested going to his office. Again, Jake came straight to the point.

"Do you know of anyone from this company, beyond Mr Kerrigan, who had any dealings with Miss McIntosh?"

"I did speak to Miss McIntosh once in this very office, but apart from that only Mr Kerrigan spoke to her and certainly only Mr Kerrigan went to her house."

"Have you ever been asked to do any work for Archibald Diamond, Prunella Holmes or Juliet Grainger?"

"Those names mean nothing to me, Inspector, though it's possible my staff might know more than I do."

"I'll have a list of names drawn up for checking against your records, if that's okay with you, Mr Gibson?" Jake then said.

"Of course. If you bring me that list I'll get one of the girls in the office check it."

"Thank you," Jake then said and got up to leave.

As he made his way back to the office he remembered that Sergeant Mathieson was now stepping out with one of the girls in the office at Gibson and Son. He would get Mathieson to take the list of the Grammar School teachers up to the company and he could spend a little time in the company of his lady friend. Jake smiled to himself at the possibility that Mathieson had possibly found his own 'Margaret'; he'd never have expected murder inquiries to be the best way to meet your life's partner.

***

The man opened the door to his house and let the woman in. As soon as the door was closed they kissed.

"I didn't think you'd come tonight," the man said.

"I just needed to see you."

The man led the way through to the sitting room and offered the woman a drink. She accepted a glass if sherry. The man poured himself a whisky and they both sat, side by side, on the settee.

"Did you get the miniature sold?" the man then asked.

"No. I got the feeling the dealer was, in some way, expecting me. He said he couldn't afford to buy it, but I'm sure he was just stalling me."

"I told you we'd have to go outside Aberdeen to sell them. Apart from the fact no one will know they are stolen, we'll get more money that way."

"But I don't want to leave Aberdeen without you and you are in no position to take time off, just at the moment."

"I'll try and arrange some time off before the school term starts. We'll only need a few days to conduct our business."

"Meanwhile, I still have the miniatures in my possession and I'm getting a little uneasy about that," added the woman.

"Then let me take them," the man suggested.

The woman eyed him suspiciously. "No, I'll hang on to them in the meantime."

"You still don't trust me, do you?" the man then said, taking the woman's hand in his.

"Of course I trust you."

"Then why won't you let me take the miniatures?"

"Because moving them might be dangerous. I don't think the police are getting anywhere in their search for either Edith's killer, or the mystery burglar. We have managed to spin a tangled web but we cannot afford to make a mistake now. We cannot be seen together, at least until the main police interest has died down. That Inspector Fraser isn't stupid and if he gets wind of us being in a relationship then he'll want to ask us both some awkward questions."

"But we may already have been seen together," the man then said, looking a little anxious.

"We can pass that off as nothing more than a business discussion. We certainly cannot afford to be seen in any romantic way or that really will have the police buzzing around us like flies. I'm not sure I want to be dealing with awkward questions just at the moment."

"Can we be that confident that the police will never solve Edith's murder?" the man enquired.

"They can have nothing to go on," the woman replied. "There is no way that they can tie us to Edith, we were careful to make sure no one saw us arrive or leave on the day she died. Had we not been successful in maintaining our anonymity then I feel sure the police would have been back, asking those awkward questions, long by now. As long as we keep our heads, we'll be okay."

"Then maybe you should refrain from trying to sell anymore miniatures until we can get out of Aberdeen?" the man then suggested.

The woman thought for a moment. "We could be doing with the money, but you may well be right."

The man squeezed her hand. "You don't regret what we have done do you?"

"I'm sorry that Edith had to die, but I don't regret the actions we took and I certainly won't regret anything once we get the money from selling the miniatures. Once we have that money then we can get away from Aberdeen permanently."

"You still want to do that?" the man asked.

"Of course," added the woman and they kissed. In the process she spilled some of her sherry, leaving a small stain on her dress. The woman laid down her glass and wiped at the mark on her dress. The man produced a handkerchief from his pocket and handed to her. She wiped some more at the stain.

"Then we just have to bide our time a little longer. In a few weeks we can catch a train to London and sell those miniatures for a price that will set us up for the rest of our lives," the man then said.

"I can't wait," the woman said, still looking down at her dress, "however, just at this moment, I'm going to have to wash this dress before the stain becomes permanent."

The man smiled. "Are you telling me that you'll have to take your dress off here and now?"

The woman smiled as well. "I am."

"In that case, we'll better think of something to do while the dress is drying."

***

TWENTY-FIVE

Friday 03rd July

The change of month had brought a change of weather. At long last Aberdeen was bathed in sunshine and finally, there was heat in the air. The temperature was around the mid-sixties in the shade and Sergeant Mathieson took his sandwich with him, in his pocket, when he made his way up to Gibson and Son with the list of Grammar School teachers.

Mathieson had been stepping out with Ruby since that first day he had gone to speak with Mr Kerrigan. They were enjoying each other's company and had even moved on to exchanging the odd kiss before parting. Ruby was beautiful and bright and Mathieson felt he might be falling in love with her. There were even notions of marriage hovering at the back of his mind, something which had never been a part of Mathieson's life before.

Ruby checked the list of teachers against anyone who may have done business with Gibson and Son. No one on the list appeared in any of the records maintained by the Gibson and Son's staff. Mathieson thanked Ruby for carrying out the check and he then waited while she collected her bag. They then made their way out in to the sun and arm in arm, walked through to the seats on Albyn Place.

They found a spare seat and sat down. Ruby produced a sandwich from her bag and Mathieson dug his out of his pocket. They chewed thoughtfully for a moment and watched other, like-minded people pass as they sought out somewhere to sit.

Little was said for a few moments and then Ruby turned to face Mathieson, her eyes wide with excitement.

"The office is alight with gossip," she said.

"Aren't most offices?" Mathieson replied.

"Possibly, but this gossip is about Mr Gibson."

"What about Mr Gibson?" Mathieson then asked, though he wasn't particularly interested in the answer.

"Word in the office is that Mr Gibson has a new lady friend," Ruby said, as if this was the most exciting piece of information ever to come out of an office environment.

"Is this unusual?" said Mathieson, not entirely sure why he was being told this.

"It's not like Mr Gibson, he's never been that comfortable around women."

"He must have felt comfortable with one woman if he was married," added Mathieson.

"That's just it, Mr Gibson has never been married. He just has the reference to a son on the business sign to make it look like a family business. He thought it a better image for his customers."

"That at least explains why I've never heard the son mentioned," said Mathieson.

"Anyway, Mr Gibson was seen, in the company of a young woman, in one of the restaurants the other week. Word is that they seemed very close and looked as if they might be in love."

"Does love have a look?" Mathieson then enquired, looking a bit vague when it came to discussing matters of the heart.

"Of course it does," Ruby added, suddenly looking very serious. "Men get all soft when they are in love."

"Soft?"

"Yes, soft."

"Do I appear soft when I am with you?" Mathieson then asked.

Ruby's face went bright red. "Richard Mathieson, what are you saying?"

Mathieson was grinning. "I'm saying, Ruby Trotter that I believe I am in love with you, therefore, by your own reckoning, I must be soft."

"Do you mean that?" Ruby said ignoring, for the moment, the question she had been posed.

"Of course I mean it," Mathieson added and reached for her hand. "I hope you have feelings for me as well?"

Ruby's face went a deeper shade of red. "We're not supposed to talk like that after just a few weeks."

Mathieson had to agree with her; it was not normal for a man to be disclosing such close feelings for a woman after such a relatively short space of time. However, he knew how he felt in his heart and even though he had not set out to open his heart to Ruby, now that he had started it seemed necessary that he continue.

"I think I loved you from the first minute I saw you," he said, "so why wait for any more time to pass before I declare that love to you."

Ruby turned a little in her seat so that she was facing Mathieson. Her face was positively glowing.

"Do you really love me?"

Mathieson took Ruby's hand.

"How many more times do I need to say it? I love you, Ruby. Look, I know this will sound insane, but I have to ask. Ruby Trotter, will you do me the great honour of becoming my wife, assuming that the Chief Constable doesn't have something to say about my proposal?

Ruby nearly dropped what was left of her sandwich. Her eyes widened in what Mathieson hoped was delight, rather than horror and her mouth dropped slightly open. She said nothing for a moment and Mathieson worried that he may have scared her with his forthright approach to the subject of marriage.

He appreciated they had not known each other for long, but he knew how he felt about Ruby and the quicker she was made aware of that the better. He continued to hold her hand and look in to her eyes. The silence continued for a little while longer before Ruby eventually found her voice again.

"Well, Richard Mathieson, this is indeed a surprise. I guessed that you had deep feelings for me, but I never expected a proposal of marriage."

"If it's too soon….," Mathieson began to say.

Ruby interrupted him. "I never said it was too soon, I just said I wasn't expecting it. Having said that, I don't feel I need any more time before I give you an answer. I would like nothing more than to become your wife."

"Oh, Ruby," added Mathieson and he leaned forward to kiss her. Ruby pulled back, looking around as she did so.

"We can't be seen kissing in public," she said, "it isn't proper."

"But we're engaged now, Ruby, surely that changes everything?" Mathieson added with a grin.

"Not as far as kissing in public, it doesn't," added Ruby and Mathieson squeezed her hand affectionately.

"In that case," he then said, "The quicker we find somewhere private the better."

And with that they stood up and began walking back to Gibson and Son by a slightly longer route than might have been absolutely necessary.

***

Lucy Gill returned to Aberdeen after a brief trip to Glasgow where her friend had printed some more documents for her that she hoped would prove very useful as she set about persuading Anthony Wilson to part with some of his money. However, after their discussion at lunch, on her previous visit, she had decided to revise her plan. The man was clearly besotted with her so she had now decided to play along with the idea of considering becoming his second wife.

Lucy was now of the opinion that she could persuade Anthony to do anything if he thought she was going to marry him. It was likely that he would do anything for his prospective new bride were he to believe that it would displease her to do otherwise. Somehow she had to persuade him to pass money in her direction without arousing his suspicion that she may not have both their interests at heart. She was, of course, confident that she could do just that. After years of conning people, Lucy was confident she could persuade anyone to do anything, if she really put her mind to it. Potentially, Anthony would be easier as he was already clearly falling in love with her.

Although their meetings had been brief, Lucy had found herself working hard at getting Anthony to become infatuated by her. She had flirted with him and laughed at all his terrible attempts at being witty. She had even agreed to spend a night in his house though the offer had been made purely to save her some money. Anthony Wilson's religious beliefs would never have allowed him to even think about putting a woman in a compromising situation; not that they would have been alone as Wilson's housekeeper, Kath, was always there.

After breakfast, on that occasion, Lucy had left for the railway station after agreeing to take the room at Wilson's house when she next came back to Aberdeen. Now, here she was, back in the city and keen to reacquaint herself with Mr Wilson. She caught a carriage at the station and asked to be taken to Holburn Street. She now knew exactly how she would play things and felt pretty sure that the next time she left Aberdeen it would be with money in her purse and no real reason for ever coming back.

***

Sergeant Mathieson got back to Lodge Walk at around one o'clock and Jake noticed the grin almost the moment he'd entered the building.

"You're looking very happy, Sergeant."

"I'm engaged, sir. I asked Ruby to marry me and she said yes."

"After only a matter of weeks, my you work fast, Sergeant," commented Jake. "Congratulations," he then added and shook the Sergeant's hand, "she's a very lucky young woman to find you for a husband."

"I still need to speak to the Chief," Mathieson added.

Police officers were not allowed to get married unless given approval to do so by the Chief Constable. Jake had gone through the same process before he had married Margaret. He had ensured that Margaret wanted to marry him first and then he had spoken to the Chief. Fortunately there had been no problems for Jake and Margaret but that didn't mean there might not be problems for Sergeant Mathieson.

Accommodation was often an issue. Police officers were usually expected to live in homes owned by the police. Married officers usually occupied larger properties, the assumption being that children would be along eventually. If properties were in short supply then Mathieson may be refused permission to marry until somewhere suitable came along. Jake and Margaret had no problems with accommodation as Margaret already had her own home.

Mathieson's expression betrayed the fact that he knew the Chief may yet be an obstacle to their marriage.

"I'll try to see the Chief Constable this afternoon," he said. "I need to know what he thinks as quickly as possible."

"I'm sure everything will be fine," added Jake.

"I do hope so, sir. If we are half as happy as you are with Margaret then everything will be just fine," Mathieson then added and both men stood and grinned at each other for another moment. They then recovered their decorum and turned back to the work in hand.

"Were any of the Grammar School teachers on the Gibson and Son list of customers?"

"I'm afraid not, sir. Mind you, I'm not sure how precise Ruby was in checking their records as she was in a state of excitement at the fact her boss, Mr Gibson, appears to have found himself a new lady friend."

"Good for Mr Gibson," added Jake. "He's not a young man and I'm sure it hadn't been easy finding feminine company again at his age. Had something happened to his wife?"

"There never was a wife apparently and there's never been a son. Ruby tells me that Gibson added the Son to give his company a sense of being a family business.

"Interesting. Did Ruby have any idea who the lucky woman was?"

"No one seems to know who she is, but she's only been in his life for a relatively short time so, no doubt, more will be learned in the days ahead."

"Unless he wishes to keep his private life, private. Meantime, assuming the Chief Constable gives you his blessing, it is Ruby herself who will become the talk of the office."

Mathieson suddenly looked very concerned. "You don't think the Chief would stop me marrying do you, sir?"

"I shouldn't think so, but you'd better clear it with him quickly before Ruby is walking the length of Union Street looking for her wedding dress."

Mathieson nodded his agreement and then both men returned their full attention to the Edith McIntosh investigation.

***

Friday evening arrived and Jake got home at a little after eight. It had been an unproductive day and he was beginning to lose heart a little. Usually he managed to find a line of inquiry fairly quickly, but here he was with two dead teachers and four burglaries but with no leads to follow-up. He had never been in this position before and he was even beginning to think that he might never solve the case. He could only hope that no more teachers would be robbed or attacked.

Margaret had cooked a meal for them of pork and potatoes. She had also bought two bottles of beer for Jake; she, herself, choosing to drink only water. They sat at the kitchen table and ate their meal. Jake marvelled at the easy way in which Margaret conjured up some culinary delight. As he ate he told her about Mathieson's engagement.

"Oh, how lovely," added Margaret. "We must invite them here for a meal some night."

"That is a lovely idea," said Jake. "Perhaps we should wait until the ring has been bought as I feel sure you will want to see it."

"We can have them here for a meal and then invite them back again once the ring is bought," Margaret then said. "I'm sure it will take Sergeant Mathieson a little while to save enough money for a ring."

"Knowing Mathieson he'll have been saving his money; not necessarily for a ring, I hasten to add."

Margaret smiled. "Who is the lucky lady?"

"Her name is Ruby and she works at Gibson and Son on Rose Street."

"How lovely for them both," Margaret said again with a beaming smile.

***

It was nearly midnight and finally dark. There were four of them, all women and all dressed in black. They were in a high state of excitement as the horse and cart, in which they sat, passed the church at Queen's Cross. Nothing was actually said as they made their way down St Swithin Street and then turned right.

They made their way to Gladstone Place where they finally stopped outside one of the houses. It was not the house that they were intent on visiting; it was a little further along the street. They did not want to attract the attention of the house occupants, so they decided to leave one of their number with the cart and the other three would proceed on foot.

They climbed down from the cart and made their way around to the back. One of the ladies picked up a tin and then they moved a little closer to each other. The street lights were casting little light down upon them and they could only just make out each other's faces.

"Are we ready?" Ada Houston asked. She could see the other two nodding, though neither of them actually spoke. "Then let's go."

They made their way along the pavement until they were standing outside Councillor Barton's home. It was nearly half past twelve and they were conscious that if anyone saw them they'd be unlikely to forget the sight of four women arriving in a horse and cart. However, all four women took solace in the fact that no one would be able to actually identify any of them.

Councillor Barton was another outspoken member of the Council who was forever putting women down and arguing that there was no place for women in politics. In fact, if Councillor Barton had his way, there would be no place for women anywhere. He was a confirmed bachelor and had, as far as anyone could ascertain, never had a proper relationship with a woman in his entire life. Some had wondered if the man might prefer men in his life, but the truth was that he had never had a relationship with anyone that went beyond casual friendship or work-related camaraderie.

Councillor Barton lived in a large house with only his housekeeper for company. She had been with him for fifteen years and was a large and formidable looking woman. It had been pretty clear to any of the neighbours that it was highly unlikely that anything even remotely romantic, existed between the Councillor and his housekeeper. She had the expression of someone eating sour oranges and he rarely had two words to say to any woman about anything.

Ada handed the tin to one of the other women. Her name was Beatrice and this was the first time she had ever done anything illegal. They made their way up the path to the front door. Beatrice then began to pour the contents of the can over the front door and also put a little through the letter box. Ada then lit a match and held it close to the door. It ignited with a whoosh and flames immediately leapt in both directions.

Some of those flames leapt towards Beatrice and her skirt was soon alight and spreading up the rest of her clothing. She let out a terrified scream sending Ada in to a panic and running for the gate. Beatrice fell to the ground, the flames now engulfing her completely. The other three hurried away from Gladstone Place, even leaving the horse and cart in their rush to put distance between themselves and what had happened to poor Beatrice.

Back at the door of Councillor Barton's home, the occupants had now been roused and the housekeeper was on the telephone to the fire service in King Street. Councillor Barton had started to throw water at the flames engulfing his entranceway but he still, at that time, had no idea that someone was burning to death on the other side.

It was nearly an hour later before the true horror of the night became apparent. The fire service had arrived and put the main fire out. They had noticed the shape lying in the doorway. They hadn't realised immediately that the shape was human until they had the fire under control. It then became apparent that the shape was that of a woman. She was dead and her body had been burned beyond all recognition. It seemed obvious to everyone that this woman had, for whatever reason, started the fire and that in doing so, she had become a victim of her own actions.

***

TWENTY-SIX

Saturday 4th July

Jake arrived at work that Saturday morning to be told about the fire and death at Councillor Barton's home. He wasted no time in walking round to the Fire Station on King Street and asking to speak with someone in charge. As it happened the officer who had been in charge of putting the fire out was still on duty. He introduced himself as being Toby Rice and took Jake in to a small office where they drank a cup of rather disgusting tea as they spoke.

"What can you tell me about the fire?" Jake had begun by asking.

Rice was a tall, athletic looking man with a cheery countenance. Clearly he was someone who enjoyed his work.

"Started deliberately, presumably by the young lady whose charred remains were lying in the door way."

"I take it there's no doubt the fire was started deliberately?" Jake added.

"Why else would the young woman have been standing there at that time of night?" Rice replied.

Jake acknowledged it had been a silly question. "How did the fire take so quickly?"

"We found the remains of a can lying beside her. She must have used an inflammable liquid of some kind and it had splashed back on her, giving the fire another route to take. I doubt if the young lady would have had any experience of lighting fires before."

"Are you happy that this woman could have acted alone?"

"She was the only one we found but there may well have been others with her, I don't suppose we'll ever know now. Safe to say, however, that if there were other women at the scene then they'll all be traumatised by what they saw. It would have happened quickly and would have been a horrifying sight."

"Do you know if the occupants of the house saw, or heard, anything?"

"The first they knew of anything wrong was when the smoke filtered in to the house and woke the housekeeper. As it was the home of a Councillor he had a telephone on the premises so they were able to alert us at once. We were at the scene of the fire within twenty minutes of it starting, but that was still too late for the young lady, unfortunately."

"Would you think there would be any way of identifying the young woman?" Jake then asked.

Rice shook his head. "She didn't have a bag with her and everything else was pretty much destroyed in the fire. I don't think she would have wanted to be identified given that she was there to commit a crime."

Jake asked a few more questions and jotted down the replies. He then thanked Rice for his help and walked out on to King Street. He made his way to Union Street where he caught the tram that would take him out Queens Road. He got off at the relevant stop and made his way through to Gladstone Place.

The frontage of Councillor Barton's property was being worked on by a team of four men. They stepped aside to allow Jake to enter. Ten minutes later and Jake was in a back room talking to Councillor Barton. It was not an easy interview for Jake to conduct as he had never liked Barton, either as a Councillor or a man.

"Do you have any idea who the young woman might have been?" asked Jake.

"Well, not specifically, but surely she has to be one of those Suffragette maniacs who will stop at nothing to try and force us men to give them rights that they simply don't deserve. I'll be very surprised if that woman was here herself last night. Mark my words, Inspector.....," Barton began.

"It's Chief Inspector," Jake interrupted. He had told himself that he wouldn't use that rank, but he had decided to make an exception for Barton. The man was a self-opinionated, male chauvinist and Jake felt compelled to put him in his place at every opportunity."

"Oh, I'm so sorry, *Chief* Inspector," Barton then said, though Jake got the feeling that Barton now felt even more important for the fact that a Chief Inspector was investigating the crime perpetrated on his home. "Anyway, as I was saying, you mark my words, these women tend to hunt in packs. There will have been others and they will know exactly what happened to that poor woman last night. I don't agree with their misguided attempts to be given the vote, but equally I feel nothing but horror for what that woman must have suffered."

"Have you received any threats recently, Councillor Barton?"

"No."

"Any eggs thrown in your direction?"

"Only Councillor Manning has been the target for eggs. I have had no previous reason to believe that these women saw me as a target for their anger."

"Other than the fact you've openly said, many times before that women could never understand politics enough as to know what to do with a vote?" suggested Jake.

Barton looked suitably offended. "I only ever speak my mind."

"Which, in this instance, has annoyed a great number of women."

"I don't see it as being your place to judge me, Chief Inspector. Our political system has survived for decades without women playing a part; there seems no reason to change that, as far as I am concerned."

"I respect your opinion, Councillor Barton, but it is a view that will inevitably invite action from the more militant section of the Suffragette Movement. We will do what we can to protect you, but you may need to review how you word your comments on women's rights in the future."

"I will not change my opinions for anyone, especially those of a violent disposition. You are making all this sound as if I, in some way, invited these women to my door so that they could set fire to my house."

"I am not condoning what they have done, Councillor, but I feel it is only right that I point out to you that your comments against women's rights, do not help the situation one little bit. These women feel as strongly about their side of the argument as you do about yours. At some stage middle ground will have to be identified or even more people may end up dying."

"I refuse to change my views, Chief Inspector, but I will concede to choosing my words a little more carefully in future."

"I would be grateful for that small concession, Councillor. Was any literature left with you before they set fire to the door?"

"If it was it would have been burned in the fire, surely," added the Councillor.

"Perhaps. Only the women behind these actions usually seek publicity of some kind and it seems strange that no one sought to claim responsibility for what they were doing."

"Unless they had planned to do so but the death of the young lady had changed their minds?" the Councillor then suggested.

"That is a possibility. It must have been a tremendous shock for them to see one of their own go up in flames like that."

"And yet they ran away like the cowards that they are," added the Councillor.

"Not a very loyal act, I grant you," Jake agreed. "Anyway, Councillor, I will keep you up to date with any developments."

"Thank you for that, Chief Inspector."

Jake left the house and walked round to catch the tram back in to the city centre. As he waited at the stop he could not stop himself from thinking that Margaret might know the young woman who died. However, before he could confirm that he was going to have to put a name to the charred remains and that may yet prove to be rather difficult.

***

Anthony Wilson sat in the dining room of the Forsyth Hotel, looking across the table at Lucy Gill and feeling, at last, that he had finally met the woman who would become his second wife. He had been delighted when she had agreed to the offer of using a room in his house, even though Kath had scoffed at the idea. She was not in love with Mr Wilson, but she did feel the need to protect him, usually from himself.

Kath had long thought that Mr Wilson was hopeless romantic whose head would have been turned by the sight of any pretty face. To Kath, Lucy Gill was far more than a pretty face. There was something about her that Kath didn't like and she certainly wouldn't have trusted the woman as far as she could throw her. In Kath's mind, Lucy Gill was the type of woman to use Mr Wilson for her own reasons and then leave him. However, she would never have said anything directly to Mr Wilson.

Lucy had picked up on the fact that Kath did not appear to like her. She assumed that Kath *did* love Anthony and that was why she was being so over-protective. Whatever the reason, Lucy knew that when she started to sow the seeds of her swindle, she needed to be well away from the prying ears of Kath.

That was why they were now sitting back in the dining room of the Forsyth Hotel. Here they could enjoy a quiet meal and Lucy could introduce whatever topic she wanted without fear of interference from anyone else.

The dining room was actually very busy that Saturday afternoon but the tables were set far enough apart as to allow for casual conversation passing unheard by others. They ordered their meal, accompanied by a jug of water. As they waited for the soup to arrive, Lucy started to drop in to character. Her expression changed to one of concern and she began to fiddle with the handkerchief she had taken from her bag. It was not long before Wilson had noticed.

"Are you okay, Lucy?" he enquired with the desired concern on his face.

Lucy took her time. "It's nothing."

"Clearly there is something causing you concern. Would you like to talk about it?"

"No, it's all right, it's just something that I need to deal with myself," Lucy insisted.

Wilson reached out a hand and touched the back of Lucy's hand as it rested on the table.

"I hope I am not being too presumptuous," Wilson began, "but I sense that we are getting a lot closer and I would like you to know that any problem you may have might be made easier by telling me about it. It goes without saying, I hope that if there is anything I can do to help you then I will."

Lucy forced a smile. "That really is very kind of you, Anthony, but I don't want to burden anyone else with my problems."

"It would be no burden to help you out if I can," Wilson added and patted the back of her hand. She made no motion to move her hand but now brought the handkerchief to her face and forced out a tear."

Wilson's concern deepened. "My dear, Lucy, whatever is the matter?"

Lucy again let some time pass before speaking. "I appear to have got myself in to a spot of trouble and I'm not entirely sure how to get out of it."

"What kind of trouble?"

At this point Lucy was of the opinion that she could have said almost anything and she would have had Anthony Wilson reaching for his wallet. As it was, she had everything thought out and now adopted the script she had written in her head.

"I'm owe someone money," she said, allowing her lower lip to quiver just a little to, hopefully, enhance the emotional impact of what she was saying. Wilson said nothing, letting her tell her story. "When I was younger and down on my luck financially, I agreed to pose for a photographer in Edinburgh. He eventually offered to pay me extra if I agreed to pose in the nude. I needed the money, so I went along with it."

Lucy reached for the handkerchief and sobbed in to it for a moment. Wilson reached for her hand again. Still he said nothing.

"Anyway, years passed and nothing more happened as a result of those photographs. That was until two weeks ago when I was contacted by a man who said he had the pictures and he would send them to members of my family as well as my friends, if I did not pay him a certain sum of money. I have a little money set aside for a rainy day, but nothing like the amount he was requesting. I have until Friday to raise the money or he is going to start posting the pictures to various people."

Lucy turned on the waterworks. "I know it was stupid to pose for them in the first place, but I never thought they would come back to haunt me in such a way. It would be beyond embarrassing to have them become public knowledge now."

"Are these photographs easily identified as being you?" Wilson eventually asked.

Lucy picked up her bag and took something from within. She held it for a moment and then handed it to Wilson. He nearly gasped in horror at what he was now looking at. It was clearly a younger looking Lucy and she was wearing nothing but a chemise that still allowed the outline of her body to be visible beneath. Wilson averted his eyes at once.

"The other photographs are worse than that," Lucy added and the shock on Wilson's face magnified. "Now you can maybe understand why I don't want them going public?"

"Of course. This is terrible. How much money is this man asking for?"

Lucy paused again. "Thirty pounds."

"Thirty pounds?" repeated Wilson, rather louder than he had intended. One or two of the diners glanced their way. Wilson's face reddened and Lucy held her handkerchief to her mouth, though now to stop her smile being seen rather than to deal with any tears. Wilson dropped his voice again. "Why would anyone think that you could afford that kind of money?"

"Exactly," agreed Lucy. "Clearly the man had no intention of being paid off, he was always intent on publishing those photographs and disgracing me."

"But why?" Wilson asked again.

"I don't know," replied Lucy. "Perhaps it is a man whom I offended in the past and he sees this as the best way to get back at me. I don't even know how he got the photographs in the first place. Ah well, I don't suppose I have the greatest reputation to ruin, so maybe I should just let him do his worst."

"My dear Lucy," Wilson then said, "there is no way that I will allow your good name to be dragged through the mud. You must contact this man and tell him that he will have his money, only you will not pay him a penny until you have both the photographs and the negatives in your possession. I will also go with you when you meet with him."

Lucy reacted to the last sentence. She hoped she hadn't reacted too quickly.

"No, no that won't be necessary, Anthony. The man I am dealing with won't agree to a meeting if anyone else is there. The best you could do is come with me to the meeting, but to stay outside the building while I go in and conclude the deal."

Wilson thought for a moment. "Very well, that is what we will do. We will both go to Edinburgh and I will accompany you to wherever you agree to meet. I will give you the money just before you enter the building."

"You don't have to do this, Anthony," Lucy then said. "After all, you don't really know me."

Wilson took Lucy's hand again. He smiled. "I know you well enough, Lucy, to want to protect your reputation. No woman should ever have to agree to such pictures being taken of them and we must get them back and destroy them as soon as possible."

Lucy paused. "If you're sure?"

"I am."

"In that case I cannot thank you enough; it feels like you have saved my life rather than just my reputation."

"And can I ask you something else?" Wilson then said.

Here it comes, thought Lucy.

Wilson then asked her to consider marrying him. He said he would give her time to think about his proposal and that, perhaps, she might have an answer for him by the time she got the photographs back. He then explained further that it was the reputation of his future wife that he hoped he was saving.

Lucy said he would have an answer as soon as she had rid herself of her blackmailer. Externally, she kept up the pretence of being upset, but inside she was elated. It was difficult to keep the smile from spreading across her face. Thirty pounds was a lot of money, far more than she was accustomed to having. All she had to do now was wait until the end of the week and she would be rich.

***

Doctor Stephen was standing over the body of the young woman; not that identifying the corpse as being that of a young woman was very easy. The body had been very badly burned and there were no obvious signs of identification by way of facial recognition.

"What can you tell me, Doctor?" Jake said as he entered the room and recoiled at the sight of the charred remains.

"Not very much, I'm afraid. We can all see for ourselves how she died but from what I have to work with, I can't tell you who she is and I can't really add anything that will be of help to you."

"She's obviously quite young?" Jake prompted.

"Even putting an age on her is not easy," Doctor Stephen replied.

"Apparently she had been using an inflammable liquid to help start the fire and it must have splashed on to her dress. Once the flames caught light she would have had no chance."

Doctor Stephen shook his head slowly. "What drives a young woman to take such militant action?"

"They're fighting for what they believe in and are prepared to go to any lengths to achieve their goal. I don't agree with their actions, but I can at least understand why they do it."

"But surely no vote is worth the loss of a young woman's life?" the Doctor suggested.

"I agree, Doctor, though they may not see it that way," Jake concluded and left the room.

He went back across to the main building at Lodge Walk and returned to his office. He sat for a moment, letting his mind wander, but always keeping it on track as regards the inquiries be was dealing with. There was something niggling at the back of his mind, something that he couldn't put his finger on. It was like an itch that he couldn't reach to scratch and it was starting to drive him wild.

Jake's biggest problem was The Aberdeen Voice for Women. No one had ever heard of the organisation and until very recently, no one had even been aware of them taking action of any kind, let alone of the militant variety. In short, Jake had nothing to work on with regard to the organisation, which was what he was finding so strange. Why would any organisation, which basically thrived on publicity, not have raised its head before now?

Wouldn't an organisation as militant as that be shouting from the rooftops of its existence and of its actions? Wouldn't they be seeking publicity at every opportunity and wouldn't they be keen to let people know more about them? It was the apparent secrecy of the organisation that was causing Jake so much difficulty. It didn't add up and he couldn't decide why.

Jake finally decided that there was nothing else for it; he needed to call in reinforcements. He needed the help from someone who could ask questions that Jake could never ask and in areas of Aberdeen that Jake could never reach. Jake got up from his desk and went for a short walk.

It was time to talk to Stinky again.

Jake arrived at the Tea and Toast, a café on the corner of the Guestrow and Upperkirkgate. It was nearly closing time, but Jake knew that Stinky would still be there, sitting in the corner with his newspaper, mug of tea and half a dozen Woodbine.

The café was busy and all eyes looked in his direction. Most of the people sitting there recognised Jake, but his appearance did not cause a stir as he was often there and usually for the same reason; his meetings with Stinky were rarely held anywhere but in public. They could be seen but not heard.

Stinky was indeed sitting at his usual table. He had just lit another cigarette and was pulling a tin ashtray towards himself when he noticed Jake coming towards him. He waited until Jake had sat down, took a drink of his tea and then spoke.

"What can I do for you, Chief Inspector?"

"I told you I wasn't going to use the title; it is only temporary after all," Jake responded.

"The Chief Constable will find a way of giving the job to you permanently; there's no one else, is there?"

"I'm the best of a bad job, is that your honest assessment of the situation?" Jake asked with raised eyebrows.

Stinky drew hard on the end of his cigarette. "It may not have come out the way it was meant."

Jake sat forward. "Anyway, I want you to ask around and see what you can find out about an organisation called the Aberdeen Voice for Women."

Stinky grinned, showing more gum than teeth. "I'm getting to look for women, I like that idea."

"It's the organisation I'm interested in," Jake explained. "If you can get me some names as well then that would be a bonus."

Jake took some money from his pocket and slid it across the table. Stinky picked it up and shoved it in to the one pocket of his jacket that wasn't riddled with holes.

"I'll ask around," he then said, "and get back to you as quickly as I can."

"Thank you," said Jake and he left the café and headed for home.

***

Margaret had cooked another amazing meal for them and again there was a bottle of beer for Jake. He had taken off the collar of his shirt and opened the top button. Margaret was, as usual, looking lovely and they sat opposite each other, in the kitchen area, eating their meal and discussing the day.

For once, Margaret had a tale to tell as well.

"I had to get out of the flat this afternoon for a little while," she began.

"Why was that?"

"A tall man in a uniform insisted that I go outside with him," Margaret then added with a glint in her eye.

Jake was very confused. "Whatever do you mean?"

"The shop on the ground level went on fire and the firemen were evacuating all the buildings until they got it under control. It was just a safety precaution as I really don't think there was ever any danger of the fire spreading. Anyway, it was all very exciting for as long as it lasted."

Jake had pondered long and hard on whether, or not, he would tell Margaret about the woman who had burned to death. Eventually he decided to tell her, but to keep his account of events as general as possible. Margaret was horrified to hear that someone had died in the course of apparently making a statement for women's rights.

Through her horror she immediately thought about Sadie Ashton. Was this her finally taking her first, tentative, steps into militancy? Might Sadie even be the woman who had died? The thought passed.

As if reading Margaret's mind, Jake's next comment was about Sadie Ashton.

"You know I'll have to go and speak to Sadie about this?"

"I do."

"Will that put you in an awkward situation?"

"They all know who I'm married to," Margaret then said, "and they all know that I have no control over the way you conduct your business. Sadie is known to have made certain comments and that would be more than enough to give you a reason for speaking to her."

"She may think you've told me things about her," suggested Jake.

"She can think what she wants, Jake. I know what we've discussed in the past and I'm happy with that."

Jake smiled. "Then I will go and see Sadie Ashton at the earliest opportunity."

***

TWENTY-SEVEN

Monday 6th July

It was a little after nine when the Desk Sergeant came in to Jake's office. He was looking concerned about something and Jake wondered what it could possibly be as he waited for the Sergeant to speak.

"There is a terrible smell at the front door, sir and it claims to know you."

Not being one of the normal Desk Sergeants, the poor fellow had never had cause to meet with Stinky before. It had, therefore, come as an even greater shock to him when the person from which the smell was emanating, had asked to speak to Chief Inspector Fraser.

"Excellent," was all that Jake said as he rose from his seat and made for the door. The Desk Sergeant followed Jake to the front door.

"Let's talk outside," Jake said to Stinky, mindful both of the need for privacy but also of removing the source of the smell from the building before it caused irretrievable damage to the nasal passages of those who had to work at the front desk.

"I have some interesting information for you, Mr Fraser," Stinky began. "Firstly, the Aberdeen Voice for Women doesn't appear to exist. The only time anyone has heard the name mentioned has been when a certain Councillor has been dishing out money and asking small groups of men to damage buildings and leave behind leaflets like these."

Stinky took a folded leaflet from his pocket and handed it to Jake. It was the same type as had been found at all the locations where windows had been broken. So, it was pretty much as Jake had suspected; someone was trying to undermine the Suffragette argument by making the women of Aberdeen appear to be dangerously militant.

"Which Councillor are we talking about?" Jake then asked.

"Councillor Manning. I believe he was supposed to be one of the victims?"

"Indeed he was. It was very clever of him to make it appear that he was a victim when, in actual fact, he was the perpetrator. Do you know the names of any of the men who smashed windows in return for Councillor Manning's money?"

Stinky provided six names and also told Jake how much they had been paid for their actions.

"Even the egg throwing," Stinky then continued," was paid for by Manning. The women involved in that particular stunt were the wives of the men I've already told you about. Apparently, Manning asked not to be told when they'd attack him so that his reaction would look more natural."

Jake shook his head. "Councillor Manning's a bit of a devious so and so, isn't he?" Jake then said.

"Do you want me to do anything more regarding the Councillor?" Stinky then asked.

"No, that's okay, I'll deal with the Councillor." Jake took some cash from his pocket and gave it to Stinky. "And thanks for getting that information for me so quickly."

"That's all right, Mr Fraser, any time. I have something else for you."

"About the Aberdeen Voice for Women?"

"No, about someone you're probably getting sick of hearing about."

Jake looked confused. "Do tell."

"I'm being told that 'The Buchan Heiress' is in town again."

Jake now looked almost disgusted. "Not again. Why won't that woman simply go away and stay away. Do you know where she is?"

"Haven't heard so far, but I'll let you know if I get an address. If she's working to her usual standards then she'll be holed up in some hotel, carrying on as if she's the lady of the manor."

"And not aiming to spend any money in the process," added Jake and they both laughed. 'The Buchan Heiress' was certainly a nuisance, but in the great scheme of major crime, she was still small fry. Jake gave Stinky another coin and thanked him for the extra information.

He then went back inside, where he found the Desk Sergeant opening the window and wafting a newspaper around, as if hoping his actions might remove the smell just a little bit quicker. Jake continued on his way back to his office, where he collected his jacket and then went to find Sergeant Mathieson.

Jake was informed that Mathieson was with the Chief Constable, so he went back to his desk and finished some more paperwork until his Sergeant was free. When they eventually got together, Mathieson was smiling, so Jake assumed it was good news on the marriage front.

"The Chief has given us his blessing," Mathieson said with an ever-widening grin.

Jake shook his hand again. "Congratulations."

"Thank you, sir."

"Now we need to go and see Councillor Manning," Jake then said.

"Why?"

"You'll find out when we get there," was all that Jake would say.

The two men made their way through to Union Street and caught a tram that would take them out Queens Road. Thirty-five minutes later and they were standing at the front door of Councillor Manning's property. Jake knocked on the door and it was soon opened by a maid who showed them through to the sitting-room, where they waited a further ten minutes until Councillor Manning finally appeared.

Once they were all seated, Jake began.

"I have some good news for you, Councillor Manning."

"You've caught the women who attacked my home?" the Councillor asked, though his tone betrayed his uncertainty as to why, exactly, these police officers had called.

"I know who attacked your home, Councillor, though arrests have not been made, as yet."

The Councillor's expression of uncertainty deepened and Sergeant Mathieson looked confused. Both men were happy for Jake to continue. He took a sheet of paper from his pocket and began to read out the names written upon it. They were, of course, all men. Manning's expression tried to look confused, but Jake could already see the understanding appear in the Councillor's eyes.

"Who are they?" the Councillor asked.

"They are the members of the Aberdeen Voice for Women," Jake replied and Mathieson's jaw nearly hit the floor," but, of course, you already know that Councillor, seeing as you paid them all for services rendered."

"Utter nonsense," Manning blustered. "Why would I pay someone to attack my own home?"

"To bring disgrace to all those women fighting for their civil rights and no doubt, to try and make your own viewpoint look that little bit more acceptable."

"I don't know where you got your information from, Chief Inspector, but I'm telling you, it's utter nonsense and I shall be having a word with the Chief Constable about this."

Jake sat forward in his chair. "I can assure you that none of this is utter nonsense. Now, we can visit each and every one of these men and take statements concerning the part they played in smashing your windows for payment and we can also speak to their wives regarding the part they played in throwing eggs at you. After we've done that we can then speak to the parents of the woman who burned to death the other night trying to carry out a militant act that she hoped would get her noticed by the Aberdeen Voice for Women. I'm sure that they will be delighted to hear that their daughter died for a cause that not only doesn't exist, but which was the brainchild of a man who stands totally against any change to women's rights."

The blood drained form Manning's face. "What's all this about a woman burning to death?"

"On Friday night at least one woman, though I suspect she was not alone, visited Councillor Barton's home with a view to setting his doorway alight. Unfortunately, the flames engulfed one woman and she died at the scene. I believe that those women were only carrying out the act of violence in response to the actions taken by the Aberdeen Voice for Women."

"But you can't be blaming me for the death of that young woman?" Manning then said.

"That's exactly what I am doing, Councillor. If you hadn't thought up the crazy notion of inventing an organisation that might give women hope for changes in Aberdeen, then those women would not have taken to the streets to emulate the actions of that organisation."

"But I never advocated burning doors down," Manning then said. "I simply wanted the public to turn against these women and the easiest way of achieving that was to paint them in the blackest form possible. No one was meant to get harmed."

"It's too late for that now, Councillor. I hold you personally responsible for the death of that young woman and I expect you to pay the price for your actions."

Manning now looked truly worried. "Good God, man, you're not going to arrest me, are you?"

Jake smiled. "Nothing like that, Councillor. However, what I am going to do is give you two days to resign from the Council and scurry back under whatever rock you appeared from when you came up with the idea of smashing windows in the name of the Aberdeen Voice for Women."

"I have been a Councillor for years……..," Manning began to say.

"In which case, you ought to have known better. I don't believe that anyone who holds office in the public domain can be seen to be taking the kind of action you have taken. Paying men to destroy buildings in a blatant effort to blacken the name of women who are doing no more than fighting for their rights, is morally irreprehensible and you need to go."

"And if I don't resign?"

"Then I will arrest you and make public everything we know about you. We might not get the case to court, but you'd be finished long before then anyway, wouldn't you?"

"That's nothing short of blackmail, Chief Inspector," Manning then said.

"Of what you have heard so far, Sergeant, would you say any of it amounted to blackmail?" Jake then asked, glancing across at Mathieson.

"No, sir. It sounds to me like you are doing all that you can to keep the Councillor's reputation intact. I mean, no one wants any of this to get to court."

"There, Councillor, even my Sergeant sees that I am trying to help you here. Just walk away and we'll say no more. Perhaps you could donate a sum of money to a charity of your choice as well; that would be a nice touch."

Manning sat and quietly fumed for a moment or two before agreeing to what Jake had requested. He and Mathieson then left the Councillor to formulate his resignation letter. Mathieson returned to the office and Jake went to see Sadie Ashton.

***

Sadie Ashton spoke to Jake in the sitting-room. She had offered him tea, but he had refused. They now sat, Jake on a chair and Sadie on the settee, with a shaft of sunshine coming through the window.

"Mrs Ashton, what do you know about the Aberdeen Voice for Women?" Jake began.

"I know of their existence, but no more than that," Sadie replied.

"How many members do you now have for your militant group?"

Sadie Ashton looked surprised for a moment, but then she smiled, as if realising something.

"Margaret told you."

"No, Mrs Ashton, Margaret didn't tell me anything, I'm a detective so I don't depend on my wife to tell me anything. You've been making noises for some time and I now wish to know how big a militant group you have managed to form."

Sadie thought for a moment. "We are still small in number, Inspector, so you need not worry about us doing anything that may concern you."

"I fear they already have done something that concerns me," added Jake and Sadie Ashton looked both puzzled and concerned at the same time.

"I don't know what you mean," she said.

"Mrs Ashton, on Friday night a young woman burned herself to death trying to set fire to the front door of Councillor Barton. I believe that that young woman had a connection to you and that the actions she was undertaken were meant to impress the Aberdeen Voice for Women, no doubt with a view to you joining forces with them."

Sadie looked horrified.

"Do you know the name of the young woman involved?"

"We haven't been able to identify her as yet. As you are known to hold more militant views, concerning the fight for women's rights, I wondered if you were aware of a plan to set fire to the front door of Councillor Barton's house?"

"I do not deny I support militant action where it might be relevant. However, I do not support putting anyone's life in danger and I would never have suggested to anyone that setting fire to a Councillor's front door was the way forward. We have an argument to make, Inspector, but lives should not be lost in the process."

"Well, I'm sorry Mrs Ashton, but a life has been lost and if there is anything you can do to help me at least identify this poor woman, then I think you should do it now."

Sadie thought for a moment. She looked genuinely distressed by what Jake had told her.

"You need to speak to Ada Houston."

"Was she intent on attacking Councillor Barton?"

"She had mentioned taken action against other Councillors who had spoken out against our cause. I never imagined, for one moment, that she would have done something so stupid though."

"Where would I find Miss Houston?" Jake then enquired.

"Probably at the university, she should be there most days."

"Thank you, Mrs Ashton," Jake then said and stood up.

Sadie Ashton stood up as well and showed Jake to the door. As he opened the front door Sadie Ashton put her hand on his arm.

"Please tell Margaret that none of this will be allowed to affect our friendship. You are married to a good woman, Mr Fraser and I do not wish to lose that friendship lightly."

"I'm sure Margaret would wish your friendship to continue, Mrs Ashton," Jake then said and started to walk down the path.

***

It was nearly six o'clock in the evening before Ada Houston was located and brought to Lodge Walk. She was placed in an interview room and left on her own for nearly an hour with only one, young Constable to keep an eye on her. Eventually Jake felt that she had stewed in her own juices for long enough and he and Mathieson went to speak to her.

Ada Houston was a pretty young woman, though when Jake and Mathieson arrived she probably was not looking her best having been crying for most of the time she had been sitting there. As soon as the two officers came in to the room she began to cry again and with even more volume. She had a handkerchief in her hand and was dabbing at her nose and eyes.

Jake and Mathieson sat down. Ada looked from one to the other and then burst in to tears again. She was still crying as she started to speak.

"This is about Beatrice, isn't it?"

"If the charred remains lying in our mortuary is Beatrice, then yes," replied Jake and the tears flowed more freely. "Do you want to tell us what happened?"

Ada pulled herself together a little more and wiped her eyes. She took a deep breath and began to speak again.

"Her name was Beatrice Hardy and she had never done anything, even remotely illegal, in her life before. However, she passionately believed in women's rights and wished to play her part in keeping our cause known to the public at large. We were all strengthened by the arrival, in Aberdeen, of a militant wing that goes by the name of the Aberdeen Voice for Women. We all wanted to be part of that organisation and thought that if we carried out a militant act they would welcome us in to their midst with open arms."

"Do you know anything about the Aberdeen Voice for Women?" Jake then asked.

"Nothing specific. We knew they had started taking action in Aberdeen and hoped that by doing something similar they might come looking for us."

"But it all went wrong, didn't it?" Jake then said.

Ada started to cry again. "I don't know what happened. One minute we were lighting the match and the next Beatrice was………"

Ada could say no more as she sobbed uncontrollably. Jake went round the table and put his arm around her shoulder. He said what he hoped would be received as comforting words and slowly she began to calm down. Jake pulled a chair beside where Ada was sitting and sat down.

"I'm afraid I have some bad news for you, Miss Houston," he then said.

"Whatever do you mean, Inspector?" Ada enquired.

"We now know that the Aberdeen Voice for Women never actually existed."

Ada Houston's expression changed to one of confusion. Jake continued talking.

"We have further reason to believe that it may have been no more than one man's attempt to blacken the name of every woman who truly does stand for the future of women's rights."

"A man, but I don't understand?" Ada added.

"What better way to damage your cause than to make you all look like a bunch of criminals?"

Ada Houston looked in to Jake's eyes with an expression of outrage. "In that case Beatrice died for nothing?"

"I'm afraid that does appear be the case," Jake replied as he returned to his seat.

"Do you know who this man is?" Ada then asked.

"It's at an early stage in the investigation and we may never identify exactly who was behind it all," Jake said. He and Mathieson knew it to be a lie, but they both knew the case would never get to court and there seemed no reason in starting a journey that could not be completed. Jake knew it was no justice for Beatrice Hardy, but the fact that Councillor Manning was finished, both as a local politician and, to some degree, as an individual, did amount to something.

"I don't understand why any man would do such a thing," Ada then said.

"It had the desired effect, Miss Houston. You and your immediate circle believed that the Aberdeen Voice for Women was the way forward and you were prepared to carry out militant acts in the name of that organisation. In doing so, you have probably set your argument back by years, but that is just my opinion," Jake added. "However, let us return to the events of Friday night. What did you think you would achieve by setting fire to Councillor Barton's front door?"

"We thought we were making a statement. We thought we were making the Council sit up and take notice of us. How wrong we were."

"And when things started to go wrong, why did you just run away?"

"Panic. Panic and terror; I hope I never have to see such a sight ever again. Poor Beatrice," said Ada and the tears were streaming down her cheeks again.

"I can understand your immediate reaction, Miss Houston, but why did you then choose not to speak to the police? If you had at least informed us of the victim's name, it would have been something."

"I know, what we did to Beatrice was unforgivable but, as I said, we were all in a state of panic and shock. I wasn't thinking straight at first and then it developed in to a state of self-preservation. I didn't want my own future to be tarnished by what we had done."

"It was a bit late for thoughts of that kind, wasn't it, Miss Houston?" Jake suggested.

"I suppose it was," agreed Ada. "So, what happens now?"

"Did Beatrice live locally?" Jake enquired.

"No, her family live in Glasgow."

"Then they will need to be informed that their daughter has been killed whilst indulging in a criminal act. There is no way that we can hide that fact I am afraid. However, as far as everyone else need be concerned, we will report that Beatrice acted alone. There seems little need to involve anyone else and destroy further lives.

Ada cried again, but this time it was from a sense of relief. Jake let her settle again before saying anything further.

"I take it that I don't have to tell you to steer clear of any further militant action. If you are arrested for anything else, Miss Houston, then I will find a way of linking it to Beatrice's death."

"I understand, Inspector and I thank you for what you've done."

"I don't feel happy about what we've done, it just doesn't seem right for poor Beatrice that she should have to take the blame for the collective actions of others. However, if in her memory you can prevent anything like this happening again, then her death will not have been totally in vain."

"I will certainly ensure that no one in the university talks of such action," Ada said and Jake thanked her for any help she might be able to give them in the future.

Ada Houston was then allowed to walk out of Lodge Walk and Jake went back to his office to write a report that was factually inaccurate, but which provided the best outcome for everyone except Beatrice. Councillor Manning kept his reputation intact and a group of young women, at university, would be allowed to carve out a life for themselves without the tarnish of a police conviction. The Aberdeen Voice for Women would disappear and hopefully, militancy would disappear from the streets of Aberdeen.

Jake went home to Margaret that night feeling very down. He was never going to be able to tell her the truth about the death of Beatrice Hardy and he did not like to lie to his wife. However, in this instance, it seemed the right thing to do.

***

TWENTY-EIGHT

Tuesday 7th July

Sergeant Mathieson had arranged to meet Ruby in the St Nicholas Church graveyard at lunchtime. It was a popular meeting place from where young people could take a walk together or simply sit and enjoy the sunshine. It had been a cloudy morning, but the Gods were obviously looking down on the love-birds as the sky had cleared and a deep blue sky now provided the perfect backdrop to a warm and inviting sun.

Ruby was looking as radiant as ever when she arrived and Mathieson let her slip her arm through his before they set off walking towards Union Street. They had little time and had decided to enjoy a walk, rather than sit down anywhere. They spent twenty minutes enjoying the warmth of the day before Mathieson saw Ruby back to her place of employment.

As they were preparing to part company, Ruby suddenly became quite excited about something and began searching in her bag. She eventually produced a piece of paper on which she had written a name.

"I meant to tell you," she began, "I was looking in Mr Kerrigan's diary for a note of when he last saw one of our clients and I came across an entry for late April, which I thought might have been of interest to you."

"Really?" added Mathieson with immediate interest.

Ruby handed the paper to Mathieson.

"Mr Kerrigan had an appointment in his diary for the last week of April to see a Juliet Grainger. That was one of the names on the list you gave me of Grammar School teachers. Now, it may not be the same Juliet Grainger, but I thought I had better let you know."

Mathieson glanced down at the name and date written on the paper and smiled. "Thank you, Ruby, that may yet prove to be very useful indeed."

Ruby looked pleased to have been of some help. Having checked that no one could see them, they quickly kissed and she went in to her work, while Mathieson made his way back to Lodge Walk, where he sought out Jake at once.

"I have interesting news," Mathieson said as he arrived in Jake's office.

"I'm listening."

"Kerrigan, the man who valued all Edith McIntosh's items, had an appointment to meet with Juliet Grainger during the last week of April. Neither he, nor Miss Grainger, mentioned anything about that."

"And it gives us that link between a Grammar School teacher and someone with knowledge of the antiques and collectables world, which we've been trying to find for a while now."

"Though, in itself, it doesn't provide us with evidence, only further suspicion," Mathieson added.

"If Kerrigan and Miss Grainger do know each other, then why lie about it unless you have something to hide?" countered Jake. He then paused and thought for a moment. "This really could change everything. What if Miss Grainger was not the first victim of the burglar but an accomplice? We only have her word for the fact she was ever a victim of anything, but by telling us that she had been burgled, she very cleverly moved herself above suspicion. I never considered the possibility that she could be involved, which is why this connection to Kerrigan changes everything. Come, Mathieson, I think it is time that we spoke with Mr Kerrigan once more."

Jake and Mathieson returned to the offices of Gibson and Son. Ruby smiled at Sergeant Mathieson and blushed when Jake spoke to her. He found that rather endearing. They waited a few minutes before Kerrigan came through and took them to a room, which he was now using as an office.

"Mr Kerrigan, have you ever met with a woman by the name of Juliet Grainger?" Jake asked, coming straight to the point of their visit.

Kerrigan gave the question some thought. "No, I don't believe that I have."

"Do you keep an appointments diary, sir?" Mathieson then asked.

"Yes I do, as a matter of fact."

"Might I see it, sir?"

"Of course," replied Kerrigan and he took a red book from the top drawer of the desk. He slid it across to Mathieson with a look of confusion on his face. Nothing else was said as both Jake and Kerrigan watched as Mathieson opened the book at a certain point and began looking down the page.

"Ah, yes, here we are," Mathieson then said. "You had an appointment for four o'clock on the afternoon of Monday, twenty-seventh of April with a Juliet Grainger. Does that mean anything more to you now, sir?"

Kerrigan looked even more confused. "Regardless of what may be written in that diary, Sergeant, I can assure you that I have never spoken to a woman by the name of Juliet Grainger. What was the date again?"

Mathieson told him. Kerrigan pondered a little longer and then a look crossed his face as if a light had suddenly come on in a darkened room.

"I remember now, I was off sick for three days that week. I ate something at the weekend, which clearly had not agreed with me and I did not return to work until the Thursday of that week."

"Would someone else have seen clients destined for you?" Jake now asked.

"I expect Mr Gibson would have dealt with any clients who came in. He's really the only person who could have done that."

"So it's possible that Mr Gibson may have spoken to Miss Grainger?" Jake added.

"Perfectly possible."

"Is Mr Gibson in the office at the moment?"

"I believe he is," replied Mr Kerrigan.

"Then that will be all for the moment; thank you for your time."

All three men returned to the front office where Jake asked if they might now see Mr Gibson. They were told that Mr Gibson had someone with him, but Jake said he'd be happy to wait. Ruby got them a cup of tea as they sat in the waiting area until Gibson was free.

Once through in Gibson's office, Jake again came straight to the point.

"Do you know a woman by the name of Juliet Grainger?"

Gibson's face twitched. "Is there some reason that I should?" he replied.

"Miss Grainger had an appointment to see Mr Kerrigan on the twenty-seventh of April, but Mr Kerrigan informs us that he was off sick for most of that week and that it seems more likely that you will have met with Miss Grainger that day."

"I may well have done," Gibson then said, his expression showing he was once more back in control of his emotions, "but I honestly don't remember every client I see."

"Miss Grainger is a teacher at the Grammar School, Mr Gibson and may well be part of a murder inquiry that is underway at the moment. Now, I'm sure that you wouldn't want to be dragged in to that inquiry as anything other than a helpful witness so I ask you again, do you know a woman by the name of Juliet Grainger?"

Gibson sat back in his chair. He seemed to be giving the question a lot of thought; far more than Jake might have expected. Time passed and Jake was beginning to think that he wasn't going to get an answer when Gibson finally spoke.

"Yes. Yes, I do."

"Are you having a romantic relationship with Miss Grainger?" Sergeant Mathieson then added. Jake felt that his Sergeant may have jumped forwards with rather more haste than was necessary, but the question had now been asked so he awaited the answer with the same interest as Mathieson.

Gibson gave the Sergeant a *how do you know that* look, but actually said:

"I don't believe that my private life is any of your business."

Jake had already noted Gibson's expression; it had actually said far more than the words coming out of his mouth.

"I'll take that as a yes then," he added.

Gibson became even more flustered.

"Look, what has my relationship with Miss Grainger got to do with your murder inquiry?"

"Miss Edith McIntosh, a teacher at the Grammar School was murdered at the beginning of June. Certain valuable items went missing from her home at the same time and some of those items have since been presented to local traders by a young woman with blonde hair."

"Juliet doesn't have blonde hair," Gibson added quickly.

"Neither does the young lady trying to sell the stolen items; she's been wearing a wig," Jake then said. Gibson twitched again, but said nothing at first. Eventually he did speak next.

"This mystery woman in the wig can't be Juliet, she'd never do anything of a criminal nature."

"Neither you, nor Miss Grainger, chose to tell us that you knew each other, Mr Gibson?"

"Surely there was no need."

"No need? Mr Gibson, this is a murder inquiry so there is a *need* for us to know everything that may of importance to the case. Two apparently separate individuals actually knowing each other could be of tremendous importance."

"But the fact that we may have known each can have no relevance to your investigation, Inspector. We believed our relationship was a private matter and that is how it should remain."

"And yet I specifically asked if you had done any business with Miss Grainger and you said that you hadn't. You deliberately lied to me, Mr Gibson and I find that somewhat suspicious," Jake added.

Gibson now seemed in complete control of his emotions.

"As I said, Inspector, we thought it unnecessary to talk about private matters, especially where they had no connection to your investigation."

"Mr Gibson, I'll decide what may, or may not, have relevance to my investigation. This case is all about someone seeking to steal a collection of valuable miniature paintings from Miss McIntosh. We believe that a colleague at the Grammar School learned of these paintings and involved a third party in carrying out the robbery. I now further believe that that colleague was Miss Grainger and that she involved you, in her little scheme, as you would have been able to put a value on those paintings once they had been stolen."

"But I was never asked to value paintings by Miss Grainger," insisted Gibson.

"Then what was the purpose of her visit in April?" Jake then enquired.

"She had a few personal items she wished to have valued."

"And those items were what exactly?"

"Oh just bits and pieces. As it turned out they weren't worth much anyway."

"Did you do the valuation?"

"I did. I went to her home and valued the items in question. I found her to be a very attractive young woman and asked her out to dinner. Thankfully she accepted and we have been seeing each other ever since."

"Whilst visiting her home on business, you asked her out to dinner?" Jake then asked, a note of incredulity in his voice.

"I know it isn't the normal thing to do but, yes, that is exactly what happened."

Jake glanced at Mathieson and could tell that his Sergeant was having trouble believing Gibson as well.

"And you still say that you had nothing to do with valuing Edith McIntosh's belongings?" Jake asked.

"None whatsoever."

Jake thought for a moment. He then asked his next question.

"If you did some valuation work for Miss Grainger why is it that there is no record of payment on your company files?"

"Because there was no payment to record. I did the work as a personal favour to Miss Grainger. As I said, I found her a very attractive young woman and her company at dinner was payment enough for me."

"And you never thought to mention any of this when we spoke earlier?" added Jake.

"As I keep saying, Inspector, I didn't think it was relevant."

Jake looked anything but impressed by Gibson's answers, but he knew that he had nothing more on the man than suspicion. Certain elements did not hang together, but Jake, as yet, had no actual evidence of wrong-doing.

"Very well, Mr Gibson, that will be all for the moment. I'm sure we'll want to speak to you again, so please keep yourself available."

Jake and Mathieson then returned to Lodge Walk. Jake asked for two Constables to go to the Grammar School and to bring Juliet Grainger to Lodge Walk for questioning. She was not to be told anything and once they had her in Lodge Walk she was to be placed in the interview room ahead of Jake being notified of her presence.

***

An hour later and Jake and Mathieson were back in the interview room, only this time, sitting at the table was Juliet Grainger. She looked prim and proper and quite unconcerned to be sitting in a police interview room. Her hair was still tied up in a bun and her overall appearance was every bit the schoolteacher. She looked at both Jake and Mathieson with an air of confidence that surprised them both. Jake wasted no time.

"Do you know Mr Charles Gibson?"

"I do."

"How long have you known him?"

"We first met when I visited his firm in late April. I had some items I wished to have valued and had been meant to meet with a Mr Kerrigan. He had been ill that day and Mr Gibson had offered to see me."

"What items were you wanting valued?"

"A few trinkets and a painting. Mr Gibson came to my house and valued them for me. He then invited me to dinner and I accepted. We have been friends ever since."

Jake felt the responses had come across as having been rehearsed in some way. Not surprisingly, they were also in keeping with what Gibson had said. The stories were the same and yet he couldn't help thinking they weren't accurate.

"Why didn't you tell me that you knew Mr Gibson when I spoke to you about Miss McIntosh's death?"

"Because it has nothing to do with Miss McIntosh's death."

"I only have your word for that, Miss Grainger. Were you to know about Miss McIntosh's miniature collection then it would be necessary for you to find someone who could value that collection. Mr Gibson would have been an ideal candidate for that role."

"Are you suggesting that Mr Gibson and I had something to do with Edith's death?"

"That is exactly what I'm suggesting, Miss Grainger," added Jake.

Jake note that Miss Grainger did not flinch. He had basically accused her of murder and yet she still sat before him as prim and proper as ever. She remained as cool as ever which, in itself, did not seem right to Jake.

"And why would Charles and I have anything to do with Edith's murder?"

"For financial gain, nothing more."

Miss Grainger readjusted her seating position and actually smiled.

"Inspector, I have known Charles Gibson for little more than a few weeks and I hardly think, in that short space of time, we would have discussed stealing items from one of my colleagues, let alone discussed killing her."

"Oh I think the discussion was only ever about theft, Miss Grainger. You see, Edith McIntosh was never meant to die that was the part of the plan that went wrong. I'm not sure exactly what did go wrong, but it did and you, or Mr Gibson, were left with no other option but to murder Edith McIntosh."

Miss Grainger did not flinch. "We had nothing to do with Edith's death," she insisted.

"In that case, Miss Grainger, I'm sure you won't mind accompanying myself and a small team of police officers back to your home where we will search for anything that will link you to this investigation. By *anything*, I even mean blonde wigs or recently used theatre make-up."

There was finally a slight twitch at the corner of Miss Grainger's left eye. She recovered quickly, but Jake knew at once that he was on to something.

"I have no idea what you are talking about, Inspector. I have never worn a wig in my life."

"In which case you have nothing to be concerned about when we put you in a blonde wig and ask two antiques' traders to tell us if you are, indeed, the same woman who tried to sell them miniature paintings, which we now know had been stolen from Edith McIntosh's home."

The twitch was there again. However, when she spoke it was still with the same confidence that she had brought in to the room.

"Play your little games, Inspector, it will get you nowhere."

Jake could now see that Miss Grainger was unlikely to buckle under the pressure of his questioning. She sat looking at him with an expression of defiance. If he was to break her down then he would need to find some real evidence.

"Very well, Miss Grainger, I'll give you some time to give this matter thought and hopefully you'll then be better prepared to co-operate with us."

"You can't keep me here," Miss Grainger added, "I haven't done anything."

"I can keep you here as long as I feel it is necessary, Miss Grainger," Jake then said and he stood up and left the room. Mathieson followed him and a young Constable was sent in to the room to watch over Miss Grainger. He was also told to take her in a cup of tea.

"She seems very cool," Mathieson then commented as they made their way back to Jake's office.

"She has every reason to feel cool, Sergeant. She knows that the most we can prove is her part in trying to sell the miniatures. It seems too much to believe that she would be our killer and I doubt if she would even have the where-with-all to be our burglar. That leaves us with her as an accomplice and for that her punishment will be very light indeed."

"But surely she played a bigger part than that?" Mathieson added.

"Oh, I'm sure she did, but we could never prove it. Proving that someone had an idea is far more difficult than proving someone committed an act. We may not be able to prove Miss Grainger's guilt when it comes to murder, but we can at least gather some evidence with regard to her part in the planning of the burglary that led to both murders. In the meantime, gather all the information that you can on Charles Gibson, I want to know everything about the man before we speak to him."

"Very good, sir," concluded Mathieson as he left the room.

Two hours later and Mathieson had spoken to a number of people connected to Charles Gibson, including neighbours and colleagues. He had been fortunate enough to meet and talk to someone who had known Gibson for many years and what he had to tell Mathieson was of the greatest interest both to him and later, to Jake Fraser when he came to interview Gibson.

Armed with this information, Jake then sent two Constables to bring Charles Gibson to Lodge Walk. While they waited for Gibson to arrive he and Mathieson sat in his office and discussed how they would approach the interviews with both Gibson and Miss Grainger.

"You're pretty sure they're behind the burglaries and both murders, aren't you sir?" Mathieson said.

"Given what we now know about Gibson and given they both chose to hide the fact they were in a relationship, we can be one hundred per cent certain that they planned to steal the miniatures from Miss McIntosh. Whatever went wrong on the day it led to Miss McIntosh being murdered. I still have no idea as to why Mr Diamond had to be burgled, let alone murdered, but I hope that will come out as we talk to both Gibson and Miss Grainger."

Mathieson thought for a moment. "If Gibson and Miss Grainger are responsible for stealing Miss McIntosh's miniatures then why did they not try to sell them through Gibson's connections? It was a terrible risk having Miss Grainger visit local outlets even if she did disguise herself first."

"Nothing more than a greed for money, I assume. Perhaps Miss Grainger could not afford to wait any longer and decided to sell some items locally. If that was the case then it further suggests that she was the dominant member of their partnership. That also further suggests that she was more involved than she will now try to claim."

"And you are quite sure that they were also responsible for Mr Diamond's death?"

"Quite sure. I have always maintained that we were only looking for one killer, even though the two murders could not have been more different. Mr Diamond was ultimately killed for the life he chose to live, I'm convinced of that as well. His murderer was most definitely a man and a man who could not accept Mr Diamond's sexuality. Once the murderer's hatred of such men had been released he was unable to control it. The number of blows that were rained down on Mr Diamond proves that he was killed in a fit of uncontrolled rage."

"So it had to be Gibson who committed the murders?" Matheson then said.

"Or a third party employed by Gibson and Miss Grainger," countered Jake. "Either way we need to get them to talk for without some kind of confession we might struggle to pull together enough evidence to build a strong case against them."

"If we find the miniatures we can at least get them on theft," Mathieson then said.

"I think the case for them stealing the miniatures will be strong enough, but I want to get them for the murders as well."

"So we need that confession, sir?" added Mathieson.

"We certainly do, Sergeant and I have a feeling that we are more likely to get one from Charles Gibson than we ever will from the ice cold Miss Grainger."

***

Charles Gibson looked very worried as he sat in the room where Jake and Mathieson had now arrived. His face was highly coloured and a thin layer of sweat was visible on his brow. He was also drumming his fingers on the table top and his eyes flicked from Jake to Mathieson as they sat down.

"You've been lying to us, Mr Gibson," Jake then said in a tone that he hoped would sound both threatening and knowledgeable.

"Whatever makes you think that?" Gibson asked. Jake noted that Gibson was finding it difficult to make eye contact, which was usually a sign that someone was not likely to be entirely truthful with their answers.

"Well we know for a fact that you lied about your relationship with Miss Grainger," Jake added.

"I've already explained that I didn't think my relationship with Juliet had any relevance to the inquiry you had undertaken."

"Ah but it did, Mr Gibson, because your relationship with Miss Grainger is what started this whole sorry mess. She had an idea to steal some miniature paintings from a colleague, but she needed someone to help her. She needed someone to steal the paintings in the first place and she also needed someone to value those paintings for her so that she wasn't swindled when she came to sell them. That was where you came in."

"I don't know what you are talking about," Gibson said, though his demeanour said exactly the opposite. The sweat on his brow was even more prominent.

"Miss Grainger let you in to her life. I'm sure you seriously thought that she genuinely cared for you but, of course, she didn't. All she wanted was your knowledge, Mr Gibson but she ended up with far more than that, she gained your loyalty, didn't she?"

Gibson's eyes flickered in Jake's direction, but almost immediately looked away again. He was trying to swallow, but his mouth was too dry.

"Might I have a glass of water?" he then said.

"Just answer a few more questions and I'll arrange for you to get a drink, Mr Gibson," Jake replied. "You had no sooner got to know Miss Grainger when she told you about the miniatures and her plan to steal them, am I right?"

"Look, Inspector........," Gibson began.

"*Chief* Inspector, Mr Gibson," interrupted Jake who felt that Gibson was someone else who needed to be put in his place.

Gibson paused for a moment before speaking again. "Very well, Chief Inspector, as I was about to say, I know nothing about any miniature paintings."

"Miss Grainger never mentioned the fact that her colleague owned some seriously expensive paintings?"

"No."

"And you were never asked to value anything of that nature?"

"No."

"So you were never in Miss McIntosh's house?" Jake then asked.

"Of course not."

"So if we had a witness who could say otherwise, you'd be very surprised?" added Jake quickly and Gibson's eye twitched.

"I don't know what you mean by a witness who could say otherwise," he then said.

Jake paused for a moment and even Mathieson wasn't sure what the Inspector would say next.

"We have a witness who told us that a man was seen arriving at Miss McIntosh's house in the company of Miss Grainger around the time that Miss McIntosh was murdered. If we were to ask that witness to come forward once more and have a look at you, is it not a strong possibility that they would identify you as being that man?"

Gibson became even more agitated. "Very well, I did visit Miss McIntosh once with Juliet, but I had nothing to do with stealing anything from her."

"Then why not simply say so in the first place?" Jake then said. "You see, the more you lie to us the more suspicious we get of you. An innocent man has no need to lie, Mr Gibson."

Gibson was now sweating profusely and the twitch at his eye was even more pronounced. Jake continued.

"So we now know that you *had* been to Miss McIntosh's house. Why were you there?"

"A social call. Juliet had some personal business and I merely went along."

"What was the nature of that business?"

"Personal, that is all you need to know."

Jake smiled. "In a murder inquiry, Mr Gibson, I can demand to know a lot more than that. Now, would you please answer the question."

"I was not in the room when Juliet discussed her business, so I have no idea what they talked about."

"You had been upstairs at the time stealing the miniatures, I assume?" Jake added quickly and the flicker in Gibson's eyes said far more than words.

"Of course I wasn't," Gibson blurted out, but Jake now knew he was on to something. However, what he said next was to take Gibson totally by surprise.

"Mr Gibson, what did you do as a profession before starting your current business?"

Gibson looked totally confused by the question. "What has that to do with anything?"

"Just answer the question," insisted Jake.

"I was a locksmith," came the rather reluctant reply.

"So you know how to pick locks or make keys?" Jake added.

"I do."

"A handy talent for someone looking to steal from others?" Jake suggested.

"Just a handy talent for someone looking to be a successful locksmith," countered Gibson.

"I used to think there was a third party involved in this investigation, but now I'm totally convinced there never was anyone other than yourself and Miss Grainger. She gathered the information and you carried out the jobs. You didn't need to use your skills on Miss McIntosh's home as Miss Grainger could get you in there very easily. However, the ability to pick locks was invaluable when it came to the other burglaries that we were meant to investigate."

"This is ridiculous, I'm not going to sit here and……..," Gibson began to say, pushing back his chair and beginning to stand up.

"Sit down!" Jake snapped and Gibson slowly lowered himself back in to the chair.

"You can have no proof for any of this," he then said.

"The miniature paintings will be all the proof we need," Jake then said and he noticed, for the first time, a look of real uncertainty cross the face of Charles Gibson. For the first time he was beginning to wonder what, exactly, the police might know.

"But I keep telling you, I know nothing about any miniatures. Even if you were to find some of them it can't, in any way, be connected to either myself or Juliet."

"A mystery blonde woman has been trying to sell some of the miniatures around Aberdeen. That tells us that at least some of them are still in the city. I'm willing to bet that they are still in either your home or that of Miss Grainger and that being the case we will find them when we visit."

"You can't go to our homes without our permission," Gibson said, though he knew he was clutching at straws.

"In the interests of gathering evidence we can pretty much do as we please, Mr Gibson. I am in the process of organising two teams of police officers to visit your homes with a view to finding both miniature paintings and evidence that Miss Grainger used a disguise when trying to sell them. Once we have that we will have all the evidence we need to charge you both with stealing the paintings from Miss McIntosh. Of course in proving that you stole the paintings we also put you at the front of the queue as a suspect for her murder, but we'll say more about that once we have the necessary evidence to prove theft."

Jake then stood up and headed for the door. Mathieson followed. Jake paused at the door and informed Gibson that he would get that drink of water now. He then said he'd be back and both officers left the room. Jake left Mathieson to arrange the drink of water and also to find a constable to wait with Gibson while he hurried to see the Chief Constable and to be given the necessary permission to go to the homes of Gibson and Miss Grainger.

The permission was duly granted and two teams were dispatched, both told not to come back until they had found the necessary items.

Jake then sat in his office and waited for news to filter back.

***

It was early morning before everyone was back at Lodge Walk. The miniature paintings had been found semi-concealed in a drawer in Miss Grainger's bedroom. A blonde wig and some theatrical make-up were also found in the bedroom. They found nothing incriminating in Gibson's house, though they did find a belt with all his locksmith's tools in it. They also found a diary, which did not contain a confession to any crimes, but did contain detail as to how infatuated with Miss Grainger, Mr Gibson actually was, including a statement that he would do anything for her.

Armed with the evidence, Jake and Mathieson returned to the room where Charles Gibson had been sitting, quietly stewing in his own juices. His eyes darted in their direction, as they entered the room and then he looked down at what Jake had in his hand. As he sat down he laid one of the miniature paintings on the table.

"Mr Gibson, this was found in Miss Grainger's home along with a blonde wig and some theatrical make-up. This obviously categorically proves that Miss Grainger was not only involved in the robbery of these paintings but also in the failed attempt to then sell them on to local dealers. All this, I believe, proves that Miss Grainger was the one collecting information from her Grammar School colleagues but it doesn't, in itself, prove that she carried out those burglaries or had anything to do with the murders. But of course there never will be any evidence to directly link her to the robberies, or the murders, as she didn't have anything to do with that. She provided the information and her male accomplice carried out the jobs. And that is where we come back to you, Mr Gibson. Here you sit, the man currently in Miss Grainger's life and a man who just happens to have the skills of a locksmith and the necessary knowledge to value antiques. In other words, Mr Gibson, the perfect accomplice."

Gibson's face drained of all colour. "You have no proof that I am that man, Inspector," he then said. "I have admitted to being romantically connected to Miss Grainger, but I know nothing about thefts and murders."

"But Miss Grainger knows who committed the burglaries and the murders, Mr Gibson and when she starts talking, as she most surely will, she will hang you out to dry as quick as look at you."

"Juliet will have nothing to say to you," Gibson said with mock bravado.

"Perhaps not at first, Mr Gibson, but once we show her the evidence and explain that without her telling us about her accomplice we will be forced to charge her with everything, I rather think we'll hear her side of the story fast enough. You see she can argue, fairly easily, that she did not kill anyone and so the worst we can charge her with is as an accessory to burglary and murder. The punishment for that charge, as I am sure you already know, will be less severe than that of the murderer himself. In other words, she will have much to gain by telling us about her accomplice, which would rather land you in it, wouldn't it, Mr Gibson?"

Jake sat back and allowed a silence to hang in the room for what seemed, at least to Gibson, to be an eternity. Whilst the silence remained, Gibson appeared to be giving his situation a lot of thought. Eventually he was ready to speak.

"It was all her idea."

"Go on," prompted Jake.

"Juliet really did come to my company to have some personal items valued. She had heard about us through Miss McIntosh. On the day she turned up Mr Kerrigan was off ill and I agreed to see her. I'm sure I loved her from the moment I saw her. I really did visit her with a view to valuing her items and I really did ask her to dinner that same day. However, once we had seen each other a few times, Juliet began to speak about a collection of miniature paintings that she knew one of her colleagues owned. She said that Miss McIntosh was keen to sell the paintings and Juliet thought I might be in a position to buy them. However, the collection is worth far more than I could ever have afforded. Juliet then suggested we steal them. I tried to dissuade her but she was adamant that we could successfully steal the items without anyone knowing it was us. We visited Edith McIntosh together and while Juliet kept Edith occupied I went in search of the miniatures. Juliet had had some idea of where they might have been kept and it didn't take me that long to find them. We were to leave at that stage and the plan was for me to come back at a later date and actually steal the paintings. That way, Miss McIntosh would never have known who the thief was."

"But things didn't go according to plan, did they Mr Gibson?" prompted Jake.

Gibson's eyes dropped and he stared at the floor. "No."

"What happened next?"

Gibson paused again. Finally he sighed deeply and began to speak again.

"Miss McIntosh began to wonder what I was doing. Juliet tried to keep her occupied but she got up and hurried from the room. I never heard her coming up the stairs and the first I knew that something might be wrong was when she came in to the room and caught me looking at the paintings. She said something about never really trusting Juliet and not being surprised that she might stoop as low as to steal from her. She turned to leave the room, saying something about going to the police. In the moment I panicked. I could see my entire reputation being lost on this one moment of madness and I simply couldn't afford that to happen. I grabbed the curtain tie caught up with Miss McIntosh at the door. I swear I had killed her before I was even aware of what I was doing."

"And where was Miss Grainger at that time?"

"Standing about three feet away from me watching. She had a smile on her face as if she were getting some pleasure from what I was doing."

"What happened next?" Jake then enquired.

"I took Miss McIntosh's body back in to the room and left it on the floor."

"And what did Miss Grainger do then?"

"She came over to me, put her arms around my neck and kissed me passionately on the lips. She then told me that I had nothing to worry about as she would never tell anyone about what had happened. She added that she would give me my reward later."

Jake looked puzzled. "What did she mean by that?"

"As soon as we got back to my home we made love. I presumed that was what she meant."

"So Miss Grainger offered you sex as a reward for killing her colleague?" Jake added, as if finding it difficult to comprehend what he was hearing.

"Yes, she's a bit strange when it comes to sex."

"So it would seem," said Jake, glancing at Mathieson.

"Okay, now you have the miniatures, why was there any need for more burglaries?"

"Juliet thought it would be a good idea for other teachers at the Grammar School to feel they were victims of the burglar as well. She hoped that if the police were looking for a burglar then they'd be unlikely to give Miss McIntosh's death any more thought than her being an unfortunate victim."

"No one else was supposed to die, were they Mr Gibson?" Jake enquired.

Gibson shook his head quietly before he actually answered the question.

"No, Chief Inspector, they were not."

"So what happened when you visited Archibald Diamond?"

Gibson face turned to an expression of absolute disgust. "No one should ever have to witness what I did. No man should ever do such things to another man, it's simply not human."

"It is no excuse for murder, Mr Gibson," Jake added, but Gibson continued to look as if he did not agree.

"I was still in the flat when Diamond came back from his walk. I was waiting for the opportunity to leave when someone called. I was trapped behind a chair in the corner of his living room and no matter how much I tried not to watch I felt my eyes being drawn to what those two men did to each other. I'm not a wholly religious man, Chief Inspector, but by whatever God you believe in, no one should have to witness what I did. As soon as Diamond's visitor left I felt my temper rise. I grabbed whatever was nearest and just kept on hitting him. My anger for everything that is wicked in the world came pouring out of me and was directed at Archibald Diamond. You say there is no excuse for murder but Archibald Diamond did not deserve to live."

Jake held back his own anger. "What Mr Diamond chose to do, in the confines of his own home, should have been of no consequence to anyone else, Mr Gibson. You chose to break in to the man's home; that gave you no right to play God."

Gibson briefly looked at Jake, but he said nothing. Jake felt a strong urge to get out of Gibson's sight. He stood up and walked to the door.

"We will be back to formally charge you, Mr Gibson," were his last words as he opened the door and left the room.

***

Jake and Mathieson then went with to speak to Juliet Grainger. When they walked in to the room Juliet Grainger actually smiled at them. She still looked unperturbed to have been left sitting in a police office interview room for hours. Even though it was now early morning, she calmly watched as Jake and Mathieson sat down opposite her. Jake hoped that his opening statement would wipe the smile from her face.

"Charles Gibson has told us everything," he said.

Miss Grainger stopped smiling, but she still did not look like a woman who was particularly worried by her current predicament.

"That's nice," was all she said.

"Mr Gibson has told us about the burglaries and the two murders. Needless to say he has also included you in his story."

"Beyond having a romantic relationship with the man and passing one or two pieces of information his way, I had nothing to do with either the burglaries or the murders."

"That's not strictly true, Miss Grainger. The idea for the burglaries came from you and when Mr Gibson murdered Miss McIntosh you weren't exactly heartbroken."

"No one was ever supposed to die. If Charles hadn't panicked, Edith would still be alive today."

"He tells us that you felt the need to reward him for killing Miss McIntosh. You kissed him as you stood over her body and then you allowed Mr Gibson to make love to you as soon as you got back to his home. That does not seem like the actions of a heartbroken colleague."

Juliet Grainger smiled. "Charles told you that? My, he does have some imagination, I'll grant him that."

"So that wasn't what happened?" asked Jake.

"Of course that wasn't what happened. I was outraged at what he did to Edith and I told him so. I haven't let the man near me ever since."

"Is that why you tried to sell the miniatures locally because you didn't want to involve Mr Gibson anymore?"

"I just needed some money a little quicker than he was prepared to get it."

"So why continue with the burglaries after you had what you wanted?" was Jake's next question.

"To keep you busy."

"I bet you weren't quite so easy going when it came to Archibald Diamond's murder?"

Jake noted that Miss Grainger's expression finally conveyed true feelings. She was no longer putting on an act as she answered him.

"Archibald Diamond should never have died. Charles let his own misguided emotions get the better of him. He was only supposed to break in to the flat and steal a few items, he was never supposed to attack the man, let alone kill him."

"But he did kill him, Miss Grainger and he killed him as part of a plan that he had hatched with you. That makes you an accessory to murder and we'll be making a case that you are every bit as guilty as Charles Gibson. If we are successful then you'll both hang for the crimes he has committed."

Juliet Grainger smiled again. "Good try, Inspector, but I don't scare easily. I may have been an accessory to his actions but there is no court in the country that will convict me of being anything other than an innocent bystander when it came to the murders. I'll confess to my part in the burglaries, but that is where it will end."

"Perhaps you are right, Miss Grainger, but the part you have played in this whole murderous charade has been far greater than you are claiming. Right from the beginning you have been lying to everyone. Your performance when I first came to tell you that Miss McIntosh had been killed was brilliant and it certainly fooled me. There you were, already in full knowledge of what had happened to Edith McIntosh and yet able to act as if everything I said was news to you. That points towards pre-meditation, which I'm sure the jury will take in to account during its deliberations after your trial."

"Do what you think is best, Inspector, but I'm pretty sure a half-decent lawyer will keep me clear of your most serious charges. I really didn't know that Charles would kill anyone and I can't be held to account for his actions."

"Think what you like, Miss Grainger. You will be formally charged with being an accessory to both the burglaries and the murders and being in possession of stolen goods. We will let the jury decide on how much they wish to take in to account before announcing your guilt."

Jake stood up and made his way to the door. Mathieson sat for a moment longer still trying to decide what might have driven this attractive, young woman to commit the crimes that she had. He wanted to ask her but decided it would be pointless. He stood up and followed the Chief Inspector out of the room.

***

TWENTY-NINE

Friday 10th July

Jake finished the paperwork on the investigation in to the murders of Edith McIntosh and Archibald Diamond. Everything was ready for the court proceedings to begin and Jake could only hope that he had connected Juliet Grainger to enough of what Charles Gibson had done, to have her included in the deliberations of the jury when it came to the verdict on murder.

He was just completing another report when Sergeant Mathieson came in to the room carrying an envelope and some papers.

"Edinburgh have put out a warrant for the arrest of The Buchan Heiress; they seem to think she might be here."

"I'll have a word with Stinky, I'd already asked him to try and find out where she might be staying," answered Jake.

At lunchtime Jake left the building and went to find Stinky. He was only ever going to be in one of three places and it was in the second of that three that Jake found him, hunched over a plate of pie and gravy with a pint of beer by the side of his plate. Stinky was on his own. Jake sat down beside him and Stinky glanced up.

"Chief Inspector, what can I do for you?"

"I'm wondering if you've found which hotel The Buchan Heiress is using in Aberdeen?" said Jake.

"Not yet."

"Can you ask around again, we need to find her?" added Jake.

"I'll see what I can do."

"Thank you," concluded Jake, standing up to leave. He dropped a couple of coins on the table. "Let me pay for your lunch."

Jake went back to the office and two hours later a message was delivered to him from Stinky. Jake passed the information on to Sergeant Mathieson and twenty minutes later The Buchan Heiress was in custody. Margaret Isabella Reid was arrested at the railway station. Fortunately for her, she had been on her own and Wilson was to be none the wiser as to with whom he had been fostering a relationship. He had gone off to buy some tobacco and had been more than surprised to find no one waiting for him on his return. He had looked around and eventually left the station having made the assumption that Lucy had decided to go her own way again.

As for Margaret Isabella Reid; she was left with the sad fact that one of her potentially most successful cons had been nipped in the bud with the arrival of the police. By the time she was released from prison any chance of conning Anthony Wilson out of his money would be long gone. Instead of a healthy bank balance and possible retirement, Margaret was off to prison for another spell. She really wasn't sure how much more she could take.

She was taken to Lodge Walk where the Aberdeen City Police were to do no more with her than keep her in custody until officers from Edinburgh could travel up and collect her. She would be formally charged in Edinburgh and serve her prison sentence there.

Sergeant Mathieson returned to a room where he could write up a report on The Buchan Heiress. He was grateful that the report was all he was required to do. The court proceedings would be for Edinburgh to deal with. However, Mathieson had taken the opportunity of suggesting to the annoying woman that she may consider never returning to Aberdeen again. He did not feel confident in her response.

At the end of the working day Jake had gone home to Margaret. She had spent the day buying the ingredients for dinner that night. Jake bought wine and beer to accompany the food and at eight o'clock in the evening Sergeant Mathieson and his fiancée, Ruby, arrived for dinner.

As the meal had progressed not a word was said about murder investigations, or anything else that may have gone on within the walls of Lodge Walk. The meal and the few hours after it, were about nothing more than friends sharing time together. As the night drew to a close both Jake and Mathieson knew just how much they were in love with the ladies in their lives.

Ruby and Margaret were what both men needed to balance their lives. A policeman's life was one that was full of sights and experiences that no one should really have to face and the only way to live such a life was in the knowledge that at the end of the working day they could go home to the love of a good woman.

After they had bade farewell to Mathieson and Ruby, Jake and Margaret went through to the kitchen to clear up.

"Oh, I forgot to say earlier," Jake then said as he turned to look at Margaret," the Chief Constable has decided to make me the permanent Chief Inspector for Aberdeen."

Margaret grinned. "Why ever did you not say that earlier?"

"I didn't want to let Mathieson know ahead of everyone else. The Chief is formally announcing my promotion on Monday."

"But that is wonderful news," Margaret then said and she put her arms around Jake and kissed him.

"I must bring home news like that more often," quipped Jake as their lips separated.

Margaret gave Jake a playful slap on the arm and then spoke again.

"Is there any chance that Mathieson may one day step up as well?"

"There will be, if I have anything to do with it," concluded Jake and with that they filled the sink with water and started to wash the dishes.

***

FACTUAL INFORMATION

'The Buchan Heiress' really existed. I have used a great deal of fact when talking about her, including her real name, but I have also built a little bit of fiction around her, just for the sake of the story. However, the Broxburn Oil Company was one of her swindles and she did live with a doctor and his family in Edinburgh as described. She was also arrested in Aberdeen on the 10th July, 1908, as described, except, of course, Stinky would not have played a part in her arrest.

I could not find any indication that the rank of Chief Inspector actually existed in 1908, but for the purposes of this story I have made that rank available to Jake Fraser. It does seem, however, that officers moved from Inspector to Superintendent. The rank of Chief Inspector does not put in an appearance until a few years after 1908. However, I'm sure you'll agree that Jake deserves his promotion.

42001293R00139

Printed in Poland
by Amazon Fulfillment
Poland Sp. z o.o., Wrocław